THE
COMFORT
of
OUR KIND

THE
COMFORT
of
OUR KIND

Tom Stoner

THOMAS DUNNE BOOKS

St. Martin's Press

New York

THOMAS DUNNE BOOKS.
An imprint of St. Martin's Press.

THE COMFORT OF OUR KIND. Copyright © 2008 by Tom Stoner. All rights reserved. Printed in the United States of America. No part of this book may be used or reproduced in any manner whatsoever without written permission except in the case of brief quotations embodied in critical articles or reviews. For information, address St. Martin's Press, 175 Fifth Avenue, New York, N.Y. 10010.

www.thomasdunnebooks.com
www.stmartins.com

Lyric quote from "Cream Puff War," by Jerry Garcia, copyright © Ice Nine Publishing Company, used with permission.

Design by Kathryn Parise

LIBRARY OF CONGRESS CATALOGING-IN-PUBLICATION DATA

Stoner, Tom, 1948-
    The comfort of our kind / Tom Stoner.—1st ed.
        p. cm.
    ISBN-13: 978-0-312-36929-3
    ISBN-10: 0-312-36929-8
    1. Eccentrics and eccentricities—Fiction.   2. Domestic fiction.
3. Religious fiction. I. Title.
    PS3619.T686C66 2008
    813'.6—dc22   2007047084

First Edition: March 2008

10 9 8 7 6 5 4 3 2 1

For
Tristan and Erin,
Morgan, Holden, and Zoë

ACKNOWLEDGMENTS

My deepest gratitude to my agent,
Matthew Carnicelli,
and my editor, Peter Wolverton,
for their advice, guidance, and candor

PART ONE

1

You know how things happen.

You're thirteen years old, working at your first real job, and one morning while kneeling in the weed-clogged flowerbed you look up because you sense a presence and sure enough, standing over you, watching you from the other side of the iron gate is a small man in a colorless suit and hat, whose face looks like he has just finished smiling; and you look from his face to his hands holding the bars and that's when you see that his two pinkies are split at the tips like snakes' tongues and he is wearing small diamond rings on each of the four clawlike tips.

He grips the gate to show you his hands; he wants you to fear his touch.

He doesn't speak, and you are too startled to do anything but look up, still kneeling and trying to reconcile the weirdness of the moment with the bright summer sun and whatever you were thinking before you noticed him standing above you.

For an eternal minute you look at each other, passing nothing between you.

"So," he finally says, in a voice no different from any man. "You're getting them by the roots?"

"Yessir."

That's it. That's all that happens. You look down because you want him to leave, and he does. Then, with your fingers curled into the dirt, tight around a knot of crabgrass, you glance up, watching him walk away.

When you were thirteen, this was just another intrusion of the adult world.

Now, when you are older, you know that was the first time you saw the Devil.

You know how things happen.

You have been seven years old for three days, and after Sunday School the preacher's boy drags you out the back door of Fellowship Hall and knocks the snap out of you in the parking lot because Annette Funicello is *his* girl. Say I love Darlene, he says as he slaps the side of your head, then yells your name as you run away. You turn, and the rock hits your face before you remember seeing it.

And later, when you are sitting in your parents' car, waiting for them to finish with Coffee Hour and you're trying not to bleed on the upholstery, the floormats, or your church clothes—you promise yourself to avoid worship of any sort.

Here's another thing that happens.

In the dark one night, in the hallway between your kitchen and the back porch, you bump into a man you soon recognize as your wife's son. He laughs when you jump; then you pat him nervously on the arm because you don't know what he wants. He's lucky you didn't nail him.

"Just dropped in for some of that home cooking?" you ask.

"I'm on my way north," he says, as if direction is the same thing as direction.

"Okay," you say. "Okay."

You both stand in the dark, trying to see each other's eyes. He wants to see if you look much older; you want to see if the spite is still there—like you've remembered.

"Okay," you say again. "Make yourself at home."

"It is," he says.

Here is the final thing.

At your parents' house is a photograph. In the picture, you are standing between your brother and sister, behind your parents, and everybody is smiling.

Every time you see the photograph you think it's funny how the proof of a moment, a snapshot, comes to represent everything that precedes and follows—even those occasional, elusive things like faith, hope, grace, and the comfort of your kind.

And you remember when you were smiling, waiting for the flash to startle you, thinking to yourself *now this is nice.*

· · ·

I'm from a family of characters. My father, when he was young, was Wes the Cartoon Man, a regionally famous host of a kiddie TV show. These days he is notorious for inventing bad history. My brother, Reggie, was the sports announcer on a Nashua TV station. Last year after he was fired, he fell apart, moved to Orlando, and now he is famous for living undetected in Cinderella's Castle for eight months.

My sister, Veronica, is unhappy, has always been unhappy. Burdened by her strangled blend of doubt and fear, she is America's most misanthropic nurse.

Our mother sees things before they happen. When she was young, she was Sister Donica Lenore, the nun who made a bargain with God.

"If you give me children of my own," she promised, "I will raise them to serve in your Army of Saints and fight for goodness on earth." God was pleased, and when He accepted her offer, Sister promptly left Pope Pius XII for Wes the Cartoon Man.

I'm known as The Man Who Caught Holy Hell.

Last month, Veronica and I flew to Orlando to find our brother, Reggie. We wanted him to come home for our parents' fiftieth anniversary. We also wanted him to make peace with our father. Reggie blames Wes for everything wrong in his own life, including his separation from the family—even though he called Wes his "idiot old man" on national TV. Typical Reggie.

We knew he was living in Orlando because we all received cards with Disney World postmarks. We spent three days sleuthing around the Magic Kingdom, watching the crowds and trying to ignore the character following us in the doofus costume.

It was Tuesday, and we were running out of time. Veronica had to be back at work on Thursday, and I had to testify Friday at a parole hearing in Manchester.

It was Veronica's idea to hire the skywriter. It cost $950 to have a stunt pilot fly over Disney World and smear these words on the Tinkerbell sky: *REGGIE, WE KNOW YOU'RE HERE. WES AND SISTER'S 50TH? CALL 407-621-6509.*

The number was our room at the Courtyard Inn.

We stayed in the room through afternoon and evening, waiting to hear from him. At ten thirty the phone rang.

"Don't yell at him," Veronica said again. "This isn't the time to be mister tough guy."

I listened for a second before speaking, trying to ID some background noise.

"Hello?"

"Hey, Boone," he said.

"Reggie, where are you?"

"At the park. I just got off work."

"Disney? You work at Disney?"

"Sort of. I made a costume that looks like a Disney character. I walk around all day entertaining the crowds."

"You made up a Disney character?"

"Yeah. I'm an older-looking guy with granny glasses and a floppy hat. I look real; nobody can figure what movie I'm from. Even Security thinks I'm legit."

"Wait a minute," I said. "I saw you. You made me hug you."

"It's a small world after all," he said, laughing in a very different way for Reggie. He didn't sound like a sportscaster anymore, with that breathless grasp of the obvious. He sounded relaxed.

"So, what's up?" he asked.

"Wes and Sister's anniversary party. You need to come home. Do you know it's in two weeks?"

"I'm not coming. I live here now. And I'm still pissed off at that clown."

"You're pissed off? *You* embarrassed *him*. You called him an idiot on ESPN."

"So? It's his fault I didn't get that anchor job. I had it locked up until they mentioned him and his freak show; now everybody thinks I grew up in a circus. People make comparisons, Boone. Idiots by association. Aren't you embarrassed by the way he acts?"

"Sure, but that's just the way he is. He's Wes. And besides, he needs our help right now."

"With what?"

"I'll tell you tomorrow. I don't want to talk about it on the phone."

"Whatever it is, he probably deserves it. And I'm not coming back."

"What about Sister?" I said. "She'll be hurt if you're not there. Come on, Reggie, it'll be a big surprise."

"Really? How do you surprise someone who can see the future?"

"Well, can we get together and talk? You, me, and Veronica? We're worried about you."

"*Now* you're worried? Great timing, guys. Where were you when I got fired and Carolyn threw me out and I was living at the Days Inn, watching some kid do my job on a black-and-white TV? Where were you and St. Veronica the Miserable when my own daughter stole my car and ran up five grand on my credit card and I got tossed out of the motel because I couldn't pay my bill? I left town with nothing, Boone. I went to the bus station with every penny I had and landed here with sixteen dollars in my pocket."

"I tried to help. I stopped by every night. *You're* the one who wouldn't see *me*."

"Yeah, that was great, too. Police cars parked outside my room."

"Reggie, it's what I drive. The point is, I tried to help. And I want to help now."

"Then go back to New Hampshire."

"Listen," I said. "I don't want to be here. I didn't come down to Florida to give you a load of shit. I wish *I* could run away and live in an amusement park, but Veronica and I are trying to put this party together, and it's going to be a complete waste of time if all of us aren't there. This isn't about you, Reggie. This is family, and it's something you've got to do. For once, you've got to help out."

"Okay, okay," he said. "I'll think about it. But I'm in the middle of something good here. I'm finally having a normal childhood, and boy, is it fun. I don't worry about anything anymore. I don't need Wes and his approval and I don't care about the Army of Saints or going to Hell. I'm doing great. I'm actually getting younger."

"That's nice," I said. "Where do you live?"

"Main Street, USA. I'm in the big castle at the end of the block."

"They rent rooms there?"

"Nope. They don't even know I'm here. I found an empty storage closet and I made my own apartment. It's really cool. I've got everything I need—bed, radio, my books—and I've got a great view. It's unbelievable at night."

"Aren't you afraid of getting caught?"

"Not hardly. I've been doing this for seven months. There's tunnels and hidden rooms everywhere. I know my way around the park better than the Mouse."

"Tell me again. What do you do?"

"I get up in the morning and meditate. I do my exercises, I go for a jog, then I put on my costume and walk around all day. I dance a lot. I hug people. In the evening I sit in a rocking chair, drink iced tea, and watch the happy families go home. Sometimes I go out at night and help Maintenance with trash detail, sometimes I help Grounds with landscaping. Last night I planted marigolds for three hours."

"They pay you for this?"

"No, and I don't care. I don't need money."

"What about food?"

"Free. I've got friends who hook me up. Employee perks."

"But you're not an employee. You don't really work there."

"Yes I do. I do what everybody does. I make people happy."

"But they don't *know* you work there."

"That's why they don't pay me, Boone."

This was going nowhere.

"So, can we see you?" I asked. "Just me and Veronica?"

"Okay," he said. "Meet me tomorrow at Coke Corner. Eleven o'clock. That's when I go on break. And don't try any fancy cop shit—I'm best friends with a bunch of guys in Security."

"I promise. Devil's stones grind my bones. You're in charge."

"Damn right," he said.

"Say God forgive me."

Reggie laughed.

The God-forgive-me prayer is what our mother always makes us say when we cuss.

"Say it," I said.

"God forgive me before my soul enters Hell for all eternity."

"Good boy," I said. "See you tomorrow."

"Sorry I flipped out, Boone. I wasn't expecting to see anybody yet."

"No problem."

We hung up. Veronica hovered, chewing on her thumbnail. "What's he doing?" she asked.

"He walks around all day in a costume. He made up a fake Disney character. He's that flumpy guy with the big head that keeps chasing you around the park."

"That bastard," she said. "Probably laughing all the time, too. Is he coming home for the party?"

"I don't know. He's changed. I can hear it in his voice. Can I have a cigarette?"

"I thought you quit." Veronica poked around in her bag and took out two Parliaments. "I need another Xanax," she said.

We lit up. I lay back on the bed.

"Nothing changes with him," she said. "He's going to ruin everything." She blew smoke at the wall. "Why does everything have to be so hard? Aren't things supposed to be easier when you're older?"

I'm 49. Veronica is 47. Reggie, 45.

Things don't get easier.

These are the judgment years—time to testify for what we have chosen to preserve or allowed to slip away: our dreams, our children, our claims of contentment, or the fading suspense of lives unfinished and our diminished power of making something happen.

For Veronica and me, life is easily measured—it's case by case. She's a nurse, I'm a cop.

Maybe Reggie is at peace with himself and has found some measure of grace. Tomorrow, we'll see. If not, it's his own fault—in spite of what he says about Wes screwing up his life.

The second time I saw the Devil I was eighteen years old. I was an Eagle Scout, hiking home over the ridge, walking back nine miles for a pack of matches. It was late afternoon, and my troop was making camp in the hills behind me—setting up tents, pranking each other, digging latrines. Wes was den leader, and he had forgotten the matches. There would be no campfire until I returned.

I knew my way. I've explored these woods with my father since I was a toddler. Jogging all my shortcuts, I could hike home and back to the campsite before nightfall.

It was the autumn of 1975. In nine months, I would graduate from high school; in less than a year I would be in boot camp.

It was Friday night. Veronica and Reggie were at our high school football game. Veronica was a junior, Reggie a freshman. Because he was so big, he was the only freshman on varsity—a great galloping lunk of a kid who was already too popular for his own good.

Sister was home, making cookies and praying to St. Christopher for the family's safe return from the woods, the bleachers, and the one-yard line.

Wes and I wanted to be at Reggie's game, but we were stuck for a night in the woods with a dozen noisy boys.

I was the oldest Scout in town, pack leader by default; Wes had been a sponsor since my Cub Scout days, leading meetings in our barn and taking us to Pinewood Derbies, Jamborees, and awards banquets. Scouting was our thing, and after eight years, this was our last campout.

It was also the last year we would all live together as a family. During my first tour of duty, Veronica would start college. During my second, Reggie would marry Carolyn and move into his new house across the valley.

I've lived in Franklin Notch my whole life.

I was three years old when Wes and Sister bought the ancient house on Talbert's Ridge. On top of East Mountain, empty and neglected for sixteen years, it was the oldest house in the county, the only house they could afford. The day we moved in, Wes and I hiked the property and discovered the Talbert graveyard, forgotten in the woods.

Inside the tumble-stone wall was a cluster of graves, their markers knocked flat and covered with weeds.

"Look here, Danny," he said. "These are famous people, the Talberts. They built our house. I'll bet they lived here when these woods were full of Indians."

I didn't see any people. All I saw was headstones broken in pieces like the cracked sidewalk in front of our church.

Wes pulled the branches and weeds out of the plot and tossed them over the fallen wall. He crawled around the small graveyard, raising the broken stones, cleaning them with the flats of his hands and laying them together like pieces of puzzles. I stumbled behind him, picking up sticks. When we finished, we sat on a rock and Wes looked around the burying ground, scratching his beard and nodding to himself.

"Yep, Danny, that's what we'll do. This will be our project, you and me. We're going to fix up the Talberts."

Over the months, Wes restored the plot and researched the Talbert family, original settlers and founders of Franklin Notch. He studied the history of the valley, driving to Manchester to copy documents he discovered in the State Archives. Somewhere, he picked up a collection of arrowheads. He speculated about a tribe of Indians he called the Sagawehs and claimed he found evidence of a treaty signed by William Talbert and the Sagaweh sachems that guaranteed peace in the valley between settlers and Indians. Wes called it Talbert's Treaty.

At the time, he was selling advertising for a Nashua radio station, and as he traveled through southern New Hampshire he kept notebooks full of folk stories and historical tidbits.

With Sister's help, he organized all his anecdotes, typed a manuscript, and had it mimeographed. He called it *History and Mystery: Stories in the Hills* and left stacks of his pamphlets in general stores and motels around the state. Nobody had ever bothered to publish anything before, so Wes became the authority on local history.

He was invited to give lectures at the library, the schools, and Kiwanis. He appeared regularly on local radio and TV, loaded with quirky home-spun tales about southern New Hampshire.

When I was in the fourth grade, Wes helped me write a heritage presentation for my Citizenship badge. Sister made the costumes. I played Jimmy Talbert, wilderness boy, and Wes dressed up as Chief Konatowitt of the Sagaweh Indian Nation. I memorized the Declaration of Independence, and Wes plagiarized Chief Logan's speech from the Ohio Valley Mingos.

I wore a three-cornered hat, britches, and a vest, and I carried a toy musket—Fess Parker issue. Wes wore a chamois shirt with strips of fringed leatherette sewn on the sleeves and a headband made from an old belt and two turkey feathers. He soaked his face and hands in Man-Tan and talked with an accent somewhere between Tarzan and Czechoslovakian.

The climax of our little sketch was the signing of Talbert's Treaty, securing peace in the valley between the Indians on East Mountain and settlers on the western side of the Notch.

At the close of the play I stood at the edge of the stage, musket at ease, giving my final speech glorifying the cooperative nature of all mankind. Wes posed behind me, his arms crossed over his chest like a shelf.

"And so after agreeing on the terms of the treaty, the two mighty civilizations worked out their differences and lived in harmony for as long as the Indians stayed in the valley," I droned while Wes nodded sagely.

Our father-son history show was so popular, Wes made it part of his lecture package. We performed at least twice a month for five years in front of every civic group from Nashua to Littleton. We appeared for a luncheon at the governor's mansion when I was in the sixth grade. I hated doing the show, but I did it five years for Wes, finally calling it off when I began the ninth grade.

Until last month, Wes was still giving lectures on local history.

As I hiked through the woods, I remembered one of his soliloquies.

"Before there was man—sachem or settler—there were secrets in the forest, mysteries in the land, deep as the stone sunk to the center of this mighty continent. And likewise, after man has gone his way—the way of all species, back to the earth—those secrets will remain, still hidden from History, guarded by Time."

I jogged through the clearings, walking where the brush was too thick, scrabbling through stands of eye-high brambles an acre deep. After an hour of running through the woods, I was finally on the backside of Talbert's Ridge, climbing over its jutting granite face. All this for a box of matches.

Near the top of the rise, I squeezed through a split rock twenty feet high and nearly fell over a boy my own age who was sitting in the middle of the crevice. He had black hillbilly hair, dark narrow eyes, and a sallow face marked with fingernail-size acne scars. He was wearing a dirty denim jacket, black jeans, and workboots with pointed toes. He was squatting in the narrow opening with his elbows on his knees, holding a burning cigarette between yellowed fingers.

"Excuse me," I said. "I just want to slide through here."

"You can wait," he said, in a voice no different from any boy.

"I'm in kind of a hurry," I said.

"Tough shit. I'm smoking." He took a leisurely drag, squinting at me through the gray cloud. The ends of his fingernails were black.

We looked at each other. I couldn't guess what his game was. I didn't want to fight him, but there was something in his arrogance that kept me from standing down, turning, and taking the long way around the rock. I leaned on the slant of the stone and crossed my arms. I wouldn't back down. I could wait him out.

I watched him smoke. I looked up the face of the rock to the fading afternoon sky. I pretended to be interested in my own feet while waiting for him to finish.

Finally, he stood up. He was very short and muscular. With his thumb and forefinger, he shot the butt at the rock above my head. Sparks scattered around me.

"Now *you* can move," he said. "I'm coming through."

I pushed myself against the wall, trying to make room for him to pass. He came toward me without turning and kicked me hard on the hip. I went down on my back like a loose fence post, wedged into the V of the split rock. He jumped on my chest with his knees, knocking the wind out of me. I couldn't move, I couldn't breathe.

Kneeling on my chest, he bent over me and put his hands behind my head. He pulled my face toward him, jammed his fist under my chin, then covered my nose with his mouth. I thought he was going to bite off my nose, but he blasted his breath into me instead. My ears popped and the smell of rotting meat filled my lungs.

He pushed my head back hard on the stone. I coughed and gagged. He jumped off my chest and scampered straight up the face of the rock on all fours like a dog.

I lay in the wedge of the rock for a while, trying to catch my breath and clear my head. I was mad at myself for letting him ambush me, and I knew Sister would be upset because I forgot the prayer to make him leave. I knew my prayer as well as my name, but I had panicked. With the Devil's knees pressed hard on my chest, I forgot everything my mother taught me.

Our mother always told us how the Devil can appear any time to confuse us and keep us from the goodness that is rightfully ours. Mr. Sticks, we called him.

She told us the story of the Fallen Angel—how the Devil rebelled, then God expelled, and the Devil claimed earth for his proxy domain. Behaving like a bitter child, he became less than human, filled with cruelty, greed, and carnal whimsy. Spiteful in exile, he still taunts God, spoiling the plan for goodness on Earth, confusing men, bungling their dreams with his antic distractions.

We learned how the Devil seduced a host of lesser angels, deceiving his demons with boasts of victory. When they destroyed the less clever angels of Heaven, they would be free to behave any way they chose, enjoying the bully pleasures of Playground Earth. They could indulge their vices, toy with people, even mate with them without consequence. Come on, he said. It will be fun.

Man has suffered since.

From the time we were babies, we were taught to believe we had the power to beat him, to make him leave our family in peace. We learned the slogans and prayers to defeat Old Sticks. With credos in couplets, homilies, and hymns, Sister taught us to fight the Devil for goodness on Earth. We were raised as three warriors in God's vast Army of Saints—the brigades of believers, both living and dead, who battle the Devil on both sides of Heaven's divide.

"Who's the best little soldier?" my mother would say.

"Me."

"And what do we do?"

"We fight for goodness on Earth."

"Good boy, Daniel. Good boy."

I asked why the Devil doesn't leave us alone.

"Because we enjoy earth the way it was intended—as a place full of goodness. He's a twisted spiteful thing, and since he can't go back to his paradise, he tries to ruin ours. That's why it's our duty in the Army of Saints to stop him."

When we were children, Sister sat with us every night and told us bedtime stories. We didn't know it at the time, but the stories were visions she had seen about each of us. It wasn't until we were older, in our early teens, and we started comparing stories and matching them with real events, that we realized she had been telling us versions of our own future lives.

As the oldest, I was first. We held hands and prayed for everybody—our family, all the people in the hospital, all the people in jail. We prayed for the United Nations, President Eisenhower, and the boys and girls with no parents to tuck them in. We prayed to see the return of Jesus, the defeat of the Devil, and freedom for all the people living behind the Iron Curtain.

When we had prayed for every component of a perfect universe, Sister told my bedtime story.

"Once upon a time, there was a wonderful family. There was a father, a mother, and three children. Like a puzzle, this family was made up of many pieces, and when all the pieces came together, it made a beautiful, happy picture. The problem was, each member of the family was missing one piece from their own collection, and when everybody laid their pieces out, they could see what the picture was supposed to look like—and it was still very pretty—but there were empty places where the missing pieces belonged.

"Well, wouldn't you know it? That was God's plan. He kept one piece hidden from each person, as a gift for them to find when they grew older. He hid wonderful gifts like Faith, Hope, and Grace inside the stories that happened later in their lives.

"The oldest boy in this family was so strong, he could do the work of twelve people. He was the best soldier in the Army of Saints, and he fought many battles against evil. He was very honest and always followed the rules. Anyone who had a problem could call this boy and he would help them.

"Because he was so good at fixing problems, he put faith in his own strength instead of trusting God's plan. He believed that his family was protected because of his own hard work. He needed to learn that his efforts alone couldn't make things right. As he grew older, he needed to find God's gift of Faith."

She smiled.

"Faith is the hardest gift to find," she said, "because it only appears when everything else is gone. Do you think the man will find his gift?"

"I hope so."

"I do, too, honey. We'll need him to keep our family together. Do you understand what I'm saying?"

"Not really."

"We're good people, Daniel, so the Devil tries to keep us apart. I'll bet you wonder how you can help."

"Sure."

"You're very important to this story. God and the Devil often bet on people's souls, and God lets the Devil test the faithful—just to beat him at his own game. As it turns out, they've made a special bet for you. Since God trusts you so much, He's letting the Devil try to keep you from finding your gift of Faith, and He's letting Old Sticks visit you seven times. You're very lucky, Daniel. Most people don't know how many times they're going to be tempted."

She squeezed my hand and looked in my eyes.

"You must remember: Never take anything from the Devil," she said. "Even it if looks like something good—something to help someone else. Promise me you'll remember?"

"I promise. Was the man scared?" I asked. "When he saw the Devil?"

"Not really, because he knew the right prayer to make him leave. Do you remember your Axis Mundi?"

"It's kind of hard."

"Let's say it together."

"Heaven and Hell, forever apart,
    Met for battle in my wavering heart.
While Goodness and Evil struggled within,
    Faith was the sword that brought death to sin."

"Good boy. Say it again."

A few years later, I realized what she was really saying: If I don't find my Faith before the seventh visit, I die and the devil gets my soul.

I never saw much goodness in that.

In fact, it's a curse—a bad place to be—stuck between my mother and the Devil. Their fifty-year battle never abates. He attacks, and Sister fights back. She has her visions, the three of us mumble our rhymes and prayers, and on the near edge of darkness the Devil crouches, keen for the moment to lure us away.

There were happier stories.

"One night, after the boy became a man, God rewarded him for his hard work. It was a cold night, and he had gone to the top of a mountain to be alone and watch for shooting stars. He didn't know it, but a shooting star with an angel inside had already fallen to earth, where she lay broken and helpless beneath him in the valley. She was too hurt to cry for help, but the light of the fallen star itself glowed like a heartbeat in the night and caught the lonely man's eye. He rescued the angel and saved her life. When she recovered, she became his own guardian angel on earth, to watch over him and be his best friend."

As the second oldest, Veronica was next in the prayer cycle.

Sister sat on the bed and told her story.

"The girl in this family was a compassionate person who wanted to ease the suffering in the world, whether it was injured little animals or people in pain. This girl was blessed with the ability to see the world through the eyes of those suffering, but there was so much pain in the world she became filled with hopelessness. The harder she worked, the more the Devil confused the people she was trying to heal. He made them covet the pity that comes with sickness. She grew discouraged and disappointed, and at the price of her happiness—and the happiness of her own family—she saw the world as a hopeless place.

"Well, wouldn't you know it? That was part of God's plan, because the little puzzle piece that He hid for her to find later in life was the gift of Hope.

"The girl craved happiness her whole life; then, one beautiful morning, she woke up in a place where a thousand eyes were winking at her. When she saw the eyes, she was finally filled with hope and joy and she was able to rise above the suffering and see the goodness all around her. From that moment, she saw the world as a beautiful place, and she lived in peace and harmony with her children and her children's children."

Sometimes I pretended to be asleep when Sister returned to pray with Reggie. She sat on his bed, across the room from mine.

"Hello, angel. Are you ready for your prayers?"

"Do we have to pray tonight? Can't we just do the stories?"

Sister prayed for world peace, Reggie prayed for the Sox to place. Then she told his bedtime story.

"This is the story of the Little King," Sister would begin. "Once upon a time there was a little boy who always got his way. Since he was so favored, he grew up believing he was better than everyone else, even his family—and especially his own father, a common man with a heart of gold.

"The boy promised himself that he would never be common, and so he pretended to be different and better than everyone else. After all, his name meant that he was a king."

"Hey, that's like me," said Reggie.

"As he grew older, he became a famous man. He lived in the company of giants, and when he spoke, thousands of people heard his voice. Acting like a king, he watched the court from a crystal chamber high above the multitude. His family still loved him, but they couldn't see him since he had placed himself so far above them. He became very confused and dizzy in his loftiness.

"Strange as it seems, this was part of God's plan. The hidden gift the Little King needed to find was his gift of Grace—the gift of comfort and love when you deserve it the least. Grace is very hard to find. Do you know why?"

"No."

"Because Grace, like a sparrow, is quick to hide
From Vanity's glare and the glow of Pride."

"And that's what finally happened," Sister said. "The Little King glowed so brightly in his own pride that he finally burnt himself out and got lost in the darkness. God had to send the Angel of Grace to find him, to show him the light of a new day and bring him home. When he returned, he was helpful and considerate to his family. It's important for the Little King to find his gift of Grace, isn't it?"

"I suppose," said Reggie.

"It is," said Sister. "If he doesn't, his piece of the puzzle will always be missing. The picture of his family will always have an empty place in it, and he will never have a heart of gold himself."

"Oh, *yeah,*" Reggie said every night when Sister left the room. *"King Reggie."*

Tired and dirty from my scrape with the Devil, I walked through the back door, into the kitchen. Sister was putting a tray of cookies into the oven, Veronica was sitting at the table, crying. At seventeen, with her wide dark eyes, brown hair, and tiny body, Veronica looked like a copy of our mother. When she saw my face, she went bug-eyed and stopped crying.

"Sweetie, what happened to you?" Sister asked, holding my head and looking at my nose. I still smelled rotting meat every time I took a breath.

I told her about my encounter in the woods. "Was it him?" I asked. "Does it count?"

"I'm afraid so," she said. "I'm sorry, honey."

I went to the bathroom mirror. I looked terrible. My nose and the skin around it were burnt bright red and beginning to blister, as if I had stuck my face in a can of boiling water.

"You could have warned me," I said. "This isn't cool. Now I've only got five times left, and I'm only eighteen."

"I didn't know," said Sister. "I don't know everything that's going to happen."

I sat across from Veronica with a cold washcloth across my face. The table between us was littered with wads of wet Kleenex. "What's wrong with you?" I asked.

"Reggie's being such an idiot," Veronica said. "He's hanging out with *my* friends, and he actually asked one of them to go out with him."

"One of your friends would go out with a freshman?"

"He's just doing it to make me mad."

"So don't get mad. If that's why he's doing it, he'll stop when he sees it doesn't work."

"So now I can't hang out with my friends? What am I going to do? Sit around here all night?"

"Take my car. That way, you won't get stuck with them after the game."

"You're letting me drive your car?"

"Sure," I said. "Have fun."

"Thanks, Daniel," Sister said after Veronica left the room. "I knew you'd have the solution. Let me put some Bactine on that burn."

She pulled up a chair and sat in front of me, her knees between mine while she patted my face with a cotton ball. "I'm so sorry this happened to you," she said. "You didn't remember your Axis Mundi, did you?"

"No. I was too busy fighting for my life. And I don't believe this guy is going to leave just because I say the right prayer."

"Oh, he will, Daniel. That's why you need to practice it. You need to keep your prayer sharp like a weapon."

"He was waiting for me. Why did he do that?"

"He's trying to distract you, to keep you from finding your gift of Faith. Don't worry, sweetie, he is the weaker power. That's why he sneaks around and ambushes people. In the end, we will win."

"I don't know how I can beat him. He went straight up the cliff like a spider."

"The only way to beat him is not to play his game. Let's say your Axis Mundi together. Come on, say it with me."

> "Heaven and Hell, forever apart,
>   Met for battle in my wavering heart.
> While Goodness and Evil struggled within,
>   Faith was the sword that brought death to sin."

"I don't even know what that means," I said. "And I don't want to see him again. I only have five more visits."

"That's plenty of time to figure it out," she said, giving me a hug. "In a way, it's a compliment, honey. He only surprises the righteous. Weak souls seek him on their own."

This was small consolation. I still had to walk nine miles back to the campsite. I might see him again, and at this rate, I could be dead by twenty.

While Veronica got ready for the game, I collected supplies for my hike. Flashlight, jacket, knife, matches.

"Will you wait for cookies?"

"No, thanks. I've got to get back. It's getting dark and they don't have a fire."

Before we left, Sister made us hold hands for a prayer.

Veronica rolled her eyes. "Oh, for Godsakes, I don't have time for this. The game has already started."

"Say God-forgive-me," Sister said.

"God forgive me," Veronica said flatly.

"The whole thing, sweetie. Say it."

"God forgive me before my soul enters Hell for all eternity."

"Good girl," Sister said, giving her a kiss on the forehead. "Have fun."

I kissed Sister good-bye. Veronica drove me to the river at the edge of town.

"He makes me so mad." She was still angry about Reggie. "He thinks he's God's gift to everybody."

"He's fifteen, Vee, and he plays varsity. That's something to be proud of."

"Big deal," she said. "I hope we lose. I seriously can't take any more of his bragging."

"Why do you let him bother you so much?"

"Because everything always goes his way. It's so annoying. Nobody should be that selfish and have that much good luck. I have to work so hard to get anything I want, and he just walks into a room and everybody's his best friend. It's not fair."

I didn't know what to say. She was right. Reggie was likable; Veronica always looked like she wanted to clean something.

"He doesn't have it that easy," I said.

"Oh, please. He's already got a car and he doesn't even have a license. He's a local sports god and he's got the perfect job—announcing college games."

"It's just an internship. He doesn't get paid much."

"Doesn't get paid much? He makes more than I do in a week at the Bob-O-Link, and he still steals money from my purse. He took eight dollars last night, Boone. I asked him about it and he just laughed."

"I'll talk to him," I said. "I'll get your money back."

"No, you won't. You'll say something, he'll deny it, and you'll give me eight bucks to keep the peace. He gets away with murder in school, he can go out with anybody he wants, and he never gets grounded like you or me because he never gets caught. Even his bedtime story sounds like fun.

Think about it, Boone. You see the Devil seven times, then you die. What's mine? I'm not going to be happy until I wake up in a strange room and a thousand eyes are watching me. No wonder I'm afraid of the dark. What the hell's that?"

"Say God-forgive-me."

"Shut up," she said, punching my arm. "Meanwhile, Reggie gets to be a king somewhere. See what I mean? Since he was a baby, they've been encouraging him to think he's better than everybody else. Our family is so weird."

"Everybody thinks their family is weird."

"Everybody thinks *our* family is weird," she said. "Who calls their mother Sister? *I'm* the sister. Not that it matters—I hate my name anyway. I'm named after a scarf with blood on it."

We were at the south end of town, at the little bridge that crosses the river.

"Don't worry," I said. "I'll talk to him. I'll work things out."

"Good luck," she said.

I walked down the culvert to the riverbed, then started my hike back to the campsite.

"Thanks, Boone," she yelled as she drove away. "Love you."

I followed the river upstream into the hills, slinking along the bank, watching every shadow.

I felt like prey.

Two hours later, I walked into the collection of tents. A grand campfire was burning, dinner was cooking. Wes was in great spirits; he had already set up my tent.

"Darndest thing," he said. "Right after you left, some little guy showed up, walking through the woods by himself, and he gave us a box of matches."

"Did he have pointy little workboots?"

"Actually, he did. Whoa, Danny! What happened to your face?"

"I'll tell you later."

After burgers, root beer, and s'mores, the kids played capture-the-flag while Wes and I sat at the campfire talking. He was smoking his pipe.

"What's going on back at the house?"

"Veronica's pitching one of her fits, Reggie's being himself, I saw the Devil on the way home, and Sister is making cookies."

"What kind of cookies?" he asked.

"Peanut butter chocolate chip."

"Those would taste good now, wouldn't they?"

"Do you want me to hike back and grab a couple?"

Wes laughed. "You probably would, if I asked you."

In the woods behind us, boys war-gamed in the dark. There were stretches of silence, then bursts of motion and noise. I told Wes what happened with the Devil.

"You can't worry about this stuff," he said. "I know what your mother thinks, but she sees things different than the rest of us. It's the way she was raised."

"Are you saying she's wrong? I know what I saw. This really happened to me." I pointed to my nose.

"No," he said, relighting his pipe. "Of course it happened. All I'm saying is, there are a million ways to live your life, and whichever way you follow is the way things turn out. It's your choice."

I broke sticks and tossed the pieces into the fire.

Wes put his hand on my shoulder. "Let me tell you about life," he said. "It's a wreck in the fog. Nobody sees everything."

We sat quietly, watching the fire. I thought of demons dancing.

"I'd like to meet this Mr. Sticks," Wes said. "I'll knock him down the stairs."

He went in the woods to take a leak.

"I hate to miss Reggie's game," he said from behind a tree. "He's having such a great year. Is he mad because I didn't go?"

"Probably. But you can't be two places at once."

"I can't seem to stay on his good side," Wes said. "I don't think he likes me anymore."

"He likes you. He thinks you don't like him."

"See what I mean?" he said. "Nobody sees the whole picture."

The noise of the boys in the woods behind us was slowly winding down. In the steady fire, sticks turned to ash.

"Oh, yeah," said Wes. "These kids filled your sleeping bag with shaving cream."

"Thanks for the warning. I guess I'd better play along."

2

On September 1, 1955, Wesley Daniel Moffatt married Teresa Marie La-Fontaine. He was known as Wes the Cartoon Man (WRDA, Nashua). She was called Sister Donica Lenore (Kingdom, of God). In the combined history of television and the Catholic Church, there were never two people less suited for marriage—much less for each other. They were opposites in every obvious way.

Wes was a wild-ass, one-man train wreck of a party. Sister was a living saint, a pure flower of the Church.

Wes was a lost soul. Sister was a nun.

Wes was a drunkard; Sister, a vessel of prayer.

Sister toiled for God. Wes was a piece of work.

Even today, people see them together and stare. Wes is a mountain; Sister, a mouse. At three hundred pounds, he is three times her size.

They are perfect for each other. Circling like mismatched moons, they balance, pulling each other into normal orbits.

They have been married fifty years and they still love each other as much as the month they met. They still hold hands in public and go out for dinner every Thursday night. They play Scrabble on Fridays, shop together on Saturdays, and sit in the same pew every Sunday, whispering and passing notes like teenagers.

In forty-nine years, I have never heard them argue. If they disagree—and it isn't often—they calmly state their case, then let the mix settle.

"Remember, Wesley," Sister says, smiling. "It's the purest thought that shines the brightest."

They are wonderful parents. They have devoted their lives to the three of us—Reggie, Veronica, and me. Wes, in his casual best-friend sloppiness, and Sister, the clear-headed authority, always agree on one thing: The family comes first.

As children, we were raised to believe that we were the most important people alive. We were encouraged to be ourselves and to follow our interests. At thirteen, I wanted to be a policeman, so Wes arranged for me to ride in a town cruiser for a few hours every Wednesday night. When Veronica showed a passion for nursing, Sister found her a job as a candy striper. Reggie was always obsessed with sports, so Wes finagled an internship for him announcing college games on the local radio station.

In our small town of twelve thousand people, Wes is a monument. Anyone who owns a television knows him as the host of *This Is My Town, with Wes Moffatt,* a local call-in cable show known for its high-energy silliness. Zoning disputes, local politics, UFO sightings, taxes, high school sports, and especially bad-neighbor bickerings, are the topics flogged nightly by Wes, head cheerleader for all cranky Yankees.

He is a huge man with shoulder-length, unruly frizzled white hair and a bushy beard that nearly covers his vast chest. At six-four, he looks like a mountain man: big flannel belly, baggy corduroy pants with fireman's suspenders, hiking boots, knotty walking stick, floppy hat, burly pipe, and granny glasses balanced on his great bulb of a schnozz. He actually blows his nose in a red bandana.

He is a riot of local color. Reggie calls him Town Clown.

Wes is one of those lucky guys who turned out complete—he is what he does. A born rabble-rouser with perfect rascal instincts, he can get anyone wildly excited about nothing at all. He is three hundred pounds of high-grade mischief, and his public access program is the most popular show in the history of New Hampshire television. Wes has been on the air five nights a week for thirty-eight years, and he has never missed a show.

A typical episode of *This Is My Town* begins with Wes pulling himself up to his little wooden table, looking straight into the camera, grinning through his beard, and asking, "So, do *you* think the county should spend seven hundred dollars on new designer furniture for the teachers' lounge?"

That gets them going.

His eyebrows go up, he pulls on his beard, he shakes his head, and for one hyper-charged hour he takes on-air phone calls from people who are wild to join the county-wide bitchfest. He takes fifteen calls, letting the heat build for half an hour; then he windbags for ten minutes more with his arms crossed over his belly, invoking the gods of reason as the voice of the little people to stem this terrible injustice, this fabulous breach of sanity.

For the last twenty minutes of his show, he returns to the phones. By this time, his audience is ready to lynch somebody—anyone who has ever paid more than a hundred bucks for a couch. He is sweating, rocking back and forth in his chair, slapping the table with the flat of his hand, rolling his eyes, roaring with laughter or sputtering in exaggerated rage.

In the final minutes of this spectacle, he channels the uproar and, looking straight into the camera, pleads with the authorities to honor public opinion.

"C'mon, guys," he wheedles. "You *know* this doesn't make any sense. Just this *one* time, put politics *aside*."

Hokey and effective. The morning after the Teachers' Lounge Furniture Disgrace, the sun came up on fourteen used sofas stacked like firewood in the high school driveway.

His show airs at six thirty in the evening. Wes calls it "two-beer time," the moment he figures the average working man or woman has been home long enough to unwind. He gives the impression that he has just walked in the door himself, and boy is he steamed.

For thirty-eight years, people in our small town have been watching Wes five nights a week with a fork in one hand and the phone in the other. In Franklin Notch, New Hampshire, more people watch Wes Moffatt than CNN.

This Is My Town is also a show of deeply running subcurrents of local intrigue. In a town where everyone owns a scanner and recognizes the voices of the callers, it is common for the night's topic to be a thinly disguised cover for a bigger fight. For instance, a show billed as a discussion about duck hunting on public property could easily spill into a private leash-law dispute between bickering neighbors with Wes playing his roles of philosopher-king, rodeo clown, and Greek chorus director. Things usually work out to everyone's equal dissatisfaction.

For the past forty years Wes has been the expert on town history. He claims to know the bloodlines of every townie family and the provenance of every inch of land in the county. I've gone with him on his Johnny Appleseed wanderings since I was a boy, hiking every hill in our part of the state.

He sees himself as the guardian of town tradition, and until recently the town agreed. People respected his authority. When he stood to speak at town meetings everybody paid attention, turning in their seats to see the big blustery man fluff his chest-length beard, hook his thumbs under his suspenders, and cut loose with a salvo of homespun anecdotes and half-cooked opinions. Nobody ever followed his advice, but he sure was fun to watch.

Things have changed. In the last month he has found himself in big trouble. He's been falsely charged with destruction of public property, misappropriating state funds, violating a cease-and-desist order, arson, desecrating a graveyard, perjury, assault and battery, slander, trespassing, theft of a town vehicle, malingering, creating a public disturbance, and malicious use of a farm implement. Eighty-one counts in all. It's a local record. If he goes to trial, they'll bury him.

Worse yet, he has divided the town. He and his so-called research are at the center of a bitter and complicated land dispute. As the self-proclaimed expert on local history, he is the only living person to see a copy of Talbert's Treaty—and now he can't remember where it is.

Two weeks ago, a woman declaring herself a descendant of the Indian tribe Wes discovered filed suit against the state. She is trying to reclaim East Mountain as it was promised by the treaty to her forefathers. Lawyers for the Sagaweh woman are trying to prove that the land still belongs to the Indians, using videotapes and transcripts of Wes's lectures as the centerpiece of their case. They say the settlers forced the Sagawehs to leave, and now the time has come to even the score.

Wes always said that the Sagawehs left East Mountain voluntarily, leaving the land to the settlers by default. The lawyers claim otherwise—that Talbert's Treaty granted East Mountain to the Indians forever. Since Wes claims he discovered the document, the burden is on him to back up his claim. The lawyers have subpoenaed Wes and his cardboard boxes of Xeroxed memorabilia, forcing him to prove that the settlers and their descendants are entitled to the mountain.

To save the town, Wes needs to produce proof of the treaty—or admit he made up the whole thing, including the Indians who are taking him to court. If he can't document his claims, he needs to admit that he's a little fuzzy about the last time he saw the treaty and maybe—just maybe—took some liberties with his imagination, beginning with his *Stories in the Hills*. Admitting he lied about his research would destroy his reputation and his towering opinion of himself, but if he doesn't clear the confusion one way or the other, the lawyers will press their case and half the people in Franklin Notch could lose their homes. Living on East Mountain himself, he could lose everything, and possibly go to jail.

He can fix the whole mess and avoid prosecution, but he needs to swallow his pride and tell the truth—whatever that is.

As his oldest son, and the chief of police for Franklin Notch, it has been hard for me to stay out of the fight between Wes and the rest of the town. So far, I've been lucky. I don't know how I'm going to handle the day when Wes needs protection—or has to be taken into custody.

For now, he is still doing his show. It's painful to watch. These days he has become the topic—and target—of all those nasty calls. Typically, he's making things worse by using his show to insult his accusers.

The night before Veronica and I left for Florida to find Reggie, I watched *This Is My Town*. Somebody pissed him off and he pulled the plug early in a fit of bluster, hurling the phone through the backdrop and kicking his table across the studio. With the camera crew following him, he stomped out the back door of the station and climbed into his truck—yelling the whole way—then backed through a fence and into the duck pond. The broadcast ended with Wes standing on the hood of his half-submerged truck, soaking wet and bellowing like a Viking, throwing his boots at his own cameraman.

Never a dull moment.

It's amazing how things have changed—how quickly Wes lost his balance and knocked himself off his own pedestal. In a few short weeks he fell from local celebrity to town laughingstock. His credibility is completely cooked, and all of his friends have turned against him.

Now when they call the house, Sister offers to say a rosary for their property values. That's when they usually hang up; and when they do, she turns away, shrugging slightly and smiling her saintly grin.

"Don't worry, Wesley," she says, hugging him. "Earthly treasures are fool's pleasures." She knows he will do the right thing. Whatever that is.

As usual, she is the only one who knows how this will turn out.

We were raised to call our mother Sister, and we never thought it odd. Everyone calls her Sister. As children, our friends called her Sister—never Mrs. Moffatt. Even Wes calls her Sister.

Catholic from birth, she was raised to respect the properly loaded nouns: Father, Mother, Sister, Brother; and when she joined the Order of the Holy Innocents at nineteen, she became a Sister of Christ for eternity. Six months later, after meeting Wes on the set of *The Cartoon Show*, she left the convent in proud defiance, keeping her title in spite of the Church.

"What God ordains, the Church disdains," she said as she walked out of the chapel, a clearheaded girl in love with the man who needed her more.

Sister is her name. Our mother, Sister.

Wes loves introducing her as "my wife, Sister Donica Lenore Moffatt." It hypes his cachet as iconoclast supreme.

As a child, she was raised by nuns to be a nun. Like the heroine in a Dorothy Gish movie, she was abandoned at night in a fierce snowstorm outside the chapel door at the Church of the Holy Innocents in Nashua. The nuns found her bundled in a dirty woolen sweater, lying in half of a broken suitcase and staring quietly upward, wide-eyed, at the winter night, the falling snow melting on her tiny face like soft manna.

They found the silent baby after Vespers, and they carried her across the courtyard to the kitchen, where they unwrapped her and checked her for frostbite and harm while they waited for the doctor. The child was healthy, but too tiny for a crib, so they laid her on a cushion in the candle box. As the doctor trimmed the umbilicus, he guessed she was only several hours old.

Born of a desperate woman, abandoned to the bosom of God.

The Nashua Church of the Holy Innocents was Gothic high, spiked with granite points and looming like twelve months of winter in the gray cluttered town. The orphanage was a dusty two-story brick building attached to the church, and between them was a bare-dirt courtyard with a collection of cement statues, rusting playground equipment, and forgotten perennials.

On the first floor of the orphanage were a nursery and a classroom used by all twelve grades. There was an exercise room with canvas tumbling mats nailed to the walls, several deflated basketballs, and a backboard anchored to the low ceiling with heavy iron pipes. Pictures of a sad Christ and severe Pope hung in every room.

The children were taught catechism four hours every day; the remaining five hours were devoted to American history, Latin, and mathematics. All the children above the age of nine learned from the same book, and every year they studied the same lessons as the year before. The brightest orphans learned how to swear in Latin and draw pornographic caricatures of the nuns.

The nuns divided their time between the orphanage and St. Mary's Hospital a few blocks away. Teaching was considered the worst of chores, and in the classroom they brandished their indifference with droning spite.

As an infant, my mother was christened Teresa Marie LaFontaine—

LaFontaine being the last name given to every orphan raised by the Holy Innocents. Like the other eleven LaFontaines, the baby Teresa Marie was raised on watery starch and solid prayer. She grew to be a tiny wide-eyed child with a bony little body and dark hair that always looked slept-on.

She was a good girl. She never disobeyed, never spoke harshly to anyone or complained about her chores. She kept to herself and always appeared to be daydreaming. She was remarkable only in her ability to be overlooked.

She seemed aloof, but in her silent way she was taking everything to heart, believing everything she heard. She was told about God, the Christ, the Army of Saints, the societies of the heavenly hosts, and the dominion of Hell, and she never doubted a word of it.

Unlike all the other children, she genuinely believed the extraordinary stories of holy men and women who were able to defeat evil with the power of a simple prayer and live forever in God's overlapping kingdoms of earth and Heaven. She believed in the miracles of the saints and all the fantastic stories of heavenly spirits and holy bones.

She was told that God created the world for goodness, but the Devil came to earth to spoil His plan. She was told she had the power of prayer to stop the Devil, and she believed it.

She believed that the Devil prowled the world disguised as any man. In this form, he was more powerful and dangerous than the unseen spirits. As a man, he could tempt, befriend, and betray, then steal a soul before its owner even knew it was missing.

She learned to spot his masquerade and scatter his demons with her holy Roman spells. She became a powerful child.

She learned that a vow from a true believer was the most powerful bond between man and his Creator, the tie that binds the fate of souls.

With her childlike spirit, she prayed constantly for the selfless things: the destruction of evil, the forgiveness of humanity, and the continued good health of the Pope. She knew that God listened and that her prayers changed things for the better, somewhere in the great troubled world.

When she prayed for herself, she prayed for children of her own, in the fantastic way that other girls would pray for a pony or lunch with an actress.

Seven times daily, she offered her vow.

"If you give me children of my own," she promised, "I will raise them to serve in your Army of Saints and fight for goodness on Earth."

She attached her childish request as addendum to her meditations every time she prayed. Seven times daily, for at least nine years, she offered her wide-eyed bargain as the ribbon that tied her bundle of Rosaries.

It became her signature sign-off, and it went the way of all prayers—token, totem, or desperate—straight to Heaven for God's disposition.

When she dreamed about her unlikely release from the shelter of the Church, she imagined her storybook family: a sober and spiritual, neatly appointed husband and several content, compatible children—all living in perfect harmony and fulfilling God's plan for goodness on Earth.

As holy property, the mongrel family of LaFontaine children was carefully tended. The boys were trained for a trade; the girls were groomed to be brides of Christ. Many had already given their lives to the Church. Four of the current seven nuns had grown up in the orphanage. They had never lived anywhere else.

The Mother Superior was a career woman who ran the place by the Book. In her early sixties, she had seen it all: devotion and distraction, piety and perversion, servitude and sabotage. She was a broad-shouldered woman of Scandinavian stock with straight blond hair that no one ever saw. She was aware of everything that happened in the orphanage and the convent and even knew most of the children's birth names. She kept her secrets in a locked oak cabinet covered by a lace altar cloth. In her desk, she kept an old photograph of her father as a boy, hamming it up in his swimming trunks on Lake Winnipasaukee. She was the only person in the building who knew how to use the telephone that sat in the exact center of her desk.

The children were plowed into an ordered life. When they weren't locked inside the classrooms, the seven boys and five girls slept upstairs in separate dorms. They ate together in the refectory and played in the courtyard in decent weather or ripped around the neglected exercise room, trying to brain each other with the flabby leather basketballs. They were allowed as many possessions as they could fit stacked neatly on the bottom third of their cots.

The rules were simple: Do your chores, obey the nuns, say your prayers, go to Mass.

Dusty rooms and dark halls were their hidden world. They were seen by a doctor twice a year and by a dentist every February. They were fed well and clothed in random castoffs from the downtown St. Vincent de Paul. They appreciated none of this.

Mockery of the nuns was orphans' sport. The nun who lisped was called

Thithter to her face. The nun who stuttered was called Sis-tit-tit-titter. Pig noises for the apneatic Sister Snort. Sister Stumpy had a clubbed foot, and the boys stomped boldly behind her chanting, "Fee, fi, fo, fum, I smell the crotch of a crippled nun."

The orphans did their best to raise as much hell as they could. The boys peed on the doorknobs; the girls made cat noises in the hall in the middle of the night or slipped into the shower room and stole the nuns' underwear while they bathed. They hoarded food, put swimming mice in the holy water and flypaper on the seats of the pews.

In grinding retaliation, the nuns regulated the orphans' lives, punishing them with indiscriminate whimsy. They told the children that the creaky night noises of the ratty building were the footsteps of old Mr. Sticks himself, stalking the halls for lazy orphans' souls.

Teresa Marie was the only happy child in the building. She never teased, never pranked. Avoiding it all, she existed on a higher plane, finding comfort in her regimen, her prayers, and her collage of a family.

She was a treasure, the perfect Catholic girl—invisible, available. She learned her lessons, did her chores, and paid attention with an open, honest face. Because she was so quiet, it was hard to tell if she objected to anything—including Mass.

In truth, Teresa Marie lived for the Mass. She loved the solitude, the round Roman phrasing, the somber tempo, the droning chants, and the holy hovering silence the moment the service was finished. She loved the musty leather-and-wood-and-incense smell and the feel of the hard floor on her knees. She loved the feeling of being in the middle of the small collection of children and holy women. She felt protected and part of some family. Mass filled a longing, and she called it love.

She was treated no better or worse than the other orphans. Her puberty and adolescence passed unnoticed. Her thirteenth birthday fell on Epiphany, and it was postponed for two weeks. Held as an afterthought, her party was an extra candle and a mimeographed pamphlet explaining menstruation. She didn't complain; Epiphany was her favorite season.

Her days never varied from one week to the next. Prayers, chores, school, Mass.

On her sixteenth birthday, Teresa Marie LaFontaine applied as a postulant; then, on her nineteenth birthday, she was accepted as a Sister into the Order of the Holy Innocents.

It was a wonderful day. The induction Mass was beautiful, with flowers borrowed from the funeral home down the street and a visit from the Bishop himself, who stopped in for some fawning and decent brandy. It was a simple ceremony with the Mother Superior dressed in red and the other nuns in standard black with their ceremonial corniculi. Teresa Marie's waist-length hair was shorn, and she was dressed in white for one bright morning as her life and soul were leased to the Church.

The other nuns sang songs and cried like bridesmaids as the nineteen-year-old girl walked out of the church at the head of the procession, carrying the chalice from the altar. After a dinner of rump roast and baked potato, Teresa Marie was confined to her small room for the night to meditate on her new life.

She carried the chalice down the gray hallway to her room and knelt in front of the small shelf that served as her altar. In the morning, the chalice would go back to the cabinet in Superior's office and she would resume her chores in the orphanage. Monday was wash day.

This was her wedding night; she was the bride of Jesus—the willing vessel, claimed and consecrated. She placed the chalice on her shelf and straightened the folds of her gown. Child, meet thy husband, the Bishop had said, the taint of Beech-Nut on his breath. There was a stain on the belly of his surplice. Agnus Dei, rise to your feet.

Today was the dividing point, the watershed of her life. Yesterday she was just a girl who lived in a church; tonight, a woman who dwelt forever in the kingdom of God.

Her fingertips strayed to her haircut. The back of her neck felt cold. When she closed her eyes, she could hear the sounds of women talking somewhere in the building and the pulse of traffic outside at the stoplight.

Using the lightness in her head, she tried to reflect in the dark. She could meditate all night; she had done it many times before. Last year during Pentecost, she prayed for two days straight without food or water. Tonight, she would be the consumate helpmeet, waiting for Jesus to come.

In the hallway, a door opened, then shut. The other nuns were going to bed.

She tried to concentrate on new feelings, any flutter of revelation, but her mind wandered to one of her favorite orphans, a three-year-old girl named Elizabeth who was alone tonight in the infirmary fighting a chest cold made worse by asthma. She was a sweet, chubby child who wore socks on her hands in the winter. Because of her honky cough, the other orphans called her Goosie. For the past three nights Sister had slept on a cot next to the child's bed. Tonight, who would fill the vaporizer?

Sister closed her eyes again. Several phrases of the *Gloria* floated into her head, then drifted away. The rump roast sat a little heavy in her belly, and there was a place under her right arm that felt itchy.

She went to her closet, shucked the white dress in the dark, and slipped into her nightgown. She sat on the edge of the bed, then returned to her kneeling-place on the floor in front of the altar.

There was peace in purpose; that's what the Bishop said. Sister concentrated on purpose, but her mind wandered instead to merely useful things: The apron hanging beside the kitchen sink—it needed to be washed. There was a broken pane of glass in the boys' bathroom. They knocked it out so they could smoke; now the bathroom was cold. And where did she leave the big mop?

She picked up the chalice and held it to her chest. It looked heavier than it was. She put it back on the shelf. Tomorrow everyone would call her Sister. Her new name was Donica Lenore. Rise, Sister Donica Lenore, the Bishop said. Bride of Christ.

Now, as a woman of God, she had the weight of eternity on her side. The prayers she offered and the vows she made carried more power and sailed more swiftly to the ears of God. Now she sat in the first circle, at His feet with the Angels on Earth and the Army of Saints.

She said her new name several times, trying to like it more.

She thought about growing old in her new life, living in this room through decades of usefulness, dying on this bed like the old nun before her. There were bones in the basement, the orphans said, to scare themselves. At night, the old dead nuns who had died in the building came up through the floor.

The edges of her room were beginning to show in the morning light.

New day. Time to pray.

She recited her battery of prayers: Our Fathers, Hail Marys, the Rosary. She said all her morning prayers once, a second time, and then a third—in honor of her new name, title, and station. As always, at the close of her prayers, she added her private, now inappropriate, addendum.

"If you give me children of my own," she promised, "I will raise them to serve in your Army of Saints and fight for goodness on Earth."

It just slipped out, but before she could feel silly about her lapse, the sun broke the day. Coming over her shoulder, the light reflected on the chalice, flashing brightly on her closed eyes. She looked up. Sunlight on silver, the cup was shimmering.

Nineteen fifty-four was the year of Ike and Mamie, Chevrolets, Chesterfields, Liberace, and TV; but the Good Sister Donica Lenore had turned herself inward, away from America the Boisterous.

She served her order, schooling the orphans, working in the laundry and the kitchen. She seldom left the building. She took her weather in the courtyard and tried planting a few doomed glads. She prayed, she sang, she remained true to her vows of simplicity, gratitude, and service. She felt herself drawing even closer to God. Out of longing or habit, she always attached her prayer for children of her own.

Then something happened, and everything changed.

Her first vision came one morning while she was washing the children's clothes in the basement of the orphanage.

The room was steamy and she was dressed for chores, wearing her heavy leather shoes, linen underskirts, and woolen dress. She was leaning over the big tin tub, stirring boy-sized wads of laundry with a large wooden rake. The pungent muddy water smelled like lye and sour sweat, and her chapped hands stung so badly she had already murmured a dozen Our Fathers to distract herself from the pain.

She paused for a moment; then, remembering that laziness was the dominion of the Devil, she began stirring again with righteous vigor.

Then it hit her, knocking her to her knees.

"I know it was a vision," she said later, kneeling again and trembling before her Superior. "It was full of goodness and light."

The Superior, who had pretended several bona fide visions herself, was skeptical.

"Came from light, you say?" she asked, her eyebrows twitching once in a spasm of brief surprise.

"Yes," said Sister. "It came over me like a flood of brightness. It was the brightest light I ever saw. It was like a light-filled waterfall, and it came *through* everything, like things around me were cutouts with the clear light shining through."

"And you stayed dark?" Superior asked.

"No," said Sister in wonderment. "No." Tears were streaming from her eyes. "I was light. I was all light. Light was coming from me, too."

Mother Superior raised her gaze, looking above the kneeling child to the corner of the ceiling where gray spiders tried to hide.

"Tell me the vision again."

Sister took a deep breath. "I was saying the Our Father, and when I got to 'Lead us not' I felt a fluttering inside me like a lot of small birds, and I felt warm on the inside, but my skin—all over my body—felt chilly. Then things turned to light."

Sister shrugged.

"And then?" asked Superior.

"In my vision, I was in a dark place, surrounded by new souls. We were waiting for something wonderful and mysterious." She fluttered her fingers. "We were quiet. There was beautiful music playing, and light began to fill the place. The light came from above and it was all different colors and it made everything bright. And then, into the room came a figure."

Sister stopped and crossed herself rapidly.

"It was like a man, except larger. He was pale blue as the sky and he floated in front of me, singing and speaking in a wondrous language not of this world. He was laughing and spinning from side to side. And he had wings—no, not wings. He had vestments that floated around him.

"I felt a lightness of spirit and complete awe for him. He was wonderful—full of life. Then he called me and I went to him."

Superior sat back in her chair. "The part about spinning bothers me," she said. "Is there more?"

"Oh, yes," said Sister, crossing herself again. "He called me forward, and I stood beside him. He gave me something to eat, divine and sweet. Then, as he moved his arms"—Sister made circular motions with her own arms—"the place became dark again, and he showed us wonderful images of all God's creatures praising Him in unison. There were marvelous animals that danced and sang. They were all so happy."

Sister was flushed and perspiring heavily. Her eyes were wide, her mouth quivering. "Was it Gabriel? The Archangel Michael?" she asked. "Was it—"

"Our Savior?" interrupted Superior. "Certainly not. He only appears dressed in the imponderable whitest of whites."

"Of course," said Sister. "Forgive me." She crossed herself twice. "What does it mean?"

"Have you told anyone else about this?" Superior asked.

"No, Mother."

Superior made her face grave. She straightened several folds on her robe, then brought her left hand upward to the heavy silver cross hanging on her chest. With her index finger and thumb she held the bottom corners of her cross. She lifted her chin, looking down her cheeks at Sister. This was her pose of reproach.

"This vision was from the Deceiver," she said.

Sister blanched, and for a moment she believed differently than she felt.

"Sister Donica Lenore, remember the words of Saint Teresa: 'In such matters as these there is always cause to fear illusion; until we are assured that they truly proceed from the Spirit of God. Therefore, at the beginning it is always best to resist them.'"

Superior leaned back, trying not to be visibly proud that she had remembered Teresa's words without error.

"What you felt was the lightness of your body as your soul briefly departed its vessel. Be careful, and be very afraid of the Deceiver. Remember Job. Remember your prayers. And don't be tempted."

"I won't," said Sister, not believing for one second that anyone had been deceived.

They nodded to each other. Sister rose and left the office.

"There's a surprise," Superior muttered to herself after the door closed behind the girl. She promised herself to watch the tiny nun more closely. She spat on her fingertips and rubbed the foamy saliva onto her eyelids.

In her room, Sister sat confused. Was this vision really from the Deceiver? Why would God allow temptation? Should she remember Job, or rather James, the brother of Christ who had been blessed with continuous visions—sometimes for days at a time?

Was this some kind of test? Of what consequence was her life that the Devil should tempt her with a lie? Wasn't it more likely that God would reward her with a blessing? The voice in her heart said yes, her vision *was* from God, and probably a test. It was a gift, not a temptation, and now she needed to pray, study, and await its outcome.

That night it happened again—and again the following four nights, as she lay wide-eyed and smiling on her narrow iron bed.

It was the same every time: a brief wave of nausea, a tingling across the top of her scalp. She felt her eyelids flutter and her fingers clutch lightly in gentle spasms. Everything around her became blurred; and then, in front of her—like a staged production she could see but not touch—the vision began. It began in darkness; then the angel larger than a man appeared. Singing gloriously in a strange new tongue, he seemed to float and flutter in the bright light. He was laughing and spinning. He made the animals dance and sing. Then he saw her. He stopped. He called her forward, into the light—to himself.

She joined the radiant blue figure in the circle of light, dazzled and unable to see beyond, back into the darkness. Her heart stuttered with joy when he offered her the sweet-tasting Host.

And then the vision always ended, as if a curtain had been dropped on a vibrant tableau.

As the scene faded, her heart found its true rhythm, her breathing became normal, and her eyesight settled on her surroundings. The lightness lifted in her head and she sank slowly, a victim of her own gravity.

Soon the lovely blue angel became the focus of her meditations. She tried to make it appear again, but the vision would not be controlled. It came on its own, sometimes sweeping over her while she lay wide-eyed before sleep, sometimes just before morning light. On Tuesday it appeared five times. If she was standing, she sagged against a wall when the dizziness came; if she was on her bed, she lay helpless as it covered her.

She kept her vision to herself, and when she found herself near her Superior—more often than before, it seemed—she managed to convey an unknowing open look.

Superior was no fool. She knew the tiny girl well enough to trust her innocence, but she was wise enough to understand the powers of involuntary fiction. Plain and simple, this was cloister fever. It was curable.

"Sister Donica Lenore," Superior said. She was standing in the hallway. Sister followed the older woman into the office.

"Have you experienced a return of your dream?"

"Yes," said Sister.

"Often?" asked Superior.

"Yes."

Superior's fingers went to the cross on her chest. Good, she thought, the girl is still honest. She pretended to improvise a plan. "I'm going to assign the children's outing tomorrow to your care. I'll find someone else to take your place at the hospital. Do you feel up to it?"

"I do. Thank you, Mother." Sister enjoyed her days helping at the hospital, but the children's outing would be more lighthearted and a good break in her routine. It was the plum chore, a chance to leave the building, to dally in the outside world.

"Thank you, Mother. God bless."

That night there was no vision.

Sister awoke the next morning feeling low and confused.

Walking down Stackman Street in Nashua, Sister Donica Lenore looked like one of the children dressed in a nun costume. She was six inches shorter than the tallest orphan, a boy named Carleton, a notorious bully who was prone to daring escapes.

Sister and the eight orphans were on their way to the WJAC building for the weekly outing. Although the station was only five blocks from the orphanage, Carleton had already slipped into a Rexall and shoplifted two cartons of Luckies and a *Gent* magazine.

The weekly outing was a visit to the local television station to sit in the audience of a children's show. The handful of orphans always sat together on the cheap wooden risers with a dozen local children, cheering and clapping as Wes Moffatt, host of *The Cartoon Show*, bumbled around the small studio telling goofy jokes, walking into shaving-cream pies, introducing scratchy cartoons, and flogging snack food.

This was Sister's first attempt at the weekly outing, and she was already regretting it. Carleton had disappeared again, only to show up ahead of the group, inside the studio with a nasty "what took you so long?" smirk on his face. Displaying classic Catholic aloofness, the other children had been casually ignoring her all morning. In the studio, they sneaked around the curtain backdrop and dug into the barrel of stale popcorn, throwing it at the better-behaved, better-dressed children sitting patiently on the risers.

Since this was her first visit to WJAC, she didn't realize she was supposed to sit off-camera with the other grownups. Instead, as the lights dimmed, she climbed up the riser and set herself on the middle row, next to Carleton. Nobody told her to move.

Twenty seconds till showtime.

Wes the Cartoon Man had been drinking since eight o'clock that morning. His life was a mess, and he had been celebrating his perennial failure. Westinghouse had rejected his bid for syndication for the fourth time, which meant his cherished dreams of California wealth and fame had again been deferred. He would spend another hard winter in Nashua.

It was four minutes until his three o'clock entrance, and he had passed out in the ancient dentist's chair the studio used for makeup. He was still wearing the light blue full-length bib when the stage manager lunged into the makeup room shrieking.

"Goddammit, Wes, don't do this to me!" the smaller man yelled, and when he spun the chair, Wes opened his eyes blearily, trying to connect.

"Blow me," said Wes.

"That's it," howled the stage manager. "You're out of here. You're on the street, Moffatt. This is the last time. I warned you. You're through."

Wes reached out, grabbed the stage manager by his throat, hauled himself out of the chair, and fell on top of him, punching him in the head. The makeup girl, who had been hovering in the corner of the room, ran out the door, wailing like a fire victim.

"He's killing me!" yelled the stage manager.

"Goddamn right," yelled Wes, as the janitor and a cameraman piled into the room. Somehow they got between the two struggling men, pulled them off the floor, and separated them. The stage manager started crying and ran out of the room. Wes shrugged off the janitor and wiggled his right hand. "Jesus," he said. "That little bastard's got a head like a walnut."

"Wes, you gotta go on," said the cameraman. "Right now."

"Out of my way," said Wes, pushing himself past the crowd that had gathered outside the door. He stumbled down the hallway and into the darkened studio. The tinny music had already started and the lights were coming up. Wes ran out and jumped into the small space in front of the risers. "Ooobie Joobie Boobaloobah," he yelled drunkenly, laughing and waving his arms.

"Oh my God," said the cameraman. "He's still wearing his bib."

Sister Donica Lenore knew. As soon as the lights faded, she recognized the hot feeling in her blood. Her tiny body began to tremble as waves of tingling warmth rushed through her. All of her senses dulled and she stopped breathing. Her body went numb as she watched the small area of empty linoleum turn dark in front of the risers. As the music started and lights came up, a big man bounced into the room.

"Oh-ho baloney, labba yabba wocky woo," sang Wes the Cartoon Man.

"Oh-ho baloney, labba yabba wocky woo," screamed the kids.

"Hicky picky nicky doo-doo. Hicky picky dicky doo."

He carried on like this for five minutes, singing gibberish, laughing and dancing his bogus ballet around the room, holding the huge baby blue bib in front of him like a spring maiden catching rose petals. He pulled the bib around so it covered his back like a cape and he ran around the small stage with his arms stretched out, making bomber noises. He slipped it over his head and pretended to be a ghost. The kids loved it, screaming with laughter.

He stopped his loopy dance, jumped and spun around, aiming his wide ass at the camera. He wiggled it like a circus beast.

Then he noticed the stupefied nun sitting in the middle of the crowd of kids.

"Holy crow!" he yelled, pointing at her. "What the hell's that?"

"Cut to the 'toon," yelled the stage manager.

The audience watched a jumpy black-and-white cartoon of barnyard animals singing and dancing the can-can. The makeup girl came out and unwrapped the tangled bib from Wes's neck. He daubed his forehead with a towel and ran his hands through his hair, trying to get himself together for the commercial. He turned to the riser and pointed at the little nun.

"Hey, Sister. Can you come here?"

She nodded.

He reached over three rows of kids and offered his hand. "Come on down," he said. She stood and put her tiny hand in his sweaty paw. He helped her step down the riser to the floor. "What are you doing up there?" he asked.

"I don't know," Sister said. She was blushing royally.

"Stay here and help me out, willya?" he said, smiling like a bartender and winking at the cameraman.

"Wes. No," said the stage manager, but it was too late.

The cartoon ended, and Wes held up a pink frosted donut. "Hi, kids," he said. "Let me talk to you for a moment about my favorite snack—Jibby Lee's Donuts. These taste great. I eat them all day, myself. In fact, that's just about all I eat anymore. I'm not kidding. Nope."

He looked through the donut hole, grinning at the camera, then munched a greedy bite. Crumbs everywhere.

The small nun was standing next to him, blinking into the camera. She was holding a pink donut.

"We're dead," said the cameraman. "And going straight to Hell."

"These are the best donuts on earth," Wes said. "Aren't they, Sister?"

"Yes," said the nun.

"You wouldn't lie to me, would you?"

"No," she said, staring wide-eyed into the camera.

"Well. There you have it," he said, taking another bite. "Divine judgment. Yum, yum, yum. Try one." He looked down on the nun and rolled his eyes. They both took bites.

"Give me another cartoon," yelled the stage manager.

While the next cartoon played, Wes escorted the girl to a chair in the adult section.

"Thanks," he said.

He thought she blinked at him oddly.

The rest of the show went smoothly enough. Wes took his pie in the face, he picked a Cartoon Boy and Cartoon Girl to spin the magic wheel, and he gave away a case of root beer to the kid who pulled the Nehi clown out of the big box.

That evening, Sister Donica Lenore lay on her bed, confused and anxious. What had happened? It made no sense at all: the shabby studio, the gibbering lump of a drunk, the cartoons, the pink donut, the humiliation.

It was too confusing. There was nothing she had learned as a devoted woman of God that could explain it. All of her thoughts worked against each other, canceling themselves. Her vision of the light blue angel had appeared so pure, but its manifestation was so corrupted. In her vision, the angel seemed divine; in person the large, loud man had been rude, worldly, drunk. In her vision she felt glorified, but the real experience left her embarrassed. She remembered the taunts of the orphans as they all walked back from the station.

"Yum-yum, eatum up. Yum-yum, eatum up."

Now, both the vision and the Cartoon Man seemed unreal.

She prayed about it. She prayed for understanding, then prayed for the vision to return. She waited. She listened to her heartbeat and held her breath. She closed her eyes tightly and watched the novas form and dissolve behind her eyelids.

Nothing.

Perhaps Superior was right—this was a cruel distraction sent from the Deceiver.

She certainly felt distracted.

3

"What an asshole," said Vee, flipping a butt off the balcony. "I can't believe he's still pulling this selfish crap."

Veronica and I were sitting at a glass-topped table on the sixth floor of the Courtyard Inn with yawning boxes of Thai takeout between us. We were talking about Reggie, the anniversary party, and Wes's problems with the Indians back home in Franklin Notch. Three miles away, Cinderella's Castle gleamed, pure as a fable. I imagined Reggie sitting in his little room in the tallest spire, watching the lesser lights beneath him, watching me watching him.

"What if he won't come back?" she asked. "Can't you get a restraining order or something? We can't have a fiftieth anniversary party without the whole family."

"I could shoot him. Then you wouldn't have to worry about him anymore."

"Maybe we should just leave him—let everybody see what a selfish little shit he really is."

"All we can do," I said, "is see where his head's at. There's no sense assuming the worst before we actually talk to him."

"I've got a bad feeling about this," Veronica said, lighting another Parliament. "So, what's happening with Wes?"

"Don't you watch TV?"

"Sure, but I'd rather hear it from you, since you know what's happening behind the scenes. Could he really go to jail?"

"He could—if the charges hold up. We'll know in two weeks, after his hearing."

"Does he have an attorney?"

"No. He needs one, but you know how he is—he thinks some miracle is going to happen and one morning all his problems will be gone. He doesn't realize how ruthless these people are."

"What do they want—just the town land, or the whole East Mountain?"

"They want it all, every inch of the mountain. They're claiming the town land, the forest, the ball fields, and all the homes between Main Street and the top of Talbert's Ridge."

"All the homes? That's half the town."

"Yep."

"But I *live* there," Veronica said. "It's my *house*. It's the *town*. They can't do that. Can they?"

"I don't know, Vee. It happened in Utah."

"Why? For a casino?"

"Sure. Gambling is big business, and they've got support from the top. All they need is a good excuse."

"Who filed charges?" Veronica asked. "That woman? Who is she?"

"She calls herself Sarah Running Doe. Wes calls her Sarah Running-After-the-Dough."

"What's her real name?"

"Nobody knows, and nobody knows where she came from."

"Is she a real Indian?"

"She says so, and if she claims she's a Sagaweh, nobody can prove her wrong. There's no record of what happened to them."

"Can't Wes figure out who she is? *He* discovered them."

"He claims he lost track of the Indians when they left the valley in the 1800s. Personally, I don't think there are any Indians. I think Wes made them up, and this woman who calls herself Sarah Running Doe is trying to cash in on his little fantasy."

"So what's going to happen to the land?"

"They'll pay full market for the homes, knock them down, and put up a ski lodge with some trails. In a few years they'll lobby for gambling and open a casino."

"What about the other side of town?"

"Well, if these guys bring in a resort or a casino, the property on West Mountain is going to skyrocket."

"Oh, that's great," she said. "I lose my house and yours is worth more. He'd better not screw this up. If I lose my house because of Wes, I'm never speaking to him again."

"He could lose his house, too—and all the land behind it."

"What does Sister say? Does she know how this is going to turn out?"

"Probably, but she's letting Wes handle it. She says she has faith in him—that he'll do the right thing."

"This is hopeless," Veronica said, rolling her eyes. "The future of the town in Wes's hands? What do you think will happen?"

"It's going to be okay," I said. "I'm working on it."

"How can it be okay?" Veronica asked. "I saw on Channel 6 that he dug up a grave and threw away the Indians' bones."

"That's bullshit. He just moved some stones up at the ball fields."

"Who was buried there?"

"Nobody. It was a replica of a burial mound that we made when we were kids. It was a Scout project."

"Then why are they saying it on the news?"

"Because they love this stuff and Wes doesn't care what they say about him. He thinks it's funny. That's part of the problem. He figures the more outrageous it gets, the less likely it is they'll indict him."

"What about Talbert's Treaty?"

"I don't think there was a treaty, either. It's something else he made up to go with the imaginary Indians."

"So the town's screwed and I'm going to lose my house because he can't show some fake Indians a piece of paper that never existed? Something like this could only happen to me."

She put her head in her hands and sighed.

"Sometimes I wish Earl was still alive," she said. "I know he wasn't the best husband and he ignored the girls, but just having him around was better than this. I don't have the time or energy to raise a family by myself. And now I've got to worry about losing my house?"

"It's not over yet. Wes has two weeks to come up with something. By the way, you've got to be careful not to say anything to anybody—even to Jessie or Catherine."

"Jessie doesn't care, and Catherine's got her hands full with the kids."

"How's her baby?"

"He's beautiful, Boone. That girl makes beautiful babies, even if they do live like hillbillies. Jessie and I are going up there Friday."

"How are you doing with her?"

"She hates me."

"I doubt it."

"No, she does. She tells me every twenty minutes."

"She's fifteen, Vee."

"I had the same trouble with Catherine at that age. I don't know where I went wrong with them."

"I thought Catherine was happy," I said.

"Happy, yes, but what a waste, Boone. This was a girl who could have had everything. She was smart, beautiful, funny, artistic—and here she sits, barefoot and broke in a shack in the woods in Vermont, married to a music teacher who can barely support them."

"Money isn't everything, Vee."

"When you're twenty-five with two babies under the age of three, driving a fifteen-year-old Toyota that you have to plug in every night to charge the battery, money is something. You and I never had it that bad. We watched out for ourselves. It's different these days. Kids don't see the big picture. By the way, how's Doctor Knock-Knock?"

"Please don't call him that."

"That's what Jessie calls him."

"He wants to be called Aero Kierkegaard."

"How did he get from Benny Fuchs to Aero Kierkegaard? Two degrees, and he can't come up with a better alias than that?"

"I don't know, Vee, it's what he calls himself. He's allowed. He's thirty-one."

"Is he ever going to get a job? Or is he just going to keep piling up diplomas?"

"He says he's still trying to define his field of expertise."

"And you're still paying for his education."

"I don't mind."

"What's he studying now? The history of chicken jokes?"

"Don't be nasty. He's writing his dissertation on why things are funny. It's called *Toward a Declension of Humor: The Destruction of Limitation*. It's a mathematical model of comedy."

"I'll wait for the movie," she said. "You're a saint, Boone, doing everything—being a good stepfather and supporting Benny all these years, being a second father to my kids, watching out for Wes, trying to help Reggie, and playing Marshal Dillon to Franklin Notch. I'm glad somebody in this family is focused. I can barely handle my own little life. How do you do it?"

"It's just what I do. Things will be better tomorrow, after we talk to Reggie. Then I can focus on Wes and his problems."

"Is he going to wear that stupid costume?"

"I hope not."

"This is insane," she said. "I can't believe this is my life. I've got a brother who lives in Cinderella's Castle and walks around all day imitating a Disney character. I've got a father who makes up American history being dragged into court by a bunch of fake Indians he invented. I've got one daughter who should have been president of AT&T living in a log cabin in the woods, and another daughter who wants to kill me in my sleep. It's no wonder I'm on medication. Look at me, Boone. I'm a mess."

"How's work?"

"Terrible. Ever since they made me shift supervisor, all I do is paper-work. Most of the patients act like they're prisoners and blame us for their pain. Not that it matters. We don't really heal anybody; we just cut out the bad parts, give them stronger drugs, and send them away. Business as usual."

"Time to call home," I said.

While I collected the dinner trash on the balcony, I could hear Veronica on the phone in the room—talking first to Sister, then arguing with Jessie. Jessie was staying with Sister and Wes while Veronica and I looked for Reggie in Florida.

"*Who*, Jessie, *who*?" she was yelling. "I can't say no if I don't know who it is. Alright, then, no. No, you can't bring *anyone* to Vermont this weekend—no matter who it is. Yes, you *are* coming with me. Yes, you are. Yes. You. Are. Jessie, put Sister on the phone. Uncle Boone wants to talk to her."

"Hey, Uncle Boone," Jessie said when I took the phone. "I'll give you sixty bucks to leave my mother in Florida."

"For sixty bucks, I'll stay myself," I said.

"Is it warm?"

"T-shirt and shorts."

"Did you find Uncle Reggie?"

"Sort of," I said.

"He's in jail, right?"

"No. He lives in Cinderella's Castle. He broke in and made himself an apartment or something. We're going to see him tomorrow morning."

"Uncle Reggie is hiding in Cinderella's Castle?"

"Hey, Jessie, this is a huge family secret. You've got to promise me you won't tell anybody. This could really damage Wes if the papers find out."

"Devil's stones grind my bones," she said.

"Thanks. Can I talk to Sister?"

"Sure. Hey, Uncle Boone. Bring me back a jacket, okay? I'll pay you. I want one with Jessie on the back."

"The cowgirl from *Toy Story*? You got it," I said.

There were a few seconds of dead air while she passed the phone to her grandmother.

"Hi, Daniel," Sister said. "Did you find Reggie?"

"We found him, but he's being difficult. We just talked on the phone. Did you hear what I told Jessie?"

"Something about Cinderella's Castle?"

"Yeah. I guess he broke in and made himself a place to live. He hides there at night, and during the day he walks around dressed up in a home-made costume. He's pretending to be a Disney character."

"Did he sound happy?"

"He sounded different—relaxed. He said he felt younger. Actually, he said he *was* younger."

"Just like St. Anthony," Sister said. "Isn't it funny how things work out?"

"I guess so," I said. "What am I supposed to do now? We're seeing him tomorrow morning, and I don't think I can get him on the plane without a net."

"Don't push him, Daniel. He's not finished yet."

"Finished doing what? He sleeps and hugs people."

"Don't worry. He's looking for his gift. Just tell him you love him. Tell him we all love him. He'll be alright."

"How are you doing? How's Wes?"

"He's good. Tonight's show was a little rough on him. Some people from a newspaper and another TV station showed up, and all the cameramen got in a big fight. I think it's going to be on national news tonight."

"You didn't watch it?"

"No. Jessie was teaching me how to tie-dye things."

"How are you holding up?" I asked.

"I'm doing good. We're making gingersnaps now. You'll be home tomorrow?"

"Yeah. Veronica and I have a six o'clock flight. I'll be back too late for Wes's show."

"Don't worry, honey. He'll be alright. Have you called Beth?"

"Not yet."

"I saw her today. She's worried about you. She thinks you're doing too much."

"I'm calling her next."

"Good. Oh, Daniel, there's something I need to tell you. It's about

Mr. Sticks. I think he may be coming to see you again. He's going to be talking about a tree."

"A tree?"

"Yes. It's from a dream I had last night. It's a tree in a hidden place. No one can pass without leaving something on it."

"This isn't good. This is my fifth time. At this rate, I'll be dead by the time I'm fifty."

"I'm sorry."

"Well, thanks for the warning. I'll keep my eyes open, and I'll call you when I get back. I love you—and tell Wes to be careful."

"We love you, Daniel. And God bless."

I hung up. Veronica was standing in the doorway to the balcony, smoking.

"You talked to Jessie?" she asked. "What did she say?"

"She wants us to pick up a jacket for her."

"You shouldn't have told her about Reggie."

"She can keep a secret."

"I don't know, Boone," she said. "I don't know if she can."

She doesn't tell *you* anything, I felt like saying.

"She wants to bring a boy to Vermont this weekend," Veronica said. "I'm not ready for this. Who's she hanging out with? Do you know?"

"It's not a bad crowd. A little aimless, but they're good kids."

"Would you tell me if she got in trouble?"

"Nope. That would be the job of the night sergeant."

"You're no help," she said. "I'm going to bed."

She gave me a sister's kiss on the cheek, patted my arm, and went back to her room. I called my wife.

"I miss you, Beth," I said. "Things are all messed up down here."

"What happened? I'm worried about you."

"Well, for starters, we found Reggie, but it's not good. He sounds different, and he lives in Disney World illegally."

"How?"

"I'll tell you later. Anyway, I don't think I can get him back to New Hampshire, and Veronica's being herself, driving me crazy with her complaining."

"Oh, honey, you don't sound happy."

"I just want to come home. I don't know what's going on, and I'm really worried about Wes. I guess things were kind of wild on his show last night."

"They were. A crowd from East Mountain showed up and confronted him."

"I should have been there."

"I'm glad you weren't."

"Maybe so. How are you doing?"

"I'm okay. I miss you. I heard from Benny. He said he might be stopping by on his way back to school. He wanted to know if you paid for the semester yet."

"Last week. I sent the check Saturday. Maybe I'll be back in time to see him. We've got a six o'clock flight, and we'll be in Manchester at nine fifteen—unless something happens with Reggie."

"Don't worry, baby," Beth said. "Everything's going to be alright. Sister stopped by today, and she's not worried. When you come back, we'll go out to dinner, have some wine, come home, and snuggle. I'll take care of you."

"I love you," I said. "See you tomorrow."

"I love you, too, sweetie."

I remember the day Beth and I married. The night before, it snowed seventeen inches. By sunrise the storm had passed, leaving the sky to its blue morning glory and the earth around us settled and soft, pure as a promise.

Beth looked beautiful. I remember standing on the back porch of the parish house, watching her walk alone in her wedding dress through the crystal pines, up the winter path. She was bright as a dream with her breath in the air and the sky in her eyes. Soft new snow clung to the hem of her dress, and when she came up the steps to give me a kiss, I watched the snowflakes on her eyelashes melt to diamonds.

"Are you sure you want to do this?" I asked her. "Sometimes it gets pretty crazy around here."

"Forever and ever," she said. "On earth and whatever comes next."

4

For three days the little nun puzzled on the meaning of her vision. It felt like a practical joke. If God was trying to get her attention, He had certainly succeeded; but what was she supposed to be paying attention to? If God was testing her, what was the prize?

Sister kept to herself, doing chores that would keep her apart from the others. On Monday morning, Superior went looking for the girl.

"Have you been relieved of your distraction?" she asked. "You seem less confused."

"I am," said the girl. She had been wiping desks in the classroom.

"I think the children's trip was good for you," Superior said. "You may go again this week."

Sister's spirit sagged. This was too much. Once was fine, but she needed more time to sort things out. She couldn't refuse, yet she knew how humiliated she would feel, walking back into the small studio. "Thank you, Mother," she said, twisting the washrag.

Coming up from her genuflect, she felt it happening again—the flutterings, like birds around her heart, and the heat deep in her belly.

"God bless," said the older woman, leaving the room.

"God bless," said Sister, starting to swoon.

When Superior left the classroom, a great dopey bear, bright red as fresh blood, waddled into the doorway. Poking his huge blocky head into the room, he looked around the doorjamb at the girl. He wiggled his snout and wrinkled his face. He looked very worried.

He wedged his body sideways through the door, grunting at the squeeze. He was so large he barely fit, and when he stood full height, his head touched the ceiling. He stood blinking in the open space at the front of the classroom, his thick droopy arms swinging loosely, like a little boy waiting in line.

"Falf," he huffed, shaking his shaggy crimson shoulders and lolling his head upward.

He looked at her as if it were her turn to say something, then plopped heavily onto his rump in front of the blackboard. He was massive. Even sitting on the floor, the giant beast was two times taller than Sister Donica

Lenore. He sat in front of her, rolling his eyes sadly, then held out his paws and made doleful sounds. It was a ridiculously mournful tableau.

The small girl stood terrified behind the first row of desks, the wet rag dripping on her shoe. The bear sat on his hindquarters, his legs splayed and his arms outstretched in supplication, as if begging for a handout. He began crying pitifully, pointing his snout at the ceiling. Huge tears the size of gumdrops rolled off his shoulders and splashed on the floor.

"What do you want?" Sister asked the animal, her body gone cold with fear. "Why are you doing this? Who sent you?"

The bear kept his nose aimed upward, nearly touching the ceiling, snuffling wetly. Then he rose on his hind legs and shuffled toward her like a man in shackles. His head knocked against a light fixture.

Towering over the tiny nun, he began to sway from side to side and sing in a soft low voice. "Ego postulo succurro," he sang over and over. The great red bear rocked slowly from side to side as he sang, and when he finished, he stood for a moment, looking imploringly at the girl. Then he shook himself and ambled out of the room, humming the Dominus and leaving behind the smell of cheap aftershave.

The girl leaned against the wall, gaping at the doorway.

One week later, things were no better for Wes Moffatt. In fact, things were much worse. Viewer outrage, always simmering, had finally exploded in a volcanic spew over his on-the-air use of the Catholic Church to sell donuts. The fistfight with the stage manager—normally considered an effective negotiating technique—became a crisis when the stage manager boycotted *The Cartoon Show* until he was promised an armed bodyguard any time Wes was in the building. Allen Walz, the station owner, took Wes to lunch and pointed out that Wes wasn't Arthur Flipping Godfrey, and if he pulled any more crazy shit he would be Ex the Cartoon Man. And, by the way, write up a little note apologizing to that nun.

Wes agreed to dilute his creative juices and to go easy on the other juice—at least during daylight hours. Yeah, yeah, postcard the penguin.

He liked Allen and he loved his job, so he stayed true to his promise for a few days. He stopped drinking at noon so he wouldn't black out again in front of the camera. He wore a clean shirt to work and thought up some new sketches. Again, it was business as usual on the set of *The Cartoon Show*. The stage manager returned, carrying a mashie everywhere he went. The show aired on time. Wes cavorted, children laughed, cartoons flickered, sponsors were happy.

And then came the Thursday afternoon show.

In fairness to Wes, Estella Papanandropolous never told him she was married.

On the other hand, he probably should have noticed the wedding ring safety-pinned to her underpants every Wednesday night for two years straight.

In any case, the look on his face was genuine surprise when the three shrieking Papanandropolous brothers raged into the makeup room twenty minutes before showtime and tried to kill him.

The makeup girl wailed and hid under the counter as Wes fought off the three screaming Greeks. He managed to pin one of them behind the door while he flailed at the other two with an empty fire extinguisher. Although Wes was still standing when it was over, no amount of makeup could prep him for his show. Both eyes were swollen shut, his hand was cut badly, his face was scraped and puffy, and most of the hair had been pulled off the left side of his head.

"Get him something from Costume," the stage manager yelled. "I don't care what it is."

The makeup girl came back with a bright red oversized terrycloth bear suit and a matching papier-mâché bear's head.

"I'm not wearing that," said Wes.

"We're not doing a horror show, either," said the stage manager. "Put it on."

"No," said the Cartoon Man.

"Wes, you can't bleed all over the audience."

The orphans were in place, the cameras were locked on stage right, and the small nun was sitting in the front row of the adult section. The ring of lights came on, and the big man in the red-pajama bear suit stumbled into the small linoleum space, his knees wobbling, his arms hanging limply, and the tacky bear's head tilted upward like a hood ornament. He staggered around the stage for a minute or two, then fell on the floor in front of the audience, a few feet from the little nun. He raised his red mittens and moaned.

"I need some help here. Somebody help me up."

"Gimme a 'toon," yelled the stage manager.

Caterpillars in grass skirts played ukuleles and danced the hula as the camera crew dragged the Cartoon Man out of the studio like a beaten boxer.

That night, Sister couldn't sleep. She sat in the corner of her room, a cup of warm milk on the small table beside her, wrapping, unwrapping her rosary through the knuckles of both hands.

She couldn't stop thinking about the giant red bear in the classroom and the moaning man in the cheap raggedy costume lying stoned and beaten on the studio floor.

God *was* trying to get her attention; now she was sure of it, but what was He trying to tell her for two weeks straight? Should she watch more television?

Who was the Cartoon Man? And what on earth did he have to do with her? He was a lost soul and he needed help—that was clear, but she was called to help children, not lumpy drunk men. Wasn't that why God made her an orphan? Wasn't that why she lived at Holy Innocents? So what if she had prayed for children of her own seven times a day for nine years. God certainly must know the difference between a child's bedtime wish and the complications of real life.

If things were different—and they weren't—she would wish for a college man with a proper office job and ten white shirts she could starch and fold. This was the kind of father her imaginary children would need, and this was the kind of man she would choose—with God's help, of course.

Superior was right, these visions were distractions because they encouraged her to pretend she had choices. She was already following God's will, and so this prayer for children of her own must be confusing to God. It's no wonder He had given her such useless visions.

"Alright then," she said, in her dark little room. "Forget it. I'll just forget it." Children, she meant, and sloppy drunks, the Army of Saints, and everything else outside the Church. The Church was her home and twelve orphans were her family. She would forget her promise. It was just a silly little wish.

"It doesn't affect anyone else anyway."

As soon as she spoke her words of denial, the room filled with a pulsing light; then, after a timeless moment, her longest, most terrible vision began.

As before—with the other visions—she felt the fluttering heat deep in her chest and cold dampness on her skin. The edge of her sight blurred and she felt weightless, then the rolling tingling nausea. She heard her own breathing as if her hands were pushed tightly over her ears and her heartbeat bounced loudly through her bones.

Her mouth slid open and her eyes fluttered upward under her lids. Under her woolen underwear she felt cold sweat dampen her belly. The back of her neck tightened and her head strained backward, pushing down into the pillow. Her body went rigid.

Through a surge of the whitest light that exploded from somewhere behind her eyes, she was hauled violently upward in a screaming arc. There was no earthly pull against her flight; it was pure velocity to the crest of vertigo. In an instant, she was torn away, sucked upward toward some gathering point in the darkening eon. She streaked outward at howling speed—too fast to think or even clutch at what was happening to her.

I'm dying now.

With searing violence she sped toward eternity—a tiny projectile, random and silent, into the reach of distant heavens.

Now she was light itself—the energy of time and motion, streaming through the red-to-violet spectrum and becoming clear brightness herself. She was piercing light, and in the raging hum of brilliance she was without mass, invisible, soaring to holiness.

Then she fell. Swift and sudden, at the apogee of a weightless zenith, she dropped instantly into emptiness, like a person being hanged. She felt the momentum change and the bottom fall out, the point of her arc curving suddenly downward.

She struggled against her fall, but there was nothing to grasp or brace against. She was falling into nothing and she felt herself sliding past the pull of earth, into a heavier darkness.

She fell forever, dropping like fury through a poison sky.

She hit the mud on her hands and knees in a carnage-cluttered valley that sloped downward in front of her as far as she could see. She couldn't see much. The air was thick, smoky, and it smelled like burning shit and matchsticks lit too close to her nose. She could barely see a hundred yards through the dusty spunked air, and all around her the ground was pocked and littered with rotting parts of torn human bodies. Sticking out of the slippery mud were pieces of arms, hands, legs—and even parts of heads and faces and larger parts of bodies that had been torn and twisted so violently that their insides had been pulled out and smeared around in great stinking heaps.

Something like a great battle had happened here, then moved down into the valley, terrible and swift. The shredded pieces of men and women had been churned into the ragged earth, becoming part of the oily stinking mud. The pulled-off skin of a face lay leering on the ground; a buttock and a leg lay half-buried. Here an arm, there a sheet of rotting flesh.

She looked around. Nothing was alive or moving. Ahead of her stretched an endless barren valley. Above her, the swirling yellow sky. The air was heavy with fecal brown smoke and the cling of decay. The stench filled her mouth and she gagged violently.

It took the girl a few moments to believe this was real. She tried to get away, but she couldn't move. She felt herself sinking into the doughy muck, cold on her bare feet. She felt it rise to her ankles. Her skirt wetly clutching her legs, she raised her foot and set it down again, trying to catch her balance. She tried to walk on the soft ooze, and she found she could keep from sinking as long as she kept moving.

By walking faster, she discovered she could skim the surface of the field like a game bird leaving a pond. She felt like a child running downhill, at the edge of weightlessness.

Her small legs pumping, her body straining, her muddy nightgown clinging to her legs and arms, she made speed enough to leave the ground and strain herself outward—off the surface of the sloping field, then upward over the ground in front of her. She skimmed the surface by force of her will, and she hovered like a damaged kite above the ravaged hillside.

She sailed vulture-like into the valley ahead of her.

Toward the center of the valley, the ground sank sharply into a wide hole like the crater of a volcano, and as she drifted closer she could see movement in the pit.

Beneath her, dust and noise rose in bursts of amber and agony, and through the yellow haze she could see an endless carpet of men and women sliding down the sides of the deep hole.

There were thousands of people sliding into the great pit, struggling against its sides and clutching at each other, deathlocked and straining. Like maggots swirling in a bucket, they writhed over each other, trying to climb the slippery sides of the bloody hole on the backs of the people below them. Kicking and shrieking, they all slid down, like sheets of blood-muddy slag, trying to twist away from the death grasp of the people beneath them. They screamed in agony as their limbs were torn from their bodies. Sister could hear their bodies being pulled apart with wet popping sounds. Legs and arms, jerking like torn insects, slid into the hole. The noise of the damned rose into the low ashen clouds in an endless keening moan.

When her shadow passed over the hole, the people looked up and their roar of pain broke for a moment, then began again in a savage burst of grief, shrieking for salvation, wailing like a nation burned alive. They clutched at the child in the sky, but with empty fists of dust and darkness, they went sliding away, their eyes like fading flames, becoming nothing forever.

The girl tried to float higher, to sail away, but felt herself falling instead—out of the brown sky and into the center of the swirling pit.

Spent, Sister fell off her narrow bed, her eyes rolling back into her skull, her mouth choked with vomit, her woolen underwear sweat-soaked and greasy with stool. Rigid and shaking, she lay on the floor, her head knocking against the leg of the bed.

She had been shown the thing she feared the most—losing God's favor, and she had been sent to the lip of Hell to see the consequence of her treachery.

These were the souls of people alive today, and the souls of their children, and the generations after until the end of humanity, who were doomed to struggle on their own without her care. Because of her selfish neglect, they never had a prayer against the Devil's sideshow of trouble and sin. Without Sister as their guide or guardian, they would live useless lives, make bad deals, and lose their souls to evil. It was her fault they would fail themselves without knowing why.

Without her vigilance and intercession, they would cover the earth like poisoned trees. Bad seeds, bearing bad fruit, twisted and bitter. Children of sinners, raising children in sin.

She had made a bargain with God; He accepted it; then she tried to break it. Never mind the circumstances, age of consent, or intent of the supplicant; this vow was a holy bond between a father and his favorite daughter. It was a promise to produce goodness, and it could not be brushed off like an insult. Once granted, it must endure forever.

It was too much to bear. For two days, the girl huddled under her blankets, refusing to leave her bed. She couldn't sleep. She lay on her side, staring at a patch of wall the size of her face. The moment she closed her eyes, she felt the familiar fluttering through her body, the heat that seemed to come from under her heart, and the empty chill that covered her like wet clothing. She clenched at every sound.

When she breathed, it was the smoke of burning men she smelled. It was yellow clouds, black rain, and the howling mouths of the damned she saw every time she closed her eyes.

Fear circled, like a serpent eating its own tail.

Now I know, she told herself. I know how it all ends.

I prayed my little prayer, I wished for something I wasn't allowed to have, and now I've made a promise I can't keep. I can't see it through, and I can't back out. I'm going to fail God, myself, everyone. He will punish me and send me to serve the Devil in Hell, along with all the souls I couldn't save because I didn't know how. I can't do this alone. I'm too small.

Jagged thoughts filled her head, and they couldn't find their right order; they wouldn't set themselves in a way she could arrange them. They swirled, noisy as bees circling their burnt-out nest.

"Sister Donica Lenore, we're worried about you," said Superior, standing at the foot of the small nun's bed. "If you aren't feeling better in the morning, I'll make arrangements for you at the hospital."

"I'm sure I'll be fine," whispered Sister, her eyes bright with fear.

The next morning they pulled her sweater around her thin shoulders, bundled her in blankets, and set her on the large wooden wheelchair. A silent nun pushed the chair nine blocks to St. Mary's Hospital. The snow had begun before dawn. It was the first snowfall of the year, and as Sister bounced over the ice-covered sidewalk on the wide wooden seat, she watched the perfect icy stars settle onto the gray blanket pulled tight across her chin, then melt to tiny silver beads under her breath.

St. Mary's Hospital covered a full city block in downtown Nashua. Built of drab brick and granite, it sat in the cold river valley looking like another factory among the mills and warehouses.

A dayroom on the second floor looked over the river, catching the afternoon sunlight that warmed the backside of the building. It looked like a large studio with a smooth wooden floor and twelve-foot windows that rose from the tops of the radiators to the high white ceiling. The room was empty, except for two wooden card tables with rickety iron legs and a handful of beat-up schoolroom chairs.

Copies of religious paintings hung on the walls. Behind a thickly carved door at one end of the room was a small, dark chapel that contained a miniature altar, six short pews, a two-foot crucifix, and one dusty stained-glass window with a sixty-watt bulb and a pile of dead flies behind it.

The long, wide room smelled like dry dust and pine oil, and in the afternoon when the lazy broad wash of yellow sunlight crawled slowly across the open floor, the room had the warm tone of an empty sanctuary.

Every day between ten and four o'clock, patients were walked or wheeled into the room to watch the river, see visitors, or read the battered books on a wooden cart near the door.

The dayroom was the best place to sit and watch the cold gray river wash past the blue-black cliffs of the far bank. It was the best place to sit and think about getting better, or wonder why dying took so long.

In 1954, all the nurses at St. Mary's Hospital were nuns, most of the doctors were Loyola men, and none of them could explain Sister Donica Lenore's condition.

Pale as a corpse, she looked like life was dissolving within her. She was burning inside, she whispered, but her skin felt cold. She lay on her back, sweating and shaking, wrapped tightly in three woolen blankets.

She wouldn't look directly at anyone, staring upward instead at the iron crucifix on the wall above her head. She smiled tightly and traded nervous small talk with her wrists crossed over her tiny chest like a child martyr and her rosary beads wrapped tight as wire through her frozen fingers.

She couldn't sleep. She ate only a few ounces of food, drank small sips of water, and refused to change her clothes. She wouldn't leave her bed and couldn't use the lavatory unless she was alone in her room with the door locked. She took twelve careful steps to the bathroom, saying the names of the apostles with each step; then she flushed the commode seven times and scuttled back into bed as soon as she was finished, reciting the names in reverse order and flipping the latch on the door three times as she ran past. Father click, Son click, Holy click Ghost.

As soon as she slipped beneath her blankets, her fears crawled upon her like stone demons. One sat on her hips, his spiny arms wrapped around her belly, his head on her breast, and his tail curled around her thigh. Another rode her neck like a log, holding her by the ears, breathing its rotting gut-breath into her face.

"Where will you go?" it asked, looking in her eyes. "Where will you sleep at night? You can't stay here forever."

The one clutching her belly laughed. "How can she save anyone? She doesn't know a soul. She'll wander the streets in the clothes she's wearing. She'll die behind a garbage heap and they'll bury her in a no-name hole."

"And what about money?" hissed the one holding her legs. "Will you pawn your dowry, Bride of Jesus?" He squeezed her ankles so tightly, the bones burned.

The one sitting on her neck pinched her breast. "You're small and ugly," he said. "No man will have you. Children of your own? Forget about it."

There was one on the mattress above her head. He had long eyes and a mouth on his forehead. "There isn't any Plan," he said, scraping her face with his nails. "Stay with the Church. You'll freeze to death outside."

"Not a chance in Hell, Snowball," said the one holding her feet.

"Do you really believe He wants you to leave?" they chanted over and over, louder and louder. "Do you really believe He wants you to leave?"

The doctors were confounded. Her fever never developed, yet her symptoms never improved. Among themselves, the nurses agreed on nervous agitation.

The nineteen-year-old nun was wasting away. She had lost eighteen pounds and hadn't bathed in seven days. Her thin face lost its color, and the flesh around her eyes darkened. Her unwashed hair spoiled in greasy tufts. She kept her head straight back on the pillow, staring upward, occasionally letting her eyes jerk from side to side. She was inert, except for the fidget of her fingers under the blankets and the frantic flutter of her dry gray lips chittering in ceaseless liturgy.

She prayed the Rosary as fast as her mind could produce the words, touching each syllable just long enough to register an impression, a logo of its familiar power. She jumbled the prayer end-to-end, never allowing an instant between cycles.

When she started her Rosaries, the demons loosened their grip and slid away. They sat around her on the mattress and on her pillow, waiting for a break in the prayer cycle—waiting for a gap in her concentration so they could jump back on top of her to resume their torments.

The more she prayed, the more she feared she wasn't praying hard enough, fast enough to keep them away. If she paused, even for a second, she thought she could feel the dark form of the Devil himself—a ranky little dog under her bed, reaching up with his filthy black claws to clutch her and pull her into the darkness.

She focused on the sequence of the rosary, keeping track of her place by slipping her thumbnail from bead to bead on its chain. Under the blankets, her hands fluttered like smothering birds, her panic building every time she approached the end of the cycle—the 108th bead.

The constant clicking of her thumbnail against the beads had worn a groove through the nail and into the skin on the end of her finger. A blister had risen, then popped wetly. The frantic sawing of the small chain drew blood, and a thick scab formed across the tips of her corresponding finger and thumb.

On her fourth day at St. Mary's, two nuns came into her room. It had been seven days since her vision of Hell.

"Okay, sweetie," said the large one. "Time for a bath."

With the look of a doomed puppy, the small girl walked to the bathroom and stood meekly as the two nurses undressed her.

They gasped when they saw her tiny naked body.

Thin as a crucifix, too weak to stand.

"Let's leave your beads here, dear. Don't want them getting wet, do we?"

Lolling frightened eyes at her rosary hanging just out of reach on the edge of the sink, she retched as they washed her in the tub.

"Mother save us, Father save us, Jesus save us," the girl murmured over and over.

Twice they filled and emptied the water. The girl floated limply, crying softly as the two nuns scrubbed her. One clucked and hummed while the other poured warm water over Sister's head. They lifted her, one at her shoulders, the other at her knees. The wasting girl leaned on the white pedestal sink with both elbows, holding her rosary over the drain, jibbering prayers in holy staccato jumble.

They dried her. "Now. Don't you feel better?"

Sister nodded, retched again, and fell to the white tile floor.

They dressed her, and then one of them pushed Sister Donica Lenore in a large wooden wheelchair down the long wide hallways, into the nearly empty dayroom.

Wes the Cartoon Man woke up in Recovery. Cold and torn, he had made it to the hospital under his own power, stumbling through the emergency room doors holding his bloody ass with both hands. He had shredded his backside and the seat of the red cloth bear suit bouncing on the pavement for two blocks, hanging on to the bumper of a taxi.

Drunk as he was, he was still in howling pain. It had taken the doctors two hours to get all the gravel out of his wide bottom. Wes passed out twice during the probing, gouging, cutting, and stitching.

"I hope you can sleep on your stomach," said the nurse on duty. It was four in the morning, she was pulling a double, and the last thing she wanted to see was the Cartoon Man's dopus.

Wes mumbled something into the crook of his elbow.

"Sign this," she said. Then she wheeled him into the padded room, where she left him.

He wouldn't be sober for another twelve hours, and when he was, he would be the sickest man in Nashua.

He needed to stay off his feet while he got clean of the booze, so they kept him in the soft room for the next six days, strapped naked on his belly to the gurney, while he heaved, drooled, raged, and screamed in cold-turkey delirium from the pain in his gut and his shredded rump. His arms were strapped to his sides, and every time he moved or coughed, the pain in his shoulder and chest nearly knocked him out. Between the hour-long waves of nausea, the big man jerked violently against the belts, crying and roaring. Twice he managed to flip the gurney over, and he lay there—still strapped and howling—until the orderlies could pick up the contraption and set it back on its wheels.

"Watch out, he's a biter."

Once a day they wheeled him into the shower room, where they pulled off the blanket and hosed him down on the gurney without releasing him. Wes cried and struggled as the cold water sprayed, stinging his large flabby body, across his butt and thighs, up between his legs, and then against the side of his head for good measure.

It had been a rude journey leading to this helpless pain.

After he was led off the set of *The Cartoon Show* in the red bear suit, Wes sat in the makeup room slamming on the bottle of Old Granddad he kept hidden in the ceiling. The bear head lay on the floor where Wes had thrown, then stomped, it. Goddamn Greeks.

The side of his head stung where his hair had been pulled off, and his right shoulder throbbed from being twisted or slugged. His knuckles were sore, and he was beginning to feel the tug of pain under his ribs every time he took a breath.

Two quick knocks at the door. Allen, the station owner, walked in.

"Ready for nighty-night?" he asked, smiling at the pajama-looking bear suit.

Wes shook his head and rolled his eyes. He held out the bottle. "Wanna slug?" he asked.

"Nope. Too early for me," said Allen. "Actually, that's what I wanted to talk about. I think you need some help with this, Wes."

"Drinking? I don't have a problem. I've never missed a day of work."

"You're not working now." Allen lit two cigarettes and gave one to Wes.

"This wasn't because I was drinking. I was attacked. I was getting ready to go on and they jumped me."

"Wes, listen to me. It's not just drinking, it's the whole picture. You're a great guy, but your own worst enemy. There's not a guy in the business who can set fire to a roomful of kids the way you do. The little shits adore you, but you can't have a career in kiddie TV and be getting in fights offstage—or showing up drunk and bloody on camera. If you weren't so good with kids I would've shitcanned you years ago. I can't carry you forever if you don't get yourself under control." Allen took a long pull on his cigarette. "Want some advice?"

"No," said Wes.

"Start with the drinking. I'm not kidding, Wes. This is a problem. I'm talking to you now as a friend."

Wes took a drink and smiled. "I already started," he said.

Allen grabbed the bottle and threw it at the sink. Piss-colored whiskey and pieces of glass shot across the counter. "Get out!" he yelled. "Now. Get out!"

Wes stood up, looking more worried than angry. He looked confused, as if he were trying to remember what he was going to say when this finally happened.

He kicked the bear head out the door, and it scooted across the hall. He left the room without looking back, without saying a word. He walked across the street into the Penguin Club, where he stayed until two o'clock in the morning, doing dancing bear tricks for his friends and anyone else who would buy him a drink.

Stone broke and blind drunk, he was walking up Stackman Street in his red bear suit, wearing the top half of the shattered bear's head balanced like a gravy boat over his eyes, when he saw the lone taxi parked in front of the hotel.

"Gimme a ride," he said to the driver. "I'm a Russian."

"A Russian?" the driver asked.

"Yeah," said Wes. "A-rushin' to get home."

"Get in," said the cabbie.

Six blocks later the driver figured out Wes didn't have any money.

"Get out."

"Okay," Wes said, laughing and lying down on the seat.

The driver pulled Wes out of the car by his ankles and pushed him down on the sidewalk. Wes stood up and sat on the trunk of the taxi. When the driver gassed the cab, Wes slid off the trunk and grabbed the back bumper.

Too drunk to let go, he hung on for two blocks.

In the morning, Veronica and I waited in the Magic Kingdom. We drank coffee in Tomorrowland while we reconned Cinderella's Castle.

"There aren't that many windows," Veronica said. "Are you sure he said he had a window?"

"He said he had a great view at night."

We watched the few narrow openings for movement.

The Disney buzz was all around us. The whole park is a walk-on stage, protected and happy. Everything about the place is different from the outside world you pay to leave when you walk through its gates. Real people dress as cartoon characters—imaginary beings walking among us, happy to include us in their world.

I posted Veronica as a decoy at a Coke Corner table. I stood inside a snack shop, looking through the shuffling crowds for Reggie. I wanted to see him before he saw me. I wanted to control our meeting.

A few minutes before eleven I saw him walking across the footbridge between the castle and Main Street. At first, I wasn't sure it was him. He looked like an early version of himself—ten years younger, thin, and happy. He was light on his feet, walking with a bounce, his arms swinging, his head bopping a little from side to side as if he were singing a jingle. He was wearing a pair of sandals, jeans, a T-shirt, and sunglasses.

His arms were muscular, no longer flabby, and there was no baby fat rolling over his belt. His sand-colored hair looked thicker, longer. He looked lean, like a swimmer.

His face was the most different. He had lost the wrinkles and bags under his eyes, the droopy mouth and splotchy skin of a bad drinker. He was tanned, tight, and healthy-looking. He was smiling for no reason at all.

He walked to Veronica's table and stood in front of her before she even recognized him. She was so startled, she didn't even stand up. He bent down to hug her, then he grabbed a chair, swung it around, and sat on it cowboy style.

It looked like he was alone, so I crossed Main Street and slapped him on the shoulder. He jumped up and gave me a killer hug. It was an eerie moment. The last time I saw Reggie, he was a spent forty-five-year-old man, tired, heavy, and depressed. The man I was hugging could have passed for a mid-thirties tennis pro.

"Reggie, I can't believe it. You look great."

"Thanks, man. You look tired. Can I get you anything?"

"Maybe another cup of coffee."

"I can smoke here, right?" Veronica asked.

"Shouldn't be smoking at all," said Reggie. "It really wipes out your serotonin."

"I know, Reggie. I'm a nurse, remember?"

"Just trying to help," he said. He winked at me, jumped up, and actually jogged to the counter.

"Just let him talk," I said to Veronica.

She shrugged and lit a Parliament.

"All we want today is a commitment that he's coming to the party, right?"

She nodded. I knew she was upset because Reggie looked so good.

"Listen," I said. "This has been a rough year for him. He deserves this—whatever it is."

"Everybody's had a rough year," she said.

I know Veronica. What she meant was, it's not fair that Reggie gets to walk away from his problems and start over on his own terms.

He came back from the snack bar with my coffee and a greenish milk shake.

"What's that?" Veronica asked.

"It's a protein smoothie. Claudia makes me one every morning." He nodded to a young girl behind the counter, who smiled and waved back. "Sometimes we go running together."

"I don't see it on the menu," said Veronica, squinting at the sign.

"It's contraband. She's got a secret blender under the counter."

Watching each other, we triangulated the round table. Nobody spoke, and I didn't know how to begin. I wanted to be in charge, not stuck between squabblers.

"I saw Carolyn last week," Veronica said. "She looked good. I told her I was coming down here to find you. She says hi."

"Her exact words?"

"She said she's gonna nail your ass if you lay one toe across the state line."

"Thanks for the update, Betty Boop. Did she mention Theresa?"

"Theresa's happy. She's dating a forward from Dartmouth."

"Oh, boy," he said, shaking his head. "The sins of the father in the eyes of the daughter. How are your kids?"

"Same old stuff," she said. "Catherine's still trapped in the hippie dream, and Jessie's a handful. I guess the babies are good. They don't have anything."

"How's Beth?" he asked me. "And Benny? What's his name now? Airplane Pointguard?"

"Everybody's fine."

"Tell them I said hey. How are you?"

"I'm okay," I said, "considering all the craziness with Wes."

"What's happening with him?"

"He's got the whole town in an uproar. East Mountain, West Mountain, families fighting each other—and everybody's mad at him. It's been a real blow to his ego; everybody treats him like a fool."

"And we could lose half the town," said Veronica.

"What? How?"

"It's not all his fault," I said. "You know how he always exaggerates things? Well, it turns out that all those years he was lecturing everybody on the history of the town, he was making up most of it. He didn't mean any harm; he just got carried away."

"Like what?"

"Like just about everything," said Veronica. "The Indians, the Talberts, the treaty."

"Talbert's famous Treaty? Why did he make that up?"

"Because we happened to live on the old Talbert homestead and it made him feel important, having them buried all over the place."

"So all those father-and-son shows you did playing Little Jimmy Talbert, Boy Patriot—were bogus?"

"Yeah, it looks like it."

"And you wonder why I called him an idiot? It serves him right for being so high-minded about his history lessons. Now I'm glad he kept me out of the show."

Here we go. The Saga of Reggie, the Outsider.

"Nobody kept you out," I said. "You refused to be in it. Wes wrote you a part. You were supposed to be King George. You said it was stupid."

"It was stupid."

"Of course it was stupid. I hated it, but nobody kept you out."

"Well, that's the way I remember it. You guys never took me camping, either. Wes told me I couldn't go."

"Maybe once when you were too young."

"No, it was all the time. It was always the Wes and Boone Club. I was odd boy out. No Reggies allowed. You guys were always laughing at me."

"You were a funny kid. You made everybody laugh. Wes always said you were the funny one."

"Can both of you shut up?" Veronica said as she clawed through her purse. "Do I have to listen to this for the *next* fifty years?"

She emptied her bag on the tabletop, brushed the lint off a loose Rolaid, popped it in her mouth, and lit another cigarette.

"Jesus," she said, squinting at both of us. "Nothing ever changes with you two."

"Say God-forgive-me," Reggie and I said in unison.

She blew smoke at Reggie. He shot a clot of smoothie at her with his straw.

"Stop it, both of you," I said, "or I'm going to cuff everybody to this table and go back to New Hampshire by myself."

They sat for a minute, giving each other the stink-eye.

"So when is Wes's court date?" Reggie asked.

"August thirty-first. The day before their anniversary party."

"Great timing. How is Sister doing?"

"She's okay, but she really misses you. That's why you need to come back. We could use the help, and you could clear the air with Wes. I know you've got issues with him, but he could use some support. It would mean a lot to Sister."

"I'm not ready to come back, and I'm not going to apologize to anyone. There's good things happening here."

"What good things?" asked Veronica. "You're broke and you're homeless."

"Wrong, Little Miss Sunshine," said Reggie. "I'm the richest man you'll ever meet. I don't need anything. I've discovered the meaning of life."

Veronica and I stared at him.

He leaned forward and looked over the tops of his sunglasses with his newbie Zen-child eyes.

"Love everything, no matter what," he said. He nodded wisely.

"Even Wes?" I asked.

He looked a little blanked. "Why? He never took me seriously."

"It's a two-way street," I said. "People can change."

"They sure can. When I came down here I was a mess. I was fat, angry, and toxic. I hated everybody. I was crazy because I didn't have ten dollars to my name. For three days I walked around the park; at night I slept under a salad bar in Frontierland. I was down to three bucks and scared to spend any of it. I watched people blow a grand in the gift shop, and I didn't have enough money to leave here and go anywhere else.

"Then one day I was sitting on a bench over on Polynesian Island, feeling sorry for myself and my three bucks. I was watching the parrots in the cages by the snack bar. These birds are unbelievable. They're a million different colors, but they live in cages so people can worship their value. As I was watching them, I noticed all the wild sparrows flying into the cage with the parrots, fluttering around in there, hanging out with the fancy birds and eating their food. When they were tired of being in the cage, they flew away, between the bars. Then it hit me: Nobody keeps a sparrow in a cage because people won't pay to see a sparrow. It's like they're invisible and completely free. Nobody covets the common things. Those little sparrows can go anywhere they want and nobody tries to trap them. So I put my three bucks on the bench and walked away from it. I haven't needed a penny since.

"All those years I spent showing off on TV, trying to be seen with famous jocks—just kept me in a cage. I thought I was so important, so famous. *I* was a famous sportscaster. Nashua's Voice of the Celtics. Nice cage, dude.

"Now I've got control over my own life. Nobody to boss me around, no Army of Saints. No more stress over money or fame. I can finally do whatever I want."

"Exactly what *do* you do?" asked Veronica.

"Well, Veronica, what *do* you mean?"

She looked up and down Main Street, USA. "Well, I don't see any prostitutes nearby."

"I don't do that anymore."

"I guess not. Don't they cost money? So what *do* you do with your life?"

"I live it."

"During the day, doofus. How do you spend your time?"

"I make people happy. I put on my costume and walk around. I've got a whole act. I pick some poor uptight-looking bastard out of a crowd and mess around with him until he smiles or gives me a hug. I'm this harmless character that makes people laugh."

"But you don't get paid for it," Veronica said.

"Even better," said Reggie. "It's a labor of love. Love doesn't count if you get paid for it. Ask Sister. I'm sure she'll agree, being a nun and all."

"So what's your plan?" Veronica asked him.

"I don't know, but something good will happen. Anyway, I'm not ready to go back. Not today."

I remembered what Sister said about not pushing him and how he wasn't finished.

"Well. We love you," I said. "Everybody loves you. I hope it works out."

"Thanks, man," he said. We all hugged.

6

On the seventh day, enough of the poison had leached out of Wes's system for the doctor to release the straps and let him find his feet. Wes held on to the railing in the long hallway and goofy-stepped sideways, his body shaking and his big baby face pinched with pain.

"How do you feel?" asked a nurse.

"Half-assed sober," he said.

He spent the morning lying in bed on his stomach, dizzy, sweaty, and shaking. After a lunch of watery broth and Wonder bread, he lay on a gurney with his chin on his hands as a stout nun wheeled him down long corridors to a hallway at the back of the hospital.

They stopped in a wide doorway. Doing a weak push-up, Wes looked into a spacious sunlit room with tall windows and a wide wooden floor.

"Dayroom," said the nun. "Doctor wants you to try walking."

She rolled him through the doorway to the far side of the room, where he could look down at the river and across it to the dark granite cliffs on the other side. The nun pushed Wes to the windowsill and adjusted the blanket across his back, then left the room. The gurney was the perfect height for lying on his belly and looking out the window. He could feel the cold glass on his brow and the warm breath of dry heat rising from the radiator beneath him. He dangled his fingers over the front of the gurney, feeling the hot air pool and curl between his knuckles.

He watched the dark marbled Hampshire River rolling flatly south to the left—the same direction as the winter wind that worried the leafless black trees.

He felt the electric jitters in his joints, the deep twisting nausea in his blood and the dull throb of his heartbeat in his head. From his hips to his knees, he couldn't move without the tight sting of pain in his ass.

Hell of a way to quit drinking, he thought.

Hell of a way to screw things up.

He had no money saved, he was two months late on everything, and now he didn't have a job. Working anywhere near Nashua was out of the question; every station for eighty miles had already heard about his problems, and nobody would take a chance on Wes Moffatt now. His cartoon days were surely finished.

He lay on the board, his forehead on the cold glass, watching the river slide by, feeling lost to his future and dead to his past.

He heard the door open and felt the closing presence of people behind him. He heard the soft shuffling of blankets and a woman whispering several feet away. He heard single footsteps leave the room and the sound of the door closing.

Still the lonely silence. Then:

"It's you," said the smallest voice he had ever heard.

Turning his head tightly to the left, he saw a thin pale girl sitting fifteen feet away, her oversize wooden wheelchair pulled up to a window, her knees nearly touching the radiator. She looked like a child bundled in the pile of gray blankets. She was looking at Wes with wide dark eyes.

"Hi, there," he said, trying to smile. She sat blinking, looking stunned. He turned back to his window. He could feel her watching him, so he twisted sideways to look at her again.

"Do we know each other?" he asked.

Wide-eyed and too shocked to talk, she just nodded.

"I'm at a loss."

"I'm the Sister," the girl said. "The nun from the orphanage. You gave me a donut."

"Oh God," moaned Wes. "I'm sorry. I meant to write you a letter—to apologize."

"That's alright," said the girl. "I know I look different—and not very good right now."

No kidding, he thought.

"You look great," he said. "It must be the menu. It's a shame—you just missed the dessert cart." He grinned boyishly.

She drew back into her blankets, still blinking at him. None of this was making any sense.

"Wes Moffatt," he said, introducing himself.

"Sister Donica Lenore. Holy Innocents."

The girl and the big man were quiet for a few minutes. He was looking out the window; she was staring at him, and he could feel the tension. He felt vulnerable, unable to look cool or move away. He turned toward her again.

"So," he said. "Why are you here? If you don't mind—"

The gray girl peered at him from beneath her pile of blankets. Her eyes had the cold shine of fear, and she reminded Wes of a baby bird caught and kept in a box. Her head wobbled. Her mouth opened briefly, then closed without warrant.

Holy Jumping Jesus, he said to himself. Get me out of this room.

"I don't know what's wrong with me," she finally said. "Nobody knows. It feels like everything's wrong. I've been in Hell," she said sadly.

"Oh," said Wes. "Was that *you*?"

The girl jerked, locking eyes with him. "Why did you say that?" she asked too quickly, as if he had insulted her.

"I don't know. I was just kidding. I didn't mean anything. I've just come through a rough patch myself and it seemed like Hell to me. Sorry."

He turned back to his window, annoyed with his lack of tact, her nervousness, and the interruption of his melancholy. He looked again to the cold river, the rolling darkness. Why was she watching him? His ass felt cold. Maybe she would get embarrassed and leave.

She couldn't stop watching him. It was too much to understand. She sat in the big wheelchair, her eyes blinking furiously and her mind spinning, throwing off pieces of shattered questions. *Why is he here? Why is this happening?*

"What happened to you?" she finally said.

Wes sighed. The window fogged in front of his face.

"Bad luck," he said. "Real bad. I kind of lost everything. I got carried away and I lost my job. I got thrown out of a taxicab and got scraped up. I came in for stitches and they gave me the treatment. Now I've been here a week."

She knew he was talking about the DTs, even though she didn't know what they were.

"How about you?" he asked. "When do you get out?"

The girl shrugged sadly. "I don't know," she said. "I don't know if I can go back."

"I don't follow," said Wes. "You lost your sponsor, too?" When in doubt, joke.

The girl looked at him oddly. How could someone joke about being sick? She looked out the window.

A few moments passed.

"So why did the nun get fired?" he asked.

She blinked a few times. "I don't know."

"She refused to change her habits."

Sister made a noise like a mouth fart—like someone had squeezed it out of her.

The Cartoon Man laughed when he heard it, then groaned from his broken ribs.

"Don't mind me," he said. "What's the difference between a hospital and a jail?"

"I don't know."

"The food's better in jail. And they have bars."

She sat blinking.

"Here's one for you," he said. "What's the difference between God and a doctor?"

"I don't know."

"God doesn't think he's a doctor."

She chirped. Heartened, he continued.

"How come doctors don't get hemorrhoids?"

"I don't know. Why?"

"Because they're perfect assholes."

At that, she blanched.

"Sorry," he said. "This one's better: What do colostomy patients and typewriters have in common?"

"I don't know."

"Semicolons."

Another surprised honk from the girl. She didn't know how to cope with this conversation, to keep up with his jokes. They're called puns, she told herself. He was the first man she had ever spoken to outside the borders of the church, and she was lost in the conversational wilderness. From all she had seen—in the television studio, and now in the dayroom—he acted like he was from another world. She wanted him to keep talking.

She worried about her appearance. She wanted the nurse to come back and save her from embarrassing herself. *What happens next? Do we keep talking? Is it my turn to say something funny?*

She tried to think of something amusing from her life.

She tried to think of anything amusing.

Nothing came to mind.

To him, being funny seemed easy. He acted like everything he said would make her laugh. Just the way he talked made her pay attention, expecting another joke. He paused before he said words that were supposed to sound funny, and then they did. Even the way his round fleshy face looked when he wasn't talking seemed funny. His eyebrows arched slightly, and the corners of his mouth turned up as if he were holding back a smile. He looked soft and pleasantly bored, like a big tired boy waiting for trouble to catch his eye. He acted relaxed—even in his broken state.

"I can't tell jokes," she finally said.

We're a pair, he thought. I can't think straight.

"I guess in your job it helps to have a good sense of humor," she offered, feeling instantly embarrassed by the lameness of her observation.

He grunted. God, how he wanted a cigarette. In front of a nun, he would sell his soul for a butt.

Sister Donica Lenore looked away from the big fleshy man on the gurney to her own tiny socks on the footrests of the wheelchair.

This was impossible. It was hard to believe that he was the same man who had stumbled around the television studio making the children laugh, and that he was the bloodred bear in her vision who had—

Suddenly, a racing thought shot through her, and she jerked backward, as if surprised by something close to her face. She caught her breath violently through her teeth. The wheelchair creaked. Wes looked over.

"You okay?" he asked. "Sister?"

She looked startled, very afraid.

She had just realized that she hadn't prayed a single Rosary since she recognized the Cartoon Man. For the first time in seven days, her obsession was dislodged. Without realizing it, she had allowed herself to be distracted. Now she was unprotected and the old fear grabbed and choked her.

The sharp jolt that made her catch her breath and sent her head back against the top of the wheelchair was the thought that the Devil would snatch her soul now—this very moment—and carry her back to Hell.

Panic flashed through her, but before she could catch herself—before she could begin praying—the Cartoon Man asked again.

"Hey. You okay?"

The moment tightened. She was confused. The girl found herself at a dividing place: to look inward and resume her ritual—or to acknowledge the big easy man in the warm open room who was speaking her way. She stared out the window.

"Yes," she said. "I'm fine."

And that's all it took.

With those three words, she stayed in the moment. She chose to pay attention, not to return to her fears. She chose Wes the Cartoon Man, making him bigger than her fear of failure and fear of Hell.

"Good," he said. "Don't spazz out on me. I'm lapsed, you know. Completely useless."

She didn't even hear him. As she said the words "Yes, I'm fine," she felt instantly lighter, empty of fear. It felt like a kind of birth, a warm wash of relief. She felt herself changing, the warmth coming back to her body—floating upward from her feet and outward from her heart. She realized that the numbness in her arms and legs was gone. She shrugged off her blanket and looked at her hands. They were steady.

Sister started crying, and she couldn't stop. She didn't care who saw her.

The big man was watching. Sweet Mary of Poughkeepsie, this is one wacky nun.

He was trapped. He couldn't ignore her, and he certainly couldn't leave. He lay on his gurney, eyes straight ahead, faking distance and waiting for her to subside.

She cried softly for several minutes, her face cradled in her hands, crying tears of relief that felt like forgiveness, washing the doubt from her soul.

When she stopped crying, she sat quietly, looking out the window, seeing the glorious starkness of winter—black trees on bone sky and the million beautiful shades of gray in the rocks and waters. She listened to her own sounds, her breath, her heartbeat, the new silence of peace in her head, and she felt warm. She shrugged off another blanket.

"Oh, my," she sighed, mostly to herself.

The man looked at her, waiting.

"Sorry," she said, smiling shyly. "I don't know what to say. I guess I needed to do that."

"No problem," he said. "I'd cry myself, but I left my makeup in my other purse." He vamped, batting his eyes like a floozy.

She snorted her barky laugh again, and he laughed along with her.

They sat in front of the windows, trading small talk for another hour. She kept quiet through his monologues. Still hopelessly shy, she missed her cues and didn't understand most of his jokes.

At four o'clock, the nurse came to wheel her back to her room.

"May I try to walk?" Sister asked.

"Good for you," said the nurse. "At least partway. Don't overdo."

Donica Lenore pulled herself out of the wheelchair. She smiled at Wes. "Good-bye," she said, wobbling away.

"See you 'round the campfire," he said, giving her a three-fingered Boy Scout salute.

While she waited for dinner, Sister sat on the bed holding her rosary, absently slipping the beads between her fingers and feeling the weight of the small chain shift across her palm.

Her demons had been scattered, shooed away, by two hours of bad puns. A fat man with nothing to his name had returned her to God's grace.

It seemed so simple now: The blue angel, the helpless bear, and her fall to Hell—these visions were story versions of God's plan for her. This was the way He chose to talk to His child. From now on, she promised, I'll pay attention to every little story—even if I don't know what it means.

Was there a saint for people who can't see God's signs because they're too busy praying? Maybe it's St. Obvious.

"Hee," she chirped. I made a joke. I need to remember that for tomorrow.

After a meal of turkey with gravy, mashed potatoes, two biscuits, carrots, milk, a brownie, and lightly sugared tea, the child nun fell asleep fully dressed, on top of the blankets on her bed.

It was her first full meal in a month, and it was her first peaceful sleep in two weeks.

As she slept, she dreamed of a sweetly scented mist that settled upon her like the breath of God. Her soul was released and she was borne away in the mist as a weightless spirit, beyond her body, outside the hospital, and above the snow-covered city. It was an easy, lazy drift, away from the frozen valley, over wide plains and shining rivers, through a cloudless sky, toward a grand ridge of fertile mountains outlined in the rising dawn.

She floated above the mountaintop and settled on the leaves of grass and trees as a million morning beads of diamond light.

As the mist rolled on, across the top of the range to the dawn of distant mornings, Sister sat glorious on the mountaintop with her knees tucked under her chin, watching the sunlight pour across the land beneath her. The breeze riffled her hair.

This was Heaven on earth, the way the world was meant to be; and this was the place where she belonged, at this locus of covenant—the nineteen-year-old daughter of God, sitting in peace, at the summit of His favor and love.

Sister walked to a spot where the soft, dark loam looked like a garden waiting for planting. She kneeled and scooped a hole in the dirt the size of a bowl. She bent over it, praying.

"I promise to keep my side of our bargain," she whispered into the earth.

When she spoke her vow, the words came from her mouth in a soft cloud and settled in the bottom of the hole. The cloud circled and swirled and formed a round azure seed, a tiny globe the size of a marble. The blue-green seed sat and shimmered like water as Sister covered it with soft earth, and as she watched, a fragile green seedling rose up, into the morning light. It grew three branches with delicate leaves shaped like the hands of children praying and delicate blossoms the color of cream. The scent of honey nectar soaked the clear mountain air. This was her promise tree, the tree of her life and testament of her promise to God. This tree was hers to tend with care, protect with prayer.

. . .

She awoke at dawn, said her morning prayers, gave thanks for her dreams, and then went to the bathroom, where she showered, happily humming to herself.

Hello. Another lovely day, she would say. No, no, no. Hi. Another lovely day, isn't it? Maybe he wouldn't think that was funny. Hello. It's still winter, isn't it? Hi, she decided she would say. Cold enough for you?

A knock. "All right in there, honey?"

"Yes. Thank you," she said.

"Feeling better?" the nurse asked.

"Much."

A clean johnny and a light blue terrycloth robe lay folded on her bed. Sister dressed and stood by the window, watching gray pigeons bluffing outside on the ledge.

The nurse returned and checked the girl's signs. Clear lungs, good heart. Affect greatly improved, she wrote in the folder. "Hungry?" she asked.

"A little," said the girl. "I'm not much of a breakfast eater. Some tea with sugar would be nice, though. And maybe some eggs and toast, please."

The nurse jotted. Appetite, good; attitude, excellent. Recommended for release.

The big man was lying on his gurney in front of the dayroom windows. For Wes the Cartoon Man, the nights were the worst—wrestling against the grinding pain of his boozy cravings. This morning, the wiry nausea still ran hot through his blood, swamping his thoughts and making his bones ache in the odd places of his neck, his jaws and teeth. He still had the shakes. Lying on his stomach, he could feel the tremors build from low in his bones, then rise in a cold shiver to the muscles on the backs of his legs. The shakes swept upward from his buttocks through his back, into the base of his neck. They came in clenching waves that lasted five minutes. The sweat poured off his back, around his wide sides, and onto the rubber sheet that covered his bed. In the morning, his blanket was always soaked and his back wrenched tight from the spasms.

When I get out, he swore, I will never touch another drink. When I get out, he swore, I will never stop drinking.

Either way, drinking wasn't a habit he could easily quit—at least not yet.

For Wes Moffatt, booze was food. Booze wasn't *like* food, it *was* food. He had been drinking hard liquor since he was nine, and all the other things he put in his belly—pastrami, hash, milk shakes, hot dogs, chowder, coffee, biscuits, fried eggs, steak, baked beans, pie, and donuts—were merely bulk. His real sustenance was marked 80 proof. There was no right or wrong to his chemistry; it was simply how he was raised, and it would take a miracle to burn his blood and bones clean of the poison.

Before this outrage, he had been happy. He was employed and he was well-liked. Women found him harmless and playful. Men envied his independence, his boisterous personality, and his easygoing way with women.

He was the big man with the funny bones.

Now this. Goddamn Greeks. Goddamn taxi, goddamn Allen Walz.

It had all fallen apart, and it seemed terribly unfair—all these bad things that had happened to him without warning. Now it was all gone: his job, his freedom, his habits, his health, his apartment and all that he owned held for back rent; and as he lay on the gurney gazing across the river and up the hills to the rocky woods, he was stunned by the blank unfairness of it all.

If they released him today, he couldn't put his hands on twenty cents— or even a set of clean clothes. He had no one to call, no one to count on for help. He had been in the hospital seven days and none of his drunken cronies or desperate girlfriends had come to see him. He was alone, lonely, and worried.

This was more than bad luck. Bad luck could be temporary and could be changed by chance. But bad luck needed something to work with, and it felt to him that everything in his life was gone. There was nothing left of his life solid enough for him to frame a plan.

Wes the Cartoon Man was in real trouble, and he needed help.

The young girl in the light blue bathrobe walked quickly through the hospital, stopping only once to rest in a stairwell. She chatted pleasantly with the nurse as they made their way to the dayroom.

"Sometimes a change of scenery is the best medicine," the nurse was saying as they walked through the doorway. The big man looked over his shoulder at them, then turned back to his window.

Sister pulled a chair from the back wall to the row of windows, being careful to sit no closer to him than she had the day before. She sat and looked out the window with her hands folded in her lap, wondering who should speak first. She sensed him stirring on her right.

The sunlight wasn't so bright today.

With the instincts of a show-off, Wes prepped for his audience. He wet-palmed his cowlick and worried whether the blanket covered enough of his legs.

"How are we doing today?" he asked, after the nurse had left the room.

"Much better," said the girl. "I feel fine. Yourself?"

"Oh, great," he said flatly. "This is a real picnic."

He snorted.

"I'm sorry," the girl said.

"Don't be. I'm just tired, is all. I'm tired of being here, I'm tired of lying down, tired of being sick. I'm tired of my life."

"That's not a good thing to say. Life is a gift."

"Yeah, yeah," he said. "I know. But you get to a point . . ." He trailed off, his voice sagging to a sigh and the window fogging in front of him.

They were quiet.

"Can I do anything?" she finally asked.

"Not unless you've got an extra cigarette."

"Alright," she said, standing up. She left the room. A few minutes later she returned with a half pack of Viceroys and a battered Zippo. She set them on the gurney by the big man's elbow. "I promised to return the lighter," she said.

"Oh, by jingo," he said. "You got smokes?" He pushed himself up, resting on his elbows. She stood by the gurney watching him light a shakey, then blow a lazy cloud at the ceiling. The big man's eyes were blissfully closed.

"You have no idea," he said, "how good this tastes. It should be a law: Nobody gets the cure without free smokes. Thank you." He popped his eyes open, wiggled his eyebrows, and took another heavy drag. He pulled on it like a drowning man.

She stood against the wall between the high wide windows, her hands in the pockets of her robe, like any teenage girl facing the morning. Her thin face was circled with curls of wavy dark hair that was cut too short for fashion. She stood straight-backed against the wall without the hint of a slouch, like a child being measured for height.

She was small, barely five feet tall, and although she was just a girl, there was a heavy quality in her nature that he couldn't work with. Her wide dark eyes had a steady, open gaze that he found unnerving. She was watching him calmly, intently, and he couldn't tell what she was thinking.

She was thinking about how everything fit together—her vision followed by his appearances in her life and the easy way he released her from her hell of fear and doubt. She was marveling at God's infinite ability to connect unlikely events with less likely characters to accomplish His purpose of goodness on Earth. She was wondering about the future and whether she found him handsome.

Wes couldn't decide if she was his type, or even if she was pretty; then he remembered that she was a nun. Christ Almighty, this was confusing.

"I'm sorry you feel so bad," she said. "What's wrong?"

"Everything," he said. He looked at her and shrugged. "I'm twenty-six. Half of my life is gone and I've got nothing to show for it except bad habits and worse luck. You don't want to hear this."

He hauled another slug on the Viceroy and tried to look matinee. He squinted through the smoke as he exhaled, and dropped his smoking hand heavily onto the gurney. He looked down at his fingernails. If he had a drink in front of him, he would have cocked his eyebrow and run a finger around the edge of the glass, shrugging fatally. It was patent barstool posing, palooka parody.

He thought it was working, but he was wasting his lines. It was all wasted theater, because this girl was the wrong audience. She wasn't watching his heavy hands in their smooth mime, and she wasn't falling for his Hollywood dash.

She didn't even know what role he was playing.

This was the girl who had never been to the movies, never flirted in a diner, never turned up her nose or turned on her heel, never lied to her mother or spied on her father, never worried a boy or covered for a friend.

She lacked the currency to buy his act. Instead, she saw clear through his hack words and shabby gestures to the nature of his soul, where she saw only emptiness. Not badness, only emptiness. It was a hollow place looking to be filled.

He didn't know it, but today he was in luck. She was the only person who could help him. She was strong and calm, and she was near. Another woman would have played along, then gone away. Sister couldn't. She didn't know how. She had never been suckered for sympathy by a man, and so she played it straight. She simply listened and cared.

"Of course I do," she said.

He lit a second cigarette. "I don't usually chain-smoke," he lied, "but it's been a week, and it helps me think. Crazy, huh?"

He tapped an ash between the edge of the gurney and the radiator. "Maybe I'll head down to New York and get a job there. Actually, I'd like to get out of kiddie TV and do some serious work. John Cameron Swayze stuff. This could be a blessing in disguise. This all sounds crazy to you, huh?"

"No. It doesn't."

"Before my accident I was talking to some people in Los Angeles. Maybe I'll follow up on that. Do you know how much they make on national television—doing the same thing I do?"

She shrugged.

"Forty thousand a year. Buffalo Bob makes forty thousand a year. Bozo—thirty-five thousand a year. Wiggly Feldstein—thirty thousand. *Wiggly Feldstein!* He ain't even funny. He makes kids cry. Seriously. Kids cry on his show." He hauled on his Viceroy and blew an O. "It's my own fault. I wish I didn't drink so much, but I do. The truth is, I couldn't stop if I had to. Sooner or later I'll be back in here going through the cure again. Here or somewhere else."

"Was it bad?" the girl asked.

"Bad?" he snorted. "You have no idea. I was out of my mind."

He lit another cigarette and started coughing. The girl sat down.

"First of all, I was really hurting when I came in here. After that accident with the taxi, I needed all kinds of surgery. Nobody told me that I was going to get clean, so they just tied me down and left me alone to dry out.

"They gave me some dope for the operation, but it wore off. Then they locked me in the rubber room and forgot about me. The next morning my ribs hurt so bad, I couldn't even breathe. Then I got the heaves. I felt like I was being twisted like a washrag. I couldn't sleep, but I wasn't really awake, either. And I couldn't tell the difference because of all the dreams."

"Dreams?" she asked.

"Oh, yeah," he said. "The worst. And they're not pink elephants, either. Cartoons I can handle. Nope. *This* was real. What I saw was as real as you and me."

"What?" she asked, somehow already knowing.

"You're gonna think I'm crazy, but I was sliding down some big muddy hole with a pile of dead people, and I was trying to fight my way out, but there were more people pouring into the hole, piling in on top of me, and we were all fighting to get out. Everybody was screaming because we knew we were going down the chute—no matter how much we fought. We were like this big squirming pile of worms, sliding into a hole. I think it was Hell or something."

He looked over at the girl. She was wide-eyed, barely breathing.

"Are you okay?" he asked. "I didn't mean to scare you."

She was staring at him.

"What's wrong?" he asked. "You think I'm crazy, don't you?"

She shook her head. "No, I don't. I know what you saw."

"Well," he said, "I never want to see *that* again. I guess that's what you see when you're dying."

"We're not dead," she said quietly. "There is always hope."

"I don't know," he said. He mashed the cigarette on the windowsill and dropped the stub behind the radiator. "I'm just about ready to give up."

"Don't give up," she said. "Have you tried praying?"

"Not really," he said. "Nothing I pray for ever works out, anyway. Maybe I'm saying the wrong prayer, or praying to the wrong saint, but nothing ever gets better for me."

"I'd be happy to pray for you. It's what I do best. If you want me to, that is."

"Okay," he said. "I'll keep it in mind—if it comes to that. Thanks."

They stayed together in the dayroom, talking for another hour until the nurse came for the girl.

"It was nice talking to you," said Wes. He reached across himself to shake hands with her. "Here," he said, handing her the lighter. "Thanks. Hope to see you again, Sister."

"Same for me," she said. She followed the nurse out of the room, her paper slippers sliding away with dry hushing sounds.

Superior was waiting in her room.

"God be praised for your recovery," she said. "You have been in our constant prayers."

"God be praised," said Sister Donica Lenore, bowing her head and crossing herself.

"The doctor has agreed to release you. You may come home now, but we must be careful with you, child." There was a warning in the welcome, and while the girl was in the bathroom changing into her habit, the Superior groped the pockets of the blue robe.

A Zippo?

. . .

That evening at Vespers, Sister Donica Lenore counted the candles lit in honor of her return. All the sisters welcomed her, but later, as she lay in her dusty room, she felt a growing uneasiness. She had never noticed how dark her room was, how close and drab were the hallways of her convent, or how shabby the rooms of the orphanage looked.

The dayroom had been so open and cheerful; she wanted to go back to the hospital tomorrow. It had been exciting to stand with her back to the windows, listening to the Cartoon Man tell jokes, talk about himself and his different life.

There was something new coming her way, something different in her life—she could feel it—and a curious sense of acquaintance with the approaching mystery.

And then she felt something else—the deep wavering in her bones.

"Oh no, dear Lord, please no," she whispered. "Not again, not now."

The lightness came over her, the rushing heat and the waves of sour tingling nausea. She felt her body stiffen, her fingertips pinching at the woolen blanket and her eyelids shivering over her straining eyes.

There was nothing she could do, so she laid her head on the pillow and waited for the light to carry her away. As always, she felt herself soaring, then sinking, but this time, something was different. It was in her eyes.

Oh God, she thought, I'm blind.

She knew her eyes were open because she could see bursts of delicate pastels spilling over her in gently rolling waves. The colors were changing—from iris to rose to jonquil, and then to a deeper violet. She could see the misty colors and feel them change around her, but she couldn't see through the shimmering corona to any of the objects in her room.

It was a soft vision. There were no images this time—only a deep, soulful sense of peace inside the swirling aurorae. It was beautiful, and she felt wonderfully relaxed.

She lay still for a while and waited calmly for something to happen. She could feel her body rolling gently from side to side as if she were lying on pillows on the floor of a small rowboat, rocking on a lazy pond.

She noticed an odd aroma that grew stronger—from the hint of a far-away kitchen to the rich smell of a banquet nearby. Mixed with the familiar scents of cinnamon, pepper, chocolate, fresh bread, vanilla, and roasting meat were strange spices she wouldn't taste again for fifty years.

The dreamy feast floated around her, and she hauled in hungry breaths of the steaming food. Peppery gravies, curry, cilantro, and lightly burnt sugars were mixed with the sweet lightness of pineapple and mint. She arched her neck and breathed deeply. Lying peacefully on her back, she was in a state of complete bliss as the changing lights and the narcotic smells poured over her.

"I want some root beer, too," she said.

"Root beer for my bride," commanded a familiar voice, as if the speaker were standing beside her bed.

The voices had begun. They were all talking, happily interrupting each other. There were six men and five women talking. It was a party of some kind. There were laughing children, and as she lay on her bed watching the lights, smelling the food, and listening to the voices, she felt excited to be part of such a happy crowd.

"Never laid a glove on me," the familiar voice said, and the group of people laughed. It was the Cartoon Man who was talking. She recognized his voice by its happy tone and the way he threw the line away—as if he expected everyone to laugh. She knew it was his voice, even though he sounded much older. His voice was softer and deeper, but he still stretched his words like a storyteller.

"That's bold," said another man. "Humility in the face of disaster." The gathering laughed again.

"What disaster?" Wes asked. "It gave people something to talk about, and we learned who our real friends are."

"Yeah. All twelve of us," said a woman. Her voice had the familiar sound of a longtime friend, and Sister strained to recall the woman and her name, but there was too much distance between the sound of the woman's voice and anything Sister could foresee.

"Root beers up," said Wes.

There was an open moment while the group arranged their salute. Then Sister could hear the clicking of glasses and cups. A child laughed.

"Bottoms up," said Wes. Then they all chanted:

"Through the lips and past the gums,
Look out, belly, here it comes."

They sipped their toast.

As Sister Donica Lenore lay on her small bed in 1954, she could taste the fizz of homemade root beer as it bubbled on her tongue a half century later.

While the voices hummed and the smells of the freshly cooked meal spilled around her and the changing pastel nimbus floated over her eyes, the young nun felt herself settling into a dreamy comfort like nothing she had ever known. It was so peaceful and exciting. She felt like an honored guest at the banquet. She felt affection for all the voices and tried to see them by straining through the misty colors. She wanted this to be more than a vision; she wanted to stay with these friends, at this party and place, forever.

The emptiness she had felt for all her short life was filled for a moment. She was warm and protected, in the comfort of her kind.

"Another toast, folks," she heard Wes say. "Another toast before we take the picture."

Sister could feel their attention turning her way.

"Here's to my bride," Wes said. "As beautiful as the day we married, and the only reason we're a family today. I've said it a million times, and I'll say it again: She saves my life every day. Thank you, sweetie, for having faith in me."

There was a light breath, then a soft brushing across her lips. It was a kiss. She felt the hot flush of her cheeks.

"I love you all so much," she heard herself say.

And then it was over. The kiss and the sound of her own voice brought her back to the real place where she lay—on her narrow bed in her bare room with a table, a chair, the iron crucifix on the wall.

The dream was gone.

7

Veronica was so whacked she smoked five Parliaments, ate another Xanax, and took a nap. Seeing Reggie twenty-five years younger and enjoying himself really pissed her off.

We had five hours until our flight, so I went back to the Magic Kingdom to buy Jessie's jacket and spy on Reggie.

The walkabout characters don't come into the gift shops, so I stood in a corner by the window, pretending to look at Grumpy the Dwarf dish tow-els for a half hour until I saw him.

He came dancing around the corner of the Fantasyland snack bar with twenty Koreans following him, doing the funky chicken. I knew it was him. I recognized the funky chicken. I knew they were Koreans because their T-shirts said so.

He was taller than everyone else, with an oversize head, floppy jacket, wide-brimmed hat, suspenders, wire-rimmed glasses, and baggy pants. His face had a funny gonna-make-ya-laugh look with bushy cocked eyebrows and a wide crooked mouth.

He stopped the Koreans in the middle of the sidewalk and had them pogo for a few beats; then he pointed at the sky. They all looked up. He stood there, pointing at nothing, until they all wandered away. He walked over to a bench and pretended to fall asleep on an old woman's shoulder, and when her husband came back with snacks, he mimed a whole honest-buddy-I-didn't-even-kiss-her schtick.

He left the old lovers and put himself in a pack of teenage girls. He picked one and mimicked her, with one foot forward, hand on his hip, head at thirty-degree cellular tilt and palm to his ear. When she tried to get away from him, he followed her with his hands together, begging to be forgiven, or shot on the spot. Her friends hooted and took pictures.

My brother, the character.

The fourth time I saw the Devil was in Hull, Massachusetts.

Beth and I weren't married yet. I had just finished the late shift and was dozing in front of the TV when the phone rang.

"Is this Mr. Boone?" It was a girl's voice, scared and shaky.

"This is Daniel Moffatt. That's my nickname, Boone."

"Well, you don't know me, but I'm with a guy who I think is your brother? Reginald Moffatt?"

"Is he okay? Where are you?"

"I'm in Hull. Can you come down here?"

"Where?" I grabbed my pen and scratchbook out of my cop jacket.

"It's Hull. Massachusetts."

"Is he breathing?"

"Yeah. He's making funny noises, though."

"Like what?"

"Like snoring, but worse."

"Yeah, that's him. What's your address?"

"I don't know. It's a beach thingy, like cottages. The Strand. He's famous, isn't he? So is there some kind of reward for this?"

"Yeah. Stay with him and I'll give you some money. What room are you in?"

"It's the last one on the end. Including the money he owes me?"

"Sure. Just keep him on his side, and if he pukes, make sure he doesn't fall asleep in it."

"Ick."

"What's your name?"

"Donna Belle."

"Your real name."

"Debbie Metzinger."

"Okay, Debbie. I'm leaving now, and it's going to take me two hours to get there. Don't leave him alone. I'm going to call you every fifteen minutes. If you have to go to the bathroom, leave the door open so you can watch him. Understand?"

"Okay. Okay."

"You did a good thing by calling me, Debbie. I really appreciate it. Please don't leave him."

"And you're going to, you know, give me a reward."

"Absolutely. Just don't leave him alone."

I drove to the station and traded my truck for the extra cruiser. I hit the road at sixty and the interstate at eighty-five. I left-laned all the way through Boston and was on the South Shore by three in the morning.

The girl answered the door in a tight no-belly tee that said LOVE SUCKS. Not a day over fifteen, smoking a joint.

The room smelled like vomit, weed, and bad meat. Reggie was lying on the floor in the corner, naked from the waist down. He had an ugly scrape on his forehead, and his arm was bent backward, under a busted-up TV.

The girl sat cross-legged on the bed. She wasn't wearing any underwear.

"Got my money, Danny-boy?" she asked in a voice no different from any girl.

"What did you do to him?"

"Everything he asked me to," said the Devil.

There was broken glass everywhere, even in Reggie's hair. I pulled the TV off him and dragged him by his armpits to the side of the bed. I checked his eyes. Pupils like empty holes. I wrapped him in the bedspread and sat him up.

The girl slid over to the edge of the bed.

"Hey, Boone, wanna fool around? I can bend myself all the way back, with my face under my ass." She showed me.

I went out to the car and opened both rear doors. When I came back into the room, she was dressed and doing her makeup.

"So why are you doing this tonight?" I asked.

"I was bored," she said. "And it didn't look like you were doing anything."

"I didn't need this."

"Sure you did. You're not happy unless you're cleaning up somebody else's mess. It's not your fault; it's the way you were raised. You're such a little martyr, always trudging uphill. But I like Reggie," she said. "He's so easy. He doesn't give a shit about anybody, does he?"

"He's my brother. We look out for each other."

"Oh, please. You look out for him and he looks for trouble."

She brushed some aqua on her lids.

"Whattaya think?" she asked. "Too much around the eyes?"

"It's an improvement," I said. "Now you just look like a whore."

I got Reggie sitting on the bed, then put my shoulder under his belly and hefted him up and out the door. I carried him to the car and set him on the backseat. I went around to the other side and pulled on his wrists. I covered him with a blanket, shut the back doors, and got in the cruiser.

The Devil came out of the room and walked to my window.

"Until next time," she said, kissing her fingertips and patting my forehead. "And tell your mother if she doesn't back off, I'll keep fucking with her favorite son."

"I can handle it."

"Not *you*, stupid."

She walked thirty feet, stopped at the edge of the driveway, and stuck out her thumb.

8

Superior was certain the little nun had lost her mind. She watched her flit around the orphanage, sweeping, scrubbing, and collecting all the dirty laundry. The girl smiled and talked to herself as she hauled the huge bundles downstairs to the basement. In the early afternoon, Superior found her standing in the kitchen by the great iron stove, dreamily watching a noisy teapot blow steam.

"When did you start drinking tea?" she asked the girl.

"I don't know," the girl said blankly.

She dusted the sacristy, then collected and stacked all the missals in the chapel. She pressed the antipodium and scraped all the wax off the floor in front of the votive table—all the while singing to herself and smiling in a private way. By three o'clock the girl had done the work of twelve impossibly happy saints. Forget the Zippo, this was all very odd.

And then, in late afternoon, the girl vanished.

"I guess he was better, Sister. The doctor released him."

"I don't suppose you know where he went, do you?"

The nurse on duty looked at the girl. "No, but he did leave under his own power. On crutches."

Sister was confused. She had slipped away from the church and gone to the hospital to find Wesley. She needed to see him. She needed answers.

The nurse watched the nun blink absently at the countertop. "Is there anything else I can help you with?" she asked.

"Oh. No, thank you. God bless," she said quietly, before turning away.

The cold wind pushed hard against her shoulders, wrapping her wimple around her face as she walked back to the church. The few people she passed couldn't see her tears.

This was true torment. How did this fit with last night's vision? Wasn't Wesley toasting her as his bride? When did they marry? Did he know they were going to be married? Of course not, but how could they get married if she couldn't even find him? And if he *didn't* know, who would tell him? She didn't even know where he had gone. She remembered his plans for

New York or California, and her spirit sagged as she lost hope of seeing him again.

She wanted to revisit the dream, and as she walked back to the church she tried to recall the sounds and smells of the peaceful dinner party. Instead, she gave herself a headache.

That evening, she mumbled through her prayers at dinner and picked absently around her food. She fumbled with her rosary during Vespers and missed cues in the Ave descant.

The next morning, she was kneeling on the floor, stashing breakfast dishes in the long wooden cupboard.

"Sister Donica Lenore." Superior was standing in the doorway of the kitchen. "You have a visitor."

They both held their gaze long enough to make sure that neither knew why.

Sister followed Superior to the front door. Standing in the vestibule, nervously picking at the clasp of her fake alligator purse, was a middle-aged rusty-colored woman with wide hips, wearing a too-tight bright blue chenille skirt, a worn-looking cashmere overcoat, and a red rayon scarf. She looked very tired. When she saw the two nuns, she attempted an awkward genuflect that nearly dropped her.

"This is Sister Donica Lenore," Superior said. "Is she the one?"

"I dunno, really," said the woman. "Was you in the hospital?" she asked Sister.

"I was."

"Well, I guess I've got a message for you, or something," the woman said, looking at Superior but talking to the girl.

"I'll let you two speak in private," said Superior, taking her leave, then parking herself around the corner where she could easily eavesdrop.

The woman made her eyes narrow. "I know this guy, and he's in real bad shape. And I think he keeps asking for you."

"Is he a big funny man?"

"If you think train wrecks are funny," the woman said.

"Is he alright?"

"Not really. I think he's sleeping now, but I need you to get him out of my apartment. He's not my boyfriend or anything, but he can't stay there. He sort of followed me home." She rolled her eyes as if the nun would understand.

"Now?" Sister asked.

"I'm real late for work," the woman said. "And I can't leave him there all day. Not after last night."

Sister walked past the woman, opened the door, and motioned her outside. They walked rapidly up the street into the wild winter wind, stepping carefully in the narrow path that had been shoveled down the middle of the sidewalk.

"You shoulda brung a coat," the woman said over her shoulder.

After they left, Superior shut the door to her office, jerked open the top drawer of her desk, grabbed her cigarettes, and fumbled thickly with the Zippo. She paced angrily for a few minutes through the hovering trail of smoke; then she went to the window, where she blew smoke rings at the glass. She liked the way the smoke bounced back off the window, toward her. It looked like it could pass through the glass to the outside, but of course it couldn't.

The woman and the little nun paused at the apartment door.

"Gotta warn you. It ain't pretty," the woman said.

The sour-sweet-acid smell of urine, vomit, and spilled whiskey poured around them as they walked into the small green apartment.

"I guess he drank most of two days," the woman said. "Let's see where he ended up."

They walked through the narrow hallway, past a bedroom, being careful to step around a broken lamp, wads of clothes, and a grand pile of puked-up macaroni and cheese. Down the hallway was a small bathroom. The door was open, and a pair of very large white feet protruded into the hallway.

"There's Prince Charming," the woman said.

Wes was lying on his back on the bathroom floor, his shoulders wedged tightly between the toilet and the tub, his arms pressed against his sides. He looked like he was lying down at attention. His head rested on the bathroom scale. It read forty-two pounds.

"Always said he had a big head," the woman snickered.

It was the first naked man the nun had ever seen. She wasn't impressed.

"His clothes are around here somewhere," said the woman. "I guess we should get him out of the bathroom first."

They each grabbed an ankle and pulled mightily. They dislodged Wes from his space and pulled him into the hallway. "Don't scrape him on the carpet," the woman said. "His backside is still all cut up. He threw his crutches out the window last night."

He woke up once and sang a few snatches of "White Christmas." The two women leaned against opposite sides of the hallway.

"Don't worry, honey. He ain't scary. He's just a big drunk baby."

They rummaged around the apartment, looking for his clothes. They found his pants, shoes, and sweater—no shirt, socks, or underwear. Somehow they got him mostly dressed and sitting slumped in the corner of the sofa. His hands were in his lap; his head lolled backward on the cushions. His eyes were closed, and he was drooling.

"What am I going to do with him?" Sister asked.

"Take him to church. Looks like he could use it."

"I mean, where does he live?"

"He don't live nowhere," the woman said. "That's how he ended up here. I felt sorry for him. Again." The woman wagged her head dramatically, sighed, then squinted at her nails.

The crucial impedance of the situation was starting to sink in. Sister realized that by default she had just assumed guardianship of a three-hundred-pound drunken man she had spoken with twice. "Maybe I should take him back to the hospital," Sister said.

At the word "hospital," Wes roared back to life. "Oh Christ, no," he bellowed. "Not the hospital." He waved his arms and knocked a lamp and a fishbowl off the end table. "Nazis," he yelled.

"Dammit," yelled the woman. "That fish was a gift." She ran out of the room and returned with a martini pitcher full of water. The two women crawled around the floor trying to pinch the flopping goldfish off the green shag rug. "He's got to go," the woman said. "And I've gotta get to work."

They hefted Wes onto his feet and out the door. They moved him down the stairway with the wide woman a step ahead, leaning backward against his slumping chest. Sister restrained him from behind, using the neck of his sweater as a leash. Step by grunting step, they made it to the bottom of the narrow stairs, where they leaned against the wall until the three of them caught their breaths.

"Ready?" asked the woman, pulling open the door. They carried him out of the apartment building and set him on a pile of snow. He belched loudly and inspected his ankles.

He seemed to accept the notion that he was outside. "My riding crop, Miss Summersby," he said to the woman, saluting her. He rolled off the pile of snow and lay across the sidewalk like a stoned ox.

"Thanks, honey," the woman said, pulling up the collar of her coat. She gave the girl a light pat on the shoulder as she walked past. "Good luck," she said, hurrying away.

"I need a drink," said Wes.

"No, you don't," said the nun.

"As usual, you're so right about that," he said. "Howsabout a drink?"

"No. Let me think."

Now what, she wondered. He won't go to the hospital, and I can't take him back to the orphanage.

"Do you have any friends?" she asked him.

"Sure," he said, waving his arm widely down the street to the row of bars. "Over there."

"Is there someplace you can stay while I figure out what to do?"

"I think I'm going to the Hamptons this weekend. Call my driver, willya?"

"You're no help at all."

"I know. I need a drink."

The hard winter wind was pushing through her dress and whipping her wimple around the side of her head. She looked down at the man. He had rolled onto his back, dreamily watching the blowing snow. He looked like he was ready to sleep. His face, his bare ankles, and the backs of his hands were already red. There was snow inside his shoes and a white dusting on his mountainous belly. This was how people froze to death.

Sister tried to race ahead of the situation, but things were moving too fast, even for prayer. She needed to do something, anything—even if it was the wrong thing.

"Come on," she said. "Get up. We're going for a walk."

"Okay," said Wes, not moving. "Here we go. I'm walking now. Hey, I'm good at this," he said, still lying on his back, making a snow angel.

"Come *on*," she said again, pulling on the neck of his sweater until he sat up. Bracing herself with a lamppost, she tugged on his right sleeve until he stood. He leaned on her heavily, almost falling on her; then they started walking down the street.

I'm going to keep walking until God tells me what to do.

They went two blocks until Sister saw a sign. It said ROOMS TO LET BY DAY. NO TRANSIENTS. GENTLEMEN ONLY.

"*You're* going to stay with *him?*"

The man behind the desk thought he had seen it all.

"He needs help," Sister said. "This is a mission of mercy."

"And who is going to pay for all this mercy?"

"I'll get the money," she said. "This is an emergency. He could freeze."

"So could somewhere else before I see the money," the man said. Figuring a nun with a drunk beats an empty house, he pushed a key across the desk. "I don't want no trouble. No noise, no mess. And he's gotta be paid up by the weekend or I'm throwing him out. I'm doing this on your say-so, Sister."

"I understand," she said. Four days, she thought. I have four days to find twenty-one dollars. "God bless," she said.

"Twenty-one bucks by Friday," he said. "Then *I'll* bless."

One step at a time, she pulled Wes to the second floor.

He fell heavily onto the bed. She looked around the stale room. One window, radiator, narrow bed with army blanket and one pillow. Dresser, chair, nightstand, lamp. Extra blanket on the chair. Tiny bathroom with sink, toilet, tub.

She pulled the frozen shoes off his feet and set them on the radiator. She pulled the blanket from underneath him, then covered him with both blankets. She sat down and rested her cold feet on the side of the heater, comparing their sizes, thinking.

Well, now. Here we are, out of the weather. We owe twenty-one dollars, and he needs clothes and food.

She remembered the Veterans Hall across town. Surely someone there would loan her thirty dollars to help a vet. She could get free clothes and food from the St. Vincent de Paul. He would have to eat canned food, and that called for a can opener. What do men need? What do I need?

First, she needed her own coat and her galoshes.

Without realizing it, she had made an amazing transition. She had taken control, faced an emergency and successfully handled it. In the space of an hour, she had transformed herself from a nineteen-year-old girl stacking breakfast plates in an orphanage to a resourceful woman responsible for another adult in great need.

And although she couldn't know it, at that moment, sitting in a hotel room with a greatly drunk fat man asleep on the bed behind her, she had claimed the role of her new life. She was the woman in charge.

I should run errands, she thought, while he is asleep.

"And you believe you can rescue him?" Superior asked for the second time. She was standing in the doorway of Sister's room, watching the girl pull her galoshes over her blocky nun shoes. A cloth satchel lay on the bed with her hasty collection inside: rosary, sweater, pencil and notebook, a copy of *The Rule of St. Benedict.*

"I don't know," the girl said. "There's no one else to help him."

"He needs a priest, not a girl."

"He needs someone to care for him," Sister said. He needs someone to watch over him, she thought.

"This is a lark. You know that, don't you? It's because of your dreams, and I forbid you to do this."

The girl said nothing. She struggled with the second overshoe.

"Did you hear me?" With every exchange, the argument was turning more domestic, sounding like a real mother talking to her stubborn child. Struggling with rage, the older woman was close to ultimatum. She actually had her hands on her hips.

"This is a good work," the girl said strongly, looking Superior squarely in the eye. "And I'm going to do it."

The Superior bit her lip and narrowed her eyes. It was a gesture she allowed herself only in moments of greatest strife. It was meant to convey barely controlled rage, but instead, it made her look like a constipated owl.

The girl responded to the jammed-up owl face. She smirked.

"Insolence," the woman yelled. "And I won't tolerate it. This is finished. For now, this is finished." She slapped the doorjamb with the flat of her hand, spun violently, and stomped down the hallway, her elbows flapping and her skirts huffing grandly around her.

At least she didn't lock me in, the girl said to herself. She pulled on her coat and lifted her satchel.

Nine men were sitting in the lounge of the Nashua VFW. It was only eleven o'clock in the morning, but they were already deep into the finger-pointing phase of their daylong dispute over who had lost Corregidor. When the nun walked through the doorway of the dark lounge, the arguing stopped. She posted herself at the corner of the grimy bar, and by the time she finished her story she had collected sixty-seven dollars, including eight bucks from the jukebox.

She hurried back to the hotel, through the curtains of snow hanging in the still sky. It would be a long lazy snow, indifferent and pure, rounding the edges of the hard town.

Wes was still asleep. Sister sat with her back to the radiator and watched the big man on the bed for a few moments; then she made a list in her notebook:

Toothbrush—39 cents
Tooth powder—19 cents
Razor—89 cents
Shaving soap—19 cents
Deodorant—39 cents
Underwear—$1.49?
Socks—$1.19?
Pajamas—$3.00?
Pants, shirt, jacket, coat, hat—St. Vincent de Paul

Thirty-eight twenty-seven left—after the rent. That's plenty for food and emergencies. She reminded herself to stop by the hospital for extra bandages, iodine, and adhesive tape.

She paced across the room at the foot of the bed; then she leaned over the Cartoon Man and laid her hand on his brow. He was moist and fevered, and he grimaced in his sleep when he felt her touch. He looked pitiful. His wide round face was mottled, splotchy red and paste gray. Moisture was collecting at his hairline, and his nose was running.

She pulled the chair to the bed, sat down, and removed her shoes. With her feet on the edge of the cot and using her coat as a pillow, she slouched into the Naugahyde armchair and fell asleep.

An hour later she awoke to movement in the room. Wes was leaning against the dresser, trying to pull on his left shoe. He was watching her carefully, trying not to wake her, and he smiled gamely when she saw him. He was red-faced and sweating savagely.

"I'm going out for a little while," he said lightly. "I need cigarettes, and

I've got a few errands to run. I don't suppose you have a dollar or two I could borrow? By the way, what are we doing here?"

"You didn't have anywhere to go, so I brought you here. Don't you remember?"

He shrugged boyishly. "Do you live here?" he asked. "Am I a priest now?"

"No. I didn't know where to take you. I was afraid you were going to freeze to death."

"I was outside?"

"You had to leave that woman's apartment. She came to the church and found me. We brought you outside; then she went to work and left you with me."

"Lucinda?"

"No. Sister Donica Lenore."

"Not you. Her."

"I don't know. She didn't tell me her name."

"Lucinda Head. That's what I call her. She's not real bright. Anyway, I've got to go now, so thanks for letting me grab some zees—and I'll see you around, I'm sure. By the way, about that couple of bucks—"

They weren't connecting. He was trying to get out the door and back to the bars; she was still playing house.

"If you're going out, maybe you could pick up a few things?"

"Sure. Like what?"

"Well, I made a list, and I'll give you the money."

"Great," he said.

"How much are cigarettes?" she asked him.

"Thirty-four cents. And I'd like to get a Hershey's."

She gave him the list and counted out seven dollars and seventy-three cents. His hand was shaking as he took the money.

"There," she said. "That's for everything on the list—and here's another forty cents for the cigarettes and the chocolate."

"Hey, thanks," he said. He looked at the money, stupefied, and put the list in his pocket without reading it.

"I'll just stay here," she said.

"Okay," he said, not even pretending that her whereabouts would affect him in the least.

"Thank you," she said. "God bless."

I forgot to tell him to save the receipts, she thought, as the door shut behind him.

Well, that's a first, he thought, walking down the stairs. Wind up in a flophouse with a midget nun who gives me eight bucks. If stranger things had happened, he couldn't remember it.

Forty-five minutes later, he had spent all the money buying rounds at the Penguin Club. So far, he had started a fire in the men's room, drunk a bottle of Shalomar on a dare, and ripped his pants trying to carry the pool table on his back. Now it was late.

It took Sister until eleven o'clock to figure out that he wasn't returning. Once again, it was very confusing. She had followed the course of divine urgings and it had turned out much differently than she expected. She assumed that events would unfold gracefully—like her vision of the family banquet—and Wes would be a willing participant in their enterprise, especially since he was the beneficiary of all this divine maneuvering.

She planned to stay with him until he could manage on his own, then return to the church in time for Vespers. So far, it had taken him seven hours to buy cigarettes. Where was he? She prayed for his safety.

This was the first night in her life that she had missed evening prayers, and now guilt was galloping neck-and-neck with her confusion.

She sat in the room and waited.

By midnight, the shabby hotel was making noises of the underworld. Drunks of all degrees were meandering the halls. Groans and shrieks of confusion or pleasure swirled through the smoky building. Rooms away, a woman was crying. The walls of Sister's room seemed to vibrate with sin's low song.

Outside, beneath the window, people were coming and going through the creaky front door. This was no refuge for a misplaced girl.

She pulled on her rubbers and slid into her coat. She shouldered herself outside, hunched into the weather, and headed for Stackman Street. She was going to find the Cartoon Man.

The snow had stopped, but the wind had picked up and the temperature had fallen to singles. Five degrees, she guessed. She shuffled down the narrow path, her shoes sliding on the frozen sidewalk. Before she had walked two blocks, her ears were stinging and her forehead was numb. Her wimple was useless in the cold wind. It flapped wildly around her head, occasionally wrapping itself across her face. It was like wearing a flag, and she had to take her ungloved hands out of her pockets to untangle it.

As she struggled down Stackman Street, she realized she was angry. She was angry with the Cartoon Man for being so selfish, but she was most angry with herself for not knowing how to deal with the situation. It was time to be firm.

The first saloon was empty, except for a wide woman at the bar who was sleeping on her forearms. It was the woman from the apartment.

Sister tapped her on the shoulder.

"Miss Head?" she said.

The bartender snickered.

"Huh?" said the woman.

"Remember me?" Sister asked. "From this morning?"

"Oh, hi," said the woman, after a few moments of realignment. "Howzit goin'?"

"Not too well, actually. I'm looking for our friend. Do you know where I could find him?"

"You should try the Penguin Club," the woman said.

Again, the bartender snickered.

As usual, the Penguin Club was packed. The bar was stacked three deep with earnest boys and distracted girls, all trying to make themselves noticed. The small dance floor in front of the jukebox was a riot of jitterbugging couples sweating, laughing, and swizzling around each other in spastic ballet.

Across the room, at the end of the bar, a loud crowd was gathered, roaring like idiots. In the middle of the crowd sat Wes, shirtless, with a huge stuffed bison's head jammed over his own. He was smoking inside the bison, and bluish puffs of smoke were coming out the ears of his shaggy headpiece. A garter belt hung from one horn. A Rube Goldberg contraption of drinking straws stuck out of the bison's nose, connecting Wes inside to a reddish-colored drink on the bar. To the glee of his audience, he was taking long drinks through the snout-siphon, violently jiggling his great bare gut and yelling something muffled like "Moolie, mookie, mookie."

Sister's eyes narrowed, her mouth set tight, her fists clenched. She marched to the end of the bar and grabbed the Cartoon Man by his arm. The great bison head looked down from the barstool, then jerked backward in surprise. A blast of smoke came out of its ears.

Half the barroom went quiet. People froze in mid-drink. In the long, loose, and occasionally violent history of the Penguin Club, nothing nearly this weird had ever happened before. This would become a legendary moment whose retelling would outlive everyone present—and even the Penguin Club itself. According to the legend, the child-size nun had real sparks shooting out of her eyes.

"Holy shit," yelled Wes.

"Take that off your head," Sister said. "Now."

After some work, Wes unscrewed the bison. "What?" he asked.

"For seven hours I've been waiting in that hotel room for you to come back."

The other half of the bar went quiet.

"I thought we were done," said Wes.

"No, we were not done," said the nun. "You got out of bed and said you were going out for cigarettes. And I've been waiting ever since."

A woman said uh-oh.

"What do you want me to do?" he said.

"You need to come back like you said you would. We need to talk."

The simplicity of her statement swung the argument out of Wes's grasp.

In front of his crowd, he couldn't explain away the obvious: He had re-neged on a promise to a nun. Whatever it was, or whatever their disagree-ment, he was clearly in the wrong—simply because she said so.

"Wes," said the bartender. "Go straighten this out. I don't want no trouble. Okay, pal?"

Frustrated with the way the moment had turned against him, he drained off the rest of his mai tai and slammed the glass on the bar. He pulled on his sweater, slid off the stool, hitched his pants, and made a grand sweeping gesture to the nun, who had already turned and headed for the door. He followed her outside, into the cold.

The path on the sidewalk was too narrow to walk beside her; the wind was blowing like crazy, so even if he had anything to say she wouldn't have heard him. He shuffled behind her, half-lit and working himself into a royal gripe. Okay, so she *had* gotten him out of the cold. What's the big deal? He had managed hard times before, and there were plenty of places he was welcome to stay. He didn't owe her anything. In fact, the way he saw it, she owed *him* an apology for embarrassing him in front of his friends. She had no business—

She knew it would be an awkward moment when they arrived at the hotel. She tried to plan her speech but didn't know what to say. This was so improbable. How could she sound convincing when she didn't even have a plan? What was she doing, walking into that bar and losing her temper? In her whole life, she had never yelled at anyone. Was this really the right thing to do? Well, here they were, baby-stepping through the snow—and he *was* following her. She considered leaving him to his own devices at the hotel and returning to the church. Perhaps Superior was right—this was a lark, and she had grabbed at something she couldn't hold on to.

Why am I following her? he asked himself.

Mother Mary, she prayed, shuffling ahead of him, what do I do now?

They arrived at the hotel and stood under the marquee. She turned to him.

"I don't know what I'm doing," she said. "But God has told me to help you."

"With what?"

"With your life, and with all the things you were talking about at the hospital."

"I don't need any help," he lied. His feet were cold.

"Well, then, maybe I do," she said. "I don't know how to say this"—she caught her breath—"but I've had dreams and they've all turned out to be true. I knew I was going to meet you that day at the TV station—and then the next time when you were wearing the bear suit. Both times, I knew what was going to happen before it happened."

"You did?"

She shrugged, shivered, and smiled thinly. "And in the hospital, when you were talking about being sick, you know, about the places you saw? Well, I've seen the same place. I was there, in my own dream—just like you—but I was flying around, over the pit where all those people were sliding down. It was terrible, and when I woke up, I was so scared, it made me sick. That's why I was in the hospital. Just like you, I thought *I* was crazy. But now I know I'm seeing all these things for a reason. I'm supposed to help you."

They were both shivering.

"Do you want to go inside?" he asked.

"I do," she said. "I'm freezing."

There wasn't enough furniture in the room, and so there was an awkward moment while they tried to place themselves between the bed and the chair. Neither knew what to say. The carousing in the hall had stopped, and although they could hear someone breathing loudly in the next room, the hotel was mostly quiet. The room was warm, and in the glow of the one nightstand lamp it didn't seem as shabby.

Sister was in the ratty chair, sitting forward with her hands on her knees. Wes was on the small bed, leaning against the headboard, one foot on the floor and the other leg stretched down the length of the mattress. He had taken off his shoes. He looked pale and weak—like a man who had just checked out of detox, then spent the next three days drinking. He was perspiring, and his hands shook when he wiped his forehead with the sleeve of his sweater.

"So you knew what was going to happen before it happened?" he asked her.

She told him about her first two visions.

"They don't sound very religious," he said.

"I know they don't. They were like bad fairy tales, and I didn't know what they meant. But I didn't think them up; they just came to me."

"Why were they about me?"

"I don't know."

"Do you know what's going to happen now?"

"No. It doesn't work like that. I get dizzy, and then I see a story, like a play. And then later, the dream happens again in real life—except that it's different. It's very confusing, but it all means something. I'm sure of that. It's the way God speaks to me."

"Very strange," he said.

"I know."

"And that's it? You just had the ones about the blue angel and the red bear?"

"No. I had the one about Hell—and then one more," she said.

"What happened in that one?"

"I don't want to talk about it yet," she said.

"Why? Was it bad? Did I die?"

"No. But I can't talk about it. Don't worry, it's good."

"Jesus Christ," he said. "What's going on here? Is this some kind of game?"

The girl clapped her hands loudly as if she were trying to get the attention of one of her orphans. Wes jumped.

"Say 'God forgive me before my soul enters Hell for all eternity.'"

"What?"

"Say 'God forgive me before my soul enters Hell for all eternity.'"

"Why?"

"Just say it. Quickly. Say it."

"God forgives me in Hell for all eternity," he said, rolling his eyes.

"No," she said. "Say it right."

"No. This is stupid."

The girl crossed herself and said something in Latin.

Wes sat up. "That's it," he said, reaching for his shoes. "I'm going. This night's young, and I want to be." He stood up, went to the door, and opened it. Sister stayed seated.

"I know you mean well," he said from the doorway. "But my life is complicated enough. I don't need strange little women having dreams about me. It's just too weird, thank you. I know things are a little rough right now, but I've made it this far and I'll be okay. All I need is just one lucky break." He nodded like a man sure of himself and shut the door behind him.

Sister sat in the chair, listening to him fade down the hallway. So that's it, she thought. All that for nothing.

She was too tired to arrange her emotions. It was too late to return to the convent, and she was too confused to make a plan. She knelt on the floor and began to pray.

"Hail, Holy Queen, mother of mercy, our life, our sweetness and our hope. To thee do we cry, poor banished children of Eve."

Her prayers were interrupted by a heavy thud on the sidewalk beneath the window.

"God fucking dammit," yelled the Cartoon Man. "You assholes ever hear of a snow shovel?"

She ran down the stairs to the street. Wes was on his side, clutching his left leg, which was bent outward at the knee. She tried to help him stand, but as he tried to put his leg under him, it hurt even more. He was bellowing like a moose in the mud, and lights were coming on in the hotel windows. The desk clerk came out, zipping up his pants, and he helped the nun slide the big man onto a snowdrift, where he sat cursing the weather and the pain.

"Maybe we should call a taxi," Sister suggested.

"And who's gonna pay for that?" asked the clerk.

Twenty minutes later, a Checker crawled up the street, sliding to a stop somewhere near the curb. Sister, the clerk, and the cabbie helped Wes across the waist-high snowdrift and onto the backseat of the cab, where he howled and thrashed, clutching his knee.

"Hospital, please," said Sister.

"Buck fifty. Up front," said the driver, recognizing Wes.

"Buck fifty?" yelled Wes. "It's six blocks, you asshole."

"You wanna crawl to the boneyard, fat boy?" asked the cabdriver. "I shouldn't even be out in this stuff."

Wes yelled at the driver every time the cab hit a bump.

"What are you doing with him?" the cabbie asked the nun.

"I don't know," she said.

A jab of morphine, some tugging and twisting. They put him in a splint and twelve pounds of plaster.

"How do you feel?" Sister asked. She was leaning on his bed in the recovery room. He looked tired and afraid, even more helpless than before. Had he been crying?

"It never stops," he said softly. "It just gets worse."

"Wo, wo, wo," said the desk clerk. "No cripples."

"We've already paid for the week," said Sister. "And I'm staying with him."

The clerk considered. "Don't let him out of your sight. He's a walking war zone."

"He can't even walk," she said.

"With him, it don't matter."

In the hotel room, Wes lay on the bed, his foot propped up on a drawer taken out of the dresser. The doctor had shredded his only pair of pants, and his left leg was in a cast from the hip down. He looked terrible. His hair was greasy and he needed a shave. His eyes looked hollow and dark; he was very pale and weak.

It was four o'clock in the morning. On a normal day, he would begin drinking in three hours, and he was already worried about how he would feel when he missed his pick-me-up. He couldn't go cold turkey again. The last time, he swore there would be no next time. Last time it was the hospital; this time they would dry him out in jail. He couldn't do it. Even with this cement on his leg, he would kill somebody for a drink. He looked at the nun-girl sitting on the chair, watching him.

"You should go," he said. "Just leave. I'm too much trouble, and it's going to get worse. There's nothing you can do. I'm hopeless."

"No, you're not," she said.

"Yes," he yelled, "I am. I'm an alky screwup. We don't get better."

"Don't yell at me," she said softly. "I may not know what I'm doing, but I will do the right thing."

That slowed him down. "What? That doesn't even make sense."

"Yes, it does," she said. "I'm not making things happen. I'm just following God's will and it's turning out this way. We have to believe that everything happens for the good." She was thinking about her vision of the family banquet.

"Well, it doesn't," he said. "My leg hurts. I'm dead broke. I even owe you money. I'm in a bad mood, and I'm going to need a drink soon."

"No drinks," she said. "That's how all this started."

She went to the bathroom and came back with a glass of water. "Here, take this." She gave him one of the three morphine pills from the hospital. "This will take your mind off the pain."

He swallowed the pill, then went to sleep.

She covered herself with her coat and tried to make herself comfortable on the chair. It was too late to make plans. In three hours the sun would rise on a very worrisome day.

In the morning, the big man was groaning. He was hurting everywhere, especially his leg, with dull pain digging in from his groin to his ankle—and a sharp razor-rip of agony biting into his knee every time he shifted his weight. Beneath the hurt on his leg, a deeper craving was building, a familiar twisting nausea that curled from inside his gut and rose to his skin in tiny acid bubbles. He was toxic. He needed his morning chemistry: a beer and two cups of coffee, then two more beers. He knew if he didn't get it soon he would be heaving yellow bile onto the floor beside the bed. He would be bent like a fish hook from the grinding cramps that would screw every muscle in his body tight as twisted wire. He would get sweats and shakes that would rattle this building like a tremor.

His groaning woke the girl.

"Are you okay?" she asked.

"Do I look okay?" he said. "For the love of God, get me a beer."

"Does your leg hurt?"

"Yeah, that, too," he said. "But I really need a drink. Anything. I don't care."

She gave him the second morphine tablet, and his pain receded to a strong headache. Before he fell asleep he tried to pretend he would feel better when he woke up.

Sister slipped out of the room and walked to the St. Vincent de Paul store.

When she returned, Wes was still sleeping. She took their only towel into the grimy bathroom, filled the tub with amber water, and took her first bath in three days.

She redressed in the same clothes, and when she came out of the bathroom, Wes was awake.

"How do you feel?" she asked.

"Like hell," he said.

"I brought you some pajamas and a robe."

"Great," he said. "Let's play canasta." He looked weak and worried. "How many of those horse pills do we have left?"

"One."

"We need more. I'm not going to get through this."

"Yes, you are."

He closed his eyes and shook his head. "You don't know," he said.

"Yes, I do."

"How? Did you have another one of your visions?"

"No. But I have a feeling."

"I do, too. And it's bad."

"Do you want anything? Some water?"

"Do you have any with the gin still in it?"

"No drinks," she said. "You're going to get better."

"No. I'm going to get worse. I've been through this before. It gets a whole lot worse. Can I have that pill now?"

She gave him a glass of water and the final morphine tab.

It was two o'clock in the afternoon. He knew in seven hours it would wear off and by ten o'clock that night he would be out of control in the crazy pain tremens of his delirium.

They both slept until he awoke at seven thirty. The room had already gone heavy in the fading winter light, and Sister was cold. She rattled the Bakelite knob on the radiator for nothing, then put on her coat. Wes lay in bed, breathing heavily, his face glistening with sweat. He was staring at the ceiling, his eyes pinched against the growing nausea.

"I'm not going to make it," he said. "This time, I'm not going to make it."

"Yes, you are. I'm staying with you. I'll see to it."

"That's no good," he said. "I get crazy. I don't know what I'm doing and I don't remember anything. You can't hold me down."

"We'll be alright. I'll be here. And I'll be praying."

"Oh Christ," he said, as the shaking started.

The tremors hit him in waves, and as each wave passed through his body, the broken edges of the bones in his left knee scraped against each other, sending jolts of slicing pain up his leg and into his hip. His body was cold, his head felt hot, and his gut was twisting. It felt like everything beneath his skin was trying to writhe out of his body. The acid taste of vomit was at the back of his throat and in his nostrils. His head was roaring with each beat of his struggling heart.

His right hand clutched at the blanket; his other hand was under his left buttock, trying to hold off the pain shooting upward from his broken leg.

When he started vomiting, he tried to twist to his right, but the weight of the cast on his left leg kept him flat on his back and he could only turn his head. With the next spasm, he tried rolling to the left, but his bad leg couldn't take his weight. Within ten minutes, his chest, the pillow, and the bed around his head were covered with puke.

He moaned and coughed and cried while the girl sat on the foot of the bed, watching helplessly.

"Get somebody," he said. "Get help."

She used the towel to sop the gruelly spew. Gagging, she rinsed it in the sink, then returned to clean the man, the bed, and the floor.

"How long does this last?" she asked him between his heaves.

"Days," he moaned.

After two hours, he was too weak to turn his head. She was afraid he would choke, so she rolled up her coat and put it under his head. He spit and drooled down his chin and onto his belly. The blanket was soaked. He had lost control of his bowels, so he soiled the bed—and himself, down into his cast.

Sister paced the small room, from the dresser to the window—three steps—and back again. She didn't know what to do. He was moaning weakly now. He looked like he could die.

She went to the side of the bed. He looked up at her, then closed his eyes.

She knelt on the spitty floor and put her right hand on his forehead. He felt cold beneath his sweaty skin.

She put her left hand on the slimy blanket, above his heart.

She bowed her head.

"Father," she prayed. "Please listen to me. You can do anything. Without you, we are nothing. Please hear my prayer for this good man. Please help us."

As she spoke the simple words, she felt a rapid searing heat come up through the big man's body—from deep inside to the shell of his skin. She felt it roar through him, so hot that she pulled her hands away, afraid she would be burned. Startled, she rocked backward and fell, sitting on the floor.

A burst of bluish fire filled the air around him. It was an explosive cough, like a burner on a gas stove. The soft blast completely surrounded him and lit the dark room like a flashbulb. He wasn't burnt, but the heat from the brief explosion flashed on the girl's face, scorching her forehead.

His eyes and mouth were open wide, and as the burst of blue fire faded, he made a long hissing sound like air escaping from a sinking box.

The room smelled like kerosene and burnt feces.

As the heat and light diminished, Sister leaned forward. She was sitting on the floor, her eyes level with his head. She could see he was trying to grab bites of air, gasping in quick choking breaths. His eyes were wide and unblinking, and his skin was bright white. His mouth was locked open in a grimace, and she could see the tip of his tongue fluttering on the edges of his front teeth.

Convinced he was dying, she was too stunned to do anything.

He arched his back and a second burst of light—less violent than the first—engulfed him.

"Nissshhh," he hissed, as if all the air were being sucked out of his lungs.

The heat and the light weren't as intense as the first blast, but the afterglow lasted nearly a minute, covering him with a pulsing blue light from crown to foot. His head moved slowly from side to side, and through the blue glow it looked to Sister like he was smiling. The nimbus hovered around him, pulsing like a heartbeat; then slowly faded. The room returned to its earthly dusk.

Sister stayed on the floor, afraid of what might come next.

"I believe in the Holy Spirit, the holy Catholic Church, the communion of the saints," she chattered as fast as she could.

It was over.

Wes was breathing deeply and evenly. His face was ruddy and clean. He looked relaxed and healthy, like he had spent an easy afternoon in the sun. His eyes were clear, and he gave off a rich pleasant odor, like cedar, or freshly turned earth.

He rolled his head and looked at Sister.

"Hello, there," he said, smiling like a cherub.

She sat on the floor, blinking at him. "Are you alright?" she asked him.

"Yes," he said. "I certainly am."

"Can I get you anything?"

"Oh. Some water would be nice."

She scrambled to her feet and retrieved the half-filled water glass from the dresser.

He sat up, drank, then lay down again.

"And my leg doesn't hurt anymore, either," he said quietly. Then he fell asleep.

While he was sleeping, Sister inspected the scene. The heat had blasted the bed and blanket; now they were clean and dry. The wall behind the headboard had been scorched to a sepia color, except for an outline of the curved iron headboard.

Above the bed, the ceiling was seared with fan-shaped marks of soot as if a dusty angel had struggled mightily upward against it, then escaped, passing through to the other side.

She lifted the blanket off his legs. The mattress was fresh; his clothes looked worn, but they were dry and crisp-looking. Even his bare feet looked healthy, pink, and clean.

Sister knelt by the window on the raggedy rug and prayed in her new style. It was holy jazz—glorious songs of deliverance swapping riffs between old Gothic cant and her new free voice. *Hail Mary, full of grace, you are my sunshine, my only sunshine*, she whispered.

After prayers, she sat in the chair and composed her note of leaving. *Mother*, she wrote, *I'm called to a different life. I can't explain it, but I'm certain now that my dreams and the things that happen to me are the same in God's eyes. In my new way of thinking, everything is real and heavenly at the same time. The world is a beautiful place and God has called me to increase His beauty. Forgive me my sins and pray for me please. By God's grace, Sister Donica Lenore.*

She tore an empty back page out of her notebook, wrote another note, folded it like a place card, and put it on Wesley's chest.

Sister closed the door and slipped down the hall, past a drunk asleep on the landing.

"We only have one towel," she said to the man behind the desk.

"So that's where it went," he said.

"Could we have another?"

"Oh, sure. I'll send it up with the bonbons. Bridal suite, right?"

She knew she was being ridiculed but didn't know how to respond.

"If you tell me where you keep them, I could get it myself."

"We don't keep them anywhere. The girl quit last week."

"So, no clean sheets?"

"Are you serious?"

"Should I wash them?" she asked.

"Don't you have a job?"

"Actually," she said. Her fingernail pecked at a button on her overcoat. "Things are a little complicated right now."

"I can imagine."

The blotter was stained with ink and coffee. His collar was blotched with old blood, and a shred of his cigar was stuck in the crease of his yellow mouth.

"God bless," she said, turning to the door. She tucked her wimple under the neck of her coat and stepped outside, into the bright and brittle morning.

Wes woke up, and he felt very strange. Clean. He didn't recognize the feeling because this was the first time he had ever felt this way. He didn't want a cigarette and he didn't feel the urge to climb out of bed and head for a saloon. It just didn't sound like fun today—in fact, it seemed wrong somehow. Even the thought of going to a bar made him feel different than before. Thinking of drinking made him ill.

His head felt different, too. He was having different kinds of thoughts. He didn't wake up feeling desperate or worried about surviving the next few hours, and he didn't have his usual pocket-money panic. As he lay on the small bed, he realized he wasn't frantic about anything. He felt like everything he would ever need was already inside his own head. He felt great.

He tried to remember what had happened to him. He remembered getting the DTs and making a mess of himself and the nun kneeling by the bed and touching his forehead. After that, he was blank.

He looked toward his feet and noticed the small placard on his chest. PLEASE DON'T LEAVE, he read. "No problem," he said.

He sat up and swung his heavy left leg over the side of the bed. He was expecting pain as his weight shifted downward, but nothing happened. This was very strange. He set his foot on the floor, then pushed down with his toes. Still no pain.

He stood up, then goose-stepped into the bathroom. His left leg supported him as well as the right one. It actually felt normal. He hopped to the toilet and released a luxurious piss the color of stout.

He stuck his head under the faucet on the sink and drank his fill of cold water; then he stumped back to bed. He lay on top of the blanket with his hands behind his head, trying to explain to himself what had happened. This had something to do with the odd little nun and her strange powers—he was sure of that. She could change things, but how did she do it? And why was she helping him? Good questions, no answers. His imagination couldn't embrace a limitless explanation, so he chalked it up to good luck.

He wondered where she had gone, but in his new ascended state, he didn't worry about it. He closed his eyes and started humming a Connie Francis tune. Soon, pleasant dreams of laughing children and dancing cows filled his great goofy head.

Sister knew she should announce herself first to Superior, but since she didn't know what to say, she went straight to the chapel. She sat in the same pew as when she was an orphan, and she felt the familiar comfort of solitude settle on her soul. She knew this place. This was her chapel. She had been abandoned in its doorway as an infant and had been carried inside for prayers as a baby, sleeping through Mass on a cushion in the narthex. She had worshipped and prayed from this pew as a child, and kneeling at the dais, she had offered herself as Christ's bride. This chapel was home. She was welcome here.

She knelt and bowed her head, trying to think of a prayer more solid than her swirling thoughts.

"To thee do we send up our sighs, mourning and weeping in this valley of tears," she began.

No, that wouldn't do. The world wasn't a valley of tears. The world was a garden of possibilities, lush and tangled. She had seen it. It was an exhausting array of variation, exciting with promise. God lived in the world, too.

"Turn then, most gracious advocate, thine eyes of mercy toward us, after this our exile . . ."

Exile? It felt more like an escape.

Ritual wasn't working, so once again she improvised.

"Father," she began, "I've tried to follow your will, but I'm still confused. I have choices I don't understand. What comes next? Please give me a sign."

"Where have you been, Sister Donica Lenore?" It was the bully voice of Superior. While Sister was praying, the big woman had maneuvered herself to the end of the pew, blocking any escape. Startled, the girl jumped up, banging her knee on the pew rack; then, from habit, she bowed to the woman.

"I was ministering to someone in need," she said.

"Without my permission," interrupted Superior.

"Perhaps," said the girl. "But perhaps you don't understand the situation."

"Quiet, you," the woman barked, clapping her hands loudly. The girl jumped again. She had never seen anyone this angry.

"Situation?" Superior shouted. "*Your* situation is obedience. *Your* situation is devotion to your station and your vows. Your *situation* is under my authority."

"I think I'm being led to a different work now. That's what I was praying about. I don't know—"

"You certainly don't know," the woman snapped. "You can't sneak off for three days, indulging your silly little dreams."

The girl said nothing. She wasn't prepared to defend something she still didn't understand, but she was beginning to feel defiant. At the least, she wanted to explain herself.

"They're not just the dreams," she said. "They mean something. In the world—where real things happen—they mean something. I can't explain it, but everything works out, and it works out for the better. It's true because I've seen it. I've seen goodness come out of evil."

Superior put her hands on the backs of two pews and leaned toward the girl.

"I'm done discussing this," she hissed. "You will be punished, Sister Donica Lenore. This will not go well for you."

In the few short seconds between Superior's dictum and her own expected compliance, Sister reviewed her options. There weren't many: Obey, or leave.

She considered the whole of her nineteen years in the same building—first as an orphan, then as a woman of God with the rowdy children and quiet matrons.

She thought about Wes, lying on the shabby hotel bed, and she felt the calling of compassion—or something deeper—for him and the whole world full of need.

She knew if she didn't return to him, then he would be lost and the parade of circumstances that led them to this point would be for nothing. She didn't know what would come next, but she was certain everything would turn out fine.

And so when she balanced the comfort of cloistered life against the fantastic events of the past two days, her decision came easily.

She looked Superior in the eye.

"I can't do that," she said. "There is more for me to do."

Superior sputtered with the rage of a mother scorned. "You will do what I say," she rasped. "You *will* go to your room. And take a chamber pot with you."

A chamber pot meant lockdown.

"No, I won't," said the girl, her gaze never flinching.

"You're just a child. You'll starve on the outside."

"Consider the birds of the air, that they do not sow, nor do they reap; yet your Heavenly Father feeds them. Are you not worth much more than they?"

"How dare you blaspheme in God's own house?" Superior said, her jaw quaking. She fought the urge to grab the girl and shake her.

"It's our house, too," said Sister. "We're God's children."

"You must obey me," said the woman. "What God proposes, man disposes."

"Like you, I serve God first. What God ordains, man disdains."

"Blasphemy," yelled the woman. "Say 'God forgive me before my soul enters Hell for all eternity.' "

Sister must have smiled, because she was remembering Wesley's lame attempt two nights ago to say the same prayer.

"What are you laughing at?"

"I'm not. Really."

They stared at each other, one trying not to laugh, the other trying not to have a stroke.

"This is your final chance," said Superior. "I'm not telling you again. Go to your room."

"No."

"Then I am through with you. Lavabo inter innocentes," said the woman, making a washing motion with her hands. She stared at the girl; then, with great lack of ceremony, she stormed away.

Sister stood for a moment, then eased herself to the end of the pew. She faced the crucifix, genuflected, turned, and walked slowly out of the chapel, across the courtyard, and into the real world. The letter lay behind her.

Sister ran back to the hotel, stood at the front desk, and tapped on the bell until the man returned. He was carrying a cereal bowl half full of gray oatmeal.

"Is the job still available?" she asked.

"What job?"

"The laundry job. What does it pay?"

"Housekeeper," he said. "Ninety dollars a week."

"Including the room?"

He eyeballed the child and remembered the godbless. "Why not," he said. "You can start tomorrow."

"Thank you," she said, reaching over the counter to shake his hand.

"Clarence Coleman," he said.

"Sister Donica Lenore. Pleased to meet you. And thank you for the opportunity."

"For sure," he said, smiling. "You're going to wear something else, right?"

In the room, Wes was sitting on the bed, chipping the cast off his leg with the room key.

"What are you doing?" she asked, afraid he was trying to leave.

"I don't need this thing. My leg is all better."

"All better?"

"All better," he said. "Short woman make big magic. How?"

"Do you mean it's healed?"

He nodded, smiling like a little boy. He had demolished the cast from ankle to knee. Pieces of it lay scattered around the room like oyster shells.

"Are you sure you know what you're doing?" she asked him.

"Probably not," he said. "But there's a first time for everything." He was working on a hand-size chunk of plaster, bending it back and forth until it cracked off. He tossed it on the floor with the rest of the shrapnel.

"I'd make a lousy statue," he said.

Sister sat in the chair at the foot of the bed. "I hoped you would still be here. I had some things to do, and I wanted to tell you about them."

Wes stopped picking at his cast.

"I got your note. I wasn't going anywhere," he said. "I wanted to talk to you. I owe you an apology."

"That's alright," she said. "Apology accepted."

"No, no. Don't let me off that easy. I've been working on this little speech all day."

He leaned forward and rubbed his forehead.

"You don't really know me," he began. "But I'm not a bad person. This is just my act—Mr. Good Time Charlie, you know? I'm the big dumb guy who gets away with everything because people think I don't know any better.

"People in a crowd—in a bar, let's say—always expect a big guy to make them laugh, because it's funnier when I do something stupid. When I break something, I do it right—I destroy it. When I fall down, I make a bigger noise, and everybody says to themselves, 'Oh, good, at least *I* didn't do *that*. At least *I'm* not like that big stupid guy.' I make their screwups look smaller. I make everybody feel smarter."

He looked at her and shrugged.

"The problem is, I don't know when to stop and there's nobody to stop me. There's nobody to say, 'Okay, Wes, you really shouldn't drink all that schnapps and then try sliding down the stairs on your belly,' because everybody likes to see me try it. Instead, they laugh and buy me another beer. Then at the end of the night everybody goes home, and I'm the guy with the sore belly and no place to live.

"I don't know why you helped me. Maybe it's your job; but if you hadn't helped me, I'd be in real trouble—maybe even dead. I was on the bottom this time.

"I was thinking about what a lunk I've been, and I'm sorry I embarrassed you at the station, and I'm sorry you had to take care of me, and I'm sorry I took off with eight bucks the other night and that you had to come out in the weather and bring me back. I wasn't trying to be difficult, I was just acting the way I always act—big, stupid, and drunk. I wasn't nice to you, and I'm really sorry. So I want to thank you for helping me. You saved my life, and I'll never forget it. Thank you."

Sister blushed. "Thank you," she said. "How do you feel now?"

"I feel very strange, like I've been cleaned out. I don't feel like drinking—and things don't feel so desperate. I feel good. I guess this is what normal feels like. Crazy, huh?"

"No," she said. "People can change when they really want to."

"Well, I can't help being big, but I'm not going to act stupid anymore," he said. "I'm not stupid, you know. I'm really not."

"I know you're not," she said. "You have to be smart to think up the things you say. Most of the time, I just pretend to get your jokes."

He smiled. "Hey," he said. "What did the nun have for breakfast after she sat on the stove?"

"I don't know."

"Hot cross buns."

She looked at him blankly. "See?" she said. "I don't get it."

He laughed so hard, the bed shook.

"Are you hungry?"

"Famished," she said. She hoped later she would get her turn to talk.

"Let me finish with this leg, and we'll go out for dinner. A buddy of mine owns a nice place where we can sit and talk. Do you like Salisbury steak?"

She nodded.

"I need to get out of this room," he said. "And I need to find a pair of pants. I've got a lot to do."

"I'll go out and get some clothes. Do you have a size?"

"Forty-eight waist. And the biggest shirt they have," he said, hacking at his cast again with the room key.

"I'll be right back. I have to get some different clothes for me, too. I'm not going to dress like this anymore."

"Okay. Don't be long," he said. "We'll have a good meal."

Either he didn't hear what she said, or he didn't understand.

9

Veronica and I argued about Reggie all the way to the airport.

"He needs to be locked up," she said. "He's completely insane."

"I don't know, Vee. Some of what he said makes sense."

"Oh, sure, if you can hide in Fantasyland for the rest of your life. Of course you don't need money if you live on somebody else's property without them knowing it and you get people to give you free food. He thinks he's some kind of monk, Boone. If he gets thrown out of there, he's going to be one of those people who walks around bus stations, yelling about invisible sparrows. He needs to be committed. *He* needs to be in a cage."

"Sister said it's all leading somewhere and he's looking for his gift. That's good enough for me," I said. "Did he look younger to you? I can't believe how young he looked. He looks like he could be his own son."

"Yeah," she said. "If that's what doing nothing all day does for you, then I should take lessons."

"No," I said. "It's more than that. It's in his eyes, too. He looks peaceful—like a little kid."

"This is one weird trip," she said. "I just want it to be over."

She was talking about Florida, but I knew she was thinking about life in general.

As I was dragging the bags to the counter, I could hear Veronica laying into the ticket agent.

"What do you mean I've been bumped? I've had this reservation for three weeks."

"I'm not sure what the problem is. I'm still checking, ma'am, but it looks like you canceled your reservation this morning."

"Canceled? Why would I cancel and then show up for my flight? Boone, why does this always happen to me?"

I was beside Veronica; Veronica was beside herself. The ticket agent, a midthirties woman with braces, held up her palms as if she were catching a beach ball.

"I don't know," she said. "It doesn't make sense, does it? But there it is."

"Do something," Veronica hissed. "You canceled me, now you can un-cancel me. I will not let go of this flight."

"Well, ma'am, it looks like we're booked full on this flight now, but I could squeeze you onto the next one. It leaves at seven thirty. Yes, I could do that," she said, looking up from her terminal with a satisfied squint.

"No. I want to be on *this* flight. *This* is the flight I made my reservation for, and *this* is the flight I'm taking. I did not cancel myself. You canceled me. Listen, I've had a bad day and a rough week, and I want to go home. *Now.*"

"Do you have two seats on the next flight?" I asked the woman.

"Um, no. Just barely one."

I knew where this was headed—high decibels and threat of property damage. I guided Veronica away from the counter.

"Vee, listen to me. Just take my seat on this flight and I'll grab the seven thirty. It's not a big deal."

"I'm not letting this go, Boone." She was jabbing her hand through her purse. "Goddamn Rolaids. My stomach's doing cartwheels. I think I'm gonna throw up."

She bit two Rolaids off the shredded little stack and chewed them viciously.

"Why me?" she asked. "Why is it always me? Two hundred people on this plane. Every one of them buys a ticket, walks to the gate, gets on the plane, and goes home. Me? I get bumped. If I get home and find out that Jessie—"

"Hold it, hold it," I said. "Listen to yourself. Jessie didn't cancel your flight."

"How would you know? Oh, that's right, she tells *you* everything."

When Veronica gets like this, all you can do is let her run her course. Eventually, she subsides. I sat on one of the benches while she paced in front of me, groaning and waving her arms for ten minutes—carrying on about being a nurse and devoting her life to helping people and now this is the way she gets treated.

"I took unpaid vacation leave, *unpaid,* mind you. Now I won't see New Hampshire until one in the morning. I won't get to bed before two, and I have to be at work—fresh and rested—at eight A.M. sharp, thank you. This wasn't even a vacation, for Godsakes."

"You done?"

"Oh, go ahead. Get on your plane. At least you've got someone to go home to—someone who likes you. *I'll* take the seven thirty. I definitely can't get on a plane now anyway, after all this agitation. I need a drink."

I helped book her flight, then sat with her in the airport bar for a few minutes.

"It's not the plane, Boone, it's everything. Nothing goes right for me. It never has. Even Reggie's happy now. I'm a nice person. Why does this happen to me? I just get tired of it, that's all. Sorry about the scene."

"That's alright. Maybe you just need a little time to unwind. Maybe this weekend in Vermont," I offered.

"Oh, yeah, that's gonna be real relaxing. Cold nights in a shack in the woods, arguing with Jessie. Crying babies."

We hugged, and I went to find my flight. As I walked past the front of the bar I looked in the window and saw her—a lonely middle-aged woman in a Minnie Mouse shirt, stabbing listlessly with a red plastic toothpick at an ice cube in her drink.

On the plane, I found my seat and adjusted myself to the space. The guy sitting in Veronica's seat looked familiar. He was dressed in an expensive dark blue suit, white shirt, and gray silk tie. He had a delicate gold bracelet on one wrist and a wafer-thin platinum timepiece on the other. He was tanned and relaxed, his thin legs crossed loosely at the knees. On his lap was a burgundy leather appointment book with the initials BH.

Bruce Hutton, motivational guru and king of late-night self-help cable. I had scrolled past his info-seminars a million times. They were all the same: slick, upbeat rallies in pricey auditoriums with thousands of eager Hutton wannabes chanting, "OH, *YES*, I AM. OH, *YES*, I AM."

He was turned away from me, looking out the window. His thin fingers held a slender gold pen that he tapped absently on his Day-Timer. He smelled lightly of a musky cologne.

When we were in the air, he opened his Day-Timer and started checking off entries, writing notes in the margins, entering phone numbers from scraps of paper tucked between the pages. He acted like he was the only guy on the plane.

After an hour, he turned to me and smiled.

"Great day for flying, isn't it?" he said, in a voice no different from any man.

"Certainly is. I think I've seen you on TV. Aren't you Bruce Hutton?"

"Oh, *yes*, I am," he said, smiling. "And your name is?"

"Daniel Moffatt. Everybody calls me Boone."

"Daniel Boone?" he said, still smiling as we shook hands. He had one of those tight shakes that hangs on a little longer than I like.

"It's a childhood nickname. It comes from exploring the woods with my dad when I was a little kid."

"Are you going home, Boone?" he asked, as if he had known me my whole life.

"I am. Yourself?"

"I've got a series of seminars coming up in Boston, and I thought I'd fly to New Hampshire for a few days—get rejuvenated, maybe visit some family."

The flight attendant brought me a beer, a vodka Collins for Hutton.

"Do you like Florida?" I asked him.

"A little too hot for my blood," he said. "But I had seminars in Miami and business in Orlando. What do you do for a living, Boone?"

"I'm the chief of police in a small town in New Hampshire."

"Are you happy with your life?"

"Yes, I am."

"Oh, *yes*, I am," he said, smiling and toasting himself with his drink. "Oh, *yes*, I am. Can you say it?"

"No, thanks."

"If I can't hear it, you must fear it. You should come to one of my Boston seminars. I can help you feel better about your life. You can be anything you want to be. You can be as successful as you want to be, beautiful as you want to be. You're in charge of your own life, you know. Oh, *yes*, you are."

"Fuck you," I said, pouring my beer on his leg. It hissed and erupted in a cloud of steam.

"No. Fuck you," said the Devil. "Today, you're a dead man, Boone. I bumped your sister so I could kill you."

"I don't think so. I die when I've seen you seven times. After this, I've got two more. What are you doing on this plane?"

"Just having some fun. I wanted some quality time with you—and Veronica is such a trip, isn't she? I love watching her. She should come to one of my seminars. She might meet somebody nice she could make miserable for the rest of his life."

"What do you want?"

"Just some honest company. The self-help field is so full of phonies. You have no idea. Hey, speaking of phonies, how's your fat-ass old man?"

"I'm not talking to you," I said.

"You can't ignore me, worm. Watch this."

He held his gold pen in his fingertips like a conductor's baton. He jerked it to the right and the plane jumped sideways. People screamed. I grabbed my armrests; my beer went flying. People lurched into the aisle. Food and small objects sailed across the plane, hitting the right wall. A flight attendant fell against the drink cart, cutting her forehead.

He held his pen flat in the palm of his hand and the plane stabilized. He moved his hand from side to side and the plane swayed like a speedboat.

He tossed the pen a few inches and caught it. Instantly, the plane jumped a few hundred feet as if it had hit a giant curb.

I tried to remember the right prayer, my Axis Mundi.

He offered me the pen. "Here you go, chief. Try it, it's fun."

"No, thanks," I said.

The pilot opened the intercom.

"I don't know what's going on here, folks. We just hit some turbulence like I've never seen before. Instrumentation says there's nothing wrong with the aircraft, and I just checked the weather for Charleston. They're not reporting anything out of the ordinary. I think we're through the anomaly now, and so we're going to press on. If we have any more trouble, I'll bring us down for an unscheduled stop—either in Charleston or some point north. Sorry for the inconvenience. Please advise a flight attendant if you need any assistance."

The Devil leaned against me. Under his clothes, his arm was hot and writhing like a great hard snake. "Wanna know a secret?" he said. "The pilot's got a colostomy bag. I just popped it. Right now, he's sitting in a pile of shit."

"What do you want?"

"Another vodka, and your full attention."

"I'm listening."

"It's about your dad."

"You can't touch him."

"I don't need to. He's confused enough on his own." The Devil laid his fingertips on my arm. "Do you want the original copy of Talbert's Treaty?"

"It doesn't exist."

"Sure it does. I just created it. And it saves his lazy ass."

"How?"

"Let's not go into the fine points until you hear what I want. You and I have a mutual acquaintance—"

"Ronnie Dolan? Forget it."

"I can't. He's family, Boone. Just like you've got a family—he's my boy. A big part of me, and you locked him up. I'm not happy with you." He poked me in the chest with a very sharp finger.

"He'll never make parole. People don't forget."

"I know that. I just want him transferred to that nice psych jail in Concord. He's served twenty-five years."

"Medium security? No way. He could bust out of there in twenty minutes."

"He won't even try. You have my word on it," said the Devil.

"It's not my decision," I said. "I'm appearing as the arresting officer. The board will never approve a downgrade."

"I think they will. But you've got to stay away from the hearing on Friday. Come on, buddy. You already got your promotion."

"Forget it."

"Don't you want to hear about the treaty?"

I missed my chance to say no.

"Here's the deal," said the Devil. "I've got it hidden, just waiting for you to pick it up—any time you want. I won't even be there to gloat. All you have to do is stay away from Ronnie's hearing. I'll make it easy for you to miss. I'll give you a family emergency."

"I don't need it. Everything's going to work out for Wes."

"Insurance, Boone. We're just talking insurance here. Listen to me. You believe Wes is going to be cleared and Ronnie's not getting moved to a psych ward. That's cool, but I happen to know otherwise. There's nothing wrong with acting on your faith—*and* covering your bases. If it goes your way, then you've lost nothing. It's a fair trade. Your dad for my boy."

I imagined myself trying to explain this to Sister.

"I won't do it," I said.

"Yeah, you will. You messed with my family, now I'm gonna mess with yours. If you don't help Ronnie, I'm going to fuck with your dad so bad, he'll wish he never met that little slit."

"Don't talk about my mother like that."

"My, my," said the Devil. "The ire rises. That's cool. I hate it when you guys give in too easy—it seems so insincere—so here's what I'm going to do."

He took his cocktail napkin off the tray and held it flat between his palms. He pressed his hands together and a wisp of yellow smoke curled between his fingers. When he opened his hands, a piece of brownish parchment lay on his open palm. It was a hand-drawn map with writing that looked like authentic eighteenth-century colonial script.

"Instant history," he said. "It's a map, drawn in 1717 by William Talbert, on the frontispiece of the Talbert family Bible. Go on, take it. It tells you where to find the treaty."

I knew it was real. I knew I could take this scrap of parchment and have it verified within fifty years of its alleged date. I knew I could follow its directions to a hidden place and put my hands on another authentic document that would save my father from harm, my family from embarrassment, my town from strife.

"Sorry," I said. "I think we'll let things take their course."

"Will we?" he said.

He set the parchment on the armrest between us. He picked up his gold pen and flipped it to the left, then aimed it at the floor. The plane jerked abruptly to port, then went into a steep fall, the front pointing straight down. Everyone started screaming. Briefcases, people, and litter slid past me down the aisle. There was a roaring noise, louder than the screams of the passengers. We were vertical, aimed at the earth beneath us. I felt weightless. I looked at him. He was smiling at me.

"Gravity," he said, wiggling his eyebrows. "It's the law."

I clutched at the armrests, my left hand covering the map.

"Take it," he said.

"Fuck you," I said, feeling myself sliding up the back of my seat as the plane screamed downward. It started to roll over. Luggage fell out of the overheads and sailed down the tube.

"Hey, Boone. How many times can you say fuck you before we hit the ground?"

"I'm not supposed to die today."

"You're right. You're the only survivor of this crash. I'm going to snap your spine in twelve places—no, make it thirteen. You're gonna be living dead, hooked up to machines for the next thirty years; but don't worry, I'm gonna visit you every ten years. Take the map."

"No."

"Take it, maggot."

I was getting dizzy from the vertigo. I shook my head.

"After I paralyze you, I'm giving your wife a job in my publishing house. How does eighty grand a year sound?"

I snatched the map off the armrest.

He leveled his pen and the plane pulled up. It sputtered and shook, but stayed airborne.

People were piled like rags in the front of the cabin, clutching and crawling over each other, crying and screaming. There was blood every-where. Loose pieces of the cabin and luggage were scattered all over the floor.

"Let's help," he said.

I went to the back of the plane and assisted the steward with the worst cases. There was a man with a deep gash on his stomach and an unconscious woman who was stuck under a seat. I looked to the front and saw the Devil holding a girl, making a tourniquet for her leg with his silk tie. I worked with the wounded for a half hour; then we settled in our seats. I could feel the warm piece of parchment in my shirt pocket.

The captain announced an emergency landing in D.C.

"Oooo," said the Devil, tucking in his shirt. "My favorite town."

As we taxied to the terminal at Reagan, he turned to me.

"Hey, Boone. Wanna know how you're really gonna die?"

"No."

"You're gonna choke to death. Wanna know where?"

I shook my head.

"In your cruiser."

"Let me guess," I said. "On a donut."

"Ain't life a hoot?" he said, laughing.

Inside the terminal, a crowd of reporters had gathered from the Washington television stations. There was a jumble of lights, microphones, and people struggling with cameras and powerpacks. Bruce Hutton, self-help guru, walked into the waiting room ahead of me. There was an explosion of noise and flashguns.

"Mr. Hutton, Mr. Hutton, over here."

He made his way to a semicircle in the waiting area and stood easily in front of the microphones. He put one hand casually into the pocket of his pants.

"What was it like?" someone asked.

"It was hell," he said. "Pure hell."

"Are you happy to be back on solid ground?" someone shouted.

"Oh, *yes,* I am," he said. "Oh, *yes,* I am."

Everybody laughed and applauded.

I was standing at the edge of the crowd, watching.

"Mr. Hutton, how do you get through something like this without losing your confidence?" a reporter asked.

He paused and collected his sincerity.

"An unshakable faith in a higher power and the abiding strength of the human spirit," he said. Then he looked over at me and winked.

I called Beth.

"Omigod, Boone. It's been all over the news. It said you were in a free fall."

"I feel like I still am," I said.

"Are you alright?"

"Yeah. Somehow, I stayed in my seat, but there were people and bags flying all over the place. I'm just waiting for my next flight."

"Is Veronica okay?"

"She got bumped to the next plane. She'll be home before me."

"Hurry home, honey. I'm not going to breathe until I see you. Love you."

I bought some cigarettes, went outside, and found an empty bench.

I took the Devil's map out of my shirt pocket. It was a small leather-looking packet, folded twice and worn shiny on the corners. It was wrapped with a string made of braided hair, and where the string was tied across the middle of the packet, it was sealed with a few drops of spit-colored wax.

I scraped off the wax with my thumbnail, untied the string, and looked at the map. It was warm and soft, and it settled over the shape of my hand like new skin.

The top half of the page was a primitive drawing of a path leading down the back side of Talbert's Ridge, into a severe geography that wasn't there. There was an extra hill, a series of caves, and a swamp circled by cliffs. There were trees drawn across the edge of the ridge, and in the middle of the pines was a larger lush-looking tree with a bright star drawn above it. Beneath the trees was a pile of rock and a scrabbly-looking tangle of brush. There was a dotted line drawn through the sketch, from the brush at the bottom to the large bright tree at the top.

I've hiked the ridge since I was five years old, and I didn't recognize anything on the map.

The handwriting under the map was written in colonial style and phrasing:

For a distance of several hundred yards, procede with prudence midway acrost the highest pointe of Talberte's Ridge (also named the Lookout Ridge) to a place marked by a great stone hewn in halves. At the cleft stone, begin marking seventy and nine paces over the ridge to a slender pathe. Going to the left waye on the pathe, proceed to a large arbor enclosing the so-called Tree of Life itself adorned with many and divers inscriptions, growing directly in the middle of the grove where no man can easily enter. Stooping low, you may discover the objecte of your intent hidden deep within an excrescence on the rooty parts, to be held fast on the hand of its owner.

I folded the map, tied it, and put it in my shirt pocket. I smoked a lot of cigarettes and waited for my next flight.

10

Wes and Sister walked into Zoda's Family Diner looking like any hungry couple. He was wearing the dark blue corduroy pants, white shirt, and pea coat that Sister bought for him. She was wearing a brown pleated skirt, beige sweater, and red plaid overcoat.

They sat in the end booth. Sister looked around the diner. The walls were brushed aluminum, the floor scuffed linoleum, the mood pandemonium.

The close air was warm and heavy with steamy smells of peppery food, grilled onions, and fresh coffee. It reminded her of her vision of the banquet, and she felt excited to be in such an exotic place with a world of choices before her.

"I come here a lot," Wes said, eager to show that he knew a place legit and well lit. "He lets me float a tab. I pay when I get some extra money." He waved to someone who was going out the door.

They talked while they waited for their food. He told her how much he missed his show, and she told him about growing up in the orphanage.

"Tonight, we're celebrating," said Wes, clinking water glasses with Sister. "Thanks to you I've got a clear head, and now I can get back on my feet. I need to find a job and a real place to stay, so I guess we won't be seeing much of each other."

Sister swallowed. "Well, that's what I wanted to tell you. Actually, things have changed for me, too. I've taken a job at the hotel." She smiled shyly. "And I've got my own room."

"What?"

"I'm not a nun anymore. I left the Church this morning."

Dumbfounded, Wes sat and blinked four times before saying a word. "Waitaminute, waitaminute. Slow down. You're not a nun anymore?"

She shook her head.

"Why not?"

"I think God is moving me in a different direction, so I went back to the church to pray. I had a disagreement with my Superior. She tried to punish me, so I left."

"So what are you now?"

"I'm still a woman of God. In my heart I haven't changed, but I know that my work is in the world now. Last night was a sign of some kind. I don't know what it means yet, but it *is* part of God's plan."

"So you quit the Church and twenty minutes later just happen to get a job? Doesn't that seem a little strange to you?" he asked. "Like *too much* of a coincidence?"

"It's how God works," she said. "That's all I know."

"Well, somebody's watching out for you," he said. "At least one of us is covered."

She smiled. "Your room is paid through Friday. After that, you can decide what you want to do."

"I'm not leaving you there by yourself," he said. "It's not safe. I'll keep the room. I'll get a good job and pay my way."

He started to say "knock on wood," then remembered how everything arrived at this point. It wasn't just luck. He remembered the first time he saw Sister and how out of place she looked sitting in the peanut gallery with the ragamuffins. He thought about bumping into her four times in one month and how she knew about the bear suit even before the Greeks jumped him and he got fired. He remembered how shocked she was to see him in the dayroom, and he recalled last night, lying on his back watching the bright light roll up and down his body like flashlights on a fence, and the heat coming from somewhere behind his heart and pouring out of him like the soul of a sun.

He remembered how scared she looked, sitting on the floor as the second blast of light faded around him.

None of this made any sense, but neither had the first twenty-six years of his life—and look what he had to show for that.

It all came down to trust. He trusted her and she trusted God. So they were in it together, the three of them—and only one knew why.

"Alright," he said, leaning back in the booth and putting his hands behind his head. His big belly touched the edge of the table. "All we need is a job for me."

Sister started laughing. She had a high sweet giggle like a child.

"What's so funny?"

"I just got it," she said, pointing at the dessert case. "Hot cross buns."

Back at the hotel, they settled in for the night. Wes lay on the floor by the bed, covered by a blanket, his pea coat for a pillow. He moved his leg. There wasn't even a hint of soreness in his knee. He was more amazed to realize that it was only ten o'clock in the evening and here he was, lying down and ready for sleep. The notion of getting up and going out to a bar actually seemed wrong. The call of the bottle wasn't even a whisper. How things change. He felt clean, content, and his belly was full.

Sister lay on the bed in her clothes, covered by the other blanket. She tried to pray but was distracted by the man breathing on the floor beneath her. She made it through a handful of Our Fathers, then realized that it was just a test of her memory. She drew a calming breath.

"Thank you, Father," she said simply. "For everything."

They were alone together for a few moments; then Wes spoke.

"What do I call you, now that you're not a nun?"

"Sister," she said. "Call me Sister. It's still my name."

"Alright. Goodnight, Sister. And thanks again."

"Good night," she said. "Thank you. And God bless."

The next morning, Wes went looking for work. He pasted his hair across his wide forehead with a dab of hand soap, then spit-shined his shoes. Sister stood on a chair, straightened his part, and fumbled with his second-hand tie.

"You look charming," she said, as if she were dressing one of her orphans. "Is it alright with you if I say a little prayer?"

"Can't hurt." His hands fluttered to his pockets, then found their way to a classic Joan of Arc pose. He scrunched his eyes shut, then peeked. The girl was holding her hands at her waist, her fingers twined, her face tilted upward.

"Father," she began, "please bless your servants in their endeavors today. And through your many mercies, guide us and protect us as we seek to further your plan for goodness on Earth. Amen."

Wes stood awkwardly for a moment.

"That's it?" he said.

"You can say something, if you'd like."

Wes closed his eyes and flexed his face.

"Okay, now. Okay. I just need some good luck," he prayed. "If you've got any left over."

He opened his eyes and saw that she was smiling at him.

They walked downstairs through the drab lobby and stood outside under the marquee. The shoveled snow was knee-high against the buildings, and the street was curb-to-curb ice, peppered with cinders. Sister hugged herself against the cold.

"Good luck and God bless," she said. "I know you'll do fine."

"Thanks. I've got a good feeling about this. You'd better get back inside before you freeze. Hey, what do Eskimos call the Grim Reaper?"

"I give up."

"Popsicle."

"I don't get it."

"I don't, either," he said, laughing. "See you later."

He pulled up the collar of his pea coat and walked toward the center of town.

Sister went inside and tapped the bell on the front desk. From the dark room behind the counter she heard bedsprings, then a man coughing. Out of the darkness, Clarence appeared in the doorway, rearranging his trousers. He was wearing the same clothes as the day before.

"What?" he coughed.

"I'm ready for work. Remember?"

"It's kind of early for this, isn't it?" He raked his scalp and coughed some more.

"By God's first light, we set it right. That's what we say at the orphanage."

"Okay, okay. Give me a minute."

While she waited for Clarence, she took stock of the lobby. The easy chair sagged like a sleeping drunk, and the velour sofa leaned like a ship going down. The carpet was worn to its backing, and the large window was clouded with smoky dust. The ceiling sagged, and the walls were stained.

Behind the counter was an old wooden desk with a gooseneck lamp and a rusty chair on wheels. On the wall was a 1949 calendar with a picture of a busty redheaded woman in a negligee cooking breakfast for a man wearing a business suit. Underneath the picture was a caption: START EVERY DAY WITH A HOT DISH.

Clarence came through the doorway, lighting a cigarette. "Let's do it," he said.

She followed him through a narrow door at the back of the lobby, then down a set of thirteen gritty steps to the ancient cellar.

A pile of moldy towels lay on the dirt floor next to a washing machine. In the weak yellow light of one hanging bulb she could see the boiler, a broken-down coal bin, and the stone frame of a dried-out well. Several loose boards lay across the top of the deep hole.

"Don't get too close," he said. "That old well is a mile deep."

"Shouldn't it be covered?"

"Nobody else comes down here, and a few more boards won't keep anything out."

The room was a tomb. Strings of old webs and husks of dead insects hung close to her head.

"Let's see what's wrong with this thing," he said, poking at the muddy slosh inside the washer with a broomstick. He jiggled the guts of the machine so fiercely that a heave of gray scum splashed out, onto his belly.

"Dammit."

He slapped the dials with the flat of his hand, and the washer made a nasty grinding noise. The tub wobbled, and a clot of bad water coughed out the back of the box and dribbled across the floor toward the open well.

A long rat crawled out of the pit and slid into the coal bin. Clarence ignored it.

"Back in business," he said, dropping the lid. "Let's go find the Kirby."

The vacuum was upstairs in a cluttered closet, under a jumble of worn and broken belongings abandoned by decades of transients.

"Lost and found?" Sister asked.

"Lost and forgotten is more like it," Clarence said. He poked through a cardboard box. "Lookee here."

He held up a jacket with a medal pinned on the pocket, the Distinguished Service Cross. The ribbon was stained and torn; the silver was pocked and crusty. A corner of the cross was bent, as if it had been used to open a bottle.

"Tommy. Tommy Ninebastards," he said. "That's what they called him. Poor guy, wore this all the time—everywhere. He claimed he took out a German gun all by himself—killed nine men. It's all he ever talked about. He'd show you this thing and say, 'Got nine of them bastards.' "

"Where is he?"

"Gone. Don't know where. Just gone."

Sister pulled a hot plate off the shelf.

Clarence looked at the bottom of it. "Some girl owned that. Used to cook in her room. Cabbage. Smelled terrible. She's gone, too. Got hurt somehow." He handed her the hot plate. "Take it if you want it."

Sister uncovered a mop, a broom, and a bucket. She rinsed the bucket, filled it, and ripped some of the old clothes into two-foot squares.

Ammonia and water, soap and brush, she scrubbed the heavy front door and scoured thirty years of bootscuffs off the kickplate. She washed the jamb and cleaned every inch of the white-tiled floor until her elbows ached. She poured buckets of filthy water on the street, where it froze to gray ice in the gutter.

She cleaned the smoky window, scraped a crust of dead flies off the sill, and shined the hinges and doorknob. She emptied the ashtrays and stabbed a broom at spiders behind the fan, then dragged the floormats into the street and shook them; clouds of plague and dust filled the air.

At noon she woke up Clarence.

"I need to find my room," she said. "It's time for my midday prayers."

He looked across the clean lobby and through the clear window to the bright morning sun. He blinked like a man seeing daylight for the first time.

"Take your pick," he said, handing her a ring of keys.

Sister chose the room across the hall from Wes.

She hung a crucifix on the outside of her door and draped a clean towel across the top of the nightstand, then unpacked her Bible, her candlestick, and *Benedict*. She arranged her belongings on the small altar.

She hung her coat and habit in the tiny closet and put her underwear in the top drawer of the battered dresser. She tested the lamp and the faucets in the bathroom, put the hot plate on the radiator, and plugged it in. She lay on her back in the narrow bed and looked out the dirty window, then stood up, turned off the hot plate, and vacuumed the floor.

Sister knelt before her altar and meditated on the moment. This was her first full day living outside the Church, and although the work was the same—scrubbing, sweeping, and cleaning—there was a new sense to her motions and a lightness in her head.

I can do whatever I want, she thought. I'm earning money, I have my own room, and when I finish with work, I'm going out to buy food and I don't have to tell anybody where I'm going. I can walk up the sidewalk and speak to anyone I choose. Feed birds all day. I can stay up all night reading if I want to.

She stood in the middle of her room and struck a childish pose. She sang the orphans' anthem:

"I'm a little petunia in an onion patch—
An onion patch, an onion patch.
Oh, I'm a little petunia in an onion patch.
Now whattaya think of that?"

There were thirteen rooms on the second and third floors of the hotel. Six rooms on each side, one room at the end of the hall. The second story was full of boarders every night; the upper floor was mostly empty, except for the weekends, when the building throbbed with subterranean carnal rhythms. The rooms were small with dirty doors and floors. The bathrooms were filthy; the tubs were scummed and the sinks crusty. There were stained mattresses on shaky beds, and the nightstands were pitted with cigarette burns and whiskey rings. The sooty windows were painted shut; there was dust and grit everywhere.

Sister cleaned all day on the second floor, hauling fresh sheets and towels up from the basement and bags of trash to the alley behind the building. The hotel was already looking better. The smell of pine oil was beginning to cut through the funk of smoke, booze, and sweat.

At five o'clock she quit for the day. She put on her coat and went outside for a walk. The day was turning gray in the early winter dusk, and the neon lights of cocktail glasses and wiggly girls blinked in the windows of the bars. This was enemy territory, Wesley's former world, and she felt like a spy in the trenches.

When she returned from shopping, she boiled water for the macaroni and cut strips of carrots and celery on the edge of the bathroom sink. She heard Wes walking down the hall, whistling.

"What a day," he said, waltzing through the door and throwing his arms wide. "I wish there was two of me."

"How so?"

"I've got two jobs. I need some advice. Two radio stations want to hire me, and I don't know which one to take. Hey, what's for dinner?"

After grace, they ate macaroni and cheese, and a Hershey's for dessert. They listened to the radio and talked, while outside the door the boarders drifted to their rooms.

"Here's the deal." Wes was describing his day. "One job is straight salary, the other is mostly commission."

"How does commission work?"

"When I sell an advertisement, I get part of the money. Ten percent."

"That sounds good, doesn't it?"

"I think so."

"Are the stations the same?"

"I like the second place better. I like the songs they play, and I like the boss."

"I think you should go with the commission plan—the second station. Since you're so good with people, it seems like you could make more money there."

"Thanks for the vote," he said, getting up from dinner to find his new employer on the radio. A popular song filled the room. "That's what I'll do."

Love and marriage in the air.

Two weeks later, they were sitting in Zoda's, celebrating Wes's first paycheck.

"Three hundred fifty dollars," he said, counting the bills for the third time. "Amazing."

"You worked so hard," Sister said, patting his hand. "You deserve every penny of it."

Wes was a new man. He woke himself up every morning. After a shower, a shave, and a clean shirt, he packed his briefcase with his appointment book and his pad of sales contracts; then he walked across the hall to spend some time with Sister. Every morning, she met him at the door with a smile and his lunch. They spent a few minutes talking and drinking hotplate coffee; Sister said a short prayer; they walked down the stairs and said good-bye in the lobby.

All day Wes beat the streets, selling air time for WNAU. Because he was a natural, his sales approach was simple: Spend a half hour telling jokes to a stranger, then ask him if he wanted to be on the radio. After two weeks, he was already top salesman for the station.

He loved his job because he could set his own schedule and pick his own prospects. He went to every office building in town, started in the lobby, and shook hands with everyone on the premises. His customers loved him. He was the only salesman at the station who actually had clients calling for him, inviting him to lunch or asking him to stop by sometime and hang out. He wasn't selling advertising so much as selling himself, simply being Wes.

He was writing six contracts a day, and the owner of the station wanted to give him a car so he could work the smaller towns outside Nashua.

His paperwork was a disaster. He kept names, dates, and ad copy in his head and odd bits of information written on napkins and gum wrappers stuffed in his pockets. At the end of the day, Sister helped him organize his contracts and appointment book.

Of all the new things in his life, he was most surprised at his feelings for her. He found himself thinking about her during the day and looking forward to having dinner every night after work in her room.

Every evening they sat and talked. She listened to his schemes of getting back into television, encouraging him to make a good plan. She laughed at all of his jokes—no matter how lame his punch lines or how far he stretched his puns. She was his best audience and his biggest fan. Sister was the first woman he had ever met who could accept his zaniness and still respect him. She never gave him advice he didn't ask for, tried to change his mind, or made him feel big and stupid when she disagreed with him.

When he considered the arc of his life so far, he saw himself on the ascent, hand in hand with his new soulful friend.

"Three hundred fifty dollars," he said again. "Let's go buy ponies."

"I'm not cleaning up after horses," she laughed. "People are bad enough."

There had been solid changes at the hotel since Sister started as housekeeper. The lobby was noticeably cleaner, Clarence was bathing every day, and it seemed like a better class of drifters had checked in. There was less noise at night, and no one had thrown any furniture out a window in over a week. There were no worn-out women lounging in the lobby anymore, no fights in the hallway, and less mess in the rooms every morning. Even the lights on the marquee seemed brighter.

Wes gave credit to the crucifix.

"I think it's scaring off the bad guys."

"I hope so," Sister said. "The sign of the cross is the Devil's loss."

After two weeks, she was still new to the notion of freedom; nineteen years of rigid obedience was a heavy burden to toss away lightly. Often during the day she found herself defending her choice of a particular chore to an imaginary overseer, and she would have to remind herself that she was in charge of her own life now, and being paid for her time as well. Now, there was no one nearby to play the role of a superior.

Staying true to her old schedule of daily prayer was the only link to her old life. Praying seven times a day was more than a habit; it was her passage between both lives, old and new. As much as drawing one breath after another, it was the way she kept her soul alive—especially in a building that seemed soaked with the stains of every last sin.

Seven times a day she prayed the sin away, and at the end of every session she still presented her standing offer: "If you give me children of my own," she promised, "I will raise them to serve in your Army of Saints and fight for goodness on Earth."

Wes was a study, and she thought about him all day. He was like a huge boy, full of earnest good cheer and mischief. He had a good heart, she was sure of that, and he was honest and hardworking—his first paycheck was testament to his ethic. She loved his stories and the way he joked without a hint of meanness. She had never heard him get a laugh at the expense of anyone's dignity, using himself instead as a foil.

"Don't play stupid with me," he'd say, "because that's a game you're gonna lose."

She loved seeing him in the morning when he came across the hall for coffee and prayers, and she waited with girlish anticipation for their time at the end of the day when they sat in her room with the radio playing, eating beans and franks with sauerkraut, then sharing a Hershey's.

"These days, the only bar for me," he'd say, breaking off two squares and handing her one.

Everything was fitting together like the pieces of a larger puzzle. It was a good beginning, she was sure of it.

The following Friday, Sister was on the third floor, preparing rooms for the weekend rush. Halfway down the hall, she noticed an unlocked door on a vacant room. She pushed the door open with a broom handle and looked inside.

A small man in a rumpled gray outfit was sitting on a straight-backed chair, looking at a photo album. His hair was peppered and tousled; his beard was short but untrimmed. He was wearing boots, loose trousers, a vest, and a gray jacket several sizes too large for his wiry frame. He had a gentle face and deadly eyes. At first sight, Sister thought it was Ulysses S. Grant.

The smell of decaying flesh filled the room. Sister put her hand over her nose.

The man looked up from his scrapbook and smiled.

"Having fun?" he asked in a voice no different from any man's.

"No, I'm not. I want you to leave."

"No can do, nunny-cunny. My playground, my rules. Your dopey little spells don't work out here in the real world. And besides, the weekend's just around the corner. This is my place, and I'm expecting some friends later."

"All things for God's glory."

"Wrong again, holy wormbag. Wanna see some pictures?"

He turned the book around. Spread across two pages was a picture of the hotel with the front of the building removed, like a dollhouse. Each room was a separate scene, moving inside like a miniature film.

In one room a man was lying on the bed, crying. In the room beneath him, a man was whipping a drunken woman with a belt. In the next room, three men were fighting over a pile of money on the floor. On the opposite page, two naked people struggled and cursed each other. Next door, a lone woman vomited in the sink. A still baby lay on the toilet seat.

"Good times, huh?" said the Devil, grinning.

"I command you to leave," Sister said, making the sign of the cross and pointing her finger at his face.

He laughed. "Wanna see pictures of your mother?" he asked.

He flipped forward a few pages to a picture of the Superior. She was lying on her bed, thick legs spread, her fingers fluttering under her nightgown, under her belly.

"Oops," said the Devil. "Wrong mother. Sorry."

"Stop it," said Sister. "In odorem sauvitatis. Tu autem effugare, diabole. What do you want?"

He shut the book, dropped it on the floor, and leaned forward in his chair.

"I want you to go away. I want you to take your fat clown and leave us alone."

"No. Appropinquabit enim judicum Dei. I'm not afraid of you."

"Of course not. I'm a nice guy. Forget what you've heard. I'll make you a deal: Leave us alone and I'll give you what you want."

"You don't know what I want."

"Sure I do. Babies. I'll give you so many babies, you'll need nine more tits. I'll give you those, too, if you want them."

Sister was quiet, forgetting for a moment that the power was hers to lose.

"Who do you think you pray to?" the Devil asked. "Who do you think gave you those stupid visions? I'm the one who got you out of that drab little life. I wanted you out here, in my world where I can play with you. You're mine now."

"I belong to God. I made a bargain with Him, and I'm keeping my side of it."

"I know all about your whore's bargain. I was there. In fact, I'm the one who told Him to take it."

"I don't believe you. You're lying."

"No, I'm not," he lied. "We were amused. In fact, we made a bet."

She took the bait. "A bet?"

"I bet Him you wouldn't survive out here."

"But I have."

"Luck. And inattention on my part. I've been busy." He scratched his thigh.

"And what did He say?" she asked.

He pulled a corncob pipe from his vest pocket, packed it, and fired it with a spark from his fingernail. He drew a long haul from the bowl. Blue smoke pooled under his eyes. "Here's the deal: You need to raise your children righteously. If they don't find their spiritual gifts, I get the soul of your firstborn. And just to make it interesting, I get to visit him seven times. If he can't find his faith by my seventh visit, he's mine."

"That's all? That's how I beat you? Just raise my son to find his faith?"

"You have no idea."

"Of course I do. I know all about faith and righteousness."

"Enough to make a teenage boy think he's not the hottest piece of shit on the planet? Good luck."

"You're just jealous."

"Of what? You?"

"Of God's faith in me," she said. "According to you, He's betting on me. I've already won."

"We haven't even started," the Devil said. "I'm gonna throw so much trouble at you and your little tribe, your boy is going to be spinning around in circles. I'm going to have him so confused, he won't have time to worry about his soul. I already know his weakness; he thinks he can beat me on his own."

"You're not getting anybody. We will defeat you."

"We?"

"My children and I. The Army of Saints."

The Devil laughed. "That's rich. I've seen the Army of Saints. Diddlers and withered little bags of piss. You'll fit right in."

"What about the rest of my children?"

The Devil made a movement as if he were brushing scraps off his leg. "Chaff," he said. "You know how we are; we're all hung up on firstborns."

"Why?"

"First fruit. Sweetest taste."

The girl stepped forward and set herself firm, an arm's length from the Devil. She looked straight into his eyes.

"You will not win. And if you hurt any member of my family, I will fly at you with every drop of blood in my life."

The Devil's eyes turned to slits behind the smoke.

"Big deal," he said. "You're a flea on God's ass, and I'm going to kill your firstborn. I'm not going to kill him right away, because I want you to suffer—and you will. With sorrow and fear you will mark the times I visit your child. Seven times, and on the final visit he will die. He will fail and die faithless under my hand, and I will take him back to my dwelling and eat him like a fig. I'm going to nail his vain little soul on my front door."

Sister felt the anger boiling in her head.

"You have no power over me," she said. "I receive power from my God."

The Devil picked up the album. He went to a page at the back of the book and showed her a photograph of a middle-aged man in a uniform sitting in a car. The man was bug-eyed dead. Spilled coffee rose steaming from his lap, and he was clutching the collar of his shirt with the fingertips of both hands.

"Seventh time," said the Devil, tapping the picture with the stem of his pipe. "Seventh time."

"Go. Now," commanded Sister.

"I'm not done smoking," said the Devil.

"*Lead us not into temptation,*" she said, loud and clear. "*And deliver us from evil.*"

He closed the book and blew a cloud of smoke at the girl.

"God, you're annoying," the Devil said, fading to darkness.

Sister marched calmly from the room, back to her homemade altar on the second floor. Her jaw was set, her fists clenched; her soul was soaring. She had met the enemy, stood her ground, and stared straight through him, and he had backed down. Power and peace surged through her as she prayed.

"For as long as I live," she vowed, "I will keep that beast at bay. I swear it."

. . .

It was late April. Wes and Sister were sitting on the fire escape outside Sister's window, finishing a tuna casserole. The weather had been warm for two weeks straight, and like the rest of New Hampshire, they were giddy with the prospect of springtime. The night sky was restless; shrouds of clouds slid across the waxing moon. The air was soaked with the rutty sweetness of springtime mud. The earth itself was breathing again. There was life in the night.

"How was your day?" she asked, handing him the salt.

"It was great. I drove up to Collins Bridge—you know, the town that had a chicken for mayor."

"What? A chicken for mayor?"

"Sure. You never heard of this? It's a famous place."

"No, I never heard of a town with a chicken for a mayor. You're making this up."

"I am not."

"Was it a big chicken?"

They had been living at the hotel for six months. Sister was running the place, doing double duty as housekeeper and desk clerk, and Wes had become the most valuable employee at WNAU, generating enormous amounts of advertising revenue. The station was doing so well, the owner was considering expanding to the television market.

They had saved over four thousand dollars together, and like the season, they were restless for change.

Day by day, their weeks were the same. They met every morning, hugging in the doorway of Sister's room, and after small talk, coffee, and prayers, they went their separate ways—Sister to her rounds and Wes to his world of schmooze.

They ate at Zoda's every Friday night and worshipped in the Epsicopal church every Sunday morning. They ate dinner together every night, talking and listening to Perry Como—Sister's favorite singer.

Dancing was difficult in the tiny room; they began their loop in the corner between the dresser and the floor lamp, then sashayed around the bed into the bathroom for two tight turns. They slid back through the doorway to the bedroom and around the bed twice more before beginning again in the corner. Their movement described a mirrored ellipse, like two question marks touching, belly to back.

They held hands while they talked between songs. Sitting at the window or on the breezy fire escape, they spoke in narrowing circles about their situation.

"Are you happy here?" he asked.

"For the moment. I think I'm doing good work." She meant the work of keeping the tares from God's earthly garden. "But it's not up to me."

"Are we waiting for a sign?" he asked, looking past the moon.

She nodded, smiling at him.

"Well, I'm sure you know what you're doing," he said.

They sat for a while enjoying their closeness in the warming night, both with private thoughts roaming the void.

Sister thought about her bargain with God, the deal she thought she had made. She was already twenty years old. How long would He make her wait for children of her own?

Wes was thinking about his own deals—places to go, clients to meet.

"I'm turning in," he said. "I've got a busy day tomorrow."

"I'm going to stay out here for a little while," she said. "The warm air feels good." She gave his hand a squeeze before he stood up. "Good night, Wesley."

"Good night."

"Wait," she said, as he was climbing in the open window. "What happened to that town with the chicken for mayor?"

"He was a bad egg, so they impoached him."

She sat on the fire escape with the night breeze blowing around her. There were stirrings in the sky, then stirrings in her soul.

It had been five months since her last vision, but she recognized the familiar rustlings in her heart and the heat that seemed to burn in her bones. She leaned against the iron steps, gripping the railing with both hands. She was afraid she would faint and tumble down to the street.

The dizziness grew. The edges of her eyesight turned gray, sparked with swirling nebulae, and she felt cold and weightless, stuck between fear and glory.

Above her, at the top of the stairway, a bright white light began to glow—as if an angel were walking across the roof, coming toward the ladder. There was no heat from the light, but it became so bright that Sister had to cover her eyes with her hand.

She heard voices. People were speaking on the roof, and she felt their footsteps above her. They came down the stairway slowly; she could see their shadows on the side of the building. There were at least three of them. She pressed her back against the brick wall and waited for them to come near.

The first was a young boy, handsome and clever-looking, wearing turquoise cowboy boots and a cowboy hat, dirty Wranglers, a leather vest over a red flannel shirt and a shiny metal star on his chest that said TEXAS RANGER. Around his waist was a tan gunbelt with a holster. It was low on his hip and tied at the tip around his right knee with a length of black shoelace. In the holster was a toy pistol, a Mattel Fanner 50.

The boy came down the stairs with his arms outstretched, touching both sides of the stairway for balance. When he came to the step above Sister he stopped, looked down at her, and smiled.

"What are you doing here?" he asked. "Are you okay?"

"I'm fine, thank you," she said. "I guess I'm waiting for you."

"Can you move it, dorkus?" said a voice behind the boy.

"Alright, I'm going," he said to the person behind him. He rolled his eyes at Sister and stepped over her.

Behind him came a girl, younger than the boy by a few years. She was dressed in a denim jumper, knee socks, and loafers. Her dark hair was in a ponytail, and she was carrying a white kitten.

"This isn't a very good place to sit," she said to Sister. "Somebody's going to trip over you and break their neck." She hugged the cat to her chest and made her way around Sister with highly exaggerated drama. The boy and the girl both passed down the stairs, where they seemed to disappear when they reached the open window of her room.

There was more movement above Sister. Someone else was coming down the steps, moving more slowly than the boy and girl. A small round child, a boy, earnestly trying to descend the stairs one step at a time. He was soft and angelic-looking with wispy blond hair and wide blue eyes. He was wearing a T-shirt that said BOSTON.

When he saw Sister, his face lit with excitement and he hustled double-time, stumping toward her on his chubby little legs. When he reached her, he fell onto her lap, threw his arms around her neck, and squeeezed her until she coughed.

"My goodness," she said. "Are you an angel?"

He pointed a finger at her nose and poked her with it. "You are," he said, hunching his round shoulders and grinning. Then he made a grumpy face and climbed off her lap, easing his way down the staircase, where he turned to mist.

Sister drew several deep breaths as the light above her faded. She sat in the dark for a few more minutes, smiling and shaking with rapture.

She stayed awake all night rejoicing in the vision of her three children. It was time for change. Now she needed to prepare herself—and she needed to test Wesley's intentions.

The next morning, she was sitting at the coffee table, her hands around her teacup in the shape of a prayer, when Wes walked into the room.

"God spoke to me last night," she said. "He revealed some things, and I think it's time to leave this place."

She had crafted her announcement with agonizing care. Word for word, she planned what she would say. Two sentences. Their future hung on his response.

He carried his coffee to the chair. He squinted as he sipped.

"Well," he said. "What are we going to do?"

First person plural. We. Two people together. It was the word she was waiting for.

To keep from smiling too much, she tested her tea.

"I guess we need to talk about it," she said lightly.

"Yeah," he said. "I guess we do."

He sounded vague, but he knew exactly what he wanted—and exactly how to ask for it. He was holding out for atmosphere. He didn't want to waste the moment over a cup of coffee in a dingy hotel.

"Do you like root beer?" he asked her.

"I do. I love it."

"Let's go out later and get some. We'll take a drive."

That evening at five o'clock, Sister settled herself on the passenger side of Wes's maroon Chevy. Its wide tires hummed like cellos as he drove it out of town onto winding country roads.

Sister watched the greening fields and granite hills as they rolled past. Like her, the people who lived in these homes and owned these fields performed their private chores and ceremonies—coffee in the morning, prayers in the night, devotion to labor in the hours of daylight.

We are all the same, she thought. God graces all with the same desires: souls at peace, dreams that matter, and the comfort of our kind.

As she watched the hills and fields wash past her window, she hoped Wes would ask her to marry him. She couldn't make it happen. She couldn't pray for it, she couldn't hint. It could only happen if it was supposed to happen. It was up to Wesley.

Wes was quiet. There were powerful urges calling him forward, holding him back. He wanted to marry this girl, but he was afraid she would refuse—and if she did, he knew he would be lost. He could never keep away from his bad habits alone, and it would be a very short fall back to his old life. He needed her, he loved her. He owed her his life, and he didn't want to lose her.

He knew it would be a hard sell. She didn't need him. She was strong enough, smart enough, to make it anywhere on her own. What could he offer? He reviewed his selling points. I'm a hard worker, agreeable, great sense of humor, and I'm dry, thanks to you. That wasn't enough, he was sure of it—but he couldn't fake credentials. She knew him better, it seemed, than he knew himself.

Oh, well. I can only play it straight. It's just me. At least you know what you're getting.

They stopped in Franklin Notch, at a general store in the center of the tiny town. It was a town settled between two mountains, with a main street running through the center of the valley.

"You're in luck," said the woman behind the counter. "We just brought ice cream back today. It's how everyone in town knows that spring is officially here."

They took their root beer floats back to the car and drove up the East Mountain to the ball field, where they parked, facing the hills on the west side of the valley town. Before them, the pale blue sunset of a cloudless day, the green hills graying in the dusk, the two white spires framing the valley.

They fished around their floats with Sweetheart spoons.

A church bell rang seven times.

It's not going to happen, she thought. Not tonight.

Okay, he told himself. Here goes.

He stuck his spoon in his cup and sighed.

"Listen," he said. He could feel his heart pounding at his bones. "I've been doing some thinking."

He looked at her. She was staring at him, her eyes as wide as the first time they talked in the dayroom.

"We're like pals, right? I mean, after everything that's happened to us."

She nodded—a little too vigorously. Where, she wondered, is this going?

"Well, I've been thinking about the way things used to be—when I was having all that trouble with the booze and no money, and no place to live when I got fired from my show. And I was thinking about how things changed for me the night you burnt the poison out of me, and how we didn't know each other then, but we ended up together anyway."

He jiggered the straw through the cross-shaped hole in the cup cover.

"It's pretty crazy, if you think about it. I mean, I wasn't really your type—at least not before."

Sister smiled.

"But I'm different now, thanks to you. I know what's right, and I was thinking how it would feel if we weren't together—if we went our separate ways when we left the hotel. It wouldn't feel right. I'd miss you, and I know I'd wish I had said something. I don't know where I want to go next, but I want us to stay together."

He paused and took a deep breath. "Here's what I'm saying. I love you, and I'm asking you to marry me. Will you please? I'll do anything to make you happy."

"Oh, Wesley, yes," she cried, diving across the seat at his great bulky chest, hugging him, then giving him a happy kiss on his wide goofy mouth.

Root beer everywhere.

"I'd love to." She laughed. "I thought you'd never ask. I love you, too. I really do. I always have. I'm so happy when I'm with you."

"We're good for each other," he said, holding her. "Aren't we?"

"Yes, we are," she said. "You're the best thing that ever happened to me."

They stood in front of the car, leaning against the hood, watching the end of the day while planning their beginnings. She was tucked under his arm, wearing his sweater. It fit her like a bathrobe.

They held hands, talking and laughing.

"Where should we go?" Wes asked. "We can go anywhere. Where do you want to get married?"

Sister looked into the valley. The town was small enough to hold in her hand. The streetlights flickered between the trees like votive candles; the white spires shone like altar ornaments. There was safety, the promise of peace in the valley—a haven of harmony for her covenant family.

"This is so beautiful," she said. "I want to live here. On top of this mountain."

11

Beth met me at the airport. We hugged at the gate, just feeling each other breathe. I love my wife. I love the way she looks; I love the way she sounds when she puts her head against mine while we hug and her voice hums *I missed you so much* through my bones.

"I was so worried about you," she said, her fingertips quivering into my shoulders.

We held hands as we drove back to Franklin Notch.

"You smell smoky," she said.

"I started again in Florida."

"Poor baby. You were doing so well. You're home now, and everything's going to be okay."

"I hope so. This trip was a waste of time. Reggie's not coming back, Veronica is actually more miserable than before, and I had a bad time on the plane."

"I know. I was glued to the TV. They said it fell six thousand feet."

"There's more to it. I saw him again. He sat next to me. That's my fifth time."

"Oh, honey," she said, putting her arm over my shoulders. "I'm so sorry. Was it bad?"

"Yeah, it was. He tried to make me a deal. He wants to trade Wes for Ronnie Dolan."

"No way. What did you say?"

"I told him no."

"Did he hurt you?'

"No. I poured beer on him."

Beth laughed. "Good for you. I wish I'd been there. I would have poked him in the nose."

God, I love this woman.

"So what happens now?" she asked.

"He's going to turn up the heat, I guess. He really hates Sister, and it's going to get nasty. All this bad stuff with the town is part of his attack. We have to be very careful."

I wanted to stop for a cigarette.

"Hell of a way to live, huh?" I said.

"What do you mean?"

"Stuck between my mother and the Devil."

"Well, at least we've got the right guy for the job," she said, leaning over with one of her best kisses.

"How's Benny?" I asked. "Don't you hate that new name he's using?"

"Seriously, yes," she said. "He's doing good, though. He says he finally discovered why the Three Stooges are funny."

"America is grateful."

"Don't be cruel," she teased. "He's trying hard."

"I know. I've just never seen the kid laugh."

We were quiet awhile. In the night, in the sky, in the darkness flying by—we were the only living things we could feel.

The folded map felt thick in my pocket, warm on my chest. I couldn't talk about it yet—even with Beth. I wondered where I could hide it until I figured out what it meant, and how to use it.

"Honey? Are you listening?"

"Sure."

"Well, what do you think?"

"About what?"

She laughed. "You are tired. I asked if you wanted to stop for a piece of pie at Hamrick's."

"Yeah. I'd like that."

"Boone, what's wrong?"

"I don't want to die. I've only got two more times."

"Oh, baby, don't worry about it. It could be years and years before you see him again. I'll protect you."

I love the way Beth feels, all wide and soft when she rolls on top of me and I slide inside her. I love the way she looks, all familiar and lazy with her smiling eyes closed and her mouth slightly open as she rocks back and forth over my hips. And I love the way I feel, surging gently beneath her, lost for the moment in the warm comfort of her kindness.

We lie together afterward, her thigh over mine.

"Can we take a vacation when all this is over?" she asks.

"I'd love to," I say. "Anywhere but Disney World."

PART TWO

12

Here is something that happened twenty-five years ago.

It started in Providence. The first body was a twelve-year-old girl, white female, headless, found sitting upright on a bench in front of the Denny's on Route 95. The head showed up later that day in Attleboro, thirteen miles north, on the self-help shelf in a Barnes and Noble. Jammed into one nostril of the child's head was a piece of paper with chilling words of wrath and judgment.

Carry to my people this message; let them know that their hour of bondage has arrived. Believe in nothing, or belong to me.

It was unsigned. The news media named the monster Holy Hell.

The next body appeared in Foxboro—a naked, middle-aged white man, found in a parked car at a 7-Eleven. His arms and legs were hacked off at the elbows and knees and stacked on his lap like four pieces of firewood. His eyeballs were in his mouth. Again the note, handwritten and apocalyptic:

You serve me well. You have named me.

The graphics for the endless TV news updates were spectacular—Gothic script over lots of flames, stylized drawings of old Mr. Sticks with goatee, horns, and pitchfork, and the sound of one bell tolling in the background. HOLY HELL: THE DEVIL IN OUR MIDST, the screens glared across the Boston area.

The experts were dizzy, talking themselves in circles; the police and the feds patrolled every inch of pavement between Providence and Boston. They were looking for pure evil; they saw it everywhere, found it nowhere.

The next body was discovered in Brockton. It looked like an older woman, but it was hard to tell with all the bite marks. Again, a note—this one signed:

The taste of vengeance lies sweet on my tongue. The stink of redemption blows hot out my ass. Holy Hell.

Providence, Foxboro, Brockton. It was moving north.

I was in New Hampshire, the rookie in a three-man police department, twenty-four years old, back home in Franklin Notch after three years in the marines. My job during the day was to sit at the south end of Main Street, waiting for out-of-state cars. At night I patrolled every street in our tiny town. My beat started on Main Street and I worked my way up both mountains, one road at a time. It took four minutes to drive slowly from the Congregational church at the south end of town to the Episcopal church on the other side. Between the two churches were Hamrick's Market, the hardware store, packy, town hall, library, the Bob-O-Link restaurant, and Dinger's Family Clothing.

In my first year as a cop, I arrested only one person from Franklin Notch: Ronnie Dolan, dubbed Holy Hell—the preacher's boy who left town under a cloud and returned in a black Fury.

People were crazy with fear in the summer of 1980, when Holy Hell was loose. Veronica was working the night shift at Manchester General, and Earl drove her to work every night, thirty-six miles each way. Reggie had just been hired as a sports co-anchor for WNAU, and he was on the road four nights a week, announcing games, scared witless. He was one of several thousand people from Franklin Notch carrying at least one illegal firearm everywhere he went.

Wes wouldn't take a gun; it went against his belief system. He believes he can talk his way out of anything, including a serial killer. I bought him a beeper that he lost in the woods.

Holy Hell was all over the news. He was all everyone talked about. He was fear, poison in the air; he was everywhere.

Sister called me one night.

"This is very bad, Daniel," she said. "And it has something to do with us. I don't know how, exactly, but in my dreams I've seen a giant of some kind. He's the worst kind of evil, and he's very close to Mr. Sticks. He's very big—bigger than everything around him. And there's the smell of candy canes."

"Giants and candy canes? Sounds like a Shirley Temple movie."

"Be careful, Daniel. Just be careful. It's coming our way, I'm sure of it."

The next day, behind a Wellesley Hills strip mall, a man and woman were discovered tied together with wire. They were bound naked, face to face—tied so tightly that the wire had cut through their flesh to the bone. They had both been whipped, raped, then left to drown in a green-water ditch nine inches deep. He was a mechanic; she was a millionaire. They didn't know each other. At the edge of the ditch, police found a chair, seventeen smoked cigarettes, and another note.

I am glory, I am the Morning Star. I am fire, feeding on the shabby little souls of straw.

Panic ripped across the region from Connecticut to Maine. People grouped in packs of six or more, taking turns huddling in each others' homes—guarding, sleeping in shifts. Nobody drove alone and no one went out at night. Everyone carried a weapon.

It didn't matter. The killing continued. Holy Hell's vicious trail meandered toward Boston, hitting three towns in two days, leaving more bodies and notes. Each victim was killed in a different way; every note was arrogant, apocalyptic.

Then he submerged. At the peak of frenzy, he hid himself for five days in the center of the stunned city. During the lull, the pressure lifted and people ignored each other again. After three days, television coverage dropped off. The authorities speculated he was wary of their extreme security measures and had moved on to less sophisticated centers of population.

He was only sleeping. The beast had gorged, and now he was soaking in the blood-memory of his deeds. He slept in his underwear in a South Boston Y, sodden, unsatisfied, his lust and rage roiling for more.

On the sixth day, it began again. The morning after he killed the three homeless men, the headline of the *Herald* screamed HOLY HELL! INTO THE SECOND CIRCLE? Boston was wired with terror while the killer wandered the town, unhurried, unchallenged in his casual slaughter. A waitress in a bagel shop, an attorney at his desk, a mother of two in a health club ladies' room. Before he headed north again, he had killed seven more times.

The next day a salesman was killed at a rest stop near Andover. The following day a boardinghouse was torched in Lawrence and sixteen people died. The police speculated that Holy Hell was moving through New Hampshire, toward safety in Canada. They still had no prints and no leads.

On July 20, 1980, I was sitting in the town cruiser, parked behind the hedges in the front corner of Hamrick's parking lot, listening to the radio and waiting for something different to happen. A black '68 Plymouth Fury coasted slowly past me, heading north on Main Street. Rhode Island plates.

The driver was a white male, midthirties, balding, with long wispy hair hanging over his collar and thick reddish sideburns that grew to his jawline.

He wore glasses and had a pronounced lift to his upper lip. He was looking straight ahead, like someone who knew not to expect much from Franklin Notch. If he saw me, he didn't react.

There was something familiar about him—maybe it was the upturned lip. I couldn't place him, but he looked like someone I should remember.

When my shift was over and I passed the cruiser to the night guy, I drove my own car through town twice, looking for the old Plymouth. I don't know why I went looking or why the sideview snapshot of the driver stuck with me. There must have been something in the moment that hooked me—the way he moved past too easily, sliding through my frame of vision, so detached from everything around us. I couldn't find him, so I went home. I figured he was a student, passing through on his way north to Henniker.

That night, I had a dream. I was a boy again, and real events from my childhood were mixed together. I dreamed I was walking in the woods with Wes the day he discovered the graveyard at the back of our property.

It was autumn, and the maples had turned to crimson and gold, waiting for the next rain to knock the color to the ground. We walked from the back of the old house across the field and through the broken gate. Wes held my hand as we went into the woods; then he picked me up and carried me against his chest, wading uphill through the brush.

Over the back side of the hill, we came to a small plot marked by a low stone wall. Wes set me down, and I followed him as he walked across the cemetery.

In my dream I pick up sticks, go to the wall, and look over it. A boy with a cruel mouth is watching me from the other side. He blows his nose in his fingers, then flicks the snot at me. He swings his other arm from behind his back, and in the slowest of inevitable motions, he heaves a rock at my skull. I can't move out of the way, I can only watch the sharp stone spinning slowly over the wall between us, toward a place on my forehead above my left eyebrow. As it spins, I see a patch of lichen on it, a few flecks of mica flashing in the sunlight, and the damp spot where it had nestled in the ground.

When the stone struck my head with a stabbing flash, I woke up and tried to separate the parts of the dream that were memories from the parts that meant something else. The phone was ringing. It was Sister.

"Daniel. It's the Dolan boy—Ronnie Dolan, old Reverend Dolan's son. It just came to me. It's him."

"I know," I said. "I remember now. I saw him today. He's in town, and I just had a dream about the time he hit me in the head with a rock. I'm going to find him."

"Wait," she said. "I'll send your father along to help."

"No, don't. He'll get us all killed." I hung up and knocked my Colt together on the kitchen counter. The phone rang again, but I didn't answer it. I stuck my gun in my belt and grabbed my stick.

I drove to the Episcopal church. It was the only building in town where Ronnie Dolan could hide and explain himself if he was discovered. I parked my car at the bank and slipped through the graveyard behind the church. The black Plymouth was parked behind the tool shed. No one was in it. I expected him to be inside the church, near the kitchen, where he would have access to water and food. I considered slashing one of the tires, then decided against it. If he got away from me and I had to call for help, I wanted him on the road, heading away from town. I didn't want him going into someone's house for another car, money, or a hostage.

I stayed low and eased myself around the parking lot to the back of the church. I tested the door on Fellowship Hall. I was right, it had been jimmied open. He was somewhere inside his dad's old church.

I lay on the ground outside the door and opened it just wide enough to slide in my nightstick. Using my stick as a lever, I slowly pried the door open, to get a clear view of the empty hall. I stayed on the ground, my face pressed to the doormat, scanning the room and listening for any movement. Nothing.

I crawled into the building. The exit sign above me washed the area with pink light, exposing me, so I scuttled to the back corner of the room and took a position behind the long wheeled cart stacked with folding chairs. I crouched and listened. I figured if he wasn't moving around, he was sleeping. I could feel him nearby, in one of the rooms, probably near a window, keeping close as possible to his car.

I sneaked around the edge of the big room to the open door beside the kitchen and made my way down the hallway to the Sunday School rooms. Another exit sign glowed above me, and I worried about throwing a shadow. All the classroom doors were open, except one. I moved across the hall, on the same side as the closed door. I had my gun in my left hand, my stick in my right.

Down low, I looked through the window in the door. Ronnie Dolan was sleeping on the sofa in the Little Miracles classroom, surrounded by toddler-size chairs and tables. So much for giants. He was sleeping on his side, facing the doorway, wearing a gray hooded sweatshirt, jeans, and running shoes.

I tested the doorknob. It was locked. If I could kick in the door, I still had seven or eight steps between me and the man named Holy Hell. The noise would wake him before I could cross the room through all the kiddy furniture. Maybe if I moved fast enough, I could be on him before he found his feet.

I took a deep breath and smashed the door with my foot. It blasted open, shattered glass flying everywhere. I ran into the room, scattering furniture. I was over him as he started to wake up. He had been drinking, and as I got to the side of the sofa, I kicked a bottle of peppermint schnapps that went scooting against the far wall, spilling everywhere.

Ronnie Dolan rolled toward me with a curved-blade commando knife the size of a tire iron. He came at me sideways, standing and turning into me with one motion, his knife aimed at my groin. I cracked him hard with my stick on a spot slightly above his left eyebrow. He started bleeding as he went down, and a flash of recognition crossed his face. As he hit the floor he smiled and held up three fingers.

I pushed the sofa across the room and handcuffed him to the radiator; then I called the state police. That's all there was to it. That's how I became the Man Who Caught Holy Hell—and edged myself one click closer to my own death.

13

Veronica looked for a spot on the lower level. It was a head game she played on herself every morning. If she scored a parking space on the lower lot— the lot closest to the front entrance—it would be a good omen, and then maybe today would be a good day. Maybe work would go better today than all the days she had to park on the upper level. The lower lot was only a couple hundred feet closer to the hospital, but that wasn't the point. Since she almost never found a good parking place and seldom had a good day anyway, she always had an excuse to expect the worst.

Come on, come on, she said as she cruised the lanes of the lower lot. She had made the loop four times already and nothing opened up. An older man limped across the lot and she tracked him; but when he got to his car, he just rolled the windows down, turned on his radio, and fell asleep.

Christ Almighty, she said. Then, God forgive me before my soul enters whatever, whatever.

Nothing. Nothing was opening up on the lower level. Dammit, she grumped. Go away for six days, and I still can't get a break. Oh, well. What do you expect.

She drove to the upper lot, where she found a spot near the back. By the time she walked down, two spaces had opened by the front door.

"How was your vacation?" one of the nurses asked when she walked out of the elevator onto the floor.

"It wasn't really a vacation," she said, grousing through her bag for the office keys.

"Well, at least you weren't in that plane, you know, the one that fell thousands of feet."

In her office, she cleared her messages, read her e-mail, then called a team meeting.

"Okay, what have we got?" she asked the handful of nurses who crowded in.

"Mostly happy customers," said a nurse. "Except for Room 262. Mr. Schreik. Refusing medication."

Veronica read his chart. "Michael Schreik, fifty-seven. History of smoking. Coughing blood, lesions on both lungs, possible obstruction. Post-op lobectomy. Refusing medication?"

"He's on a morphine pump," said the nurse, "and sometimes he just shuts it off for no reason. He says he can't think when he's medicated."

"How is he today?"

"He's downstairs now, in Radiology. Scheduled back by eleven o'clock."

"Find me when he comes up. I'll talk to him."

The nurses filed out. Veronica closed the door to her office, then called the junior high school.

"Just checking," she said to Jessie's guidance counselor. "I was gone for six days, you know, and I want to stay on top of things."

"Everything's fine," said the counselor. "I wouldn't worry if I were you."

"I'm a little concerned with the people she's involved with. Do you think it's a good group? I mean, do you know if she's attracted to anybody in particular?"

"What do you mean?"

"Well, like a boy. Someone she hangs around with a little bit more than the others?"

"I couldn't really say. At this age, fourteen, fifteen, they have their own crowd and they all hang out together. Like I said, I wouldn't worry if I were you."

"So she doesn't have a boyfriend?"

"As a person, she seems to be pretty open—very sure of herself. Maybe this is something you could talk to her about. She's extremely artistic, you know."

"I know," said Veronica.

She called her oldest daughter, Catherine.

"Hey, Mom, how was Florida?"

"Hot and crowded."

"Are you still coming up this weekend?"

"I want to, but I'm having trouble with your sister. Now she doesn't want to come."

"Really? I talked to her last night and she was all excited about it."

"She wants to bring a friend and I said no. Now she says she won't come at all. I thought maybe you could call her and tell her there isn't enough room for any more people at your place."

"Why? We have plenty of room."

"Not really, you don't. You have one bedroom, and that sofa. There's barely room for one person."

"Mom, I'm not going to call Jessie and do your dirty work. I'm not conspiring. We've got plenty of room. If you don't want her bringing someone, then you tell her."

Veronica sighed. "How are the babies?" she asked.

"They're doing great. Molly can't wait to see you, and you won't believe how much Vedran has grown. Charlie says he's got little musician fingers."

"Great," said Veronica. She sighed again.

"What's wrong now?" Catherine asked.

"Just about everything, honey," Veronica said. "That name, for one thing."

"What? Vedran?"

"Yes, Vedran. I can't tell people I have a grandson named Vedran. It sounds like a sinus medication."

"First of all, it's pronounced Vay-drahn. And second of all, that wasn't very nice. You know, Mom, for someone who just got back from vacation, you sound pretty stressed."

"It wasn't a vacation. Uncle Boone and I went down there to find Uncle Reggie."

"Did you find him? Is he okay?"

"No, he's not okay, but I don't want to talk about it on the phone."

"Well, it sounds like you need a real vacation. You can relax this weekend with us. We've got lots of good stuff planned. We're going to a cookout on Saturday. There's going to be music and everything. We'll have fun."

After Veronica hung up she locked the door to her office, then groped in her bag for cigarettes. Kneeling on the floor behind her desk, she lit a Parliament and blew smoke into the vent under her computer table. She sprayed a couple shots of room freshener at the ceiling and went into the hall.

She patrolled both sides of the floor, checking the closets and cabinets and looking into each room briefly before stopping to see the man in 262.

He was lying on his back, looking at the ceiling, his face gray with pain. He had a sharp, hooked nose, feathery receding hair, and dark, round eyes. His lips were pulled tight across his teeth, and the cords in his neck were straining. His thin fingers clutched the bedsheets.

"Mr. Schreik. How are we feeling today?"

He looked at her and shook his head tightly.

"Is there some reason why you're refusing medication?"

He nodded. Two quick jerks of his head, then a long twisted grimace of pain.

"This is not a good idea," Veronica said. "At this point you should be trying to make things easier for everybody. You need to tap your pump if you hurt too much. Do you understand?"

His face pinched together like a baby suddenly hurt. He nodded.

"Okay, then. I'll send a nurse down to check your pump."

Veronica left the room, went to the station, and put together a tray of meds. She gave it to the young nurse, went to her office, and called her house to see if Jessie had ditched school. No answer. This is stupid, she thought. If she's there, she's not going to answer the phone. Maybe I should call Boone and ask him to drive by.

She sat for a while and pounded through some budget stuff, then crawled under her desk for another cigarette. She ordered roast beef and pie for lunch, tried calling her house again, then went back to see Michael Schreik.

He looked very sick, but he was more distracted now, medicated above the pain. His thin hands were turned upward, fingers curled. His head was pulled to the right and he was looking blankly at the air conditioner.

"Hello, Mr. Schreik. It looks like you're more comfortable."

The sick man swung his head loosely to the left, looking at Veronica with liquid eyes. He made a chewing motion with his jaw.

"Can you sit down?" he rasped.

"I really don't have time to chat. I've been gone for a week, and we have a lot of other people on this floor to worry about. What do you want?"

"Writing things," he said. "My final request." He tried to smile.

"Like what?" Veronica asked.

"Paper, envelopes, blue Pilot pens. I need to write some letters."

"You're not dying, you know."

"Yes, I am."

"I'll get your things," Veronica said, halfway out the door. Room service, she hissed as she stomped up the hall. It's not a fucking hotel.

She went back to her office, locked the door, and called Sister.

"Hi, honey. How are you feeling? I heard about your airplane adventures. When did you get in?"

"Two A.M. I'm exhausted."

"Oh, I'll bet. It must feel good to get back to work, though."

"Not really. I'm up to my eyebrows in problems. I've got the usual whiners and some idiot who won't take his medication."

"I'm always amazed how people act when they don't like themselves," Sister said. "But I'm sure you'll get it all straightened out. You're so good at what you do. How's Reggie doing?"

"Weird. Except for being so selfish, he's a completely different person now. He looks ten years younger, and he's not making any sense. I know he never made much sense before, but now he's going through this midlife thing where he doesn't want to own any possessions or money. He lives in that stupid castle and pretends to be an animated character that doesn't even exist in a movie. Personally, I think he needs intervention of some kind."

"Honey, what should we do? Sit him down and make him take some money?"

"How come I'm the only one who thinks this is wrong?"

"Maybe because you want him to be happy on your terms. He is happy, isn't he?"

"Village idiots are happy. That's what he is—a village idiot. He walks around all day talking in *parables*. He's like this idiot grinning hermit who gets younger."

"Well, dear, St. Anthony is his namesake. You need to pray to St. Anthony that Reggie finds his gift of Grace and doesn't return to his old ways."

"But when do I get to be happy?"

"You remember your bedtime story, don't you?"

"Yeah, yeah. The miserable little girl will be truly happy when she wakes up in a room, watched over by a thousand blinking eyes and finds her gift of Hope. What the hell does that mean?"

"Don't curse, honey. Say God-forgive-me."

"No. I'm at work."

"Say it."

"Okay, but when do I get to be happy? What day? What year? I'm tired of things going against me all the time. Boone's happy, Reggie's happy. When do I get my turn?"

"Say it."

"God forgive me before my soul enters Hell for all eternity."

"Good girl. Don't worry, everything's going to turn out fine. You shouldn't worry so much. It's not good for your health."

"That's another thing. I'm feeling so old. How come Reggie gets to be younger?"

"I don't know, sweetie. In judgment fair, sits God everywhere. You need gingersnaps. I've got some left over from the batch Jessie and I made last night. I hid them from Wes. Come over and sit on the porch with me. We'll pray and eat gingersnaps."

"What fun," Veronica said dryly. "Maybe next week. I'm going to visit Catherine tomorrow for the weekend."

"Oh, that's right, Jessie told me. I can't do it tonight anyway. I'm going over to Daniel's house to watch Wes's show."

"Are we going to lose our houses?" Veronica asked.

"I don't think so."

"Don't *think* so? Aren't you worried?"

"Not at long as everybody does their part in the Army of Saints."

"This isn't a religious question. Should I call a realtor like everyone else in my neighborhood?"

Sister laughed. "For someone who just came back from vacation, you're not in a very good mood."

"Forget the vacation. This all looks pretty hopeless to me. Anyway, thanks for watching Jessie."

"We had a great time. We tie-dyed T-shirts."

"You did? Isn't that messy?"

"Not really. We used buckets in the yard and we dried them on the clothesline. I'm wearing one now. I borrowed it from Wes and it fits me like a nightgown. Jessie figured out how to get a pattern of a cross on it. I love it."

"So she was okay?"

"She was fine."

"Did she talk on the phone much?"

"Of course. She's fifteen."

"Was she talking to boys?"

"Probably. I didn't eavesdrop. She's a good girl, Veronica. Just like Catherine."

"I don't know. It's so hard knowing what she's up to," Veronica said. "There's not enough of me to go around. I can't work and raise a family alone like this."

They hung up, and Veronica walked down the hall to the nurses' station. She poured herself a cup of old coffee, leafed through the charts, and chewed on some sugar cookies that were in a box next to the phone. She collected the writing supplies for Mr. Schreik and took a Sharpie to the calendar, drawing a big black X through today.

I was changing the plugs on Beth's car when Wes and Sister pulled up.

"Hey," he yelled from his truck as Sister climbed down. "What do you say to a one-legged hitchhiker?"

"I don't know."

"Hop in."

"You're in a good mood for somebody on the hot seat," I said.

"What do a toilet and the electric chair have in common?" he asked.

"I give up."

"The end is in sight."

"Got any more?"

"Sure. What's the end of everything?"

"Nuclear war?"

"Nope. The letter *G*."

"Are you coming in?" I asked him.

"After the show, and I want to hear about Reggie. Hey, what do you call a nudist going through menopause?"

"I don't know."

"A hot flasher. See ya."

I walked Sister to the house. She was wearing a huge tie-dyed T-shirt over her girl-sized overalls. It was a swirl of cumulus-looking splotches in reds and blues with a giant goldenrod cross in the middle, like a crusader's tunic. She was carrying a small forest of Technicolor dahlias.

"How do you keep up with that?" I asked her.

"I don't. I just laugh at everything."

She looks great. At seventy, she has more energy than most teenagers. She walks three miles a day—often with Beth; she does stretching exercises and her Richard Simmons video every morning. She never learned to drive, so she does all of her in-town errands on foot, year-round, walking a mile down the mountain to Main Street, then home again with her shopping in her little backpack. It's no wonder Jessie and her friends adore her. She's like a little mountain elf, bringing happiness and pixie wisdom to us mortals in the town below.

She's no taller than my shoulder and weighs ninety-five pounds—not an ounce more than the day she was married fifty years ago. Her mostly gray hair is cut the way she's always worn it—short, with bangs. Her dark eyes still sparkle like a sparrow's behind her wire-rim glasses.

Beth met us at the door.

"Hi, sweetie," Sister said to Beth. They hugged. "Here's something for your table," she said, handing over the flowers.

"Great shirt," said Beth.

"Don't you love this thing?" Sister held it out at the hem and twirled on the balls of her feet. "Jessie's so good with this stuff. She's got a pile of them she's going to sell."

Sister helped Beth with the fajitas. I finished working on the car while they arranged dinners in front of the TV.

Beth and Sister are best friends. No secrets between them, and I don't mind.

They see each other at least once every day, and when Beth drives to

Manchester or Boston, she always invites Sister. They serve together on committees at the church; they co-chair the local arts guild and a dozen other groups like the quilting club, book club, and a Bible study that Sister has been hosting in her home for forty-seven years.

They watch out for me: Beth in the day-to-day, Sister in the near-after.

At six thirty, we are three of twelve thousand people in Franklin Notch watching *This Is My Town, with Wes Moffatt.*

The show opens, as always, with "A Taste of Honey" over a jumpy film of Main Street, moving from one end of town to the other. The name of the show hangs over the whole montage in white globby-looking flower-power letters.

It's a piece of film that Wes shot in 1977 with a Super 8 camera while standing up in my VW, with most of his huge body hanging out the sunroof. The film is jumpy because while we were shooting, he was yelling at everybody on the sidewalk to smile and wave. There are people coming out of the bank, talking in pairs, starting across the street then stepping back, out of the way of my car. A dog barks at us, then runs around the corner of the liquor store.

It's eerie to watch. Nothing on Main Street has changed since then, but some of the people grinning and waving at us have been dead for twenty years. Wes refuses to update the opening; he says it reminds people of their history, which is an ironic thing to say, considering.

The cheesy graphics fade, and the camera comes up on Wes sitting behind his little wooden table in front of a dark curtain. He's wearing a tie-dyed T-shirt, his red suspenders, and a Red Sox cap. His shoulder-length frizzy gray hair is pulled back in a ponytail, which makes his chest-length beard look even longer and more full than usual.

He looks into the camera and grins, his eyes crinkling at the edges.

"Hey, folks," he says. "Last night's show was something, wasn't it? We're still trying to repair the damage to the set, which is why I've got this curtain behind me tonight. I'd like to thank the four or five people in town who didn't come down to the station and try to beat somebody up, and I'd like to thank our friends at WMCH in Manchester for letting the rest of the world see how silly we look. I've been told that CNN is showing an interest in our little circus and may send a crew to Franklin Notch sometime this week, which gives everybody a day or two to get their hair done and mow the lawn.

"I know what everybody wants to talk about tonight, but that's not what we're going to do. I don't want to talk about town land and treaties and subpoenas and what Sarah Running Mouth said in the *Union Leader* this morning. Tonight I want to talk about water rates and do they really need to jump a full six percent? That sure seems like a lot to me. That's the topic on the table, so let's stick with it."

He looks at his speakerphone and punches a button. "First caller, you're on the air."

"Wes, this is Marty from Bent Branch Lane. What the hell am I going to do if I lose my house? I've got kids in school here, and my wife has family on the other mountain. What are we supposed to do, move in with them? And one more thing, how come this is all up to you? If I lose my house, I'm suing your ass."

Wes listens and looks straight into the camera. His face is already getting red. "Did you hear what I said? I don't want to talk about this tonight. And it's not my fault some wacko—"

"Wacko? That's a good one, Wes. While you're out digging up graves, it sounds to me like she's the one with a plan. How come nobody on our side has got a plan to stop these people?"

"Is this the same Marty from Bent Branch Lane who got caught last winter throwing flammable waste into the Dumpster behind the bank?"

"I swear to God, Wes—" the caller yells, then hangs up.

Wes looks at the camera and shrugs.

"I'm going down there," I say.

"No," say Beth and Sister. Beth grabs my arm. "No, honey. He's got to get through this. You can't take his side. It would make it worse." Sister nods, but I can tell she is worried for him.

"Next caller?" says Wes.

"Hi," says a young woman. "I'm a first-time caller, and I'm actually calling from Hanover, and it seems to me that what's happening is sort of like justice for Native Americans because of the way they were treated, being killed and pushed off their land and everything."

"Nobody killed any Native Americans in Franklin Notch," Wes says.

"How do you know?"

"Let me put it this way. There's no record of any strife between the settlers of Franklin Notch and the Sagawehs."

"See, that's the problem," the girl says. "Of course there's no record. Why would white men bother to keep a record when they didn't even think of Indians as human beings?"

Wes has his head in his hands. Like a bear in a baseball hat, he shakes it slowly from side to side.

"Please hang up," he says.

"No. People need to realize that history has a way of balancing—"

"'Bye," he says, poking another button on the phone. "Next caller, you're on the air."

"Hey, Wes," says a gruff-sounding man. "Is everybody invited to the town meeting next Wednesday?"

"Yes, Carl, they are."

"And anybody can ask questions?"

"Yep."

"And are you going to be there?"

"Yep again."

"Well, I know a lot of people who have a lot of questions, and you'd better be ready with some answers."

"I'll do my best," says Wes. He is looking tired, and he still has forty-five minutes to go.

I couldn't watch any more. I went to my gun case in the living room, unlocked it, and took the Devil's map out of the ammo drawer. I put it in my shirt pocket. It felt warm on my chest, over my heart.

I walked outside and sat under the tallest oak in my front yard and looked across the valley to East Mountain. I remember when both mountains had fewer houses and Main Street had no traffic to speak of and Wes and I could yell to each other across the valley, over the town, and hear each other perfectly. Standing in the front yard of his house near the top of East Mountain, he would yell, "Ivanhoe!" and I would yell back. I could hear him laughing.

After Beth and I married, I moved into this house—her house. Benny was seven. Born without a father attached, he wasn't real keen on losing his mother to a local cop, especially me.

He ignored everyone except Beth, acting like he was just putting in time, waiting for the day he could return to his own dark tribe.

We all tried to get on his good side. I took him for weekly rides in the cruiser, but he just sat against the passenger door, head down, playing with his Game Boy. Even Wes, children's ambassador to the adult world, couldn't get through to Benny. Wes included him in his get-broke-quick schemes—the root beer brewery, mail-order whirligigs, and handmade arrowhead keychains that shredded your pockets. Reggie called them Moffatt's Leg Bleeders.

Benny never allowed himself to be part of the family, never took our last name as his own, making up names for himself instead. Last year he was Bronx McVee, urban poet.

I remember throwing a thirty-foot rope over a branch of this tree and rigging a tire swing for him. He never used it, and it became another symbol of our stalemate. He refused to accept the gift, and I couldn't remove it. Classic stepfamily standoff, one of a million spurned overtures. He could reject me, but I couldn't withdraw the offer. There were channels: Beth would request things on his behalf, and he would accept only if she carried my offer.

For years, the long swing hung in this big tree, the rope turning gray, the branch swelling around the knot, the tire spinning and swaying with every breeze that moved up the mountain. Fifteen years later I cut the swing down—the day Benny left for Henniker. He's a good kid—as much as I know him. I wish we could be closer, but until then, I'm waiting for the day when he's old enough to see us both on the same side of life.

Right now, Benny isn't my biggest problem. I need to figure out what this map means, and if I can use it. I know it's a bad thing and it comes from evil, but I need to consider all my options, keep something close for backup. It can't do any harm; it's just something to think about.

Over my heart, the map felt warm, soothing.

I heard Sister walking behind me. She sat next to me on the grass, pulling her knees up to her chin like a little girl.

"How are you doing, honey?" she asked, patting my shoulder.

"Not so good. I was thinking about the family. We're falling apart—out of control, and I'm the only one trying to keep us together. It's getting harder all the time, and I feel like I'm not doing my job."

"Maybe you need to see things a little differently."

"I know, I know. Have faith in God's plan for goodness on Earth."

She looked at me over the tops of her glasses.

"Sorry," I said. "But when I see Wes shaking the ant farm, and Veronica complaining all the time—how can I help these people when everybody is off on their own little trip? Look at Reggie; he's more immature and selfish than before."

"Well, he is getting younger. He's like Wes when we first met—so full of himself."

"Oh, that's encouraging," I said. "The Doofus Brothers."

"Daniel. What's wrong with you? You're acting so angry."

"Sorry. I'm running out of patience, and I'm running out of time. I'm afraid I can't fix this mess before my next two visits. Sometimes I wish I had some magic medicine-stick I could shake to make things right."

"What do you mean 'next two visits'? Did you see him again?"

"Yeah. On the plane."

"You weren't going to tell me?"

"I didn't want to worry anybody."

"I'm sorry, sweetie. No wonder you're bothered." She put her arm around my waist. "I thought there was something fishy in that plane falling. Do you want to talk about it?"

I shrugged. "The Devil wants to trade Ronnie Dolan for Wes, and he wants me to miss the hearing tomorrow. He said if I promise to skip the hearing, he would back off and spare Wes from jail."

"Did he give you anything to hold?" she asked.

"No," I lied, and before I could stop myself or even see where I was headed, I knew I had strayed over, veered around the back of some ancient barrier of restraint—and I found myself instantly distant, off balance and sliding away on a mythic descent. I could feel it. For every second I let the lie settle, I slid a mile.

Like a carcass, the lie hung between us. We were quiet a long time.

"Anyway, that's my point," I said. "Everybody looks to me for help, and nobody knows what it's like being in the middle. I can't afford a mistake. They have faith in me, so I need faith in myself. If I doubt myself for a second, I could lose control of a situation. I almost died on that plane."

"Daniel, your job is to fight the Devil, not play Little God. Just do your part and have faith in the goodness of everything. It will raise you up— above the Devil's confusion. Your problems will look smaller, and they'll be easier to deal with."

"But things aren't good. There's too many things wrong. There's too much evil in the world."

"There *is* evil in the world, but it doesn't belong here. It's just mud on the windshield. Clean it off, honey, and enjoy the scenery."

She hugged me and gave me a kiss on my temple. "Remember your Axis Mundi?"

> "Heaven and Hell, forever apart,
>   Met for battle in my wavering heart.
> While Goodness and Evil struggled within,
>   Faith was the sword that brought death to sin."

I wasn't in the mood for slogans. I looked away.

She was smiling, and she put her arm across my shoulder. Maybe it was the sunset, but it looked like she had a halo.

"Daniel," she said. "You worry about everyone else, but I never worry about you. I remember when you were a little boy and Wes would take you over the ridge for those long walks in the woods. I never worried about him getting lost as long as he was with you. You were only five years old and you could always find your way home."

"That's me," I said. "Daniel Boone."

"It's one of your best gifts," she said. "Knowing the right way. That's why I don't worry about you. You'll do the right thing."

We sat under the big maple, watching the evening shadows climb the other side of the valley. We talked about the old days, when everyone was younger, dizzy with innocence and promise. We talked about hawks and how we never see them anymore circling over the hills, and how the deer have disappeared.

I felt terrible. I couldn't believe that I lied to my mother and separated myself from her trust. Tonight, after they leave, I'll burn the map and forget the treaty. Tomorrow morning, I'll call Sister and apologize. She will forgive me. She understands the pressure I'm under.

After a while, we went back to the house, back to Beth.

An hour later, Wes returned, and we all sat at the kitchen table. Sister, Beth, and I ate ice cream while he polished off the last seven fajitas. He didn't seem fazed at all by the hostility on his show.

"Nobody's going to hurt me," he said. "And it's not because Boone is chief of police, either. I'm the only one who can straighten out this mess. I'm the only one who knows what's real and what's not. There's truth, and then there's truth."

"No, Wesley," Sister said. "There's truth, and there's confusion."

"Well, in this case, there's confusion, and then there's truth," he said, stuffing half a fajita in his mouth. "It's all gonna work out. Trust me."

Sister looked at me and rolled her eyes.

"Hey, how's Reggie?" he asked.

"He's good. He looks good."

"So he's living in a castle? What a hoot. When is he coming back?"

"I don't know."

Wes looked thoughtful. I knew he was thinking about Reggie's "idiot old man" mistake.

"I know he blames me for getting fired," he said. "I wish we could have talked before he left. I really miss him."

"Why don't you write him a letter?" Sister offered. "He'd probably like that."

"Yeah, I think I will. Hey, Boone, I've got to pick up a load of firewood tomorrow. Wanna come?"

"I can't. I've got cop business in Manchester. It's a parole hearing for Ronnie Dolan. He's up for approval to a medium-security psych hospital in Concord, and I'm supposed to testify. I want to make sure they don't move him."

"Why would they?" Wes asked.

"He claims he got religion. The way I see it, if he's got religion, he can practice it where he is."

"Amen," said Beth.

The phone rang. It was Veronica, and she was crying.

"Boone," she said, "I've got an emergency here. I can't find Jessie. We were arguing and she took off—grabbed her backpack and went running out of the house. Can you help me find her?"

"What do you want me to do? Walk around town in the dark, calling her like a puppy?"

She made a moist, fading sound—like tears chasing gin. "Don't yell at me," she cried. "I don't know what to do."

"Okay," I said. "I'll call the station and have the guys watch out for her. I'll call you if I hear anything. Don't worry, she's safe. I'm sure she's with a friend."

"Who? What's their number?"

"I don't know. I don't know her friends."

"I think you do."

"I have to hang up, Vee. Sister and Wes are getting ready to leave. I'll call if I hear anything."

My parents went home; Beth and I went to bed. She fell asleep, but I stayed awake for a long time, thinking about the problems that were piling up around me.

Except for the college girl, I knew all the people who called Wes's show—all old friends, but tonight they were edgy and hostile, genuinely pissed off. I don't know why he doesn't understand his situation, blundering around like a carnival bear.

Count the days. Twelve days until the anniversary party, and nothing has been done. We rented the room, that's it. We don't even know how many people to expect. Two months ago, when we booked the Bob-O-Link, Wes and Sister had friends. Veronica, Beth, and I planned for two hundred guests, and we agonized over who to snub in the head count. Now the list is eroding. In the past week we received seventy-five cancellations—none of them gracious. The way things are going, we could cancel the room and have the party in a window booth.

And then there's Reggie. I don't know what to expect. The old Reggie would have stubbornly stiffed us, demanding an apology from Wes before backing down on his boycott of the party. New Reggie could show up in his Muppet suit carrying a skateboard and handing out lotus blossoms. I worried that his return could cause as much confusion as his absence.

I looked at the clock. Two thirty. I can't believe I'm still awake and I've got to drive to Manchester in the morning. It has been twenty-five years since I caught Ronnie Dolan. I wondered what he looked like now. He scared me when we were kids; he still scares me. I felt cold, and I crossed my arms over my chest.

The map. Where was it? In a panic I realized I had lost track of it, maybe left it where Beth would see it. I eased myself out of bed and went to the chair where I always leave my clothes. Pants, sweater, no shirt. I went to my knees and felt across the floor. No shirt.

The phone rang.

"Anything?" Veronica asked.

"Vee, just go to sleep. Don't you have work tomorrow?"

"Fuck work. Goddamn sick people."

"I can't talk now. Don't drink any more."

Beth woke up. "Honey? What's wrong?"

"Did you touch my clothes?"

"Everything's downstairs. In the washer."

"Did you wash my shirt?"

"Boone. Boone. Do you think I killed Earl? I mean not like I gave him a heart attack, but I'm such a bitch?"

"Veronica, I can't talk now. Beth, did you wash my shirt? Did you take anything out of the pocket?"

"I don't know, honey. Everything's in the washer. Why?"

"Boone. Boone. Who's a good realtor?"

"Veronica, go to bed."

"Really called about Jessie."

"Did she come back?"

"Nope."

"Go to bed." I was running down the stairs to the basement. "I'll find her. I'll get dressed and find her."

"I know," she said.

I missed the light switch at the top of the basement stairs and yanked the string on the bulb above the washer. I opened the lid and looked inside. Dry. Beth had left the wash for morning, so the noise of the old machine wouldn't keep us awake. I groped through the load for my shirt. On the back side of the bin I felt something warm. My shirt. The pocket. My map.

I sat on the edge of the toolbench, catching my breath, holding the map between my palms. I could feel the heat spreading back, up past my wrists.

I sat for a few minutes, holding the map and thinking about the absolute nature of imaginary things. I saw Indians slipping through the woods where this house now sits. I saw the lonely parade of a displaced race, hiking down this mountain with their raggy bundles and skinny dogs, fading over the next set of hills into the dawn of a much worse day. I heard a noise above me, someone walking in my kitchen.

I dropped the map in my pajama-shirt pocket and grabbed a hammer off the bench. I pulled the light string and slipped across the basement in the dark and up the stairs. I crouched behind the door, raised the hammer, and waited. Someone was moving toward me in the hallway between the kitchen and the back porch. I stepped out as a man came around the corner and bumped into me, full-front. Something hot sprayed on my chest. Instinctively, I covered my face with my left hand and aimed my weapon at the center of his head.

He looked at the hammer. "Fixing something?" he said.

"Benny. You shouldn't do that. Sneak around, I mean. You're lucky I didn't drop you." I was shaking.

"It's Aero now," he said, correcting me. "And I'm not sneaking around. I'm going to watch TV. Sorry about the coffee." With him, it's hard to tell, but it looked like he was smirking more than usual. "Is my mother up?" he asked.

"She probably is now," I said. "So, how have you been?"

"I've been good. Yourself? Still fighting crime?"

"Yeah, keeping the bad guys out of Dodge."

He gave a little snort.

I heard Beth coming down the stairs.

"Just dropped in for some of that home cooking?" I asked him.

"I'm on my way north," he said.

Beth walked into the hallway and turned on the light.

"Benny," she said, smiling when she saw him. "What happened?"

They hugged.

"We collided. I spilled his coffee," I said.

Beth had her arm around her son, hugging him at the waist. They don't look anything alike. She is short and big-boned, a Norwegian Earth Goddess. He is tall, lanky, dark, and brooding. Mother hen and nighthawk.

"I'm going back upstairs," I said. "See you in the morning, Aero. Make yourself at home."

"It is," he said.

Beth apologized with her eyes.

I left them downstairs to talk. When I changed my shirt in the bedroom, I touched my chest. Over my heart, beneath my skin, there was a hot raised lump the size of the map. It felt puffed-up and tender, like it was filling with infection.

The next morning I was in my blues, reading the paper and drinking my coffee, waiting for Beth to wake up so I could say good-bye. Ronnie Dolan's hearing was scheduled for ten o'clock. I hate these things. I get nervous in front of people, and today I was supposed to stand before the State Board of Reviews and read a statement opposing Dolan's upgrade. It was standard procedure; any member of the law enforcement community was allowed to offer a recommendation. The attorney general's office called me to testify against the request. Because I was the arresting officer and chief of police from Ronnie's hometown, they thought my statement would carry more weight.

I had my speech and the map in my shirt pocket.

My stepson, Aero Kierkegaard, walked into the kitchen and made himself a cup of coffee.

"So," I said. "Keeping busy?" It's hard not calling him Benny.

He tilted his head and nodded to himself as if he were deciding whether he could spare me the time.

"I suppose so," he said.

"What have you been up to?" I asked. "Working?"

"Working and research. I've got a situation where I can do both."

"Really? That's great. What do you do?"

"I work at Blockbuster," he said with a straight face.

He took a sip of coffee and considered it for a moment. He held the cup with his fingertips.

"So you get to watch funny movies?"

"Yes," he said, rolling his eyes in a fleeting show of impatience. "I watch funny movies. Not because they're funny. I watch them for my thesis."

"What will you do when you graduate? Be a comedy writer?"

"No," he said, scoffing. "I'll be more of a consultant, advising producers and writers on what is funny."

"Doesn't everybody already know what's funny?" I asked.

"Yes, but no one knows how to quantify comedy. If someone can come up with the template—the formula for all humor—they can pretty much write their own check. Comedy is a seventeen-*trillion*-dollar business." He nodded as if he already had the check in his pocket.

The phone rang. Beth wandered into the kitchen and picked it up.

"Sure," she said, handing it to me.

"Boone, it's me," said Veronica. "Sorry about last night, but I just got a call from the school. Jessie didn't show up this morning. What should I do?"

"Leave the door open. She'll be back."

"I think she ran away. You know this has always been my biggest fear. What if she's in Boston, or worse? Can you help me?"

"What do you want me to do?"

"Help find her."

"Vee, I've got a meeting in Manchester at ten."

"This is a family emergency, Boone. If I don't hear from her by noon, I'm filing a missing person report."

"Veronica—"

"Boone, I need help here. My family's falling apart."

"Okay, okay," I said. "I'll look for her."

"Call me, one way or the other. I'll be at work." She hung up.

I hugged Beth, shook hands with Aero Kierkegaard, grabbed the Disney bag, and drove to Veronica's house. I knocked on the door.

"Hey, Uncle Boone. Come on in," Jessie said. She was wearing her pajamas and her hair was wet.

"I brought your present. Hope you like it."

She opened the bag and pulled out her Jessie jacket.

"I love it," she said, putting it on over her pajamas. She checked herself in the mirror. "It's me, huh? She's feisty and not afraid to fight for herself."

"I don't know why your mother worries about you."

"She won't have to. I'm moving out."

"Where are you going?"

"Anywhere. She treats me like I'm a criminal. I think if somebody has a problem, they should work it out themselves—not take it out on everybody else."

"Were you safe last night?"

"Sure. I stayed with a friend. We did an art project together."

"We were worried."

"Sorry for the confusion," she said. "But this whole thing isn't even about me. It's about Catherine and how embarrassed Mom is because Catherine and Charlie live in a little place and don't have any money. Mom doesn't want anybody from town to see how they live. I want to take some-one to Vermont this weekend, and she says no—just because she's embar-rassed about Catherine. Is that fair?"

I shrugged.

"Seriously. Then it gets all weird because I won't tell her who I want to bring. She starts yelling about how I'm too young to have a boyfriend. I don't even have a boyfriend. I could ask ten people to go to Vermont with me and none of them would be a boyfriend. It doesn't matter anyway. She's always in a bad mood. She'll say no to anything I want."

"She's under a lot of stress," I said, "with planning the anniversary party and Uncle Reggie and everything."

"She's always under a lot of stress," Jessie said. "She pitches a nutty if she can't find her checkbook. Then she blames me."

I remembered how Veronica thought Jessie had canceled her flight.

"How about if I talk to her?"

"Saying what?"

"I'll say that she ought to ease up a little bit—that you're not involved in anything bad, and that you're a well-balanced person who needs a little space."

"And not to yell at me."

"And not to yell at you."

"Good luck," Jessie said.

"She'll listen to me. I'm the big brother."

I called Veronica at work. I talked to her, then she and Jessie talked. Jessie promised to go to school and go to Vermont. Veronica promised not to yell at her.

It was nine-fifty. I had missed the hearing. It didn't matter. There was no way the state was going to take Ronnie Dolan out of maximum security.

Jessie and I talked for a few minutes.

"Is Benny back in town?" she asked.

"Just for the day," I said. "But we're not calling him Benny anymore." I said his new name and tried to explain what he was doing. "He's applying mathematics to jokes, trying to figure out what makes them funny," I said.

"Here's one," said Jessie. "If Aero Kierkegaard married Will Smith, what would he be?"

"I give up."

"Aerosmith."

Veronica hung up the phone. It was time for her to make the rounds.

She paused at the doorway to Michael Schreik's room.

He had fallen asleep with a pen in his hand. There was a half-finished letter written on the tablet, and his open checkbook was on the tray. He woke up when Veronica walked into the room. He smiled and moved his hand across the checkbook, covering it from her view.

"How's it going today, Mr. Schreik? Have you been taking your medication?"

He cleared his throat. He cleared it again. He tried to take a deep breath and winced in pain. "Later," he said.

"I thought we agreed that you were going to do your part."

"It makes me drowsy."

"Morphine is supposed to make you drowsy."

"I can't write my letters," he whispered. He pulled his breath sharply between his teeth as he reached away to the nightstand on the other side of the bed. His hand shook as he opened the drawer and pulled out six envelopes addressed with jagged writing. "Can you mail these?"

"I don't know if I'll have the time. I'm going out of town this weekend."

"Just drop them in a box, please." He strained back to the nightstand and lifted his wallet. "Postage money," he said, dropping the wallet on the bed. He fumbled over his wallet with his left hand, spreading some bills on the sheets. Veronica noticed that several of the letters were addressed to Schreiks.

"Mr. Schreik, why are you doing this? What's the point of going through all this pain if you don't have to?"

He arched his neck a few inches. His forehead tightened and his eyes pinched shut. When the spasm passed, he turned his eyes toward Veronica, fear flying between them like a curse.

"Pain for pain. Please mail my letters."

The six letters rode between them on the seat.

"Whose writing is that?" Jessie asked, picking up the top envelope.

"One of the patients at the hospital. I forgot to mail them after work."

"He looks really sick."

"He had part of his lung removed. He's in a lot of pain. That's what happens if you smoke."

"Mom, I don't smoke."

"I didn't say you did."

"Well, you said it like you thought I did, and I'm just letting you know that you don't have to worry about it. I don't smoke."

They drove in silence for a half hour. Jessie opened her backpack and took out her sketchbook. She leafed through it absently, then put it away. She pulled out her iPod, fiddled with the buttons, gave up, then rummaged through her backpack.

"Can we stop for batteries?" she asked. "Can you loan me the money for batteries?"

"What happened to the money I gave you last week at Sister's?"

"I spent it. It was only sixty dollars. And it was a week ago."

"You spent it? On what?"

"Never mind. I'll wait."

"You say 'only sixty dollars' like it was nothing."

"I said I'll wait. I'll wait until I get to Catherine's."

"You're not going to borrow money from Catherine."

"I didn't say I was." Jessie looked out the window, her head tilted for distance.

"I didn't say I wouldn't give you the money," Veronica said.

"I don't want your money. I can get my own money. I'll have money tomorrow."

"Tomorrow? How?"

"I'm selling T-shirts at the Drumfest. I'm going to make two hundred dollars."

"You mean at the cookout?"

"Yeah, Mom. The cookout."

"Well, I don't know. I didn't know you could sell things there. Is it like a craft fair? How am I supposed to know what's going on if no one tells me? You never tell me what you're doing."

"I don't need to. You spy on me all the time."

"I do not."

"Oh, come on, Mom. I know you go through my backpack. I know you call the school every day, checking up on me. What do you think? I'm a terrible person and I'm just hiding it from you? You're making me have this secret life that isn't even bad. I have a lot of friends. People like me. They think I'm a good person."

"I don't think you're a bad person. I just don't want you to make the same mistakes as Catherine."

"Catherine? She's the happiest one in the whole family. She's the normal one."

"She looks happy," said Veronica. "But all these bad decisions are going to catch up with her, and I'm just trying to protect you from having that kind of life."

"I like her life. I wish I had her life right now."

Veronica snapped.

"Listen to me," she yelled. "You think you know what you're talking about, but you don't. You think you know what Catherine's life is like, but you don't. She looks happy now, but wait until things start getting complicated and going wrong and there's not enough money to go around. Wait until the kids grow up and need things—basic things, like clothes and doctors and money for school and insurance and food. Wait until all these choices she's made catch up with her. I know what I'm talking about. Everybody acts like life is so easy. Well, it's not. It's hard, dammit. It's real hard."

Jessie was looking at her sideways. "Why are you always so miserable?" she said. "You're never in a good mood."

"I've been through a lot, Jessie, with your father's death and all."

"Daddy died eight years ago. And besides, you were miserable when he was alive."

"That's not true."

"Yes it is. Catherine and I talk about it all the time. You used to sit in the kitchen and cry all weekend. And Sister says you were miserable even before you married Daddy."

"She said I was miserable?"

"She said you were burdened. I think that was the word she used. Sounds miserable to me."

A raging sadness, sour as pain, swept through Veronica, and she felt like crying. She felt like howling. *Burdened.* She felt like jamming down on the gas and flying off the road into the landscape, ending the arguments and bitterness forever. She felt like turning around and going home. She felt like stopping and buying batteries and saying here's your goddamn batteries. She felt like pulling over, jumping out of the car, running into the woods, and screaming the anger out of her body.

She clutched the steering wheel and watched the dark road sail beneath her.

They didn't speak to each other until they arrived at Catherine's.

"Forgot to mail your letters," Jessie said, getting out.

Catherine was in the garden, putting vegetables in a basket, when they drove up the hill. Her baby was in a wicker buggy in the shade of an apple tree, waving his feet at the clouds. Two-year-old Molly was marching around her mother, dragging a sunflower stalk behind her. Catherine stood and waved when she saw Veronica and Jessie. She picked up Molly, set the child on her hip, and pushed the buggy down the path to the driveway.

"I wanna walk," said the little girl.

"Sorry, sweetie," Catherine said. "I forgot. Next time, you can carry me."

Jessie gave her sister a hug, then squatted in front of Molly. "Remember me?" she asked.

The girl nodded and pointed to a red mark on her left arm.

"She whacked herself with a sunflower," Catherine said, smiling. "We're going to be reliving this for a week."

Jessie picked up Molly and kissed her on the forehead.

"Hi, Mom," Catherine said, giving Veronica a lazy, loose hug. "I'm so happy you guys came up. This is going to be a great weekend. It's going to be so much fun."

With the back of her wrist, she brushed a long strand of hair off her face. Her fingers were dark with garden dirt and she left a muddy smudge across her forehead. Catherine was thin and pretty. She had long sunshine hair, wide green eyes, and a mouth that smiled higher on the left side. She was wearing a white cotton blouse and a tangerine peasant skirt. Tanned and trim, she looked more like a teenage lifeguard than a midtwenties mother of two.

"Where's your baby brother?" Jessie asked Molly. The girl pointed at the buggy. Jessie carried her over to the baby boy, who smiled grandly when he saw his sister.

"How old is he now?" Jessie asked Catherine.

"Six months next week," said Catherine. "He wants to crawl so bad, it's driving him nuts. He just woke up, so he's real mellow right now. He loves being outside."

At that, the baby let out a whoop of joy. The three women laughed, and then the little girl Molly, who leaned back in Jessie's arms and brayed at the sky, trying to recapture the moment and the attention for herself.

"Show-off," said Catherine, giving her daughter a loud kiss on the neck.

"Where's Charlie?" asked Veronica.

"He has ensemble practice on Friday afternoons. It's a Renaissance group that he started last year. They're really good. He built a viola da gamba all by himself and found a bunch of people to play recorders and all these other weird instruments. They're even letting him teach a Pro Musica course next year. He's so proud of himself; it's all he talks about. Anyway, he'll be home in a little while. I hope he remembers to pick up noodles and a package of tofu."

"So he leaves you out here without a car?" Veronica asked.

"Mom, don't start," said Catherine. "Come on inside. You need a glass of wine."

"Sack butt," said Molly, poking Jessie in the cheek.

"Jessie, do me a favor," said Catherine. "Go pick some more carrots and corn, and bring the whole basket inside. See if you can find more snow peas, too. I've got to give Vedran his bath before dinner. Mom, grab your stuff. Time to unwind."

Catherine winked at Jessie. "Can't wait to talk to you," she said, grinning. "You look great. Nice jacket, too."

"Thanks," said Jessie.

"Let's go, Mr. Vedran Smailovich Cooper," Catherine said to the baby, turning the buggy toward the tiny house across the yard.

"That name," said Veronica, shaking her head and following her daughter.

"Hey," said Jessie to Molly in her arms. "I forgot what corn looks like. Can you help me find some?"

The little girl hugged Jessie around her neck and pointed to the garden.

"It's over there? How did the corn get all the way over there?"

"You're a bad cow," said the little girl.

"No. You're a bad cow," Jessie said, tickling her and wading into the weeds.

"I don't know if it's better having them close together or not," Catherine said. She was on her knees by the tub, pouring clean water over her little boy, who was slapping at the bath with the flats of both hands.

"I think he's trying to save his toes from drowning," said Catherine.

Veronica was sitting on the toilet seat, holding a half-empty glass of red wine. "I don't think it matters. I was glad you and Jessie were ten years apart, especially after your father died. Does Charlie have life insurance?"

"Oh, yeah," said Catherine. "He's insured for seventy billion dollars. Mom, lighten up. It's the weekend. Have some fun. Enjoy my babies."

Veronica took a sip of wine. "What are we doing tomorrow?" she asked. "I mean, what time is the cookout?"

"Sometime around two. It doesn't really get going until later, though."

"And it's like a craft fair, where people can sell things?"

"Sure," said Catherine. "People sell things, but it's more like an autumn festival, you know, with music—mostly drums—and lots of food and dancing. It's called Drumfest. Charlie was one of the founders, back when he was in school here. It's just an excuse for everybody to get drunk and make some noise."

Later, when the babies were settled and sleeping, Catherine and Charlie, Veronica, and Jessie sat in the tiny living room, listening to music and talking. Jessie was drinking tea; the adults were having wine. Veronica was feeling drowsy; the others were going strong.

"Okay, Jessie," Charlie said, untangling himself from Catherine. "I've got a present for you."

He left the room. "Close your eyes and hold your hands out flat," he said from the bedroom. "This is something you'll need tomorrow."

Jessie sat up, closed her eyes, and held out her hands.

"Nope," said Charlie. "Palms down," and he placed a large djembe under Jessie's open hands. He gently pushed her hands down to the surface of the drum. "Open your eyes," he said.

"Omigod," squealed Jessie. "For me?"

Catherine laughed. "He traded one of his students guitar lessons for it. It's practically new. He was so excited about giving it to you, I thought he was going to explode."

Jessie pulled the drum between her legs and pattered her fingertips over the head. She was grinning and she did a little twisty dance, sitting in her chair. "Oh, yeah," she said. "Oh, yeah."

"It's a really good one," said Charlie. "Tomorrow I'll show you how to take care of it. You'll be banging away by noon."

"Can you teach me crossbeats?"

"In about twenty seconds," Charlie said.

"Omigod," said Jessie, jumping up and giving Charlie and Catherine a three-way hug. "My own djembe," she said.

"Where can you play that?" asked Veronica.

"Anywhere," said Jessie.

Veronica looked worried.

Catherine was happily buzzed. She kept laying her head on Charlie's shoulder, slipping her fingers between the buttons of his shirt. Jessie tapped the djembe nonstop with her fingertips, bopping her head and shaking her shoulders. Veronica talked about her weary trip to Florida.

"This isn't funny," she complained.

"Uncle Reggie is a cartoon character?" Catherine was howling. "That's the funniest thing I've ever heard."

"No, it's not," Veronica said. "He's not even a real cartoon. He just pretends to be one. He's going to end up in jail if he doesn't stop it."

"Not to worry," said Jessie. "It'll be an imaginary jail."

"Well, he's causing the rest of us a lot of real trouble—as usual," Veronica grumped. "He won't come back for Wes and Sister's anniversary party, and he's not doing anything to support Aunt Carolyn. In the meantime, Uncle Boone and I are running out of time. We have spent a lot of money and energy trying to plan this party that's going to be ruined anyway."

After a while, she stood up.

"Time for me to turn in," she said. "It's been a long week."

"Sleep good," said Catherine. "Molly's is the coziest bed in the house."

Veronica smiled, gave a tight little wave to everybody, and left the room. She went through the kitchen to the tiny bedroom at the back of the cabin. She closed the door, put on her pajamas, lay on the little girl's bed, and went to sleep.

"You two aren't getting along, are you?" Catherine asked Jessie.

"Not hardly. She's on me like a hawk—or a vulture. She thinks I'm into all this bad stuff, and I'm not."

"It was the same with me," said Catherine. "Except I think she's getting worse. I don't know how she's going to survive tomorrow. She thinks it's a cookout."

Charlie laughed. "She's going to think we're on Borneo."

Jessie reached for the wine and poured herself a finger in her teacup.

"Oh, my," said Catherine. "You are such a bad cow."

14

"Spankaporkie."

"That's not a real word. You're making it up."

"I am not."

"What does it mean?"

"Exactly what it sounds like. Of, or pertaining to, the discipline of pigs."

Sister laughed. They were playing Scrabble, their Friday night tradition. The score was 781 to 26.

"I thought you were smarter than that," Wes teased.

"The only reason you're winning is because you hid the dictionary."

"I did not. And besides, you don't need a dictionary to recognize a good word."

He fumbled around the diminishing pile of tiles on the table between them, pretending to drop them letter-side up until he found a vowel he needed.

"Your turn," he said.

Sister looked at her tray. O, P, I, D, S, R, M. "I can't make anything of this," she said. "You've got all the good ones."

"Why don't you ask me if we have anything to eat, and when I go to the kitchen to get you another piece of pie, you can go through all the letters and find something you need."

"Is that what you do?" she said, pretending to be shocked. "I had no idea."

"Only when I'm hungry," he said.

"That explains why I haven't won a game of Scrabble in fifty years. You're always hungry."

"I'll start my diet tomorrow. I'm going jogging."

"I'll warn the neighbors," she said, laughing.

Wes pushed back from the table. "All this talk about food has made me hungry. Want a piece of pie?" he asked.

"Just a little one. Thanks," she said. When he left the table, she shuffled the letters on her tray.

"I'm worried about Daniel," she said. "He's working too hard."

"He always works too hard. He's not happy unless he's trying to fix the world. It's what he does. He'll be okay."

"No, there's something different about him. He looks sad. And very distracted. He's really worried about you."

"Me? Why?" Wes came back to the table, a smear of whipped cream in his beard.

"He thinks you're not taking your legal problems seriously enough."

"I don't have any problems. Everybody knows they're fake charges—all made up."

Sister looked at the Scrabble board. Fartapple, tubenose, jabillycooth.

"That doesn't mean you can't lose," she said.

When she got up to get him a napkin, he looked at her letters. He took two of his own vowels and put them on the table, close to her tray.

"It's not just you," she said from the kitchen. "He's worried about Reggie and Veronica, and the party. And he saw the Devil again. That's why the plane fell out of the sky."

"There's the real problem," said Wes. "Somebody needs to knock that guy out of the picture. I wish I could put my hands on him. I'd tie his tail in a knot."

Sister returned to her chair. She looked at the game, her elbows on the table, her chin on her hands.

"It would do some good if you talked to him," she said. She discarded the D and picked up a vowel.

"That's a good idea," said Wes. "I was thinking of brewing some root beer for the party. I'll call him and see if he wants to help. That's always a good time."

On her tray, Sister moved two letters to the right, another to the opposite side of the row, and she put in her new vowel in the middle.

PROMISE.

"Oh, my," she said.

"What?"

"I think I need to pray now."

"Is it serious?"

"I can't tell yet," she said. "We'll see."

"Well, I'll make the tea," said Wes.

She put the letters in her pocket. "I'm going to hang on to these for a while," she said. She gave him a kiss and went into the bedroom.

Wes put the game away and went to the kitchen. He filled the teapot and set it on the stove. He turned on the gas and watched the blue flame flatten against the bottom of the pot. Inside, water struggled against itself, sizzled and hissed, escaping the heat by turning to mist.

Sister went to her closet-chapel to pray.

In the back of the little chapel was a simple cedar chest, and inside the chest were the treasures of her life: Veronica's Brownie uniform, Reggie's first football jersey, my Jimmy Talbert shirt, a huge sweater of Wes's from their romance days, and her habit from Holy Innocents.

Tonight she opened the chest before praying. She unfolded her habit and held it against herself. It looked ancient and severe in front of the flannel shirt and jeans she was wearing. She put it back in the box and crossed herself. She lit a candle.

Sister kneeled at her altar and arranged the Scrabble tiles in a row. PROMISE.

"Thank you, Father, for the mercy of your attention," she prayed. "I patiently await the discernment of Promise."

She could feel the eye of God turning her way. She felt the welcome warmth spreading outward from her bones and the lightness in her head that meant she was leaving her body for a while.

She was borne up in the sweet scented mist, the same breath of God that carried her away from the hospital bed when she was a child. It lifted her up from the chair in the chapel and carried her through the kitchen unseen, where she kissed Wes on the top of his fuzzy head as he boiled water.

She sailed across the autumn valley, over the house of her oldest son. He was sitting alone in his den, reading words of evil from a page of flesh. There was darkness around him, and although she tried to move closer for comfort, he had retreated into the darkness, sealing his spirit inside.

With sorrow, she left him and floated over an ancient landscape, to a familiar mountain standing in the sunset. She settled on the mountaintop and found the place where she had breathed the word "promise" as a child and planted the azure seed.

She expected to find a tall tree, fifty years healthy and strong. Instead, there was a stumpy bush with three weak branches, dark leaves, and withered fruit that gave off a discouraging smell. The trunk was squat and stone-like. The leaves were dry and curled like husks. Two of the branches were growing aimlessly, unformed and fruitless. The third branch was bent to the ground, overloaded with brittle pods that rattled like bones in the wind.

Sister dug around the dirt at the base of the tree. The roots were shallow and moldy.

"What kind of promise is this?" she wondered. "How can this be my family tree?"

It was clear—God was chiding her, displaying the state of her unresolved promise to Him. The message was stark: He had given her the beautiful azure seed, but this tree of her life had gone untended and barely survived. She was not keeping her side of the bargain. None of her children had found their spiritual gifts of Faith, Hope, or Grace; none had increased the goodness of anything. Her family had become a silly-looking collection of strangers, each lost in their own confusion. Instead of behaving like disciplined soldiers in the Army of Saints, they were acting like rodeo clowns.

Sister picked at the rubble around the base of her tree.

"I'm sorry," she said. "I know things look bad right now; but don't worry, I'll keep my promise. I have faith in my children. When the moment comes to change their lives, they *will* find their gifts. They will remember their stories and prayers. We will increase goodness on Earth and you'll win your bet with the Devil. I promise."

She felt sunlight, like a smile, turning her way.

"But it won't be easy, will it?" she asked.

A piece of fruit the color of cement fell off the tree onto her head.

"Ow," she said, and as she went unconscious, she began to dream within her dream.

She was floating above a tortured terrain—like her childhood vision of Hell. It looked like her neighborhood and the mountain behind it, but parts of the landscape were in the wrong places. There was an unfamiliar hill, a line of unlikely caves, and a swamp circled by cliffs. On the top of the ridge she could see her own house turned sideways, and behind it was a clearing that had been burnt clean of all life. In the middle of the desolation was a great pile of thorns.

There was a terrible battle raging in the clearing. People were running, falling down and being shredded like rags beneath the grinding engines of war. There was smoke in the sky and fire in the earth. There was death and dust in the air and the sounds of iron on stone, steel and spirit colliding. The mountain was soaked with blood.

Seeking comfort and safety, Sister turned away, settling in the garden beside her home, surrounded by late-season dahlias and the smell of strawberries.

15

It was early Saturday morning, before sunrise. I was sitting in my kitchen, drinking coffee, watching our countertop TV. I don't work weekends anymore; being chief has its privileges. On my free mornings, I sit at the table, read the paper, watch the sunrise, and wait for Beth to wake up so we can hang around for a while, then plan the day. After more coffee with Beth, I take the garbage to the dump, go to the bank, and drop by the station for an hour to read the night log; then we drive to Manchester for the afternoon. We always go to the mall, grab a pizza and beer, sometimes a movie, then we come home.

Today we are running last-minute errands for the party. With Veronica out of town, I'm left with all the planning. I still have no idea how many guests to expect. Beth suggested we buy food for fifty and freeze what we don't use.

Wes's show doesn't air on weekends, so I don't have to worry about him making things worse for two days straight. Veronica is in Vermont, so there won't be any agitation from her camp.

We still haven't heard from Reggie. I tried to bring him back from Florida, but like Wes says, "You can lead a horse to water, but he's got to put on his own swimming suit."

I thought about filing a phony warrant, calling Security at Disney World, having him arrested and put on a plane. I decided against it after I got a call from Carolyn, his ex-wife.

"Boone," she said, "what's this about Reggie being arrested for breaking and entering in Florida?"

"That's not true."

"Then what is it? I need to know."

"He's in Florida, but he's not in trouble."

"So you've seen him?

"Yes."

"Where is he?"

"I'm not going to tell you that right now."

"You have to. I'm his wife. It's against the law to withhold information from a spouse. You and your whole family have all caused me a lot of strife. Is he coming back for your parents' party?"

"I don't know."

"Liar."

"I'm sorry you're having such a hard time, Carolyn, but I've got to draw the line somewhere. He's still my brother."

"I'm serving notice, Boone. If you take his side, I'll ruin you. I'll sue the town and get everything you own. By the way, I'm changing my name back to Herschelflamm. I'm sick and tired of being ridiculed as a Moffatt."

"That's nice. Tell Theresa I said hi."

The next two weeks are going to be difficult, but we'll make it—with a little hard work. The town meeting is Wednesday, four days away. The following Monday, Wes will be in court. The fiftieth anniversary party is the next day.

Wednesday's town meeting will be Wes's last chance to clear up the confusion in front of everybody. The meeting is scheduled for six-thirty in the high school gym and is going to be broadcast as an episode of *This Is My Town*. Wes's show is going to be aired regionally and covered nationally.

Town meetings are usually poorly attended and grindingly boring. This meeting is going to be gladiatorial, Wes against the world. We are expecting at least two thousand people.

Thanks to Wes, Franklin Notch has become the national flashpoint of the week. The news media has locked on to the issue of Native American reparations—the sins of our forefathers against America's original landowners. *WHAT PRICE ATONEMENT?* wailed the cover of last Sunday's *Union Leader Magazine*, under a picture of Sarah Running Doe standing at the top of East Mountain, looking extremely put out. She was wearing a lumpy sweatshirt, a clunky turquoise medallion, and a feather in her hair. Her arms were crossed and she was scowling mightily. She was holding a fistful of broken arrows.

Town Hall is already freaking out. We have been bombarded with requests from the major networks for broadcast space, and we are expecting all the Manchester and Boston stations, the big three, CNN, and Court TV. Next week, my little town will be crawling with suits and microphones. I'm already feeling the pressure of my three conflicting roles as protector of the town, gracious host to the media carnivores, and son-defender of the town's biggest scoundrel.

My first loyalty, of course, is to my family. Beth and I already agreed that I will resign before I take Wes into custody. In the meantime, I can't appear to show him any favoritism. I'm not accustomed to this level of subtlety in my job. It's just a job, and rules are rules: You break the law, I lock you up. I drive a black-and-white, not a gray.

The problem with the Indians is much more complicated. The resort people have found the perfect angle—attack the ringleader to confuse and conquer. The charges against Wes are bogus, and he is being squeezed to split the town.

Typically, he isn't making things any easier. He does his show every night and drives around town in his truck all day acting like nothing is wrong. Even though his feelings are hurt, he can't stop being Wes. He's enjoying the attention, and he's downright giddy over the prospect of appearing on national television. He even bought a new flannel shirt for the town meeting.

Everybody hopes he has something new to say. People want proof that

Talbert's Treaty existed, and that it gave the eighteenth-century settlers the right to claim East Mountain if the Sagawehs ever moved away. In the absence of any proof, people want to hear Wes admit he made up the whole thing.

"Hey, you know what?" they want to hear him say. "I got carried away. I wanted everybody to respect me for something, so I dreamed up the whole thing. Back in '58, I found a cemetery on my property with my three-year-old boy. I did a little research on the people who were buried there, then I got carried away. I wanted to be an authority on something, so I made up some stories, gave some lectures, wrote some columns, and got a TV show. I pretended to know what I was talking about, and you all bought my act. And now, here tonight, in front of all these cameras and friends and family, I want to make it clear: I invented a whole tribe of Indians, there was no treaty, the Talberts were just average people trying to survive, and I'm an idiot. Thank you and good night."

Not likely.

Pending any revelations Wednesday night, Wes will be in court the following Monday morning, when he will stand in front of a judge while the charges are read against him. The judge will listen to the plaintiff—Sarah Running Doe and her attorneys—then listen to Wes, without an attorney to advise him. He will enter a plea of not guilty, and the judge will schedule a jury trial sometime in the next ninety days. Bail will be set, bail will be met. Wes will go home and get ready for his fiftieth wedding anniversary the next day.

The party plans are incomplete. It's hard to imagine the family without Reggie. Catherine, Charlie, and the babies are coming from Vermont, and Aero Kierkegaard is driving down for the weekend from Henniker. All we really need is each other.

As usual, Sister is steadfast, even with all the confusion roiling around the family. She isn't worried about anything—next week's town meeting, Reggie, Wes's court date, or her anniversary party the next day.

"I know how it looks," she says. "Just remember: Day to day, God makes our way."

Across the valley, above East Mountain, the sky was changing from night-black to morningblue, with the top of Talbert's Ridge as the jagged edge between earth and Heaven. A ribbon of geese trailed south, down the center of the valley.

Autumn is my favorite time of year.

"Ronnie Dolan—" said the television.

I held my breath. The anchorman for Channel 6 was standing in front of the Concord State Hospital.

"—better known as Holy Hell, New Hampshire's most notorious serial killer, currently serving thirty-seven consecutive life sentences for fifty-three murders committed in the early eighties. He was granted permission yesterday by the State Board of Reviews for a transfer from maximum security in Longerville to this medium-security psychiatric facility in Concord. According to authorities, Mr. Dolan, a former preacher's son, has been a model prisoner for the past twenty-five years after rediscovering Christianity during his imprisonment. Advocating for Mr. Dolan yesterday was Dr. Bruce Hutton, the nationally acclaimed author and life-management expert."

The camera panned to the right.

"Standing with me now is Dr. Hutton, who is a recent convert to Christianity himself, following a near-death experience during an air travel mishap earlier this week. Dr. Hutton, how would you describe Mr. Dolan's frame of mind?"

Bruce Hutton looked through the camera, directly at me. I could feel the heat of the Devil's glare, burning through the front of my eyes, into my skull, straight to the heart of my soul. I went cold from the inside out, but the skin beneath the map in my pocket stung as if I had been branded.

Sweetly, he smiled. Softly, he spoke.

"I've spent a considerable amount of time with Mr. Dolan over the past ten years, and I would describe him as sincerely repentant and extremely grateful for the chance to atone for his sins in an environment more nurturing to his spiritual growth. In my opinion, he is living proof of the redemptive powers of our Lord and Savior, Jesus Christ, and I would like to personally thank the Board of Reviews of the State of New Hampshire for their mercy and their humanity."

I felt sick. This was the worst news for Wes. Since the Devil was right about Ronnie Dolan, I knew he could manipulate and accelerate the confusion surrounding Wes. I called Sister.

"I was just about to call you," she said. "I had a dream last night. We need to talk."

I was sure she had seen my lie.

"Maybe later," I said. "Right now, we've got trouble. I just saw on the news that the state granted Ronnie Dolan's request. The Devil was there, at the hearing I missed. He was disguised as the same guy who made the plane fall."

"You didn't go to the hearing?"

"I was dressed to go, then something came up with Jessie. It was a setup. The Devil knew I'd choose family over duty. I'm afraid for Wes. If he can spare Holy Hell, then he can hurt Wes."

"This is serious," she said. "Let's focus, Daniel. I'll worry about your father. You worry about Ronnie Dolan."

My cell phone rang.

"I've got to go," I said. "Town business on the other line."

"Please call me later," she said. "Love you."

I picked up the other call. It was one of the guys from the station. "Boone, you'd better get your ass up to the ball fields. The place is crawling with Indians."

"What?"

"Yeah. They put up thirty teepees in the middle of the night."

I went to the bedroom and changed into my uniform. When I took off my shirt, I saw the skin on my chest had gotten worse—burnt and blistered over my heart.

16

The next morning, Veronica was the first one awake. She lay in bed for a moment, letting her first-light anxiety overtake her the way it did every morning. Michael Schreik's letters. It's Saturday. I have to get to the post office before it closes at noon. This place is filthy. I wonder if they even have a bottle of Top Job. She looked around Molly's room. Dust and cat hair everywhere, like snowdrifts in the corners. This was no way for a baby to live. She made a list in her head: vacuum cleaner bags, paper towels, dish soap.

She reached for her Rolaids and cigarettes. She put on her shoes and walked through the kitchen to the living room. Jessie was asleep on the sofa, covered by a sleeping bag. Her jacket was draped over her new drum.

Veronica looked into the other bedroom. Catherine, Charlie, Molly, and the baby were sleeping together on the wide bed, tangled in quilts. Catherine was facing the doorway, curled around her baby. Her nightgown was unbuttoned, and one breast was exposed over the little boy's face. Veronica fought the urge to go into the bedroom and pull the blanket up over her oldest daughter.

She went back to the kitchen and made a pot of coffee. The sink was full of dishes, the table was crusty with last night's dried food, and there were piles of newspapers, books, sheet music, Molly's drawings, and mail everywhere.

She opened the refrigerator. Inside was a bottle of ketchup, a box of baking soda, a bowl of crusty macaroni salad, and three Jell-O singles.

"Good Lord," she said.

She took a quick shower, threw on her jeans and sweater, and drove into town.

When she returned two hours later, she had a car full of food and cleaning supplies. Charlie was sitting in the middle of the garden, playing his cello. Jessie was in the front yard, bent over her djembe, flailing, filling the air with whack-poppas. Molly was dancing in front of Jessie, waving a muffin tin and a long wooden spoon.

"Jessie. Help me unload this car," Veronica yelled.

Charlie looked up and waved. He picked up his cello and carried it high over the weeds, back to the house.

"Mom, this is so great," said Catherine as they carried in bags of food and supplies. "Perfect timing. Charlie doesn't get paid until Wednesday. We were going to exist on leftovers from the Drumfest. Thanks so much."

She gave Veronica a big hug.

"Yeah, thanks," said Charlie. He stepped forward like he wanted to hug, too, but he chickened out.

"Nobody wants to eat leftovers all weekend," Veronica said. "I'm going to start cleaning."

They all dispersed to their projects. Veronica began scrubbing the refrigerator, Jessie took a shower, Charlie tried to start his car, Catherine put food away, Molly kicked empty grocery bags around the kitchen, and Vedran Smailovich Cooper sat in his seat, digging the chaos.

By noon Charlie had tinkered the old Toyota to the point where it would start, more or less when he expected it to.

"Watch your fingers, honey," Catherine would yell from time to time out the back door of the cabin.

Jessie helped Catherine collect and pack all the equipment for their two-baby assault on the outside world; then Jessie organized her own inventory, stacking her tie-dyed T-shirts by color and size while Molly helped by saying ooooo nice and pulling apart the piles.

"We're going up to the orchard now," Catherine said to Veronica. "We're going to help set up."

"I'll be fine," said Veronica. "There are a few more things I need to do. I'll join you later."

She wanted the cabin to herself. She was on a mission. She wanted to clean every room, scrub every fixture, and dust every surface. She wanted to fill all fifty garbage bags with the raggedy crap that Catherine and Charlie had accumulated and toss them into a big hole. This was no way to raise babies, she said to herself, over and over.

Catherine, Charlie, the babies, their car seats, backpacks, and strollers, and Jessie with her drum and duffel bag full of T-shirts all squeezed into the little Toyota station wagon and bumped down the long rutted driveway.

Veronica collected all the dirty clothes and started an assembly line between the washer and the dryer. She stripped the covers off the sofa and pushed all the furniture into the center of the living room; then she vacuumed the cabin ceiling to floor and scrubbed all the doorframes and windows with disinfectant. She cleaned the bathroom on her hands and knees. She swept the mudroom and the front hallway. Then she started on the kitchen.

She scraped the floor around the table with a putty knife, then sponge-mopped and dried it three times. She scrubbed the oven with steel wool, scraped the counter, and cleaned it with bleach. She threw the slimy old dish rack in the trash and replaced it with a new wooden one, emptied all the drawers and cabinets, and collected every dish, pan, and piece of silverware she could find. She started washing, filling one sink with hot soapy water and letting each load soak for a few minutes before she attacked it with a scrub sponge and scalding water.

Veronica was standing at the sink looking out the window at the garden when a movement in the weeds caught her eye. While she watched, not even thinking of anything, a peacock scooted out and ran across the backyard toward the garage, its head down, its mouth open, and its long broom tail bouncing through the high grass. A few seconds later, two more wild-eyed peacocks dashed out of the weeds and sprinted in jerky tangents toward the garage. Behind them came a man walking quickly, crouching slightly. He was wearing jeans, a denim workshirt, and sandals. He was average height and very thin. He had short light brown hair and blue eyes, and he was wearing wire-rimmed glasses. He was in his midforties, she guessed. He was light on his feet, and he was laughing.

From the moment he walked out of the weeds, moving past the kitchen window, Veronica was attracted to him. It was the surprise of seeing him; it was the way he moved and the way he looked, but it was also more than just his presence in her field of vision. There was mystery in the possibility of the moment.

He ran past the window, toward the garage. The scene was so sudden—the three peacocks running under the window and the thin man with the sharp happy face chasing them—that Veronica wondered if it had actually happened. It was a flash of activity that didn't fit with anything.

Veronica walked outside. The man was crouching in front of the open garage door with his arms spread wide. He was moving slowly toward the door singing "I'll Be Your Baby Tonight." He saw Veronica, and he smiled. "Hi," he said. "Sorry for the invasion. It's the drums. It's got them all crazy."

Veronica stood at the edge of the driveway, still wearing her bright yellow cleaning gloves.

"Do me a favor, willya?" he said. "Just stand right there." He pointed to a spot several feet to the right of where he stood. Veronica could hear shuffling noises coming from inside Catherine's garage. She moved next to him and stood stiffly.

"They like this song," he said. "Sometimes it calms them down." He sang a few more lines. "Okay," he said. "I'm closing the left side of the door. Just stay where you are."

The door scraped on gravel as he pulled it, and from the back of the garage came a noise that sounded like three women wailing.

"They've lost it," he said. "They can go on like this for days. They won't eat, drink, or sleep when they get this excited. I think they're past Code Zimmerman."

"Are they your birds?" Veronica asked.

"They are," he said. "I have two more, and they went up a tree. Right now I've got to catch these guys and get them home before they give themselves embolisms."

"What do you want me to do?"

"Have you got any rags? Like bandana size?"

"Sure," said Veronica. She went into the cabin, to the bathroom, where she gaped at herself in the mirror. Pretty grotesque, she said, teasing at her hair with her fingertips. She grabbed one of the ragged towels and ran back outside.

"I was cleaning," she said. "I don't live here. I'm visiting my daughter."

"Catherine? She's your daughter? That's great," he said. "You must be so proud of her."

Veronica didn't know what to say. Proud? Her response of habit was sarcasm, but she held her tongue. There was something about this tableau that skewed her mood—the happy, healthy-looking man smiling at her in the autumn morning sun, the way the sky, earth, and air seemed to frame the moment, and the curious warmth she felt pouring through her.

"Doc Barringer," he said, holding out his hand.

"Veronica Marston," she said. His hand was lean and strong.

"Really?" he said. "Great name, Veronica. The most fearless and graceful move in bullfighting."

He ripped the towel in pieces. He shoved three rags in his back pocket and handed Veronica the remainder.

"Peacocks are really stupid," he said. "Especially the males, which makes them very brave. They jump sideways and they've got claws like steak knives, so don't let them get near you. Just wave this at them. I'll grab one, then carry him back to my place. Then I'll come back for the other two in my truck. I hope I can get them home before they hurt themselves."

"We can put them in my car if you want," Veronica said. "I'll drive you back, wherever you're going." She couldn't believe she was saying this, but she had to know more about him. Did he say he was a doctor?

"Really? That would be great." He hadn't stopped smiling since she saw him run past the window. He tucked in his shirt. "What a way to spend a morning, huh? Alright, it's time to round up the pretty boys," he said, stepping into the garage.

The wailing started again, followed by the sounds of a brief struggle. He came out with one of the big birds under his right arm and a piece of towel tied around the peacock's head, covering its eyes. He was holding its legs with his other hand.

"I got lucky," he said.

He put the bird in Veronica's Camry. It sat in the middle of the backseat, bobbing its head.

After another sortie in the garage, Doc emerged with the second peacock. He put it with the first one, where it sat pecking halfheartedly at the door lock. Doc headed back into the garage. "Now for the ringleader," he said.

A few minutes later he walked out with the last bird. He was holding it in front of him as if it were going to explode. Even with the rag over its eyes, it was squealing like a fire alarm, and when he put it in the backseat, the other two took up the skree, howling and swinging their heads from side to side.

In the kitchen, Doc washed his hands in the sink.

"Sorry about the mess," said Veronica.

"Looks great," he said. "You oughta see my place."

While Veronica showered and changed clothes, Doc finished washing the dishes, then hauled the trash to the garage.

The birds were still yurping like airhorns when Veronica and Doc climbed into the Camry and drove down the driveway.

"I live on the other side of the hill," he said. "I hope we can get through. The kids are having a bash in the orchard tonight. This place is going to look like Woodstock in about an hour."

"The Drumfest?"

"Yeah. We do it every fall. It's great fun."

"I know. Catherine and my other daughter are already up there. She came with me. She's fifteen. She's going to sell T-shirts."

"Great," he said. "I'll have to buy a couple. Are you going?"

"I was. Maybe later."

"Good. We can go together. There's a path from my place to the top of the hill."

"Okay," said Veronica. Afraid to smile, she pretended to struggle with the driveway.

She wanted to rewind this adventure and start over. She felt she had presented herself badly, made a nondescript first impression, and now she wanted to reintroduce herself with more presence. She didn't know how. She felt shy and incidental. She felt plain.

It didn't seem to matter; things were happening anyway. Here she was, driving around a mountain, sitting beside an easygoing, attractive man with his three yowling peacocks in the backseat of her car. Clearly, the adventure was well under way and they were already friendly. Maybe it was too late to worry—he seemed to be enjoying her company. She glanced at him, hoping to catch some sense of his intentions. He caught her look and smiled back. This was excitement, not fear, she reminded herself—this fluttering in her chest.

"Turn here," he said.

They drove down a long lane, over a stream, and up to a large, long farmhouse. Veronica slowed down in front of the house.

"Keep going," he said. "I'm around the back."

"Is this your house?" she asked.

"Probably," he said. "It's a long story."

Veronica drove around the house and followed a narrow path between the trees. Several hundred yards into the woods, she came to a clearing that looked like a gypsy camp. In the middle of the clearing was an ancient sky-blue RV. It looked like an old school bus, with rounded edges and Buck Rogers-style chrome trim. It hadn't been moved in a long time. It was resting on a frame of cinder blocks and railroad ties. A flower garden had grown up to the windows. A wide yellow awning hung off the side of it like a circus tent, suspended by poles and guywires. A thick, bright tangle of morning glories, hyacinths, and grapevines covered the back half of the camper like a soft cocoon. On the roof of the ancient RV was a wooden platform with a telescope and several lawn chairs.

Scattered around the clearing were brightly painted sheds and outbuildings. On the far side was a row of five solar panels that looked like Ping-Pong tables tilted on their sides.

"Okay, boys, we're home," Doc said to the three bobbing peacocks in the backseat. "Wander around," he said to Veronica. "Make yourself comfortable while I put these guys in the pen."

One by one, he hauled the goofy birds out of the Camry and pushed them into a lavender coop on the other side of the clearing. Veronica walked through the garden. There were sunflowers, snapdragons, dahlias, and staked plants heavy with vegetables.

Chickens roamed around the clearing and through the garden. A flock of six wild turkeys hovered near the edge of the woods, watching Veronica nervously. In a corral near the peacock pen, several goats and a pair of emus stopped eating to consider the scene. A llama poked her head out of a pink and blue shed, hay hanging out of her mouth. A cat poured itself off one of the chairs and walked halfway to Veronica, where it stopped, then looked back over its shoulder.

The woods around them seemed to vibrate with a low throbbing sound. It must be the drumming, Veronica reminded herself.

"Try the grapes," Doc yelled from the back of the clearing. "They're just coming around." He was pouring feed into shallow buckets for the goats. One emu pranced around the pen, trying to peck him on the neck. "Beat it, Gretchen," he said.

Veronica picked a brownish-purple grape and bit into it. In her mouth, the bitter skin slid off the pulp. The meat was sweet, the seeds slippery grit. She picked a handful and walked around the front of the RV. The roof over the cab had been fitted with glass, converting the cab into a greenhouse. The seats had been removed and replaced with shelves and hanging pots of nonflowering plants—spices and herbs, Veronica guessed.

Doc came across the clearing. "Come on inside," he said. "I'll give you the tour."

An ancient three-legged yellow hound crawled from under the camper. He looked at Veronica and mouthed a toothless yawn. He lay on his side and appeared to stop breathing.

"Is this dog okay?" she asked.

"I wouldn't stand behind him. He farts something fierce."

They sidestepped the dog and went into the RV.

It was a wizard's den. Across the front of the camper, behind the greenhouse cab, was a long table piled with books, bottles and jars, a mortar and pestle, a cutting board, and a hundred brown extract bottles with black eyedropper tops. A long wooden flute lay across the table.

Bunches of drying plants hung from hooks in the ceiling. Rows of shelves had been built into the walls of the camper, and they were packed with a thousand books and natural curios like birds' nests, buckeyes, and chunks of quartz.

There were books everywhere. They were piled on the floor and stacked on the little table in the eating nook—even inside the microwave.

On the wall behind the refrigerator was a framed diploma. JAMES AARON BARRINGER, COLLEGE OF MEDICINE, DARTMOUTH UNIVERSITY. 1986.

"You're a real doctor," she said.

"Yeah," he said, from the back of the camper. He had gone into the back bedroom and closed the door behind him. "It's hard to tell without the lab coat and attitude, huh?"

"I thought maybe Doc was just a nickname," Veronica said.

"Like one of the Seven Dwarfs?" He came out of the bedroom, buttoning a clean workshirt. "It used to be a title; then it turned into a nickname when I moved back to Crawfordsville. Now it's my first name. I like it. It's got a Wild West ring to it."

"I'm a nurse," said Veronica.

"Really? My condolences," he said, smiling.

"Do you have a practice?"

"I've got a great practice. I've got the dream practice, the one everybody prays for. I run the free clinic in town. Are you hungry?"

"Sure," said Veronica.

"I'll be right back," he said, stepping out the door. "I'm going to find us some breakfast."

Veronica sat at the little table in the breakfast nook, looking through some magazines. She stood up and looked again at the diploma. 1986? He was forty-eight, she figured.

On a shelf over the sink were a dozen photographs, none of him. She washed her hands.

Doc climbed back into the camper, carrying a bowl loaded with eggs and greens.

"Huevos rancheros with goat cheese," he said. "Juice, coffee—if you want it. Corn muffins or fresh-baked bread? Your choice."

Veronica sat at the table, sipping fresh-pressed apple juice, watching him make breakfast.

"You run the free clinic?" she asked.

"Actually, I started it—eight years ago, when I came back. It's something I wanted to do when I retired. Circumstances conspired and I took advantage of the moment."

"You retired early?"

"Sort of. I quit. I had a practice in Syracuse—a partner and three clinics. It was hell. Miserable patients, miserable employees, miserable partner, and a miserable wife. Everybody miserable, including me. Thirty patients a day. Hi, howya doing, hey that's too bad, here take this. Typical stuff—medicating people against their own lifestyles.

"For a while I dug it. We were making plenty of money. We owned the space, started our own billing service and temp agency. We had the market covered. I was working ten, thirteen hours a day, smoking, drinking coffee all day and Manhattans all night. I was living on crullers, cigarettes, and Seconals. I had it all—panic attacks, incipient ulcer, galloping obesity. Paging Dr. Elvis."

He set two plates of eggs, brown rice, and salad on the table. "These are the best eggs you'll ever eat," he said. "I've got the happiest chickens in America because they wander around free all day, in and out of the coop. They work hard, keeping the bugs off my tomatoes."

"Aren't you afraid they'll get lost in the woods?" Veronica asked.

Doc laughed. "We're already lost in the woods," he said.

They sat at the small table, eating and talking. The late summer breeze blew through the window, the animals rustled around the clearing, and the feeling of life was all around them. He was right, everything tasted better.

"You grow everything yourself?" she asked. "Even the apples?"

"I make my own wine, too. There used to be a working orchard between us and the house. It goes from here to the top of the hill. It's overgrown now because nobody has tended it for years. I don't have the time. The apples are still okay, but not great. They used to be the best in the county. Now they're only good for juicing and wine."

"So this drum party is on your property? In your orchard?"

"Yep. I grew up here. I grew up in that house," he said, pointing his fork over his shoulder. "My dad was the town doctor, and that's where we lived."

"Why don't you live in the house?"

"I can't. When I sold my share of the practice, the shit hit the fan. Now everything's tied up in court, including the house, the land, and everything in Syracuse. I'm not worried. Sooner or later, it'll work itself out."

"Am I being nosy?" Veronica asked.

"Not at all. I'm glad you're here," he said. "I had a feeling something good was going to happen today. And besides, everybody else knows the story."

He settled into the corner of the alcove with a mug of apple juice.

"I was driving home from work," he said. "It was a Friday afternoon, and I was in a hurry. We had a plane to catch. My wife and I were flying to Barbados for five days. I was stopped at a light, the light changed, and the car in front of me pulled into the intersection. Another car came flying through and hit it. I grabbed my cell phone and called 911. I didn't even get out of the car. I went home, picked up my wife, and drove to the airport. It turned out that both drivers were actually patients of ours. That night in Barbados I drank a pint of rum and fell into the hotel pool, too drunk to swim. A girl who was walking home from work jumped the fence and pulled me out, and before we left I went to her house to thank her. She lived in a shack smaller than this camper with her parents and two brothers. They wouldn't let me leave without dinner. Plantains and rice, that's all they had to eat. I asked if I could do anything for them. 'Oh, no,' they said. 'We can't afford doctors.'

"I had a complete meltdown. I started crying on the plane and didn't stop for a week. When my head cleared, I sold out to my partner and made plans to move back to Vermont. My wife refused to move and divorced me. She wanted to be a real doctor's wife, so she married my partner. She took me to court, got the house in Syracuse, the condo in Vail and the one in St. Pete. She wants this place, too, so she got an injunction keeping me out until the court decides who owns it.

"After I left Syracuse I bought this motor home, traveled a bit, then drove up here and parked it in the woods. A year later, I started the clinic. I've been doing it for seven years, and I love it. I'm doing a lot of work with natural remedies. It's real medicine—compassion and clear thinking, not pills and paperwork. We teach people to heal themselves.

"I get to spend time with my patients and actually talk to them. The kids bring me little presents, and they say thank you when they leave. I don't have to worry about lawsuits or office managers stealing meds. Another year in Syracuse and I would have been on Thorazine."

"That's the way I feel," Veronica said. "I'm doing budget requests now, and it's such a waste of time. I stay in my office all day—unless there's a problem on the floor. I smoke too much. I don't sleep. I eat garbage. I don't even have time to learn anyone's name. By the end of the day, I don't know what I'm doing. People act like it's a spa and we're janitors. I've got a guy who refuses medication so he can write letters to his family."

"Maybe he's looking for permission to live," Doc said. "When people hate themselves, they try to cover guilt with pain."

"That's what my mother says. I don't even feel like a nurse anymore.

After thirty years, it's like housecleaning. It's such a grind and it feels so hopeless. I try so hard, but nothing ever turns out right. Even my daughter hates me."

"Catherine?"

"No. Jessie, my fifteen-year-old. Catherine just puts up with me. Jessie and I argued the whole way here—about nothing. It makes me sad, but I can't get close enough to change things. Everything I say comes out wrong. I just want to be a good mom. I just want my girls to be happy. I want to be happy. I'm complaining, aren't I?"

"Not at all," Doc said. "Somebody has to stand guard."

"That's it," she said. "I feel like I'm always on guard. It's so hard, doing it alone. Do you have kids?"

"No. My wife didn't want them."

"That's too bad," Veronica said. "You would have been a good dad. You've got that gentle nature."

"Thanks," he said. "I always thought so. I love seeing the kids at the clinic. Molly and Vedran are two of my favorites. If you worked with us, you could do Vedran's well-baby checkups."

"Catherine comes to the clinic?"

"Catherine, Charlie, Molly, Vedran. We call them the Happy Clan. She's a great mother. You did a good job with that one," Doc said.

Veronica didn't know what to say. She was still in the habit of blaming herself for the shortcomings of her children. Praise confused her. "Thanks," she said. "I don't know how much of it she got from me."

"Everything, I'm sure," he said.

Veronica smiled.

They sat at the small table and talked for a while. Somewhere in the woods, the two missing peacocks screeched, and they were answered by the others safe in their coop. Beyond the peacocks, the sounds of drumming grew louder.

"Can I ask a personal question?" he said.

"Sure."

"Are you seeing anyone?"

"No." She smiled at the wild improbability of the question.

"Then can we hang out today?" he asked.

"I'd like that," she said. "I'd like that a lot."

"Great. Let's go to the party," Doc said.

. . .

The drumming was louder as Doc and Veronica followed the path up the hill. In the woods around them, groups of people carrying blankets, baskets of food, and musical instruments straggled upward, toward the orchard at the top. Doc carried a backpack and his flute; Veronica carried the blanket. As they came out of the woods at the top of the hill, Veronica felt the buzz of gathering and noise.

The orchard was full of people—mostly young—talking in groups, dancing, lying in pairs, sitting in clusters. There were tents, and children chasing each other. The apple trees were decorated with colored banners; the sky quivered with kites. The smell of marijuana was everywhere, and beneath it all was the steady throbbing of a hundred drums.

On the crown of the hill was an open area, and arranged in a great circle around the clearing were the drummers. There were people of all ages, playing drums of all sizes—djembes, timbalas, bongos, and tubanos. They were playing together, beating their drums with their hands or knobby-looking sticks. They were a joyous engine, syncopated and powerful. Layered over the steady pounding were intricate variations of backbeats, crossbeats, and the occasional eight-bar freakout of someone who had just lost both mind and sense of time in the tribal throbbing.

There were people inside the wide circle, dancing and spinning, or sitting calmly with their eyes closed.

Veronica walked with Doc through the ragtag camp.

"Security sweep," he said.

They strolled between tents and groups of people gathered in the orchard. Everybody knew Doc and he greeted them all by name, stopping to talk and hug. He worked the crowd like a gracious host, introducing Veronica.

"Catherine's mother," he said, to everyone's approval.

They found Charlie with a group of guys, trying to level a row of porta-potties.

"Who said you guys don't know shit?" Doc said.

He and Charlie hugged. "Hey, Missus M," Charlie said, giving Veronica a wry look. "Where did you find this guy?"

Veronica tried not to look flustered. Doc told the story of the fugitive peacocks.

"Catherine and the babies are up at the circle," Charlie said. "We'll get together later, okay?"

"Sure," said Doc. "We'll find you."

They went to the drum circle, looking for Catherine. She was in the center of the circle with Vedran, dancing slowly to the drums. She was holding the baby close to her waist with one arm while supporting his back and his head with her other hand. She spun slowly, dancing with her boy, singing to him and watching his face. He was leaning back, grinning with joy, wide-eyed at the spun sky, his arms stretched over his head, fingers brushing through the clouds.

Veronica saw Jessie. She was sitting across the circle, playing her drum with her head bent back and her eyes closed. She was bouncing the flats of her hands off the rim of the djembe in strong slaps. Her face was twisted in rapture, in the ecstasy of noisy communion. It was an expression Veronica had never seen on her daughter. Molly was standing next to Jessie, watching her face and tapping an empty spot on the drumhead with one chubby finger.

"You need a picture of that," said Doc, taking a camera out of his backpack. He focused, then shot the frame just as Molly looked back over her shoulder and smiled at him, her little hand resting on the lip of the drum.

When Catherine saw her mother, she came out of the circle. It took a moment for her to realize that she was with Doc.

"What's this?" she asked. "A drum date? Doc, you don't have my permission to turn my mother into a hippie. What will the grandchildren think?"

Doc laughed and reached for Vedran. "Come here, cello-baby," he said. The little boy came to him easily. He held the baby up to his face and, in a smooth motion of habit, checked his eyes, nose, and ears. He put his ear to the baby's chest and checked his little fingernails. He turned Vedran around, hooked a finger in the child's waistband, and looked down his backside. He looked the baby in the face and made a startled face. When Vedran smiled, Doc sniffed the child's breath and looked down his throat. He gently pinched the baby's thigh.

Veronica's heart was melting.

"Is he getting enough fluid?" Doc asked Catherine. "He seems a little loose in his skin."

"Maybe not," she said. "I think it's me. I think I'm drying up."

"It's autumn," Doc said. "Your body is trying to save nutrients; it's preparing for winter. Drink more water, drink a glass of wine—red wine with no nitrites—every night. And in the morning take some anise tea. It'll boost your milk. It's good for colds, too. Give him plenty of apple juice."

"How do I make anise tea?" Catherine asked.

"I'll send some extract back with your mother," he said. "Two drops per cup."

"Thanks, Doc," Catherine said. She took Vedran, held him at eye level, and wiggled him. She hugged him and gave him a ripe mouth-fart on his neck. The boy squealed and pushed at her face with his fists.

"Gotcha," Catherine said, rubbing noses with the squinch-faced baby. "Gotcha."

Doc and Veronica made camp near the drum circle, on the back side of the hill. They spread the blanket behind an apple tree and Veronica sat cross-legged while Doc lay on his side, propped on one elbow.

"Are you having fun?" he asked.

"I'm a little overwhelmed," Veronica said. "This is different."

"Yeah, it is," said Doc. "That's why I like it here. It's why I came back. I like the freedom to try different things. I like it loose."

"I'm too strict," Veronica said. "The girls always said I was a worrier."

"A warrior?"

"No. I worried. I worry too much. I worry about everything. I know it bugs them, but I can't help it. It's no wonder they keep secrets from me. Now I feel left out—like I'm not part of their lives, and that makes me worry even more."

"What do you worry about?"

"I worry about Catherine. They don't have anything. I mean, they don't even have enough money for food until Charlie gets paid on Wednesday. I bought them a whole refrigerator full of stuff. And Charlie has to work on that car for an hour every time they want to go anywhere."

"Have you heard him play the cello?"

"Not really," Veronica said. "I guess he's good. Catherine says he is."

"He's incredible," said Doc. "He's extremely gifted. He's writing a concerto for cello and twelve-piece orchestra that people in Boston want to perform."

"But they're starving," said Veronica.

"But they're learning," said Doc. "And they're happy. They're smart kids, and that shack's full of love. They'll be fine."

Veronica sighed. "I don't know," she said.

"Are you sad?" he asked.

Veronica shrugged. "Just confused, I guess. Tense. Sorry. This is where I usually take a Xanax."

He got to his knees and crawled behind her.

"Lean back," he said.

He was kneeling behind her, and she settled back against him. He put his hands on her shoulders.

"Close your eyes," he said. "I want you to imagine you're sitting on a hill in an apple orchard. The sun is warm on your shoulders and on the top of your head, and the breeze is blowing softly through your hair and over your face. Imagine you can smell the ripe apples."

"It seems so real," she said, smiling. "It's like I'm really there."

"Don't get happy on me now," he said. "I charge by the hour."

"And what is it, exactly, that you are doing?"

Her back was pressed against him, and she could feel his voice vibrating inside her own body. He spoke in a soft, low singsong rhythm that fit the heartbeat drums pounding behind them. "I'm taking away all the tension and all the worry," he said softly. "I'm taking it away, taking it away."

He had his thumbs on the back of her neck, at the base of her head, and as he spoke, he rolled them gently into the muscles. A drowsy warmth flowed through Veronica, and she felt the hardness and tension being drawn out of her body wherever he touched her.

"How are you doing that?" she asked.

"I don't know," he said. "It's some kind of medical thing. Stop thinking about it, and just relax."

For an hour Veronica sat, leaning against Doc as he coaxed the tension out of her shoulders, her arms, and the muscles of her back with his fingers and the heels of his hands. Neither of them spoke; there was only the steady sound of drumming from the hilltop and the voices of people at play in the orchard around them. When he finished, they sat side by side, touching at the hips and shoulders.

"I feel like a baby," Veronica said. "A little girl with nothing on her mind."

"Another successful exorcism," he said, smiling.

They sat quietly. It was late in the afternoon, and they watched the sun slide off the sky and behind the hills to the west.

"We should go back to the circle," he said. "I've got to make sure they don't burn down the mountain."

At the top of the hill, Charlie and his crew were piling pallets and logs in the center of the circle. The drummers had dwindled to twenty. It was a new crowd, and they were flailing halfheartedly, not making much noise.

"What are they doing?" Veronica asked. She was so relaxed, it didn't even sound like her own voice.

"Everybody is resting up for the grand finale," he said. "In a few hours, they'll light the bonfire and all the drummers will come back and make a bigger circle. People who brought instruments will jam until midnight. Everybody else will just bop till they drop. We can leave whenever you want," he said.

Jessie came toward them, out of a crowd of kids. She was wearing a woolen poncho, and she had her drum slung over her shoulder.

"Taking a break?" Veronica asked.

"Yeah. I played for three hours. I'm getting so good at this. Charlie says I'm a natural."

"We've got a good picture of you playing," Veronica said. "Molly's standing next to you."

Jessie realized her mother was with a man—and standing close to him. She couldn't hide her surprise.

"This is Doc," Veronica said. "Dr. Barringer. He's Catherine's doctor."

"Hi," said Jessie.

"Hi," he said, shaking her hand. "Your mother was telling me about your T-shirt business. How's it going?"

"Great," she said. "I made a hundred and eighty dollars. I've only got seven shirts left." She was watching the two adults very carefully.

"Save a couple for me?" Doc said.

"Sure. Thanks." Jessie looked at her mother. "Are you okay, Mom?" she asked.

"Sure. Why?"

"You look kind of spacey."

"I'm fine, honey. Isn't this fun?"

Jessica Marston looked at her mother as if she had never seen her before; and for as long as she would live—but especially at the time in her own life when she would be the age her mother was now—she would remember this moment as the point when everything between them changed. From this moment, when her mother said she was fine and was having fun, Veronica became a natural friend to her daughter—and the daughter allowed her.

"So much fun," Jessie said, hugging Veronica. "It's so much fun."

As she walked away, back to her friends, she turned, smiled, and waved. "See?" said Doc. "She likes you."

The bonfire blazed in the middle of the drum circle. People crowded behind the wide curve of drummers, watching the fire and the people inside the circle dancing and playing instruments. People danced alone, in pairs, in groups. They danced graceful serpentines, frantic herky-jerkies, and delirious tarantellas. They stripped naked; they bounced like flubber and jiggled like tapioca. They slow-danced, bunny-hopped, cartwheeled, and jitterbugged around the fire. Surrounding them, the powerful pounding of a hundred drums never stopped, building to a fearsome rush of sound and rhythm.

Veronica stood with Doc, watching Jessie on her drum and the dancers flirting the fire. She reflected on the moment and the way she felt. There was heat from the fire on her face, and a growing warmth the length of her body where she was pressed against Doc. There was also a gentle glow that had taken life in the darkest part of herself—the corner she had always preserved for her own self-doubt. It would glow like prayer, then flame like hope, to cauterize and sanctify. Now she knew for sure; things could change. She could change.

"I'm ready to go—if you are," she said.

They walked through the orchard, and when they had gone beyond the reach of the fire's light, Doc used his flashlight to guide them past the trees to the edge of the woods.

Veronica put her hand on his shoulder as they picked their way down the mountain path. When they came into his clearing at the bottom of the hill, the peacocks cut loose with a skreeling shriek.

"Watchbirds," he said, as he swung his light across the clearing. "Beautiful idiots." The last two peacocks were standing outside the pen, brooling with the other three. Veronica followed him across the clearing and stood to the side as he opened the door for the last two birds.

They sat at the little table in the breakfast nook, drinking homemade apple wine. The mood was mellow with candlelight and Fauré. The drumming had stopped on the top of the hill, and the night was finally quiet.

Veronica told him about Wes and the fake Indians who were taking him to court, and how half the people in town could lose their homes because he made up all the local history. She told him about Reggie's lifetime aversion to responsibility and his selfish refusal to show up for his own parents' fiftieth anniversary party. She told him about Sister and her Gothic orphanage upbringing and how she sees the future and still makes everybody recite novenas to protect themselves from God knows what. She told him about the Army of Saints and her older brother, the chief of police who has seen the Devil—the real Devil—five times already and somehow has to balance the laws of the World with the fears of the Other.

"No wonder you're so stressed out. You're the only one in the family who has a normal life."

"I know," she said. "They always called me a cranky little girl, but all I really wanted was a normal family. I just wanted to call my mother Mom."

"Why don't you?"

Veronica looked at Doc blankly, as if she were trying to remember an answer that he could understand.

"I don't know," she finally said.

"Maybe you should try it," he said. "Seems reasonable."

"Yeah. Why not?" Veronica smiled to herself, then laughed. "What a perfect idea," she said, and she gave him a hug. "Thank you."

It was well past midnight and they were still talking. They spoke of attractions and distractions, the arcs of lovers and friends and the sweet refuge of loneliness. The quart of wine was finished. Outside, the voices of peepers and crickets soaked the night with their busy gossip. Somewhere beneath the camper, the ancient hound sighed in his sleep. It was late, and the later it became, the less Veronica felt like leaving.

Doc stood and offered his hand. "Will you stay with me?" he asked.

"I'd love to," she said, her heart beating like drums.

He blew out the candle and took her hand, leading her in the darkness to the bedroom at the back of the camper. The sweet smell of hyacinth filled the room.

They undressed in the dark, then crawled under a quilt on the soft wide bed.

Veronica gasped when they slid together, feeling the naked length of their bodies. They jostled and explored each other, touching those places where they wanted to be touched themselves. It was eager love the first time, then slow and easy again with whispering kisses. And when it was over, they lay together, enjoying the fit of themselves, hugging and talking.

"Why are you attracted to me?" Veronica asked, her head resting on his chest.

"Because it feels so natural," he said. "Like an old friend. Doesn't it feel like you knew this was going to happen?"

"Like I always hoped it would," Veronica sighed.

They kissed again and he pulled her closer, tucking the quilt tighter around them.

Even before Veronica woke up, she knew she was happy. There had been lazy dreams of summer scenes, and the sleepy childhood feeling of safety and warmth—being close to someone who loved her.

The sun had come up while they slept, and as Veronica awoke, she opened her eyes to a glorious sight.

The walls of the small bedroom were covered with peacock feathers, and as the morning sun shone through the vine-covered windows, a thousand gold-and-turquoise eyes blinked in the brightness.

"Oh, my goodness," she said to the spirits of joy around her. "Oh, my goodness."

The thousand sunny eyes winked down on Veronica as her new love lay sleeping, breathing easy on her shoulder. I hope, she said. I hope this lasts forever.

"When can I see you again?" Doc asked later that morning as they walked to her car.

"Next weekend?" Veronica said. "Friday night?"

"Friday night," he said, hugging her. Softly they kissed. "I can't wait."

Twenty minutes later, Veronica walked into Catherine's kitchen. Catherine, Charlie, and Jessie were eating waffles at the table.

"Alright, Mom," Jessie said, giving her the thumbs-up.

"What?" said Veronica, blushing.

"What?" the three of them said, in unison.

Molly wandered out of the bathroom, without her pants.

"What?" she said. "What's what?"

17

I drove the cruiser down the hill, across Main Street and up East Mountain. There was a news truck ahead of me on the narrow road, so I flashed my lights and gunned past.

The scene at the fields was carnival surreal.

The town ball fields are a ten-acre parcel of open land with diamonds set in three of the corners and a picnic-playground area with a log shelter on the far side.

This morning there was a circle of teepees in the middle of the field. They looked like a regatta—bone white and twenty feet high with streamers and ribbons fluttering off the tips of the poles. Each teepee was flying an American flag, and several had black-and-white POW flags and DON'T TREAD ON ME banners.

The teepee closest to the parking lot had a sign tied across its back. I HAVE BEEN TO THE MOUNTAIN, it said. MARTIN LUTHER KING.

They were arranged in a wide circle a hundred feet across, with their doorways facing the center. There was a prefab wooden shed outside the circle with three generators inside and a row of porta-potties downwind from the encampment. Parked behind the circle, over second base, were a water truck and a house trailer with a satellite dish on the roof.

Ten men dressed in battle fatigues and carrying walkie-talkies patrolled the perimeter of the camp. A heavyset man in a biker jacket sat on a lawn chair in front of the generator shed with an ax handle across his lap.

I walked to the nearest Indian.

"How are you doing?" I asked.

"Pretty good. How are you doing?"

"I'm doing great. This is my favorite time of year." I held out my hand. "Boone Moffatt," I said, introducing myself. "Chief of police for Franklin Notch."

He looked at me like he had a grudge. Three more guys walked over.

"So who's the sachem?" I asked.

"The what?"

"The sachem. You know, like Muttawump or Shoshanim. You guys are Sagawehs, aren't you?"

"Do you mean who's in charge?"

"Yeah," I said. "Who's the chief? Like me."

"She's not ready to see anybody yet. We're still setting up."

"Okay," I said. "I'll be back around seven o'clock tonight. A-won-o-tay-bet."

"What?"

"That's good-bye in Sagaweh," I said, walking away.

I didn't want to get into a confrontation until I knew what was going on, and I could see the news crews were taping our powwow. I also needed to make sure my family was safe, so I called Wes and told him not to leave the house. Then I called Beth.

"It's already on the news," she said. "What's happening?"

"It's a stunt to get public opinion on their side. I'm going back to the station to make some calls. I need some advice before I go back up there. Call me if anybody comes near the house, and don't open the door for any-one except family. I'll be home in a couple of hours."

As I drove down the mountain, I saw Wes coming up the road in his truck. When he saw me, he ducked into a side street, trying to outrun me in his '86 Ford. I put on my flashers and pulled him over.

"What the hell are you doing?"

"I want to see the teepees," he said.

"Well, you can't—not until I figure out what's going on. Go home and I'll call you when it's okay to come out. Go home or I'm going to lock you up."

He laughed. "Okay, okay," he said.

"I'm serious."

"I know. That's why it's funny."

As I drove to the station, I heard the Channel 6 helicopter flying up the valley.

I spent the day talking to the DA's office, the state police, and some guy from the Governor's Council for Indigenous Peoples.

"These aren't real Indians, you know," I told him.

"It doesn't matter," he said. "We can't appear to be insensitive to their demands."

Late afternoon, I drove past Wes and Sister's house. His truck was in the driveway, so I went home.

I watched the five o'clock news with Beth. The teepee protest was a big deal, and all the stations were calling it a camp-in. There were aerial shots of the village and interviews with experts on land rights and reparations.

The air was full of lightweight predictions and heavyweight buzzwords like Wounded Knee and Custer's Last Stand. People speculated on the terms and whereabouts of Talbert's Treaty.

I dressed for my meeting with Sarah Running Doe. No uniform—just jeans, boots, shirt, jacket, badge, and gun.

"Be careful," Beth said, hugging me.

"Piece of cake," I said. "I'll pick up some ice cream on the way back."

The ball fields looked like a movie set. Surrounding the circle of teepees was a clutter of RVs and news trucks with light towers and satellite dishes. There were snack wagons, ice cream trucks, and vendors selling T-shirts and plastic tomahawks. The slogan of the moment was GO TELL IT ON THE MOUNTAIN. Generators hummed, and people milled around as if they were at a county fair. The Channel 6 helicopter sat idle at the far end of the field, near the playground.

I parked the car at the edge of the road and walked through the media muddle unnoticed.

"Sorry I'm late," I said to the guard. "Let's go see the lady."

He announced me on his walkie-talkie, and two more guys showed up to escort me into the circle of teepees. A bonfire was burning in the middle of the village, and somebody was playing ZZ Top on a tape deck. "Tush."

There were fifty people standing around, looking surly—mostly late-twenties lock-and-load types. There were a few kids and an older guy with a ponytail in a wheelchair.

We walked to one of the teepees, and the guard waved me inside. He followed me and stood behind me in the doorway with his arms crossed.

The teepee was furnished like a small apartment. There was all-weather carpet, a small refrigerator, TV, bed, desk with a laptop and a cell phone in its charger. There was a roadcase with a pile of clothes on top.

A wide, tough-looking woman wearing jeans, a sweatshirt, and moccasins was sitting at the desk, typing on the laptop. She had thick black hair with reddish roots that was tied in braids. She pretended to ignore me; then she stood up and crossed her arms. She was wearing a heavy necklace made of imitation turquoise.

"Well?" she said.

"Are you Sarah Running Doe?"

"I am."

"I'm Daniel Moffatt, chief of police for Franklin Notch, and I'm serving notice that you are camped illegally on town land and that you have two hours to vacate the property."

"Daniel Boone Moffatt?" she said, smirking. "Aren't you named after the white devil Indian killer?"

"No, I believe you're thinking of Kit Carson. Daniel Boone was actually a nice guy. In any case, I wasn't named after him; it's just a nickname I picked up when I was a kid."

"Well, Mr. White Devil Indian Killer—we're not leaving. In fact, we're serving notice that you and half of your town are on property that still legally belongs to the Sagaweh Nation, and before this is over, you will be vacating our property. We're prepared to die for what is rightfully ours."

"Remember Ruby Ridge," said the man standing in the doorway behind me.

"I'm just telling you what the law says. You're trespassing on town land, and you have to leave."

"We're not leaving," Sarah Running Doe said again. "When the dust settles, there's gonna be bodies all over this mountain. We're going to own this whole town, and your idiot father is going to be shaking his fat ass for the brothers up in Longerville."

"We know where he lives," said the man.

I lost it. I spun and grabbed the guy by his jacket and backed him against the roadcase. "Listen, asshole," I said. "You can pretend to be anything you want, but you lay a finger on any member of my family and I will personally hunt you down and hurt you. Understand?"

He smiled. "Sure do, Indian killer."

I left the teepee village and walked to my car, shrugging off reporters along the way.

I went home and called Sister, making sure that Wes hadn't slipped out of the house again; then Beth and I watched the ten o'clock news.

The camp-in was the lead story on every station. We settled for Channel 6, broadcasting live from the ball fields.

The anchorman was wearing a fishing vest and a plaid shirt.

"Earlier tonight, the chief of police for Franklin Notch, who is ironically named Daniel 'Boone' Moffatt after the old frontier Indian fighter, and is also the son of controversial television personality and local historian Wes

Moffatt, served notice to the reparation rights activists that they were trespassing on town land. Channel 6 has obtained a videotape of the confrontation."

The camera had been hidden in the pile of clothes on top of the roadcase. The tape had been professionally edited.

I was standing in the middle of the teepee; Sarah Running Doe and the
guard were off-camera.

"I'm Daniel Moffatt," I said, "chief of police for Franklin Notch, and I'm
serving notice that you are camped illegally on town land and that you have
two hours to vacate the property."

Sarah Running Doe's voice comes from off-screen. "We don't want to
cause any trouble," she says. "We just want the chance for people to understand what we believe is the truth."

"I'm just telling you what the law says. You're trespassing on town land
and you have to leave."

Behind me, unseen, the man speaks. "Yeah," he says. "We just want the
freedom to explore our true identity as Native American patriots. Why
don't people believe us?"

The tape shows me spinning around, grabbing the guy and slamming
him against the roadcase, barely two feet away from the camera. I look like
a madman.

"Listen, asshole," I yell. "You can pretend to be anything you want, but
I will personally hunt you down and hurt you. Understand?"

They showed the doctored tape twice. When they finished, I had to lie
down. Beth disconnected the phone.

I didn't want to go to church the next morning. I didn't want to leave the
house. Wes and Sister came to pick us up. I thought twice before bringing the
map, but I didn't want it in the house in case anything bad happened to me.

We drove down the mountain to Main Street. The town was flooded
with strangers—fake Indians and newscasters everywhere. People were either talking into microphones or holding them.

We've been going to the same church since I was born. We sit in the
same pew every Sunday; we stand in the same spot in Fellowship Hall
every week after church, drinking coffee and talking with our friends. Today was different. I felt like a stranger, walking down the aisle to our pew.
Everybody was watching us; everybody was watching me.

Before the offertory, our pastor always asks for prayer requests. This morning, Sister stood and spoke.

"You all know us," she began. "We've lived in this town for fifty years. We've been good neighbors and good friends. Every Sunday we all sit together in this church and pray for goodness to overcome evil in the world, as if an imaginary battle was happening somewhere else. It's not. It's happening right here. For some reason, the Devil has chosen this moment and our little town to test our faith. Today, this place is the battleground between the darkness of confusion and the light of understanding.

"In my heart, I know everything is going to turn out fine, so I'm not asking anybody to pray for Wesley, Daniel, Beth, or me. I just want us to pray like we always do—for goodness to overcome evil in the world. This morning, I'm asking everybody to pray like we really mean it."

Sister started praying the Lord's Prayer in her clear quiet voice. No one joined her, except for Beth, Wes, and me. It sounded like the pastor was whispering from the pulpit, but I couldn't be sure, because the longer Sister prayed, the more fervent she became. By the time we got to "Thy will be done," her voice had reached a timbre and volume that filled the air with her swirling angels of war. The Army of Saints was on the march.

I looked at her hands clutching the pew in front of her. Her knuckles were white, her arms straining as if she were trying to pull the whole building upward, out of the earth itself. Her eyes were pinched shut, her face was twisted into a grimace of ecstasy.

"—the kingdom, and the power, and the glory forever. Amen."

Her loud, clear voice was still bouncing around the sanctuary when she sat down.

No one moved or breathed.

I held her hand. It was hot, vibrating as if a great engine were roaring inside her.

I was very proud of her, and ashamed I had carried Hell so close to my heart, so deep within her refuge of righteousness.

For the first time in fifty years, we skipped Coffee Hour. After church, we went to our homes. Wes watched baseball; Sister made brownies. Beth read a book; I went to bed and didn't wake up until the next day.

Monday morning, the attorney general's office called—some hotdog lawyer with his diploma up his ass.

"Chief Moffatt, the attorney general wanted me to touch base with you and make sure we're all reading from the same playbook. I guess you had some trouble down there last night."

"Not really. Just some people camping out on town land. They'll leave."

"We see that, but what's got the office a little bothered is the way you handled the situation—with the media. And just to keep you in the huddle, I thought you should know there's some talk this morning about an inquiry. You're all over the Internet, you know. It's pretty ugly."

"That was a doctored tape. The guy threatened my father."

"Well, it's making us a little nervous that we've got a chief of police who threatens Native Americans. This is a sensitive issue with the attorney general—civil rights and all that. Nobody wants to give the ball to someone who is going to throw it into the stands."

"What are you saying?"

"To be honest with you, there's some talk about bringing in a new team."

"State police?"

"Possibly, possibly. But what we really want is for you to make this happen. You know, see it doesn't go into extra innings."

"I'll keep my eye on the ball."

"That's what we want to hear. You know, everybody still talks about the time you popped Holy Hell."

"Thanks."

"I guess he's doing good over at Concord. Model prisoner, Bible studies, all the right stuff. Good report."

"I think it was a mistake," I said. "I've got a bad feeling about him."

"Then maybe you should have come to the hearing and mentioned it."

"I wanted to. I had a family emergency."

"Seems like you've got a lot of that lately. Hey, speaking of family, you're related to Reggie Moffatt, aren't you? The Voice of the Celtics?"

"He's my brother."

"We used to listen to him all the time—out at the quarry, slamming down Guinness, listening to the games on the car radio. Haven't heard much from him lately. Is he still in radio?"

"No. He lives in Orlando now."

"Retired? Good for him. I remember the night he called Kevin

McHale's wife nine miles of slippery road. We laughed our asses off. I guess they fired him for that one."

"No. Not that one."

"Well, anyway. When you see him, tell him people still ask about him."

"Thanks. I will."

18

Once upon a time, there was a beautiful princess who came from humble beginnings in a neglectful household, and through a series of serendipitous events involving a nationwide talent search and crystal footwear, she captured the heart of the ruling monarch—a young man who was willing to overlook her lack of pedigree for the rest of the package. They were married, and they governed their kingdom graciously for many years. They were loved by their subjects; even in their dotage they were an attractive couple who always drew a good crowd. After a storybook reign spanning decades, the king died, leaving his wife to rule their imaginary country alone. With no heirs to perpetuate her legacy, she transitioned the kingdom to a market-based hedonocracy and retired to one of her properties—an ostentatious fortress built incongruously in the middle of a Florida swamp, where she died a few years later and was carried to Heaven by unicorns to be reunited with her husband-king.

From the north came a man run aground by his own shallow pursuits. Homeless and penniless, he sought refuge in the moderate climate and enchanted protection of the queen's magic castle. He was a tired man, confused and lonely. Full of pride and selfishness, he had wandered far from the comfort of his kind and didn't know how to go home.

In the castle he discovered an empty storage closet with a small window. He scavenged a collection of essentials—a sleeping bag, a foam mattress, and clothing. He hid in his castle room, a brooding hermit regent, observing the world beneath him. At night he sat in his tower, watching the stars, reflecting on his own glimmering childhood and fading future. For many months he rested secretly in the safe haven of the magical kingdom, and as he pondered the wreckage of his graceless life he regained strength and found his peace of mind. He became wiser and magically younger. No longer depressed and self-destructive, he wanted to live happily ever after.

Reginald Anthony Moffatt woke up in his secret cell in the highest tower of Cinderella's Castle. It was a stone box of a room, just Reggie's size. Lying on his back with his arms outstretched, he could almost touch the walls with the four points of his body. On one side, a narrow window. Opposite, a door.

From somewhere deep in the castle a generator thumped, then hummed. It was Reggie's angelus, waking him every morning.

He floated up from sleep and lay on his back thinking. Eight months of solitude had taught him to meditate every morning on the first few notions that washed into his head.

In his old life, his waking thoughts had been carnal. Breakfast, money, sex. Now, without possessions or cravings to distract him, Reggie's mind was free to drift in the deeper currents of his life, and as he waited for the dawn in his Goofy sleeping bag, he considered his new course. Melancholy.

For the seventh morning straight—since the day he met with his stressed-out brother and worn-down sister—he woke up missing his family.

Missing his family was a reversal of desires, and difficult to reconcile. For forty-five years he had convinced himself he had risen above his upbringing—achieved dignity in spite of his family's sideshow image. My father is a clown, my mother is a fortune-teller, he complained when he was young. People laugh at us, and my parents don't care.

He was the normal Moffatt, he promised himself—the one who didn't look under the bed every night for Beelzebub, the one who didn't dress up like Johnny Tremain and recite the Bill of Rights at the drop of a musket. I'm okay, he told himself. I'm not miserable like my mousy sister or completely oblivious like my great waddling boob of a dad.

I can't believe I live with these people.

Remember? Our house was chaos. Wes was always knee-deep in some useless project, and Sister lived by her stupid convent clock. Everything that went wrong was the Devil's fault. Look out now, old Mr. Sticks is screwing with the Dodge again. God forgive me for this, God forgive me for that.

Just my luck—getting these two as parents. Pippi Longstocking and Smokey the Bear. What a freak show. Marriage made in Heaven, my ass. Marriage arranged by Ripley's is more like it. Sure, they got along, but who else would have either one of them? Wes couldn't keep two thoughts straight at the same time, and Sister couldn't let go of one in a week. He couldn't say no, and she couldn't say yes without asking twelve saints first.

Do you remember how you could be talking to Sister about something important and she would get that dreamy little look and disappear into her closet for an hour to pray?

Remember when she had one of her visions at the movies and had to run home to call LBJ on the phone?

How about the time she made Boone climb the water tower and write some Latin gibberish four feet high in gold paint?

And those bedtime stories? Who tells their kids how their lives are going to turn out every night before they go to sleep? I didn't sign up for the Army of Saints.

Poor Wes—so open-minded his brains had leaked out of his skull.

Poor Veronica. She'll probably give the undertaker a hard time.

Poor Boone, the universal mule.

It's a miracle I turned out normal, he always told himself. After all, I'm the famous sportscaster. If it weren't for me, this family would be wards of the state.

Sweet Jesus, get me outta this nuthouse.

But now, after eight months of solitude in his eight-by-eight room, Reggie missed his family, and he wanted to go home—not to the house of his brutally helpless wife; he wanted to return to the haven of his birth, blood, and soul—to his parents' home on top of the ridge.

Eight months of being alone had merely made him lonely. Now he remembered the good things, and he missed them all.

Remember the time Wes filled the bed of his pickup truck with water and drove the neighborhood kids around town in a portable swimming pool? Remember how he took me and all my friends out of school every year for Opening Day at Fenway? Remember Sister's backyard Easter egg hunts for every kid in Franklin Notch?

Remember Veronica's field hospital in the barn, full of wounded animals? And the time Boone drove to Boston in a nor'easter to bail me out?

I took it all for granted.

The day after Carolyn tossed me, Sister came to see me at the Days Inn.

She sat on the bed and tried to pray with me. I got mad, stomped out, and drove around for two hours until I was sure she had gone home. When I came back, I found one hundred dollars in the motel Bible. That was the last time I saw my mother.

I was so ungrateful.

I cheated on Carolyn at least twice a week for twenty years straight. I spent more money on hookers than I did on home improvement. I was making ninety grand a year and bouncing mortgage checks. They repo'd Carolyn's car three times.

I wiped out Theresa's college account, betting on the Rockets in the '86 playoffs. For her sixteenth birthday, I gave her passes to a Nets game and a Hooters T-shirt. I actually thought that was funny. What the hell's wrong with me? I don't even know my own daughter.

When I was a kid I stole everything that wasn't nailed down. When my mother went into her closet to pray, I pawed through her purse for cigarette money.

I told all my friends that my sister had herpes.

I took Boone's car and totaled it in the creek. I never paid him back, and how many nights did he let me crash on his sofa because I was too drunk to go home?

I thought I could get away with anything.

Remember the night we were snowed in with the team in Detroit and I hurt that girl in the parking garage at the Sheraton? Five grand and four days later, the cops finally let me leave Michigan. I missed the next two games, and when I caught up with the team in Seattle, I got so loaded that I wrecked the rental—drove it into the back of a street sweeper, four in the morning.

I bogeyed expense accounts, bolted checks, stiffed cabbies, and shoplifted like a junkie—but it was okay; I was Reggie Moffatt, Nashua's Voice of the Celtics, King of the Granite State Airwaves. When I spoke, thousands of people heard my voice. I sat high above the playgrounds of giants. I described the motions of stars. We were the greatest—Champions of the World. Number One, and I traveled with the team. I won awards. I was engraved on plaques. My name would live forever.

What a poser.

My first year in the booth, 1984. I was Mr. Stats, the new guy with the instant recall, the guy who knew everything about everybody in the league. Bird: Forty-nine percent from the floor, seventy-nine games, *ten-point-four* rebounds per game. Kareem Abdul-Jabbar: Fifty-*eight* percent, eighty games. Magic Johnson, fifty-seven.

I was obsessed with the locker-room life. I had to be seen with the team. If someone aimed a camera at one of the boys, I had to be in the background, acting like a player. I ate where they ate, shared the same flights, and weaseled my way onto the team bus like a cheap groupie. I dropped names like spare change. To hear me talk, you'd think Red Auerbach couldn't dress himself in the morning without consulting me first.

I was so selfish.

Half-whacked on Stackers and blow, I called my own father an idiot on national television.

"Well, folks, we've got a new face in the booth tonight for the pregame rundown. Reggie Moffatt, from one of our fine New England stations, WNAU, is helping out with the play-by-play. Welcome to ESPN, Reggie. It's always good to have a fresh face in the booth."

"Thanks, Matt. It's a real pleasure to be here."

"So, Reggie, I hear you come from a long tradition of broadcasting. Isn't your father a fixture on the local cable scene back in New Hampshire?"

"He's been around."

"Isn't he the one who got everybody in town to run outside and make moose noises in the middle of the night?"

"Yep. That's my idiot old man."

Pucker up, asshole, and kiss the career good-bye.

Reggie slid out of his sleeping bag. His window faced east. He sat cross-legged in the spot where the sun would appear and bathe him slowly with the day's first light, from his aura to his half-lotus feet. Reggie closed his eyes and savored the sound of sweet morning air rushing through the center of his body, the tidal flow of life all around, within him.

Reggie imagined his parents far to the north, rising to the light of the same day. Sister would be kneeling at the window of her little chapel, in the sunlight herself, saying her morning prayers. Wes would be in the kitchen, making breakfast, trying not to make any noise. He would carry a cup of lemon-honey tea to his wife.

Reggie wanted to be there with his parents, but like a dream, the scene seemed a lost and distant hope.

I want to go back, he thought, and not just for the party. I want to go back to the way it could have been before I screwed it up with my snotty demands, tacky fights, insults, and sabotage. I want to give back the money and take back the lies.

I want to tell everybody I'm sorry. I'm sorry for all the times I lied to my mother and ridiculed my father. I'm sorry I treated my brother like hired help and my sister like an insect.

"I'm sorry," he said, alone in his cell. Sadly for himself, it simply sounded lonely.

Who am I kidding? After all the bullshit I've pulled, how could they ever forgive me? I've done too much damage, hurt too many people, and it would be an insult to show up for their party. I've got nothing to offer. Nothing but sorry. Here's poor Reggie again—worse off than ever and looking for a place to crash. Sorry Reggie. Sorry, Reggie.

How could I ask for that much forgiveness? How could anyone forgive me?

During his first few weeks in Cinderella's Castle, Reggie stayed in his room, sleeping on the concrete floor, slipping outside only at night to forage and explore. He fished day-old pastries out of hotel dumpsters and filled empty soda bottles with water from the men's-room sinks.

He needed to rest. Life, and the bus trip south, had taken everything out of him.

He was in terrible shape. His boyish face was thick and pulpy, and his nose looked like a sponge. Twenty-five years of heavy smoking and drinking had soaked his greasy flesh heavy with poisons. Big-boned like his dad, he weighed 285 pounds when he hit Florida. His tallow skin hung from his bones like suet, his jowls sagged, and his bloated neck looked like a pig's ass in a girdle. He had trouble breathing and he hated the way he had to heave himself out of the car, out of bed, out of a restaurant booth. His pinkish eyes were always crusty, and the knuckles of his right hand were scorched from his endless battery of burning Luckies. His thinning hair was sloughing off his mottled scalp, he had eczema on his elbows and a case of jock itch older than his daughter. Only forty-five years old, he already smelled like death with a dose of Right Guard.

Sweat soaked his collars and dripped down his back. The armpits of his undershirts were perma-stained yellow; the waistbands of his trousers curled under the spread of his gut, and all his pants were threadbare where his thighs chafed.

His ankles were weak, he had sores on his ass, and his back hurt. He hadn't seen his penis in nine years. It didn't matter; after he moved to the Days Inn and started drinking all day, he couldn't even rise to the pay-porn.

When he wasn't sleeping, Reggie spent his days sitting in his castle room with his flabby back against the cool cement, watching the sunshine rhombus slide across the floor, bend up the wall, then fade to gray at the close of the day. Without smokes or alcohol, he was paranoid-jumpy, holding his breath at every sound, preparing to look flustered if the door ever opened. For three weeks he sat in the same corner, eating his foraged food, staring at the floor and the window, picking at his cuticles, and trying to imagine what comes next.

When he was tired, he slept. When he craved a smoke or a drink, he did without; and cell by cell, his body began healing itself. His kidneys, his marrow, his liver, and his lungs strained to drain the poisons from his body.

High in his secret retreat, Reggie soaked up the sun and the rare citrus air, and he heard the sounds of happy families playing in the park beneath him. Like pilgrims at a shrine, they circled the base of the castle, glorifying and praising its majesty. Worship and wonder filled the air, floating up to the highest tower, where the broken man sat with his back to the wall.

Amazing alchemy. Magic and medicine, the powers combined. The empty man filled like a vessel with goodwill and good health; then, miraculously, his decline reversed.

In the beginning, Reggie didn't realize he was getting younger. He thought he was just losing weight; he thought his hair was getting longer, not necessarily thicker, and his eyesight was improving simply because he was sleeping more.

He thought the liver spots on the backs of his hands had faded into his tan and he was breathing easier because he couldn't afford cigarettes.

After six weeks of solitude, something interesting popped up. Reggie woke up with an erection. Lying on his back, he looked down the pasty dough-pile of his slightly diminished belly at the curious crown winking above his gutscape.

"Hey, old buddy," he said, giving it a good handshake.

Afterward, he went for a walk—his first daylight trip outside the castle. He stopped by Lost and Found and claimed some clothes that fit him better; then he wandered around in the Florida sun, mingling with the wide-eyed tourists, digging the Disney vibe. He watched the walkabout characters, fascinated with the effect that real people in costume versions of imaginary figures had on other real people. Tourists stopped cold in their tracks, then lit up with rapture when they saw another person dressed like a drawing of a mouse.

Reggie sat in a rocking chair on the porch of the hospitality center and watched the giddy crowds. A girl in ragtime gear served him a free lemonade. "Enjoy yourself," she said.

This was a new day, with definite changes in body and soul. Reggie felt lighter, relaxed, and less confused. He had come south to hide, perhaps to die. Improving his condition was the last thing he expected—but he did feel better. He felt slightly purified, sanctified by the solitude and invigorated by his wake-up tune-me-up. With some effort, who knew what could happen if he tried to get in shape? How good could he feel?

Beginning that morning, Reggie reversed directions. His retreat became an advance. He decided to get healthy.

It started with the water. That night, Reggie found the ground-floor room where the five-gallon plastic jugs of spring water were stored. He swiped a bottle and carried it to the foot of the stairwell, calculating its weight as he caught his breath on the bottom step. A pint is a pound the world 'round. Forty pints, forty pounds. Piece of cake.

He picked up the jug and bow-legged himself up the staircase, his gut and thighs straining against his size 48 Levi's. He went ten steps before he stopped, waiting for the tunnel vision and buzzing to recede.

It took him over an hour to haul the five-gallon jug of water sixteen flights of stairs. This is pathetic, he told himself, lying on the hard floor of his little room, oozing grease like sausage on a grill.

The next day was worse. He blanked out on the sixth floor.

He drank spring water and ate raw foods stolen from salad bars at the hotels. After three weeks he noticed that his clothes fit loosely and his thighs didn't chafe from his crotch to his knees when he walked. He could do one hundred push-ups, one hundred sit-ups, then run in place for twenty minutes without losing his breath. He did his little workouts eight times a day. The haze in his head cleared, and his urine didn't smell like sewage anymore.

One week later, he could jog sixteen flights of stairs without stopping, holding a forty-pound jug of water over his head.

The age spots on his forehead faded; his arms and legs trimmed and toned. All over his body, his skin tightened. He lost his jowly look and his stomach went flat. He hung out at the employee health center, lifting weights and pounding the cardio gear. He made friends with people in their early thirties; he joined the racquetball club and placed third in the young singles employee tournament.

"How old do you think I am?" he asked when asked.

"You look great for thirty-four," everybody said.

Between exercise and sleep he sat at his window, watching the sky and the crowds below, meditating on his renaissance.

This was fun. This was more fun than the first time he was young. He tossed paper airplanes out of his castle window, taught himself how to yodel and throw the boomerang. He stayed up late and played the harmonica, read poetry, and kept a journal. He went to bed happy and he woke up relaxed. At night, he helped the trash crew, driving golf carts around the park at three in the morning. He hadn't carried money for three months.

He spent a lot of time eavesdropping. Grownup conversation bored him. Money and envy, medication and sex. I can't believe I used to be one of these guys, he said.

Now that he was young and had most of his life ahead of him, he needed to think about a career. He admired the Disney walkabouts, the people who roamed the park dressed as cartoon icons—secret celebrities with a license for silliness. It would be the perfect job. Now that I'm younger, he asked himself, who can I be?

Reggie's three-piece costume hung from hooks on the back of his door. He had made the head and most of the suit from fabrics and foam scavenged from a Dumpster behind Productions. The shoes were modified hiking boots, and the pants were made of loose-fitting washed denim padded with foam around the belly and butt.

His jacket was a new barn coat he found in the parking lot. He sewed pads of foam into the sides to give his character some bulk and make him look heavier, older, harmless, and common. Seven months ago, this jacket would have been too tight; these days, it hung loose on his lanky frame. He had a gray slouch hat that matched the jacket perfectly.

The head was made of foam, polyester, and cotton. The face was a slightly larger-than-life caricature of a happy, fleshy middle-aged man with a monklike bald spot, round spectacles, and a bushy white mustache. He had a wrinkled laughing face with a wide grin, friendly blue eyes, and one eyebrow higher than the other. He looked like a cross between Gepetto and Jed Clampett.

Compared to most of the Disney walkabouts, Reggie's costume head was closer to normal size and the features were more human-looking. Instead of a person dressed to look like an animated character, he looked like a cartoon man trying to pass for a human being—a friendly older guy, slightly overweight and completely harmless. He looked like a gardener or a Lit professor.

Reggie finished dressing for work. He pulled the pants up around his thin waist, picked up his head, set it on his shoulders, and adjusted it so his eyes were aligned with the small black screens behind the spectacles. He tucked the excess fabric of the head into the collar of his jacket, then shrugged himself around inside the suit, enjoying the way it felt, all loose and cozy.

By nine thirty, the crowd noises had grown louder below Reggie's castle window. Beneath him, visitors were wandering around the kingdom, eager for an audience.

He did a shuffly little dance, then lumbered out the door.

A crowd gathered around him as soon as he walked into the sunlight at the base of the castle. There were children and grownups, older couples, and a group of people wearing light blue polo shirts who were pushing a convoy of wheelchairs across the footbridge.

Reggie went for the wheelchairs. He stood in the middle of the bridge and raised his hand like a traffic cop. The wheelchairs stopped, and Reggie paraded back and forth in front of them like a mime general addressing his troops; then he marched to the first chair, took the handles, and wheeled a young girl twisted with palsy to the bronze statue of Walt and Mickey, where he pretended to introduce them. Reggie picked a flower for the girl, then went down on one knee, performing a proposal to her.

"Hey, look," said a woman to her two children. "There's that guy from that movie, you know, that movie you like? You know, that funny guy who plays the dad who always messes things up."

"Oh, yeah," said one of the kids vaguely. They ran over and gave Reggie a big hug.

He wandered around Fantasyland, dancing with grandmas, doing loopy little skits for the babies, high-fiving the teenagers, and goofing on the middle-aged men.

The middle-aged guys were his favorites—the ones who were happy to look bored or impatient. When he found one standing by himself with his arms crossed and scowling at his family, Reggie would stand behind him and imitate his pose. If he looked at his watch, Reggie looked at his own wrist and sighed. If the guy took out his wallet, Reggie would pretend to count money and act like he was in pain. When the rube finally caught on, he usually perked up, happy to be the center of attention. If not, Reggie tried to get him to play air guitar or slo-mo football or challenge him to a quick-draw shootout.

If the guy wouldn't budge from his funk, Reggie would simply follow him and mimic his every move until the poor bastard escaped into a building.

Inside the costume head, Reggie's field of vision was limited to the area in front of his shoulders, and his biggest fear was falling over someone shorter than himself. He learned to perform in front of buildings with big windows so he could watch himself and his immediate surroundings, and as he watched his own reflection mugging and dancing in his costume, he felt a quirky Zen distance between the reflection, the suit, and himself inside. He felt like a loose spirit, free to inhabit any host.

He was doing the Twist in front of the Tomorrowland snack bar, watching himself in the windows, when he noticed a girl standing behind him. He saw her again, spying on him, reflected in a gift shop window on Main Street. In Frontierland, he caught her eye as she stood by herself around the corner of a toolshed.

She had a round face, clever eyes, glasses, shoulder-length hair, and a big-boned body still soft with baby fat. She was wearing a grey Pluto sweatshirt, jeans, and a different hat each time she showed up. She had a pleasant quizzical look about her. Reggie guessed she was thirteen years old.

He couldn't place her with anybody. She was by herself in Tomorrowland, but on Main Street she appeared with a collection of kids being shoved around by four women wearing DARE sweatshirts. Later, Reggie saw her having lunch with a large Asian family, and in Fantasyland she had her picture taken sitting on a bench eating french fries with an older couple.

All day, she popped into Reggie's field of vision. He saw her standing under an awning at Splash Mountain with an older boy. She poked the boy and pointed at Reggie. The boy said something, and they both laughed. Later in the day, she waved as she rode past on a courtesy cart with a guy who looked like Mickey Rooney.

It seemed like she was stalking him, teasing him, placing herself near enough to let him know she was wise to his scam.

By late afternoon, Reggie was intrigued enough to reach out. He saw her standing in a crowd of kids wearing City Year T-shirts and motioned her over, miming an invitation to waltz.

She came to him, eyebrow cocked and smirking.

"You're not real," she said as they danced.

"Yes, I am."

"Oh, yeah? What movie are you from?"

"The one where the dad always screws up and the kids have to bail him out."

"That's every Disney movie ever made. I know you're not real."

"How can you tell?"

"You're not fake enough to be real."

"So this can be our secret, right?" Reggie said.

"Sure. I don't care. I think it's funny."

He twirled the girl. She was smiling. Just a kid.

"Are you here with your parents?"

"No thanks."

"Where are they?"

"Skiing. In Colorado."

"And they left you here alone?"

"Not really. They don't know where I am."

"So how did you get here?"

"I took the train. Amtrak doesn't check IDs."

"You took the train from where?"

"New York."

"New York? How old are you?"

"Thirteen."

"You took the train from New York to Florida all by yourself?"

"Sure. I take trains all the time—all over town. What's the difference?"

"About fifteen hundred miles."

"Not a big deal," she said. "It's just another train. I come down here every time my parents go away."

"By yourself?"

She nodded. "But this can be our secret, right?"

"I suppose," Reggie said. "And they don't care?"

"If somebody found out, they'd care. Otherwise."

"What do you mean?"

"I mean they're not going to take me to Colorado, and they never check on me anyway. I can do whatever I want as long as it doesn't get out and make them look like bad parents."

"They told you that?"

"They don't have to. That's the rules. It's cool; they don't like me anyway."

"I'm sure they do."

"They don't. They told me. I'm too fat. But I'm smarter than they are, so they're actually kinda scared of me."

"Where do they think you are?"

"Home."

"Alone?"

"With my sister. She's sixteen, but she's gone, too."

"Is she here?"

"Nope. She went to Bermuda with her boyfriend. He's thirty-two. She's really pretty."

"What if your parents call?"

"Cell phones," she said. "I could be in the kitchen, I could be in Cancun."

"Right. Where do you stay?"

"Here. With a friend. He lives here, in the park. He's a shadow."

"A shadow?"

"That's what they call themselves. They find places to live behind the scenes. He made an apartment out of one of those old submarines from *20,000 Leagues Under the Sea*. It's actually really cool. He's even got a TV. He's kinda messed up, though. He thinks he's that guy from *The Matrix*. I shouldn't be telling you all this."

"So how long has your friend been living here?"

"As long as I've known him. A year, maybe more. There's a whole bunch of them."

"Shadows?"

"Yeah. They live all over the park. It's mostly kids, but there's a lot of grownups, too. One guy has been here twenty years. He's like a legend. Nobody has ever seen him. I guess he used to be a famous guitar player or something. Most of the older ones never come out, but I know all the kids. I know this girl who lives inside one of the Swiss Family Robinson trees, and there's a guy who's got a two-bedroom apartment that he built in the Haunted Mansion. He's got plumbing, a sofa, the whole deal."

"That's ambitious."

"Actually, I think it's kind of pathetic."

"Why?"

"Well, basically these people act like it's so profound to survive without doing anything. The fact is, they wouldn't be here if there wasn't so much free stuff to pick up on. I mean, if Disney World wasn't here, do you think they'd all be living together in a cornfield in the middle of Florida? The only thing they have in common is nothing. The only friends they have are other people who don't have any friends or family, either. Can we stop dancing?"

"Sure. Sorry. Let's walk. I've got to keep moving," Reggie said.

"Like a violation."

Reggie laughed. "You're a very smart person."

"I know. Everybody always underestimates me."

They walked up Liberty Lane. Reggie waved to the tourists and did his shuffly little two-step.

"Don't you feel silly?" she asked.

"Not really. It's not me they're laughing at, it's the character."

"What do you mean, it's not you? That suit jumps around by itself?"

"People aren't laughing at me. They can't see me."

"But you can see them."

"Yeah. So?"

"So why are you hiding from the people you're trying to get close to?"

Something about the question bothered Reggie.

"I don't know. I guess it would look weird if I was doing this without the costume."

"Makes you think, doesn't it?" she said.

He stopped dancing and walked in a straight line.

"What do you look like?" she asked.

"I'm a middle-aged guy."

"Like thirty-something?"

"Sort of. I'm actually younger than I used to be. This place makes me younger."

"I know what you mean," she said. "I used to be nineteen."

Reggie stopped and looked down at her.

"Just kidding," she said. "I used to be twelve." She laughed.

"I think you're a little old for your age, actually."

"Thanks," she said. "I decided a long time ago not to hold anything back. Hey, we're having a party tonight. You ought to come and hang out with us."

"Who?"

"Me and Steven and a few friends. We're meeting on the boat in Pirates of the Caribbean. You can get us beers."

"No."

"Why not?"

"I don't drink anymore."

"That's cool, I guess. I think we're all set anyway. Somebody's getting a bunch of stuff from the Hilton. So stop by. You can meet some shadows."

"Yeah, I might. Where do I go?"

"Come to the maintenance side of Pirates at ten o'clock. I'll be there."

"What's your name?" he asked. "I'm Reggie."

"Gracie," she said. "Gracie Jellico."

"Gracie? Pretty name."

"Thanks. I'm named for the mansion. My dad's supposed to be mayor someday." She shrugged and pushed her glasses up with her finger. "Can't hardly wait," she said, rolling her eyes.

They shook hands, and Gracie walked away. She stood by herself for a moment, then sauntered into the center of some Muslims.

Reggie went back to his room. Now it all seemed slightly shabby and predictable. How special was this new life of his, now that he knew he was part of some subterranean squatters' community? How many people had run away from real life and settled unseen, behind the scenes in this place? How many like himself were here now, wandering around the park? Twenty? Thirty? One hundred shadows? Enough to make the place a little darker, anyway.

Friends without friends or family; the ultimate lonely trip.

It made him feel like a cliché, and it made him tired to think about it. He took off his costume, lay down on his mat, and closed his eyes. He wouldn't go to the party.

As Reggie slept, he dreamed two dreams. The first was a wishful fantasy; the second, a forgotten wish.

He is at his parents' house in New Hampshire, in the small three-bedroom Cape where he was raised.

It is morning.

Wes is making breakfast while Sister prays in the bedroom. Reggie is sitting at the kitchen table, watching his father and drinking coffee.

"How many eggs, Reg?"

"Two or three. Thanks, Dad."

The sun is shining through the bay window in the breakfast nook. The shelves in the window are loaded with house plants, statuettes of saints, and rows of sports trophies. Shadows and sunlight stretch across the table-top. Among the shadows of vines and flowers are silhouettes of narrow men with raised crosses and chesty boys offering laurel leaves and footballs to the morning light.

"Hey," says Wes. "What did the baby chick say when the hen fell asleep on the fruit basket?"

"I don't know."

"Oh, look at the orange marmalade."

Reggie is waiting for his brother to show up. They are borrowing their father's old truck to pick up two loads of firewood. It's a whole-day affair, driving ten miles to the woodlot, splitting and loading it themselves to save a few bucks. They will drop a cord at their sister's house, have lunch with Veronica and Jessie, then pick up another load for the woodstove in the barn.

This is a boyhood tradition, fetching the family's winter wood together. The brothers still argue over the truck keys and who splits the most oak. It's little things like this that keep them connected and close.

"I wonder where Danny is," Wes says. "It's not like him to be late. Actually, I hope he takes his time; I never get to spend time alone with you. So how's work?"

"Pretty good," Reggie says. "They offered me a promotion. They want me to be director of program integration for the local affiliates. I'll be making deals. Not just the Celts, but the Sox, the Bruins, everybody."

"Hey, that's great. But aren't you going to miss the road? You know, traveling with the team?"

"I'll tell you the truth, Dad, it's a younger man's job. It's time to move up and make room for the kids. I don't even care about the money, I just want to spend more time at home."

"I know that's going to make your mother happy. Maybe you and Carolyn will work things out."

"We'll see," says Reggie. "So, how are you doing?"

"Not so good," says Wes. "I've got myself pretty jammed up with this

Indian treaty business. These lawyers are squeezing me to prove things against myself, and I feel like I'm trapped in bad versions of my own stories. The worst part is the way everybody treats me now. I'm not funny anymore. I'm just a fool."

"How can I help?"

"I don't think anyone can help," Wes says. "I really stepped in it this time, and I don't know what to do. I've got Sister praying for miracles."

Wes brings breakfast to the table. "Just the way you like it," he says, setting a plate in front of Reggie. He sits across the table and wiggles his eyebrows.

"I don't know why this coffee tastes like mud," he says. "It was ground this morning."

In the second dream, Reggie is twelve years old, lying in bed and waiting for his mother to finish praying across the hall with his sister. His brother pretends to be asleep on the other side of the room they share.

"Hello, my favorite child," says his mother, sitting on the edge of his bed. "You know you are my favorite, my angel, and I love you so much more than my other children. Anything you want, anything that catches your eye, anything you favor—no matter how trivial, I'll get it for you, my favorite. Just ask, and I will drop everything to keep you happy.

"Now here is the story of your future: For your whole life you will be entitled to do anything you want—no matter how selfish—and you will never be punished. Little King, Little King, Little King. Gifts, gifts, and more gifts. Little King, Angel of Grace, gifts, gifts, and more gifts. Do you want anything right now? Just say the word and I'll get it for you, my favorite child."

"Hold it," says Reggie in his dream. "Is that what you usually say?"

"No, my love, it's not," says his mother. "And it's a shame you can't remember what I really said when you were a boy, because you could use the advice now. I wish you had paid more attention to your bedtime story when you were younger, because today is the day I was talking about. Good luck."

It was night when Reggie woke up. For a long time, he lay in the dark room, struggling with his unsettled conscience, wishing he could go home.

At ten o'clock he was hiding in a line of shrubs behind the Pirates of the Caribbean building. I can't believe I'm going to a party with twelve-year-old kids, he thought. If I get any younger, I'll be back in day care.

Behind him, a door opened and he scooted inside.

"What's the password?" Gracie asked.

"I don't know."

"You're right," she said. "Follow me and don't fall off the pipes."

They crouched through a four-foot-high utility tunnel jammed with conduit, cables, and wires. Bent at the waist and pressing his hands against the narrow walls for balance, Reggie eased his way into the darkness on a six-inch pipe.

"These wires have millions of volts of electricity," she said. "And we're thousands of feet above a cavern lined with razor-sharp spikes. I'm trying to make this more interesting."

They crab-walked twenty feet and went through a doorway into a large, dark room the size of a gymnasium. There was a life-size replica of a pirate ship floating in shallow water next to a mock-up shoreline of a Mediterranean village. There were mannequins of pirates frozen in postures of slapstick revelry on the shore and on the ship. Except for red exit signs every fifty feet, the room was dark. Reggie thought he saw cigarettes glowing ahead of them on the deck of the pirate ship.

He followed Gracie across the set to a wide wooden ramp that ran up the backside of the fake boat. Reggie walked onto the deck. It was laced with wires, hydraulic equipment, and half-dressed mechanical pirates.

"Watch the generator," somebody said.

On the far side of the ship, a dozen people—mostly young—were sitting on lawn chairs, drinking beer and whiskey from Styrofoam cups, smoking cigarettes and weed. A CD player was on.

A thin boy, fourteen or fifteen years old, wobbled to his feet, came to Gracie, and gave her a hug. He looked at Reggie over her shoulder.

"Anybody follow you?" he asked.

"Don't be so paranoid, Steven," Gracie said.

Reggie shook hands with him. He was dressed in black and was wearing black leather gloves and a cape.

"The circle widens. Our influence grows," the boy said. "Welcome to our world." He swept his arm dramatically toward the dark room around them.

"Just visiting," Reggie said, already regretting the evening.

"We are all visitors in this sphere," the boy said.

"You're all visceral in your sphincter," Gracie said, punching him on the arm.

Reggie made his way to the crowd in the bow of the boat and introduced himself. There were a couple of people in their thirties, but most were younger—late teens, early twenties. They all looked like homeless tourists; everyone was wearing lost-and-found trademarked Disney gear—sweatshirts, denim jackets, baseball hats. They were sitting on Disney director's chairs, smoking with Disney lighters, and carrying Disney backpacks. They were talking about investments.

"I wouldn't buy Disney stock," said a skinny man with stringy blond hair and no teeth on his upper gums. "The way it goes—up and down, up and down—you'd lose all your seed money. That's the part about investing that nobody understands. Once you lose your seed money, you're pretty much fucked."

"Just like everything else," said a pasty-white girl with a nasty scab on her nose.

"And that's the problem I had from back in Indiana," continued the skinny guy. "I didn't have no seed money per se, but I had an investment partner who was like family to me, and my fucking brother goes and tells him all about some shit I got myself involved in years ago—and it wasn't even my fault—and the next thing I know they're opening up a car detailing franchise down in Evansville together, or somewhere. Shit."

"What are you gonna do?" said a heavyset guy who was sitting on the floor drinking Robitussin and rum out of a Lion King thermos. "Seriously."

Reggie looked across the ship and saw Gracie trying to squirm away from the boy in black. He had his arm around her neck, and she was pushing on his chest with both hands.

Reggie walked over.

"Everything okay?" he asked, in a voice that reminded him of his own brother.

"Not really," said Gracie, straightening her glasses.

"Why don't you come over here for a little while?" Reggie said, taking her arm and leading her away.

"I think I will," she said. "Gladly."

"I'm leaving," Steven said. "Are you coming, Mafia princess?"

"No."

The boy made a gesture, sawing his fist with the edge of his other hand, then trailed the backs of his thumbs across his eyelids.

"Destiny is an unfathomable lover," he said.

"You're an idiot," said Gracie.

"You're not all that smart."

"Yes I am," she said.

Reggie took her to the other side of the boat.

"Why do you come down here?" he asked her. They were drinking Diet Cokes from a Scrooge McDuck cooler.

"Because I get lonely," the girl said. "I'm not happy anywhere."

Reggie looked at the child and wondered if his own Theresa ever felt too lonely to stay home.

"I'm not, either," Reggie said. "I thought I was."

"Now I wish I was home."

"Me, too."

"Do you have kids?" she asked.

"Yeah, a daughter."

"I'll bet you were a good dad."

"I wasn't. Now, I think I could be. But no second chances, huh?"

"You're so wrong. If my dad came back from Colorado tonight and wanted to take me out for a hot pretzel, I swear to God I would love him for the rest of my life."

It was the saddest thing Reggie had ever heard, and he groaned beneath the rush of grief like it was his last breath, and then he started crying. The sadness smothered him before he could bow his head, and so he cried standing, looking straight out into the near-darkness of the fake lagoon. The misery of loss poured out of him in heaving waves, and he gripped the edge of the boat as forty-five years of confusion and selfishness swept through him like a cold fire. He cried for every person he had used, pushed aside, and forgotten, and every moment he had manipulated for his own fleeting gratification. He cried like a man buried before dying. He cried for his life.

The girl leaned against him, unsure.

"I'm sorry," she said. "What do you want to do?"

"I don't know," he cried. "I don't know. I'm such a fuckup. I need to get out of here."

"Where do you want to go? Do you want to go home?"

He nodded. She put her hand on his back.

"Come on," she said. "I'll take you home."

He dried his eyes, and she led him off the boat by his sleeve.

They were halfway through the utility tunnel when the lights went on.

"What's happening?" Gracie asked.

Reggie was close to the inside door, so he opened it an inch and looked back at the pirate ship.

"Wo," he said, shutting the door. "There's Security and cops all over the place in there."

Inside the building, the roundup had begun. The lights were on, and men in Security windbreakers were chasing shadows around the room, herding them into a corner near the control booth. A few of the bold ones had bailed off the side of the pirate ship and were slogging their way through the shallow water toward the exits. Two crews of Security guys were circling them in inflatable boats.

"What do we do?" Gracie asked.

Reggie looked down the short tunnel. On the floor at the far end was an air-conditioning unit with a removable metal front piece. He put Gracie beside the unit and pulled off the cover. He set it in front of her, hiding her from the sightlines of both doors. He unscrewed the overhead light and climbed behind the little barricade with the girl.

"I'm dead," Gracie said. "If I get busted in Florida, I'm dead."

"Pretend you're a kid and this is hide-and-seek."

"I am a kid."

"Well, pretend you're invisible."

They sat in the darkness, holding the panel and listening to the commotion in the big room. There were loud voices and heavy things being pushed around. The door to the tunnel opened twice and someone leaned inside, sweeping it with a flashlight.

After a few hours Security had captured all the shadows, and the cleanup crew appeared. A maintenance guy poked his head into the tunnel and flipped the light switch a couple of times.

"Let's go," Gracie said, grabbing Reggie by the hand and leading him outside, into the morning light.

They huddled between two dumpsters.

"What are you going to do now?" Gracie asked.

"I'm going home," Reggie said. "I've got a lot of apologies to make. How about you?"

"Me, too, and I'm going to sleep for a week."

Reggie looked worried.

"What's wrong?" she asked.

"I don't have any money. I have to hitchhike back."

"Ride with me." She opened her wallet. "I've got my credit card," she said, showing him. "I'll pay. It'll be my gift."

Reggie looked at the name on the card.

Grace D'Angelico.

19

He was in good shape when he came to the Concord facility, and he volunteered for every physical job on the daily work sheet. When he had gained their trust, he asked for permission to start a garden. Permission granted, and every morning, after he signed out a shovel, a rake, and a wheelbarrow, he went to work on his flowerbed.

Every day, before he started digging, he sat cross-legged on the lawn, reading his Bible and praying for half an hour. He took a Bible break at noon, and another at two o'clock, before he returned his tools to the shed.

It was a nine-by-twelve plot that he dug up and filled with soft, dark loam. He placed his flowerbed behind the hospital, across the sidewalk from the back of the building, but still fifty feet inside the high brick wall with the barbed wire on top. The sun was better, he said, and the bed was far enough away—thirty feet or more from the back of the building—so the shade of the four-story facility covered it for only an hour in late afternoon. Someone standing in the second-floor supply room could look out the narrow window and see him directly below, digging the bed six feet deep, making what he called a French planter.

"Several reasons for digging it so deep," he explained. "I want it to last a long time, so I'm purging the soil of weeds and trash. Some of the plants I'm growing have deep root systems—like gladiolas. When I water it, I want to nourish the whole system."

A couple of the other inmates teased him about digging a tunnel in broad daylight.

He smiled. "I'm just lucky to be here," he said. "So grateful, praise God."

He got himself into two Bible studies—one on Friday nights, hosted by the assistant pastor from a local church. During the week, the pastor often thought about the Bible-wise inmate with the hellish past.

"He's a real testament to the healing power of the Spirit," he told his wife.

20

Monday morning, Veronica drove past the first lot, straight up the hill, where she parked in an open area three rows from the back. She sat in her car, listening to the end of a song she liked, waving her peacock feather to the music.

Some of the trees around the lot had turned poinsettia and marigold against the darker greens of the hillside. A veil of birds feinted and banked over the lower lot, then swarmed noisily into the side of a big maple.

Veronica walked down the hill and through both lots, without the aid of a Parliament.

"How was Vermont?" one of the nurses asked when she walked off the elevator.

"It was so much fun," Veronica said. "We went to a drum concert and a cookout. It's so nice up there, and the babies are doing fine."

In her office, she straightened her desk and threw out her workstash of cigarettes, Xanax, and Rolaids. She dug the little radio out of the back of her filing cabinet and found a classical station. She pinned the peacock feather to the wall above her computer.

"Pictures," she said to herself, promising to remember enlargements of the girls and the babies.

She shut the door, sat at her desk, and looked at the phone before dialing.

"Hello," said Sister.

"Hi. Mom?"

"Veronica?"

"Hi."

"You called me Mom."

"Is that okay?"

"It sounds wonderful. I love it. I love the way it sounds."

"You do? Then why have we been calling you Sister all these years?"

"I don't know, honey. I guess it was important at one time and then everybody got in the habit." She laughed. "Sounds like one of your father's bad jokes, doesn't it? How was Vermont?"

"It was wonderful. Guess what?"

"What?"

"I'm truly happy. I actually found my gift. The thousand blinking eyes were peacock feathers."

"Of course," said Sister. "That makes perfect sense."

"Doesn't it?" said Veronica. "I feel so good about everything." She laughed. "And there's more. I met a man. He's the nicest person I've ever met, and we have so much in common. He's even a doctor. He's Catherine's doctor. And Jessie and I are getting along. We're actually friends now."

"That's wonderful," said Sister. "I'm so happy for you."

"Can we get together tonight and talk? I've got so much to tell you."

"I'd love it. I'm going to Beth and Daniel's tonight to watch Wes's show. Why don't you join us? I've got bad news on the gingersnaps, though. Your father found them yesterday."

"I'll bring snacks," said Veronica. "See you guys tonight."

"Alright, honey."

"I love you, Mom."

Sister smiled with her voice. "I love you, too," she said.

Veronica went to the nurses' station. She reviewed the charts and checked for new admissions; then she walked her rounds, humming to herself.

Michael Schreik was staring at the ceiling when Veronica walked into his room. His forehead was tight, wet with perspiration. His throat was trembling, and his eyes were distant, buried in pain.

"Good morning, Mr. Schreik. How are you feeling?"

He shook his head.

Veronica slid a chair to the side of his bed and checked his pulse.

"I owe you an apology," she said, leaving her hand on his arm. "I'm sorry I was so cranky on Friday."

He smiled tightly. "That's alright," he whispered. "I know I'm a burden. How was your weekend?"

"Wonderful," said Veronica. "The best. My daughter and I stayed with my other daughter and her family."

"You're lucky," Schreik said.

"I am lucky, and I'm just figuring that out. I mailed your letters. Your family will be happy to hear that you're alright," she said.

"Let's hope so," he said.

She wanted to call him Michael.

"You're not taking your medication, are you?" She leaned forward and looked at his neck. "Do you mind telling me why?"

"Pain for pain," he said. "I've hurt a lot of people."

"But they won't forgive you just because you're in pain. You've done the right thing—you wrote your letters. When they read them, they'll see how sincere you are. They're your family. That's what counts, Michael."

He carried his hand to the place where his body had been opened. He turned his head toward her. A tear eased from the edge of his eye.

"I think I'm out of time," he said.

"You're not dying. You need to be rested when they come to see you. And you need to be healthy to enjoy your second chance."

A slow nod, a tight smile, then he reached toward the rack beside his bed and pressed a button on the pump. Within a minute, he was asleep.

Veronica sat watching him for a moment; then she dried his forehead and left the room.

There was a crowd at the nurses' station. As she walked up the hall, the group of nurses turned toward her and smiled.

"Aren't we the lucky one?" one of them said.

In front of the switchboard was a cart with the largest vase of flowers Veronica had ever seen. The vase was the size of a bucket, and the arrangement was three feet across.

"They brought it up on a cart," said one of the young nurses, wide-eyed.

Blushing royally, Veronica wheeled the vase into her office. The forest of flowers engulfed all the space between her desk and the far wall. She sat at her desk and read the card:

I already miss you was all it said.

I spent Monday morning covering my ass. I needed twenty troopers for crowd control, so I called Manchester for backup. I called attorneys for advice. They said I was screwed.

By noon, Main Street was packed with out-of-state cars, news wagons, and hucksters; and now the second wave of disaster groupies was rolling into town. Old hippies, New Age wizards, human rights activists, writers, bums, swindlers, attorneys, and talk-show bottom-feeders were wandering the sidewalks, chasing the buzz.

Folksingers and street performers had set up shop in front of the bank. Somebody wrote a song called "The Ballad of Talbert's Ridge" about a white girl who fell in love with a Sagaweh brave who didn't want to leave the valley so he jumped off a nonexistent cliff into an equally fictional lake. Everybody was humming the chorus.

> "So he sank to the bottom of the cold clear water,
> Drowning his love for the pioneer daughter."

I stayed in the station all day, organizing traffic details and security for the ball fields. The phone never stopped ringing.

At five o'clock I stopped by the Indian village on my way home. I met Sarah Running Doe in the middle of the no-man's-land between the news trucks and the circle of teepees with a herd of newscasters surrounding us.

I served her the warrant for illegal assembly on town land. In front of the cameras, she set it on fire and did a phony little war shuffle on the burning scraps.

I went home. Sister, Veronica, and Jessie were there for dinner and to watch Wes's show.

Before she started telling her story, I knew something good had happened to Veronica. Her eyes were wide and sparkly and she was smiling—actually smiling. She was talking with her hands like an awestruck child, describing the happiest moment of her life.

"Peacock feathers," she said. "A room full of peacock feathers. Can you believe it? Oh, Mom, I'm so happy. It was just like my bedtime story. The morning was winking at me with a thousand eyes."

"Are we calling you Mom now?" I asked Sister.

"If you want to," she said.

Beth laughed. "I want to call you Mom."

I sat at the table as the four women talked in the kitchen. Veronica and Jessie were acting like sisters, teasing each other.

"She didn't come in until the next morning," Jessie said.

"I'm allowed," said Veronica. "We were talking about medicine."

"Lo-o-ove medicine," said Jessie, wiggling her eyebrows for my benefit. Veronica tried to pop her with a dish towel.

"How do you know this guy is for real?" I asked.

"Because I hung out with him," Veronica said. "And he's Catherine's doctor."

"Just because he passed the first audition doesn't mean he's got the part."

"Lighten up," she said, patting me on the head. "It's my bedtime story coming true. What's wrong with you? You're such an old woman these days."

Sister laughed. Beth gave me those back off eyes, so I went to the den and turned on the six o'clock news. It was eerie, watching myself playing the part of the bad guy, serving the warrant to Sarah Running Doe.

The Channel 6 anchorman was flogging the father-son connection between Wes and me—ten minutes before *This Is My Town*.

"It's hard to say how this show will end," he said. "The curtain may be coming down on the dynasty of deception in the hamlet of Franklin Notch."

Beth brought my dinner from the kitchen, and the five of us settled in to watch Wes. Sister, Beth, and I sat on the couch; Veronica and Jessie sat cross-legged on the floor, sharing a plate of nachos.

The show starts the same as it has for the past thirty-eight years. Jerky footage of Main Street in grainy Super 8 color, cheesy graphics, fade to Wes.

The lights come up on the big guy sitting behind his little table, wearing a blue workshirt, his red suspenders, and a Red Sox cap. He must have blow-dried his beard; it looks like he's wearing a sheep around his neck.

The flimsy table bends in the middle as he lays his heavy arms on it and leans forward. He looks directly at the camera and smiles.

"Hi, neighbors," he says. "Wow, what a week, huh? And it's only Monday."

He shakes his head, takes a drink of coffee, and chuckles to himself.

"I'd like to welcome our new viewers to Franklin Notch, the curiosity capitol of the world. I used to be the biggest curiosity in town, but tonight I feel like a flea on the back of an exploding horse. I haven't seen this much confusion since old Mrs. Loomis—God rest her soul—called one night screeching about spaceships landing on her house. Anybody remember that?"

He looks off-camera and shares a laugh with someone in the studio.

"Turns out it was Deke Loomis with a flashlight, nailing some plastic around the chimney. It's a miracle she didn't shoot her own husband off the roof. I guess she came pretty close, though, for an eighty-year-old drunk woman on crutches.

"Anyway, here we are with a town full of visitors, and I think it's great. I even wrote a poem to commemorate this whole episode, and I'd like to read it now."

He fiddles with his granny glasses and several sheets of notebook paper. I looked at Sister. She shrugged.

Wes pretends to clear his throat.

"On the field where kids play baseball, we've got an amazing event.
  I heard an Indian war call from an Indian circus tent.
We know they came to plunder, we know they came to pillage.
  The only thing we wonder is: Who paid for this fake village?"

"What's he doing?" I asked Sister.

"He's trying to piss them off," said Jessie.

"Say 'God-forgive-me,' " the three women said in unison.

Wes continues reading, smiling to himself.

"We've got Sagawehs driving Caddies who bully us and beg us
  To believe they're not bad guys–spaghetti Indians from Las Vegas.
They've got caterers and cell phones, RVs and a Hummer.
  They look more authentic than me, and that's a real bummer.

They claim they own the mountain, they claim they own the valley.
  They claim they're going to scalp us with attorneys hired by Bally.
They want to build a ski lift, they want to build a lodge.
  Now they're getting angry when we say, 'Get the hell out of Dodge.'

Anyone can live here. This is the land of the free.
  But try to take my town, and I say, "Don't Tread on Me."
If they really want a land war, we're not going to lose,
  Even if they ambush us by lying on network news.

So, if you want to get attention, set up some prefab teepees,
  Then get a phony squaw and pretend you're Indian wannabes.
But if we smoke too much peace pipe, circle the wagons and head south,
  We've lost the war of cheap hype to Sarah Running Mouth."

Offstage, someone is laughing uproariously. The screen is shaking as the cameraman tries to control himself.

Wes starts laughing and can't stop. He throws back his head and bellows great Falstaff bleats at the ceiling; he puts his head on the table and shrieks into his hands. He pulls out his red bandana and wipes his eyes and blows his nose. Then he starts up again. He spends five minutes of his show laughing uncontrollably.

"Oh my God, is that fun," he says.

He goes to the phones. "You're on the air."

"Yeah, Wes, you're a trip."

"All aboard," says Wes.

"So what's your plan for Wednesday night? You know, the town meeting? Are you just going to read poetry and giggle yourself silly?"

"I guess I'll stand there and answer questions."

"Or maybe our beloved chief of police should hunt down all Native Americans and beat them up."

"That isn't the way it happened," Wes says. "That tape was edited to make Boone look bad."

"I believe what I see," says the caller. "And to me it looks like we're the laughingstock of the whole country, and I'm sick of it." The caller slams down his phone.

Wes takes a few more calls; then the big one.

"You're on the air," he says.

"Good evening, Mr. Moffatt," says a woman with a scolding velocity to her voice. "This is Sarah Running Doe, and for your information our camp-in is funded by private citizens and is not affiliated in any way with organized crime."

"Okay," Wes says. "And I'm a Playboy bunny."

"Well, I suppose if your bobo son can keep his job as chief of police, then you're entitled to be anything you want to be, too. The fact is, our gathering is a peaceful demonstration of our lawful right to free assembly on land that still belongs to us. Your ball fields are on top of our burying grounds. You said so yourself, and I've got a videotape of one of your lectures to prove it. Right now I'm walking over the bones of my great-great-great-grandmother, and her spirit cries to me from her resting place. How would you feel if someone built a playground over your parents' graves?"

"I see your point. A ski lodge would be nicer."

"You can make your jokes now, Mr. Moffatt, but when the American people hear our side of the story, things are going to change—and we're not leaving until that happens. I think you'll find they agree with us."

"What is your side of the story?"

"It's simple. We were run off our land and not given the chance to live peacefully with our new neighbors. History has been tweaked and tampered with. We did not leave our homelands willingly, and now we want them back. You're just mad because you were caught with your pants down. You're the one who is looking silly after making claims you can't deny."

"Let's go back a little bit," says Wes. "How are you connected to the original Sagawehs of Talbert's Ridge?"

"Through my mother's side," says Sarah Running Doe.

"And what proof do you have?"

"There is no proof. That's the point. We were run off our land. It was a holocaust, an American holocaust. We lost everything, including our history. All we have is what was passed down through the generations. I only know what I heard from my grandmother, who heard it from her grandmother, and so on."

"And what was your grandmother's name?" Wes asks.

"It doesn't matter," she says.

"Yes, it does. What was your grandmother's name? Better yet, what was your name before you decided to play Indian?"

"It doesn't matter," she says again. "What's important is that I'm reclaiming the heritage that was stolen from my ancestors and my children by your town."

"You have children? What are their names? Billy Jumping Goat and Jenny Freaking Catfish?"

"I'm not going to sit here and listen to some big monkey insult my family," she says tightly, starting to lose her cool.

"Why not? I have to sit here and listen to your bullshit. See, that's my point. You know everything about me because I have nothing to hide. So. What is the name of the family I'm insulting? What was your grandmother's name? And while we're asking questions, who is really paying for the cell phones, the walkie-talkies, the water truck, the food, satellite dish, porta-potties, and the RVs with rental plates? Do you know how much each of those generators costs? Do you? Do you know how much a generator costs?"

"I don't buy generators," she says. "My job is to—"

"Exactly," Wes yells, slapping the table with the flat of his hand. "Somebody else buys the generators. Your job is to make people feel sorry for you, and it ain't working, lady. You're not a good enough actor. This isn't *Last of the Mohicans*. This is real life."

"I'm not answering any more questions," she says. "I'll see you at your town meeting. And you'd better be ready for war."

Reinforcements showed up the next morning. Manchester loaned us six state troopers. Three patrolled the ball fields; one was parked at either end of Main Street; one cruised around town. I hired a retired Manchester cop to watch Wes and Sister's house, and I had one of my guys drive past every hour to keep the reporters off their yard.

I called Sister early.

"When Wes wakes up, don't let him leave the house."

"He's already up. He's locked himself in the barn with a pot of coffee. He's working on some project."

"Keep him there. I don't want him going out at all. It's getting too tense."

"What about tonight? He won't give up his show."

"I'll get somebody to follow him to the studio. Don't let him leave until you hear from me."

"Can you come by so we can talk? I want to tell you about my dream."

"Maybe later."

I spent the day at the station, coordinating security and dodging the media. I felt like a prisoner in my own job.

I called Beth at noon.

"There's news trucks in our driveway," she said. "I walked down to get the mail and some guy called me Annie Oakley." She laughed.

"Don't talk to them."

"Boone, we can't be afraid. We need them on our side. I called Sister, and we decided to bake cookies for them."

"Bad idea."

"No, it's not. I think it's perfect. If we act scared, they'll think we're feeling guilty. Let's just be ourselves. We're nice people."

"There's a lot at stake here. Nice doesn't count. Wes could go to jail."

"He's not going to jail. Sister says so."

"Sister doesn't know everything that's going on behind the scenes. Right now, everybody needs to keep a low profile."

"Have a little faith in us," Beth said. "You're carrying the whole load, so let us help. We can lighten it a little."

I called Veronica.

"Are you baking cookies, too?"

"Jessie is. She's got a crush on the guy from Channel 4."

"Good Lord."

"Boone, don't worry so much. I can handle this. It's too exciting to turn out bad."

"I never thought I'd hear this from you."

"Hey, what can I say? I'm a happy girl now. I got flowers from my new boyfriend and I'm getting along with Catherine and Jessie. Have you heard from Reggie?"

"No."

"I feel bad about him, and I wish I had been nicer to him in Florida. I should have apologized for being so self-righteous when he lost his job, and that crack about hookers was really cruel. Is it okay with you if I try to get in touch with him?"

"I suppose. Why?"

"I want him to be happy, too. I know it sounds corny, but he needs to find his gift—just like I did. Mom was right. There *is* a plan for everything. Things *do* fit together, like pieces of a puzzle."

"It sounds strange—calling her Mom."

"It feels good, Boone. You ought to try it. Lighten up a little. Enjoy life."

This was too much. I couldn't keep up with the changes. I needed solitude.

I took the cruiser out of town and drove the county roads through the hills around Franklin Notch. I stopped at the crest of a hill and sat on the hood of the car. This was my favorite vista because I could look in every direction and see nothing man-made. This is the way it should be—undefiled, unspoiled, free from the greed of my kind.

I tried to make myself comfortable. Any person driving over this hill would come around the bend and see a uniformed officer lying on his back on the hood of his cruiser, barefoot, watching the clouds.

This is the way I clear my head. Since I was a child, I have gone to the woods to sort things out. There are lessons of balance in the hills: beauty and decay, movement and monument, earth and air, flower and stone. I can imagine this land—fragile as moss, solid as a mountain—before the first European dug in his heels and wrote his own deed. It must have been beautiful before the first stones were pulled out of the ground and stacked for walls that snaked between new English farms, before the carving-out and pounding-down of all those gritty roads.

I believe in balance, the elemental tension of opposing forces.

I've learned to live between the forces that control me: Sister's bargain and the Devil's bet, and I know where I'm headed with my faithless heart—far from the comfort of my kind. Without faith, I'm a lost soul; but Ronnie Dolan changes everything. I need to watch him carefully, and I need to fix Wes's problems before the Devil throws him into the mix. I need to move fast, and all I've got is this map.

Faith can wait.

Searching for my gift in this rush of confusion is a job for the man with time to kill. I've got the opposite problem: Only two more times, and the Devil kills me.

I've come to believe that faith is a luxury, not a gift—for people born with less to lose. For those of us born with souls on the line, life is a desperate business, and I need to gain the advantage with every trick in the bag. I need to make my own plan and use the map against the Devil who gave it to me.

I took the map out of my pocket and read it. It seemed simple enough to find the Devil's Tree.

Thursday, the day after the town meeting, I'll take this map and follow it into the woods. I'll find the tree, grab the treaty, and run—just like a game of capture-the-flag. After I get the treaty, I'll take Wes up to the ball fields, let him wave it around, and watch the media do the rest. My plan could work—as long as nobody finds out about the map in the meantime. And if the Devil sees me at the tree, all I've lost is a visit. I was going to lose it anyway, and I'll still have one chance left.

I looked down, over the side of the road.

I remembered the cold night twenty-five years ago when I found Beth at the bottom of this hill. That night, I had come to the top of this hill to be alone and watch the stars. That night, I parked in this same spot, turned off the headlights, and sat on the hood of the old Fairlane cruiser.

While I watched the winter night, I noticed an uncommon light beneath me in the valley.

I slid off the hood of the car and walked across the road. To my right, I could see where the guardrail was splintered, and down the hill, I saw the car resting on its side, its turn signal blinking like a heartbeat in the darkness.

I called for the ambulance and charged down the hill. I pulled her from the car, tied off her shredded leg with my belt, and carried her up to the road. I sat beside her on the drive to the hospital and stayed with her all night.

Today, I lay on the hood of the new Crown Vic and watched a trio of carrion crows circling over a creekbed. I tried to lose myself in their lazy pattern, but I couldn't relax. I couldn't evade my own dark fates hovering above me. I couldn't see the end of trouble.

I put the map back in my pocket, tied my shoes, and drove back to town.

I went to the station and called the ex-cop watching my parents' house. He was inside, eating cookies with Sister. I talked to Sister.

"Your father is already at the TV station. He's all excited about the show tonight. What's up, honey?"

"I just wanted to tell him something," I said. "I'll be home, if you need me."

I went home to watch *This Is My Town* with Beth.

Wes has a dangerous twinkle in his eye.

"For those of you who missed last night's show, we had an interesting surprise. The Queen of the Nevada Sagawehs called in and dished out a serious dose of crap about what they're doing on our ball field. If you missed the show, we've got a tape of the conversation that we're going to play for you now. This tape has not been altered in any way. I repeat, this tape has *not* been altered in any way."

"Oh, no," I said to the television. "Don't do it." Beth held my hand.

Wes grins at the camera and rolls the tape.

"Good evening, Mr. Moffatt. This is Sarah Running Doe, and I'm looking for a monkey to tweak my bobo."

"You're what?"

"I'm looking for a monkey to tweak my bobo."

"You are? How do you plan to do that?"

"I walk around town with my pants down."

"That sounds interesting. Where did you learn to do this?"

"I heard from my grandmother, who heard it from her grandmother, and so on."

"So how long do you plan to stay in Franklin Notch?"

"Until I find a big monkey."

"Well, it sounds like you know what you want."

"I'm looking for a monkey to tweak my bobo."

The tape has a jerky, hacked-up quality to it, and while it plays, Wes looks into the camera with an expression of complete seriousness, nodding along with the nonsense. It plays a second time and he hams like a bad schoolboy while the crew falls over themselves in the background.

For the rest of the show, Wes patches the tweaky bobo bit into everything that happens. Basically, Tuesday night's show was about middle-aged men who can't stop laughing.

He was still laughing when he called me from home after the show.

"Sister said you wanted me to check in," he said, all raspy. "What did you want to tell me?"

"Nothing, really. I just wanted to remind you not to antagonize those people."

"Oh, okay," he said. "See you tomorrow."

21

Reggie and Grace sat in the club car, playing pickup sticks with a box of toothpicks. They had been talking all night. They were six hours away from New York.

"I want to be a nun," she said.

Reggie laughed. "No, you don't."

"I do, I really do. They don't have to worry about anything. They can sit around all day and read, and nobody cares what goes on in their heads. They don't have to worry about being pretty or pretend they care what boys think."

"You don't want to be a nun. Trust me. My mother was a nun."

"Get out."

"Seriously. She was a nun before she got married and had babies."

"Did she like it?"

"Which?"

"Being a nun?"

"Apparently not. Actually, she still is a nun, in some ways."

"For instance?"

"She prays all the time, and she's got all these little sayings—a million of them—one for every situation."

"For instance?"

"If somebody has been selfish and she wants to remind them that they need a little grace in their program, she says:

"*Grace, like a sparrow, is quick to hide*
From Vanity's glare and the glow of Pride."

"Oh, I like that. Did she make it up?"

"I think so. I've never heard anyone else say it."

"I don't like the part about the sparrow," she said. "I think of myself as an African gray."

"A parrot? Why?"

"Because they are highly intelligent birds, they mate for life, and can live to be over ninety years old. Did you know that a woman in Pompano Beach taught an African gray to recite her own funeral?"

"Really?"

"Yeah, and she even taught it to sound like it was crying. Crazy, huh?"

Reggie thought about his own family and gave the episode honorable mention.

Grace tried making a little teepee out of toothpicks. "If you ask me, the really crazy part is that nobody cares about the lady, but everybody remembers the story because it's about a parrot who recited somebody's funeral."

"Maybe nobody showed up for the funeral and it was just a parrot and a dead woman in an empty room."

"Sounds like my funeral," said the girl.

"You've got friends."

"Not really. I think I'm going to buy a hundred African grays and teach them all to sing 'Midnight at the Oasis.' It's my favorite song."

"Now that's a funeral I'd go to."

Grace laughed. "So now I've got a hundred African grays and a fake cartoon character at my funeral. Perfect. Send me a picture."

"I'll have my mother get in touch with you. Why don't you have any friends?"

"Because everybody is so predictable. I want to find somebody like me, and I don't want to act stupid just to have a boyfriend. Being smart is all I've got. I'm not pretty, I don't dress like everybody else, and I read all the time."

"I think you'll be fine."

"Thanks. How about you? Are you married?"

"I don't know. I was, before I left home."

"Are you going to try and get back together?"

He shrugged. "We'll see what happens."

"I don't think you should."

"Why not?"

"First of all, she's too old for you now."

Reggie laughed. "I guess so. I hadn't thought about that."

"And don't take this wrong, but I don't think you're the predictable type, either."

"Thank you." He smiled.

"What? What did I say?"

"A good thing. I just realized why I'm going home. It's not because I'm lonely or desperate. It's because that's the only place where everybody is like me. I used to think I was different from them, but I missed the point. Everybody else is different from us. I hope they take me back."

"They will."

"Why?"

"Because if they're just like you, they'll want to be with you, too. All anybody wants is to be comfortable with their own kind. They'll take you back. Just say you're sorry."

"How do you know all this?"

"Because I lie awake every night listening to my parents talk about their careers and all the deals they do with people they hate, and I wonder why nobody ever comes to my door and says, 'Hey, Gracie, do you need anything before you go to sleep? Hey, Gracie, want to come in and watch a little TV? Hey, Gracie, I could use some company. Come on, get up. Let's hang out and have some ice cream.' "

She looked at him over the tops of her glasses. She was crying.

Reggie put his arm around her as she sniffled into the sleeve of her sweater. After a while she fell asleep against his chest.

22

My phone rang the next morning at five thirty. I knew it was Sister, and I knew it was bad news.

"Daniel, somebody poured red paint all over the front yard. The cat tracked it in, and I've got little red pawprints everywhere."

I drove Beth's car across the valley. I got there at the same time the camera crews showed up and the ex-cop woke up in his Lincoln.

"What the hell, Bobby. You were supposed to watch the place."

"Sorry, Boone. Damned Indians slipped right by me. I guess I wasn't counting on them being so sneaky."

"They're not real Indians, and they probably didn't even see you. All you had to do was stay awake and blow the horn."

"Sorry."

The front yard was covered with bright red latex goo. The driveway was painted with the words TWEAK THIS.

Inside the house, there were little red cat tracks everywhere—across the counters, the floors, and the furniture.

Wes and Sister were sitting at the kitchen table in their pajamas, holding cups of coffee. Blood red pawprints meandered around the tabletop between them.

"Maybe I went too far," he said.

"Just maybe," I said. "I can't believe you did that, considering the town meeting is tonight."

"I know," he said. "I'm sorry."

I spent the morning riding herd on crazy town. Everybody was on edge. Rumors ricocheted across the valley: The Indians were on a hunger strike, the National Guard was coming, someone had poisoned the water, the Indians were setting Jeep Cherokees on fire.

There was a bomb scare at the high school, and Jessie came to our house early to wait for Veronica.

"Somebody said they were going to do that ceremony where they dangle themselves from a pole with hooks in their bodies," she said.

Early afternoon, I went to the high school gym with Wes to check on arrangements for the town meeting. The gym looked like a convention arena. A small stage with a microphone was set up in the foul lane at one end of the floor. A banner was spread across the back wall that said THIS IS MY TOWN, WITH WES MOFFATT. There was a clutter of cameras and lights spread out across the floor to midcourt, and a wall of video gear was stacked on risers against the back of the gymnasium. The parking lot was a small city of satellite dishes.

I watched Wes as we walked around. He had the sly look of a kid who just hid the whoopee cushion.

He tested the PA and the feed to the station. He tinkered with the microphone on the floor where people with questions would stand.

I checked the doors, the bathrooms, and the open spaces beneath the bleachers. Then I drove Wes home and waited for the town meeting.

Two by two, the Sagawehs paraded down East Mountain Road, dressed in full costume, beating drums and chanting. At the head of the column was Sarah Running Doe, her face painted with ocher zigzags. She was wearing a buckskin dress and a beaded headband with feathers. She was carrying a wiggly walking stick wrapped with feathers, bells, and strips of leather. She was moaning and shaking her stick at the houses and the sky, weaving back and forth across the road like a drunk woman looking for her glasses.

Most of the Indians looked self-conscious; a few acted belligerent. The first two were carrying a banner that said NATIVE AMERICANS ARE AMERICA'S FIRST HOMELESS.

The road was packed with people watching the procession. There were signs in the windows of most of the houses. NO SKI LIFT IN MY BACKYARD. MY MOUNTAIN, MY HOME.

They came down the mountain to Main Street, where they turned left and walked four blocks to the high school driveway. The sidewalks on Main Street were filled with protesters and supporters waving posters and plastic tomahawks. There were camera crews and photographers standing on the roofs of news vans.

When they hit Main Street, Sarah Running Doe went into hyper-wail. She cut loose with a primal moan and fell to her knees in front of the Channel 6 van. The parade stopped while she shook her stick for the cameras.

Still wailing, she took a handful of ashes out of the pouch on her belt, patted some on her face, and tossed the rest in the air.

Inside the high school gym, we waited for the show to start. The place was packed. The bleachers were jammed shoulder to shoulder with townspeople, and the perimeter of the floor was solid with broadcast gear and technicians.

There were state troopers in the parking lot and three of my guys posted at the doors to the building. They had orders to keep the tourists outside.

Protesters of all kinds were clustered on the sidewalks and in the parking lot. There were old hippies with guitars singing Buffy Sainte-Marie songs; there were politicians handing out bumper stickers; beer-belly survivalists were standing at attention around a Hummer, and women from the DAR were selling brownies off a card table. There were townies having a tailgate party in the corner of the lot and a mime version of Custer's Last Stand going on in the handicapped spaces.

Inside, I was standing out of sight behind the first set of bleachers.

Wes sat alone on the little stage under the hoop. He was wearing a blue flannel shirt, red suspenders, khakis, and workboots. His beard covered his chest; his hair was tied in a ponytail. He was holding a small notebook.

If he was nervous, he didn't show it. He scanned the bleachers, occasionally waving to a friend. His cameraman scampered onto the little stage to tinker with the microphone and give last-minute advice.

It was six twenty-five. Five minutes before airtime.

Wes stood and walked to the microphone.

"Okay, folks," he said. "We're getting ready to go on the air, and I want to make sure everyone understands the rules. I'm the moderator tonight, and this microphone on the floor is for anyone who wants to say something. We'll form a line across the front of the bleachers, and when it's your turn to talk, just step up to the mike and speak clearly. We're asking everybody to limit themselves to three minutes. Remember, we're broadcasting to a lot of the networks tonight, so let's show the world how civilized we are."

There was a buzz around the gym as Wes counted down the seconds.

Crews hunched into their equipment; the audience settled and shushed.

"Four, three, two, one—and welcome to a special edition of *This Is My Town*. My name is Wes Moffatt, and we're coming to you live from the Franklin Notch High School gymnasium in beautiful southern New Hampshire. Tonight we're broadcasting our town meeting as the show, and we're going to discuss ways to resolve the current conflict between our little community and a group of people who claim they still own half of it. There's a lot of opinions on this issue, so we've got an open mike on the floor for people to express themselves. Go ahead, sir, step up and ask your question."

I heard a deepening sound. It was my heart beating faster, or drums drawing closer.

"My name is Carl Vickers, and I live at 1142 Birchwood Lane."

A narrow, nervous man was standing at the microphone. He was turning a hunting cap with his fingertips while he leaned into the mike.

"And I was wondering what proof these people have that the mountain still belongs to them?"

"Good question, Carl." Wes tugged on his beard and nodded his head. "Unfortunately, the only record of ownership is a collection of stories dating back to colonial times. There's a story about a treaty signed by the settlers and the Indians that allows both to share the valley—the Indians on East Mountain and the settlers on the West. It was called Talbert's Treaty, after the man who negotiated it for the settlers."

Wes was playing to the cameras. This was part of his old script, and I could see it was making people nervous.

"What about these stories?" asked Carl. "Are they real?"

"Yeah," somebody shouted from the bleachers on the right. "Stories is stories. That's all they are. They don't mean nothing."

"That's a good point," said Wes. "If nobody believes them, then I guess it's like they never happened."

"Well, did they?" the nervous man at the microphone asked. "Did they happen?"

"What?" said Wes. "The stories, or what the stories are about?"

"What the hell's the difference?" somebody else yelled.

"Well, I suppose if the stories are made up and you believe them anyway, then it don't matter," Carl said to the voice in the bleachers.

"Sit down, Carl," someone shouted. "Your three minutes is up."

Carl Vickers nodded, scratched his forehead with his pinkie, and sat down.

A middle-aged woman wearing overalls and a stocking cap stood in front of the microphone. She read her question from a piece of yellow paper.

"Here's my question," she said. "Why doesn't the government offer these people low-interest loans so they can buy houses like the rest of us?

They're welcome to live on my street as long as they keep their place nice and mind their own business. Thank you." She walked back to her seat.

The next person—a young man—was walking toward the microphone when the doors were shoved open at the far end of the gym and an explosion of noise filled the building. Seventy-five people dressed as Indians danced into the room, banging on drums and shouting. They paraded around the basketball court twice, inside the ring of cameras, doing a hotfoot parody of a war dance; then they spaced themselves several feet apart around the perimeter of the floor, slamming on their drums in unison.

I hit the walkie-talkie.

"What happened?" I yelled. "How did they get in here?"

"That crazy bitch kicked Eddie in the nuts. They ran right over us, Boone. What do we do now?"

"Nothing," I said. "It's their show now. Wedge the doors open in case we've got a stampede out of here."

Sarah Running Doe made her way to the microphone. In one breath, the crowd turned nasty. People started booing; cameras swept the bleachers like searchlights.

She did a stompy little sidestep for the cameras, then she aimed her hex-stick at Wes. He took a step backward; I took a step toward him.

"Liar," she screamed. "Thief," she shrieked. "You stole the bones of my ancestors. Where are they?" she howled.

"I have no idea what you're talking about," Wes said. His voice was barely audible above the pounding of the drums.

She carried on like an evangelist.

"You have *stolen* our mountain, you have *stolen* our freedom, you have *stolen* our spirit, you have *stolen* our heritage, you have *stolen* our lives." Each time she said the word "stolen," the drums thundered in unison and she shook her stick at Wes.

People were standing in the bleachers shouting at her to be quiet, to leave the building. She turned to each side of the gymnasium and shook her stick defiantly at the crowd.

The place went crazy. People in the bleachers were yelling at the circle of Indians on the floor of the gym. Sarah Running Doe was yelling at Wes. Wes was waving his arms to calm everyone. News guys with minicams were scooting around the front of the stage to get a shot of the angry Indian woman. The circle of Indians pounded their drums and shouted their phony war chant.

I'm not sure what happened next. I think someone dropped a cherry bomb under the bleachers. There was a loud noise, and for a second, there was a gap in the chaos before everybody ran for the exits. It was a miracle that no one was seriously injured. The frightened crowd poured out the front doors of the building, swarming over the DAR and the hippies, around the Channel 6 van that was parked in front of the gym. Fights broke out as some of the rowdies chased Indians down the driveway. The survivalists took off across the football field in their Hummer.

I grabbed Wes and hauled him out of the gym through the exit behind the bleachers. I locked him in the back of the cruiser and ran around the front of the building to help with the riot.

Vehicles were flying out of the parking lot, driving over curbs and into each other like bumper cars.

There was a clot of people around the ambulance being treated for scrapes and twisted ankles. There was broken glass and litter everywhere. People wandered in and out of the gym looking for their shoes and belongings. Volunteer firemen ran lines of hoses through the front doors. Groups of news crews stalked the crowd for interviews.

I walked past the Channel 6 van and saw Sarah Running Doe sitting inside, drinking a beer. She gave me the finger.

I stayed in the parking lot for two hours, until every person from the town had gone home. We did two sweeps of the school and taped off the front of the gym. We made a list of the cars left behind, and we posted cruisers at both driveways.

I checked on Wes every half hour, and finally at ten thirty I drove him home.

We sat in his driveway, in the front seat of the cruiser with the lights off.

"You actually locked me in the car," he said.

"Yeah, I did. It was for your own protection. A lot of people don't like you right now."

"I know," he said. "I'm so sorry. I don't know what to do, Danny. I don't know what's happening. I know it's my fault, but I don't know what I did wrong. Why are things so complicated?" He put his head in his hands and started to cry. "I'm so embarrassed. I don't want people to hate me. What should I do?"

"Why don't you just tell the truth?"

"About what?"

"About all those legends and stories. Just say you made everything up."

"I can't do that," he said. "I didn't make them all up. Some of those stories are hundreds of years old."

"But they didn't really happen."

"That's not my fault," he said. "See, that's what I mean. I don't know what I did wrong. I repeated some stories. Big deal. It's like that story about the beer cart rolling down the hill in Henniker, spilling beer everywhere, and how all the pigs in town got drunk and wandered around for two days, bumping into things. Who cares if it's real? It's a good story."

"What about the treaty? Talbert's Treaty? Did you make that up?"

"I don't know, Boone. I don't remember. That was fifty years ago. It's a story about something that happened two *hundred* and fifty years ago. Maybe I made it up, maybe I heard it somewhere. Maybe I heard part of it somewhere and made up the rest of it. I don't know, and it shouldn't matter. Even if I did make up the whole thing, it shouldn't have caused all this trouble."

We sat quietly for a moment. He took off his glasses and wiped his eyes with the knuckles of his thumbs. I put my hand on his shoulder.

"What am I going to do?" he said. "I'm such a fuckup."

"No, you're not," I said, patting his back.

"Yes, I am. I ruin everything. I messed up my own family. I made Reggie feel like an outsider. I made him leave. I really miss him, Danny. Why didn't he come home?"

"I don't know."

"He was right. I'm just an idiot old man."

"No, you're not. Things are just a little out of control now, but it's going to be okay. I've got a plan. It's a secret, and I can't tell anyone about it, but I can fix everything. I'll take care of it."

He leaned against my chest, weeping like a child.

After I left Wes, I called Beth to tell her I was going to be late coming home. I wanted to drive around and make sure the town was quiet for the night.

It was almost midnight. I started at the ball field and worked my way down East Mountain. The lights were still on in many of the houses—an unusual sight for this time of night. I drove down to Main Street and turned left toward the Congregational church at the south end of town.

The Channel 6 news van was in the parking lot of the church with its lights on. It was a white van with bold red graphics on its sides—slanting rows of three sixes that overlapped, shading from light to dark. The anchorman was standing in front of the van, talking with one of the cameramen. When he saw me, he waved for me to stop. On impulse, I turned into the driveway. He walked toward me, across the lot.

He was a smooth-looking, overgroomed man in his midthirties with blond hair, sharp features, and impossibly white teeth. He motioned for me to lower my window. He leaned on the side of the car and smiled at me.

"Marshal Earp," he said, in a voice no different from any man.

"What are you doing here?" I asked him.

"Just having some fun. Tonight was a trip, wasn't it?"

"Don't people complain about your breath?" I said.

"You're the only one kind enough to notice," he said, blowing it in my face. I wanted to retch. "Got the map?"

"No."

"I know you do. It's in your shirt pocket. Let's go for a ride. I'll take you up to the tree right now."

"No, thanks."

"What's wrong, Boone? You're not so spunky tonight. No fuck-yous for old Mr. Sticks?"

I just looked at him.

"Oh, I get it," he said, tapping the big Channel 6 button on his lapel. It was white with the three sixes logo and a slogan that said CHANNEL 6: THE TIMES OF YOUR LIFE. COUNT ON IT.

"Number six?" he said. "Sixth time? Pretty clever, huh?"

"I can handle it," I said.

"You've got no choice, worm. Once I heard about your lame little strategy, I had to regain my advantage. I had to use the sixth visit before you grabbed it. It rushed the program, but what the hell. I guess you'll need another plan—now that you've got only one chance left. Bummer, huh?"

I didn't know he could read my mind.

"I can't read your mind," he said. "But it's always the same half-assed scheme with you guys. We call it the Reverse Trojan Horse. It never works. Nice try, though."

"I saw you on TV with that asshole Hutton. So you were interviewing yourself about yourself?"

"You're never lonely if you can entertain yourself. Remember: I am legion and I can divide as many times as I want—and I get stronger every time I do it. Hey, let's go drive around. I'll show you some really neat tricks. We can watch what people do in the dark."

"No, thanks."

"How about the treaty? Let's go get it. I've got it up at my place."

"I'm never going up there. Ever."

"You'll do it."

"No, I won't."

"Then give me my map."

"I don't have it with me," I lied.

He laughed. "Didn't your mother teach you to tell the truth?"

"Why are you doing this?" I asked him.

"What?"

"Tormenting our family."

"Hey, Chief, I didn't start this. I was poking along back in the Fifties, minding my own business, and your withered little bitch of a mother started screwing with the system. She was supposed to stay in that convent, but she takes off, and all of a sudden, things get all complicated. She makes a promise to God, I make a bet for your soul, and now we've got deadlines, bargains, and bets piling up in the next few days. Want to know something? I don't care about you and I don't really give a shit about your soul. You're just a small-town cop, but thanks to your mother, it's turned into this whole big fight that nobody can afford to lose. It's her fault. She's a sniper, Boone. She torments me, so I fight back, and now it's on your head. Tell her to back off and I won't spook you anymore. You could live forever."

"I'm leaving," I said, shifting the car to reverse.

"Do you want to know how your wife dies?"

"No."

"Then go for a ride with me. Let's go get the treaty."

"No."

"Brain tumor. Wanna know when?"

"I'm not going up there. Not tonight. Not ever."

"Tonight would be a good night, after all that's happened. And besides, if I go with you now, it doesn't count as the seventh time. If you go later and I'm waiting for you, it's bye-bye maggot. You'd better go up there tonight while I'm in a good mood. There's some real bad stuff coming your way, buddy. Real soon, too."

"Forget it." I started to pull away. As I was backing out the driveway, I heard him say something.

I stopped the car. "What?" I asked.

"Next October," said the Devil, grinning and touching his temple with his fingertips.

Beth was waiting for me with a glass of merlot.

"Bad night," she said. "Are you okay?"

"I don't know. I'm kind of shell-shocked."

"Let's go to bed. We'll snuggle"

Under the comforter, she tried. I couldn't. I worried where she would touch me, maybe feel the map in my pocket and the lump on my chest.

"Sorry," I said.

"Don't be."

Through the blackblood night, I could feel him watching us.

"I need to talk about something."

"Okay," she said.

"Something else happened on the plane. The Devil gave me something—something that can solve everybody's problems. A map."

"What kind of map?"

"It's a map to a place where I can find the original Talbert's Treaty. If I get it, Wes will be cleared and all this Indian stuff will go away."

"This is scaring me, Boone."

"I know. But I don't know what to do."

Beth raised herself on her elbow.

"You're going to get rid of it," she said. "Right?"

"I wanted to talk about it first—let you know what's going on."

"You have to get rid of it. I'll help."

"There's more. I saw him again tonight, and he said real bad things are going to happen soon, and now I only have one more chance to try and fix this mess."

"So you thought you could use the map, waste a visit, grab the treaty, and not get caught?"

"Yeah, I thought had a plan, but when I saw him tonight—he already knew about it."

"You can't outwit the Devil. Where is the map now?"

"At the station," I lied. "I keep it locked up. Don't tell anyone, okay?"

"I thought we didn't keep secrets, but if that's what you want—okay. Does Sister know about it?"

"No, and please don't tell her."

"Boone, we have to get rid of this thing before it gets into your head and comes between you and everything else."

"I'm just thinking about Wes," I said. "Trying to help him."

"But this map's not real. It can't fix real problems."

"None of this is real, Beth. The Indians, the treaty, Reggie's little trip, my life."

"I'm real. Your family is real, you're real—whether it feels like it or not. We're good people. Don't let this map confuse you and pull you away."

"That's easy to say if you're on the outside looking in, but all these problems are in my face every day. I can't pretend they don't exist."

"But they don't. They're fake. You said so yourself. He made them up to confuse you. Don't let him win by trying to fix his lies. Stay focused on all the goodness around you; the Devil will go away and find somebody weaker."

"But I've only got one more chance. I'm out of time."

"You're never out of time. Every minute is a new beginning."

"Not anymore. Every minute could be my last."

"Honey, listen to yourself. You're just waiting to die. Let me help you turn this around. Let's go down to the station right now, get the map, and burn it in the middle of Main Street. He'll get the picture. Then we'll go to Hamrick's, get a piece of pie, and make a list of all the things that are bothering you. Tomorrow we'll gather the whole family and brainstorm. We can fix anything together, and once you get a little breathing room, you can start enjoying life—for a change. Okay?"

"Okay what?"

"Let's go burn the map on Main Street. Grab your coat."

She was sitting up, so clear, alive, and strong in her flannel pajamas.

"Hold it," I said. "There's something else—something he told me tonight. It's about you. He said you were getting a brain tumor."

"Brain tumor? What are you saying?"

"I'm just telling you what he said."

"Brain tumor. Me? I don't have a brain tumor."

She looked scared and confused, trying to assign meaning to the part of her mind that was questioning its ability to question itself.

"This isn't real, is it? How can I have a brain tumor, just like that?"

"I don't know. That's just what he said. We'll get you tested. Then we'll know."

She held her hand to her forehead. "Right. Okay, okay. I'll get tested to-morrow, or something. I'll call Veronica. She'll know what to do."

"What will you say?"

"I'll say I need a good doctor for a test. A brain scan. Why?"

"Because the Devil told your husband?"

"What difference does it make? I want to know if I have a tumor."

"I'm just thinking—maybe you should say it runs in your family, or you have headaches. Let's keep this quiet until we figure out what it means."

She was pressing her fingers across the top of her head, along both sides of the part in her hair. "What's it supposed to feel like?" she asked. "A lump inside?"

"Headaches," I said. "I don't know."

"I'll call Veronica in the morning."

"She'll know what to do," I said.

"Boone," she said, beginning to cry, "I don't want a brain tumor." She fell back on her pillow.

I couldn't risk a hug, so I held her hand. We lay side by side under the comforter, holding hands. She turned to me, wanting me to hold her. I rolled toward her—close enough for a half-hug, but not close enough for her to feel the map in my pocket. After a few minutes, I felt her muscles go slack and her breathing change.

There was darkness around us, darkness between us. I lay beside her, thinking.

You know how things happen. One day, you're nearly fifty and you realize you've been doing the same things most of your life. You know it's normal, but now it makes you nervous, thinking about the dwindling ration of your remaining days. Some nights you can't sleep. Wired, awake in your fragile shell of a body, you can feel yourself drifting toward that solid blankness of death, no longer so distant. Lying in the dark, with your arms straight by your sides—or crossed over your chest—you can almost imag-ine being gone. Your throat goes tight as if you've been caught in a lie, and your spine turns cold. You can't move your mind off the point: It could happen anytime.

I go through this every day. I'll be standing in a line somewhere and get that feeling of dread. I look around, checking the faces of the other people in the room, wondering if he is nearby, if he has set himself just out of sight, only a few degrees of darkness between him and me. I watch each face for that spark that chills.

Sometimes I think I see him in the act of doing something simple, like coming through a doorway, holding it open for me with a shrug and a nod; or sitting alone with his cigarette and coffee, blowing smoke with a wink and a smile; or driving past me, our eyes briefly connecting.

Every time I've seen him, he has caught me by surprise, and so I've convinced myself that if I keep looking, he can't surprise me—and maybe I'll never see him again. Of course, that's not true; it's just a game I play in my head: Hide the dreaded thought. I know it's a fool's wish; he can find me whenever he wants, and it's just a matter of time before he grabs me and keeps me. Like kids playing hide-and-seek, everybody gets caught. It's the suspense of the search that wears me down, because I'm always the prey.

The next visit could happen anywhere, and it could be anyone—the guy coming out of the bank, or the woman in the Saab asking for directions. It always begins as a random encounter and ends with the drawing down of my life. I can only see him one more time, and then it's over.

Tonight, I was off balance, badly cornered in the Devil's game, and closer than ever to the end of my days. What did he say? Deadlines, bargains, and bets.

I know what he's doing. Tonight, he made Beth part of his strategy, spreading his game, raising the stakes higher than I can afford to defend. He is separating me from my wife and my mother, my guardian angel and chief protector. He's drawing me out, into the open.

I'll take the bait. I can still win. All I need is a new scheme, and I need to act fast. Tomorrow, I'll sneak the map into the boxes of evidence in Wes's barn, then lead him to discover it. He'll be like a kid at Christmas, and when the lawyers find out, the court will send somebody else to the Devil's Tree. I won't have to go, and if they can't find the tree, the map is still proof that Talbert's Treaty could exist. It will confuse things enough to give credence to Wes's claims and swing some momentum his way. Perfect.

"Boone," she said. "Are you still awake?"

"I thought you were sleeping."

"No. I'm really scared. I hope the Devil is wrong, or this is one of his mind games. But if not, we'll beat it. Right, honey?"

"Yeah," I said. "We'll beat it."

23

In the morning I called Sister.

"I'm worried about Beth," she said. "She told me all about it."

"All about what?"

"The headaches and going for tests. She's calling Veronica for the name of a good doctor."

"I know. She's pretty scared."

"I'll pray for her."

"How's Wes?"

"Not so good."

"Don't let him sneak out," I said. "Tell him if he leaves the house, I'll put him in a cell. It's for his own good."

"He's not going anywhere. He's been sitting in the barn all morning, drinking coffee and looking out the window. He's so miserable. I've never seen him like this. I told him I was making brownies and he just shrugged. How are you doing?"

"I've been at the station since four this morning. I couldn't sleep, so I came down here to get a jump on the paperwork. I've been on the phone with attorneys and insurance adjusters. The town wasn't covered for this, so the school is closed until we can find money for repairs. Veronica said the emergency room was so packed last night, they were seeing people in the cafeteria. It's a miracle nobody was killed."

"That's what Wes said. It's been all over the news. CNN called it a riot."

"I know, I've been watching here at the station."

"Terrible, just terrible," she said. "And they're blaming his show. That's what hurts him the most. It's not all his fault."

"Yeah, but I still wish he could restrain himself—when it really matters. It sure would make my job easier."

"I know, honey. This is a test for all of us.

'Man is the portal between darkness and light.
Through all deeds mortal we carry the fight.'

"Are you and Beth coming up later?" she asked.

"Sure. I could use some brownies."

"Good. We'll make a nice dinner. It's going to be hard for your father. This is the first show he's missed in thirty-eight years."

"I know, but don't let him change his mind about going in. See you later."

"Love you, Daniel. We still need to talk."

"I know. See you later."

The nurses at the station looked embarrassed when Veronica walked off the elevator. They were reading the *Union Leader*. On the front page was a picture of Wes and Sarah Running Doe from last night's town meeting. She was snarling and pointing her stick at his face; he was backing away with his arms raised like a man trying to fly. The headline read INDIAN PROTESTERS MAKE CASE AT TOWN MEETING.

"Good morning, everybody," Veronica said pleasantly. "Floor meeting in ten minutes. Can I read that when you're finished?"

She went to her office and fussed with her flowers, easing the wilted ones out of the vase and rearranging the survivors. It was Thursday morning and she was excited about the coming weekend. Tomorrow she would be on the road with Jessie, driving to visit Catherine, Charlie, the babies, and Doc.

Saturday night they were all going to Charlie's fall concert at the college. His new ensemble was making their debut appearance, playing a program of original concertos Charlie had written for the group. Sunday morning, the family was having a picnic at Doc's clearing in the woods. Veronica had never been this excited.

The nurses wandered into her office in pairs.

"How's my new best friend in 262?" Veronica asked.

"Schreik. Stable," said a nurse. "But still not taking meds on schedule. Asks all day if he got any mail. Scheduled for transfer to rehab this afternoon."

"I'll talk to him," said Veronica. "And now I have something to say about my father and my brother." She picked up the *Union Leader*.

Several of the nurses looked to the floor.

"There's a lot of things being said and written about my family that simply aren't true. I'm not embarrassed about my father or brother because they haven't done anything wrong, and I don't want to talk about what's going on at home because it has nothing to do with our jobs here. Maybe when this is over we can all go out for drinks and tell stories, but for now I would appreciate your help guarding my privacy."

Everyone nodded.

"Thank you," Veronica said. "Now let's get to work."

She checked her e-mail. One from Doc: *It's almost Friday and I feel like a teenager. Can't wait to see you.* She printed it and put it in her pocket. Then she called the *Orlando Sentinel.*

"Rickey, City Desk," the man said.

"I think I've got a story for you," said Veronica. "My brother is living in Disney World and nobody knows about it."

"It happens all the time," he said. "It's like Woodstock out there."

"Well, he actually invented a character—with the suit and everything. I don't want to get him in trouble; we just want him to come home. Maybe if you did a story about him, he'd feel like he accomplished something. He had a hard time before he left New Hampshire."

"I'll check it out," he said. "If I find him, I'll have him call you."

"Thank you. We would be very grateful."

After she hung up, she read the article about Wes, changed her shoes, and went to visit Michael Schreik.

He was sitting on the edge of his bed, his back to the door, looking out the window.

"Good morning, Michael. I see you've been walking."

"Is the mail here yet?"

"No. You know it's too early. When it comes, I'll bring it down myself."

She looked at his chest. "So you're getting a new neighborhood," she said. "They're nice over there in pulmonary rehab. We'll miss you. I'll miss you." She smiled.

"How do I get my mail over there?" he said.

"If it comes while you're gone, I'll make sure you get it. I promise. It's only been a few days, you know." She patted his shoulder. "I'll come to see you before you go."

Veronica made the rest of her rounds, moved a mountain of paperwork, then went back to her office and called her mother.

"How's Wes doing after last night?"

"Not so good. He's taking it pretty hard. At least nobody was hurt."

"Do you need anything?"

"No, thanks, sweetie. We're just sticking around the house today. Beth is coming up later and we're going to make dinner. Did she call you?"

"Yes. I gave her the name of a good doctor. She's got a test Monday."

"Call me if you hear anything. And stop by later, if you feel like it."

"Okay. I'll call. Love you."

"I love you, too."

Veronica walked into the hall just in time to see a tall man in an overcoat turn away from the nurses' station, toward the elevator. It was Michael Schreik.

"Mr. Schreik," she called. The man turned. Schreik features, but a younger version.

"Yes?" he said.

"I'm sorry," said Veronica. "I thought you were one of our patients."

"His brother. I'm his brother. I left something for him. Over there." He pointed to the desk.

"That's great," said Veronica. "I know he's been waiting for something. I'll show you his room."

The man looked to the floor and shook his head.

"Don't you want to see him?" she asked.

"No," said the man. "I don't think so."

He turned and stood in front of the elevator with his back to Veronica. When the doors opened, he entered and stood sideways, still looking at the floor.

The envelope was a padded mailer, legal size.

Veronica took it to Michael Schreik. He was lying on his bed, propped up against the headboard. He turned off the TV when he saw the mailer.

"Merry Christmas," she said.

"How did that get here?"

"I guess somebody had it delivered."

He pulled the tab at the edge of the envelope and tilted the open end toward himself. A thousand tiny pieces of checkbook-blue and tablet-yellow paper poured onto his chest like confetti, spilling over his body, the bed, and the floor.

He looked inside the envelope. More dusty shreds floated onto his bandaged chest. Now it was empty.

He brushed the confetti off his chest.

"I'm so sorry," Veronica said, pulling little piles together with the edge of her hand.

"Leave it," he said. He wiped his eyes. Little pieces of paper stuck to his cheek.

"What can I do?"

"Nothing," he said. "Just leave me alone."

"I can stay."

"Leave. Me. Alone." He moved his arm toward the door and a cloud of shreds drifted off the bed to the floor.

"Alright. I understand. I'll send somebody down to clean up."

Veronica patted his arm and left the room. She went back to her office, closing the door behind her. She sat for a while, reading Doc's e-mail, filling the spaces between the words with snapshots of hope. The noise in the hall and the songs on her radio drifted away, somewhere behind her memories of the weekend. She considered calling him.

The phone rang.

"Veronica Marston? This is John Rickey in Orlando. We spoke earlier about your brother."

"Yes?"

"Well, it turns out that Disney Security evicted a bunch of squatters two days ago, but your brother wasn't in the group. I called one of my sources at the park, and they checked out the castle. They found his room, but there's nothing there. Empty."

"Are they sure it was his room?"

"They found some trash—pages from a notebook with his name on it."

"He could be anywhere," Veronica said, her spirit sagging. "I don't know what to do."

"You could try Busch Gardens."

"No, no," she said. "He's gone. I can feel it. Oh my, what have I done?"

She sat at her desk for a minute, then left her office. When she stepped into the hall, one of the nurses ran toward her.

"You're here?" she said. "We needed you. Schreik in 262. He killed himself."

"What?" Veronica felt her knees buckle.

"He bit through the feed on his pump and swallowed about two hundred units. Your door was closed. We thought you were at lunch. We had you paged."

Veronica ran down the hall to Schreik's room. A security guard was leaning against the closed door, cleaning his thumbnail with a toothpick.

"We're just waiting," he said.

Veronica went into the room. The body of Michael Schreik lay on the bed. The sheet was pulled up, covering his head, exposing his pale, skinny legs from the knees down. Veronica lifted the sheet and looked at his blank face.

She sat on the edge of the bed as confusion and guilt surged through her.

The door opened. A woman, the coroner, came into the room. "Was he family?" she asked. "Is he your brother?"

Veronica shook her head.

"Can you sign this anyway?" she said, holding out a piece of paper.

Veronica picked up Schreik's yellow tablet to use as a hard surface. On the first page was a note written to her. She finished the paperwork and took the tablet to her office. She locked the door and read the note.

Veronica Marston,

I had to do this. They left me no choice.

I'm sorry for any trouble I caused you or this hospital. I know you tried. You're off the hook.

You probably think I don't know what I'm doing, but you don't know everything. I know I'm a bad person, but everyone deserves the chance to set things right. If people won't listen, then they can all go to hell.

I was dying anyway.

> *Michael Schreik*
> *By his own hand*

Veronica picked up her purse, the newspaper, and her shoes. She made a copy of Schreik's note, put it in her pocket, and went home. If this doesn't count as a sick day.

Jessie was watching TV when Veronica walked in.

"What are you doing home?" she asked.

"Bad day," said Veronica. "What are you doing home?"

"No school. Closed. Tomorrow, too. Wes is a god. Can we go to Catherine's tonight?"

"I can't, honey. I'm too weirded out." She went to her room and changed into jeans and a T-shirt. She came back to the living room and sat on the sofa with Jessie.

"Are you okay?" Jessie asked. She clicked off the devil box.

"Not really. One of my patients killed himself."

"Are you serious?"

"Remember the letters we took to Vermont last week? Him."

"Why?"

"He did something to his family—I don't know what—and they wouldn't forgive him. He sent them money to make up for it, and they sent it back. He couldn't handle the rejection, so he bit through the line on his pump. God help me, Jessie, all I could think about was Uncle Reggie."

"He wouldn't do that."

"No, he wouldn't, but I couldn't live with myself if he stayed away because I was too cruel to him. I should have been nicer when we saw him in Florida. I said some bad things."

Veronica started to cry, and Jessie scooted across the sofa. She hugged her mother.

"He'll come back, Mom. He can't stay there the rest of his life."

"I don't want him to fade away. It's funny, last week all I wanted to do was yell at him; now I just want to say I'm sorry and have him back here, where he belongs. Things go by so fast, Jessie. You get locked into a way of doing things and you get used to doing them wrong; then before you know it, it's all over. Like my patient today—by the time he figured it out, he couldn't go back."

"Did he leave a note?" she asked.

Veronica showed it to her.

"Why does this bother you?" Jessie said. "This guy sounds like an asshole."

"Because I don't know what I'm doing with *my* life. I'm not enjoying it. I'm not doing anything for my kids; I'm not paying attention to you guys. And I've got grandchildren who need my help. Isn't that what good moms are supposed to do—help their daughters raise their children? I got all pissy when Catherine married Charlie, and I almost cut myself off from them. I basically hate my job, and I took it out on you because you were the only one around. I stayed mad at Uncle Reggie too long, and now he's gone. I took a vow to preserve life, and then I get patients who don't care if they live or die. Why do I bother? What am I doing with my life?"

"'Watch what you're doing with your time,'" Jessie said. "'All the endless ruins of the past must stay behind.'"

"That's good," Veronica said. "Is that from the Bible?"

"No. The Grateful Dead."

24

I stayed at the station most of the day, trying to keep the heat off the town. The governor's office called, offering to send the National Guard, and some TV guy faxed a proposal for a reality show named *Notched*.

At six o'clock I drove to the ball fields to break up a crowd of kids who had surrounded the teepees and knocked over a Harley. It looked like half the town was there, spoiling for a fight, so I sent everybody home and put a cruiser at the entrance of the park. I posted another on Sister's street to protect her neighborhood. All over the valley, the mood was getting ugly.

Wes was sitting in his chair looking at a blank TV. I sat in the other chair.

"What did the guy say when the horse went into the bar?" I asked. "No, that's not right. There's this bar, and a horse goes in—"

"Is this the only joke you know besides me?" Wes said. He looked old. "I'm sorry, Danny, that wasn't fair. This just ain't one of those funny days."

It was six forty-five—fifteen minutes into his show. It was killing him, not being on the air.

"What can I do for you?" I asked.

He shook his head. "Nothing. It's all over. I can't show my face in this town after what happened last night. I'll give up the show—if that's what it comes to. I just don't want anybody to get hurt. I don't want anything bad to happen to you."

"I'll be alright, and nobody's going to get hurt. I promise. You and I need to go through those boxes of evidence tomorrow—just to see what's in there."

"Sure," he said. "Come on over."

I could see his reflection on the dark screen. His head was down on his chest, and his eyes were set on a spot near the wall. He looked like he was going to cry.

Sister and Beth were talking quietly in the kitchen. After a while, I went to the fridge and got a couple of root beers. Wes held his bottle, absently picking at the label with his thumbnail. No belching contests tonight.

When Beth came out of the kitchen, I stopped her.

"You didn't tell her about the map, did you?"

"Boone, stop it. Of course not. We were talking about me. But I think you should tell her. It's not right—keeping secrets from each other. You got rid of it. Right?"

"Yeah, I did."

"Then what's the big deal?"

We sat down to Wes's favorite dinner: Salisbury steak with fried onions, mashed potatoes, gravy, applesauce, yams, cornbread, and buttermilk. For dessert: pecan pie and vanilla ice cream.

"So, have you heard from Benny?" Sister asked.

"He's doing good," said Beth. "He's writing a paper about the Pavlovian stimuli in laugh tracks."

I looked to Wes for a punch line. He was making a volcano out of his mashed potatoes.

"It looks like the Sox won another one," I said.

"They're doing good," said Beth.

Sister gave me her worried look, and Beth squeezed my hand. The mood was morbid, like being trapped in a bomb shelter.

We were having coffee when my cell phone rang—the theme from *The Good, the Bad, and the Ugly*. Caller ID said Unknown. Nobody has this number, except for family and the station.

"Boone," said a voice very different from any man's. It was heavy and guttural, deep, as if he were speaking without breathing, without tone or emotion, dark as death itself. When I heard it, I felt myself weaken and start to fall.

"It's time," the voice said. "I'm taking you away now. It's over."

"Who is this?"

"You know who."

"Now? Why now?"

"Why not? I'm bored."

I sat on the chair, my stomach churning and my sight going gray on the edges. My chest felt tight, and I couldn't catch my breath.

"What's wrong? Boone, what's wrong?" Beth looked in my face. "What is it?"

"It's him. He wants to take me now. I'm not ready, I'm not ready," I said.

Sister grabbed the phone.

"Hello," she said. "What do you want?"

She listened for a moment, her face going fierce with fear. "Adepto te secundum mihi," she said. She listened some more, and I could hear the voice insisting, growling, impatient. "Reverto ut abyssus, Diabolus," she said. Then she dropped the phone and ran out of the room. Wes came over and stood beside Beth.

I picked up the phone.

"Let's go," said the voice. "Right now. I'm outside, so say your good-byes, maggot, and prepare to serve me."

"No, no, this can't be right," I said.

Sister ran back into the room with her crucifix. She grabbed Wes and pulled him to the door. She set her jaw and hunched her shoulders like a wrestler squaring off. Wes picked up a stick of firewood.

"Open it," she said. "This shall not happen."

I stood. Leaning on Beth, I followed Sister and Wes to the door, standing behind them, my hand on Wes's back.

"I can't do this," I said. "I can't."

"We must face him," said Sister. "Stay together, don't step outside, and pray like there's no tomorrow." She crossed herself. "Now open the door, Wesley."

Wes opened the door. Sister stepped in front of him and held her crucifix high in the porch light. "Adepto te secundum mihi," she called in her strong, clear voice. "Say your prayer, Daniel—your Axis Mundi."

I was too weak to speak.

We looked to the darkness just beyond the edge of the yard. A tall figure in a long black cape was standing still as a corpse in the dark, his hideously misshapen head staring at us without expression. He began chanting in a muffled voice. It took a moment to catch the words.

"Happy Anniversary to you, Happy Anniversary to you," he sang. Then he opened his cape and stepped into the light. He was wearing a T-shirt that said KISS ME, I'M SATAN.

"Dammit, Reggie," I yelled. "You almost gave me a stroke."

"Gotcha good, huh?" he said, taking off his cartoon head.

In two jumps, Sister was across the yard and into his arms.

"Reggie," she squealed, hugging him and bouncing on the balls of her feet like a cheerleader. "You're here, you're here. You're really here. Look at you!"

I caught Wes's eye, and for a man who claims to have seen everything, he looked wonderfully stupefied. His eyes were bigger than his glasses, and he was moving his mouth like a guppy.

Reggie stepped toward him and took his hand.

"Hi, Dad," he said. "How are you doing?"

"I'm doing great, now," Wes said, pulling him into a spine-bending bear hug. "I missed you. I really missed you."

"Me, too, Dad."

Beth grabbed him; then Sister started again with the second round. They stood in the front yard whooping it up for twenty minutes. Wes put on Reggie's Disney head and chased the cat. Sister hung on to Reggie and couldn't stop giggling. Beth stayed pressed against me, her arm around my waist.

Reggie was digging his role as homecoming king.

"Are you hungry?" Wes asked.

"Are you kidding? I've been on a train for two days."

"Are you here to stay?" I asked him.

"Do you want me to?"

"We could use the help."

"Cue the cavalry," he said. "Reinforcements are here."

We went inside the house and Beth called Veronica to come over. Vee was crying when she jumped out of the car.

"Nothing ever changes," Reggie said.

"No," she said, hugging him. "No, no. I was afraid I'd never see you again. I'm so sorry, Reggie, I treated you so bad. I'd be miserable if you never came back."

"What? You're happy now?"

"I'm so happy to see you."

He looked at me, bug-eyed, completely flummoxed.

"But that was my speech," he said, hugging her and grinning.

The five of us sat around the table, watching Reggie eat.

"What happened to you?" Wes asked. "You look great."

"I went to Disney World and got younger. I guess that's why they call it the Magic Kingdom."

"So how old are you now?"

"Thirty-two, give or take a few months."

"You look better than the last time you were thirty-two."

"This is what healthy looks like. Actually, I never eat like this anymore. I think I'm getting drunk on gravy."

He told us about spending two days on the train with a thirteen-year-old girl who understood more about pride, sorrow, and forgiveness than a cathedral full of saints. While he told his story of coming home with Grace, Sister closed her eyes and smiled, nodding to herself—as if hearing the best part of a favorite song.

"What are you going to do now?" Veronica asked.

"Get a job, find a place to stay until I get back on my feet. I've got to see Carolyn and try to clear up everything, and I want to find Theresa."

"Why don't you stay with Jessie and me? We'd love to have you. You can have Catherine's room and drive Earl's old car."

"Thanks, little sister," he said.

Wes was in high spirits.

"So what's going on with you and the Indians?" Reggie asked.

"Like the hunter said to the duck, 'It's all over except for the shooting.' "

"Who's the hunter and who's the duck?"

"I don't know, but I'm quacking under the pressure."

"Do they have a good case?"

"Somewhere between a case of beer and a case of hives," Wes said.

"Oh, honey, you're so punny," Sister said, giving him a hug.

"Punny?" said Reggie. "It's more like punishment."

After the last piece of pie, Sister picked up some plates and went to the kitchen.

"Wesley, can you come in here and help me?"

"With what?"

"Something. Can you just come in here?"

"I want to stay out here."

"Wesley."

"What? I want to stay out here with the kids. We're having fun."

"They need to talk about things. Like private things."

"Oh, I get it—the P-A-R-T-Y." He winked and shrugged, stood up, and started for the kitchen. He turned and came back. "No strippers," he whispered. "It wouldn't be A-P-A-R-O-P-E-I-A-T-E."

"What are you trying to spell?" Veronica asked.

"I don't know," he said. "See you later."

Beth, Veronica, Reggie, and I sat at the table

"You couldn't have picked a better day to come back," Beth said. "He was a mess before you showed up."

"Yeah, it's funny how it all fits together," Reggie said. "Last week I was afraid to face you guys. I thought you wouldn't take me back."

"I know," said Veronica. "Last week I was monster bitch. I almost lost Jessie. Then everything changed overnight. Now I wake up every morning in a good mood. I'm not obsessed with things going wrong. I don't smoke or medicate anymore. I get along with my kids, and I like my life. Imagine that. Who could believe those bedtime stories were the real thing? There really was a gift I was supposed to find when I got older. Amazing."

"How about you?" Reggie asked me.

"I'm good," I said.

"No, he's not," said Beth. "He's a wreck."

"You look kind of worn down," Reggie said. "What's up?"

"Nothing. I'm okay."

"I think you should tell them," Beth said.

"Tell us what?"

"I don't want to talk about it," I said.

We sat and looked at each other, nobody speaking.

"Okay," said Veronica. "This is almost weird enough."

"I don't want to talk about anything," I said. "It's my problem. Wes, the town, the Indians, and now this thing with Beth."

Beth looked down at the table. I knew what she was thinking. Blaming her. This thing.

"Don't worry," said Veronica, touching Beth's hand. "These tests are easy. Non-invasive. And they get the results pretty quick. If it's just headaches you're having, it's probably premenopausal."

Beth nodded. I felt Reggie looking at me.

"Well, it's been a good night," I said. "So I guess we'll say good night." One of Wes's lines.

"Let's get together tomorrow and talk," Reggie said. "I'm here to help. I want things to be different now."

"Okay," I said. "Maybe tomorrow."

It was late. It had been a mind-bending day, and everybody was tired. Reggie was going to stay at Wes and Sister's tonight, in our old bedroom. We all hugged good-bye. Beth and I followed Veronica to her house, then drove up the other side of the valley to our place.

"I'm sorry," I said. "But I didn't want to talk about the map. It's my business."

"It's our business, Boone. It's family business. I was just trying to help."

"I know, but it's too complicated to get everybody involved."

"You burnt it, right?"

"Of course."

"Then why not tell them about it, and the last time you saw the Devil?"

"Because I want to tell Sister first. And because it sounds like I can't do my job."

"But it makes me sound like I'm freaking out over hot flashes. I think you're jealous."

"Of what?"

"Reggie, and the whole fatted calf thing."

"I am not. I'm glad he's back. It's a good thing. It's good for everybody. I'm trying to figure out how he fits in."

"Fits in? He's your brother. He's one of us. I think you feel threatened because Veronica and Reggie have found their gifts, and they did it on their own."

"No."

"It's a natural reaction, honey—especially since you've worked so hard to keep this family together."

"I don't feel threatened," I said. We were crossing Main Street, and I looked both ways for the Channel 6 truck. "I'm happy for them. I really am."

Of course she was right.

By dumb luck alone, Reggie and Veronica have found their gifts. Veronica is happy, hopeful, and reconciled with her children. Reggie has enough grace to be patron saint of Franklin Notch. The guy can't stop apologizing. That leaves me—the only one without his God-given gift, the only one still struggling to make sense of his life.

I couldn't tell if Beth believed me about burning the map. It didn't matter. One more day, then I can come clean with everybody—as long as my new plan works. When I get this fixed, I can 'fess up, as Sister says.

I stayed downstairs long enough to let Beth get ready for bed. I couldn't risk her finding my map and taking it while I slept.

"Are you coming up?" she asked.

"I think I'm going to hang out for a while and watch TV. The late news."

"Good night," she said.

"Good night."

I put a sleeping bag on the sofa and slid inside. I looked out the window, into the night, and tried to get control of my battle plan. The Devil was outflanking me. I saw his hand in everything—even Reggie's return. This was the Devil's way: first raise the stakes by threatening my wife, then throw me off guard by sending my brother home. Reggie's homecoming looked like a good thing, but it was just a trick to isolate me from my family. While everyone else rejoiced inside, I had to stand guard outside, on the edge of darkness.

Reggie means well by offering to help, but it's not him talking. It's the Devil's script, the Devil's show. He's sending me unseasoned reinforcements to slow me down. Very clever.

Sister thinks she knows best, but if I hadn't taken the map from the Devil, I wouldn't have a chance to beat him at his own game. As usual, Wes is oblivious. He doesn't even know he's in danger. While he and Reggie stage their prodigal lovefest, I've got to protect them both.

Veronica is too distracted to back me up. This new crush of hers is probably another one of the Devil's tricks.

As usual, it's all up to me, and just to be safe, I'll assume the worst. I can't trust anybody. That's okay. I can handle it.

25

The next morning, Jessie packed her stuff while Veronica called Reggie.

"I'm worried about Boone," she said. "What do you think he was arguing about—last night with Beth?"

"I don't know. I'll call him later. He said he wanted to hang out."

"I'll stay if you think I should."

"No, go to Vermont. Have fun. I can handle it. And give me some credit on this responsibility thing. I already made a pot of coffee."

"Reggie, I'm serious. He still thinks he can save the world."

"Vee, I can handle it. I'll be driving around all weekend apologizing to people; I might as well keep an eye on Boone."

Halfway to Vermont, Veronica and Jessie went on a shopping spree for Catherine, Charlie, and the babies.

"What do you think of this?" Veronica held up a tank top.

"She's not really the tank-top type," Jessie said.

"I was asking for me. I like this."

"Looks good. While we're at it, how do these look on me?" She was wearing a pair of round-rim sunglasses.

"Janis Joplin junior."

"Life is just like a baw-aw-awl and chay-ay-ain," Jessie sang, twisted up in soul and pain in the aisle of Marshall's.

Catherine was kneeling in her garden, cutting shocks of purple-gray sage and piling them in a basket. Molly was standing beside her, wearing Catherine's wide-brimmed straw hat and supervising the project. For late September, the garden was surprisingly lush. Fall perennials were blooming, and the vines tied to the fence were still heavy with sun-colored gourds.

When Molly saw the Camry, she squealed and ran through the gate toward the driveway. The hat sailed off her head, and her pigtails bounced around her happy face. Catherine stood, grinned and waved, then followed Molly.

"What's your name again?" Jessie asked Molly, scooping her up.

"Foof," said the little girl, holding up three fingers.

Charlie came out of the house carrying Vedran.

"You're early." Catherine gave her mother a hug.

"She needs pampering," Jessie said. "She's had a bad week."

"Poor Momma," said Catherine. "Let's get you a glass of wine and some babies to play with."

"Hi, Missus M," Charlie said, giving Veronica a hug. He handed her the baby and picked up the duffel bag. "Trade ya."

"Charlie, call me something else, okay?"

"Sure. Like what?"

"How about Mom?"

"Sure," he said, smiling, "Mom."

Going into the house, Veronica gave the baby a great wet smooch on the neck. He squealed and grabbed her hair.

"Actually," said Veronica, inside the house, "I want to go into town first. How do I get to the clinic?"

The Free Town Clinic was a neat-looking white frame house one block from the center of town. The front parlor was a waiting room, and sitting around the room on a Friday at four-thirty was a collection of mothers with their children, an old woman with a pale teenage girl, and a worried-looking boy wearing jeans, workboots, and a T-shirt. He was holding an ice pack on his collarbone. A sign on the wall read NO ONE DENIED HEALTH CARE. PAY IF YOU CAN, WHEN YOU CAN. A sign underneath said BARTER ACCEPTED. NO MORE CHICKENS PLEASE.

Veronica walked to the receptionist's window. A middle-aged woman in a wheelchair smiled up at her.

"Could you please tell Dr. Barringer that Veronica is here?"

The woman rolled herself away. A minute later Doc opened the door, wide-eyed and smiling.

"You're early," he said. He kissed her, and they hugged for a long moment. "I'm so happy you're here."

"I couldn't stay away," she said. "It's been a wild week. I need to talk to somebody."

"I'm your guy. What happened?"

"Reggie came back. That's the good news. But that lobectomy killed himself. On my watch."

"I hope you're not blaming yourself," he said.

"I don't think so, but it really shook me."

"I'm sorry," he said. "Come on back. You can help me with some healthy sick people." He walked her through the door with his arm around her waist, picked a stethoscope out of a drawer, draped it over her neck, and kissed her again. "I'd love to talk later."

He tapped on the door of an examination room, opened it for Veronica, and followed her in. Reading a book on a bench by the window was an older woman. Veronica guessed she was in her mid-eighties. She was thin and bright-eyed with a swirl of fine silver hair piled on top of her head. Her face was creased with laugh lines, and she smiled with a full set of perfect teeth. She was wearing jeans and a white cowboy shirt.

"Hello, Jimmy," said the woman, closing her book.

"Hello, Mrs. Dykstra. This is Veronica Marston, from Manchester. She's a nurse, and she's a good friend of mine."

Veronica shook the woman's hand. Delicate as cornsilk, dry as a husk.

"Mrs. Dykstra is the healthiest woman in Crawfordsville. I see her once a year, whether she needs it or not." Doc sat beside her on the bench, and as they talked he casually examined her—rolling up the sleeve of her shirt to take her pulse, holding her hand to check her fingernails, feeling her spine at the base of her neck, and gently touching her throat beneath her jawline.

"Alright, Cinderella," said Doc, dropping to his knees in front of the woman. "Let's check that ankle."

He untied the woman's shoe and slipped it off her narrow foot with the sock. He cradled her foot in his left palm and rotated her swollen ankle, lightly pressing the joint with the fingertips of his right hand. Veronica could hear the ankle click.

"You're not wearing your brace when you walk, are you?"

"Nope," said the woman. "It slows me down."

Veronica knelt beside him to look at the woman's ankle, and when their shoulders touched, she felt the soft rush of closeness.

"Should we take it off at the knee?" Doc joked. He left the room while Veronica dressed the woman's foot with a bandage and replaced her sock and shoe. When Doc returned he was carrying an Aircast and two small brown bottles.

Veronica braced the ankle while Doc explained the medication.

"This is goldenseal. Take two drops in the morning for five days straight. It's an anti-inflammatory, and it's good for your swollen glands. Wear the brace every time you take a step."

Doc helped her stand. She gave him a peck on the cheek. "Thanks, Jimmy," she said. They walked her out of the room.

"She'll have that off before she leaves the driveway," Doc said, watching her walk out the front door.

Veronica laughed. "I need to go back to Catherine's. Jessie and I brought them some presents, and we're taking them car shopping tomorrow. Don't say anything, it's a surprise."

"What a good mom you are. Can I see you later?"

"I'll sneak out," she said. They kissed again.

Gumbo, home-grown salad, cornbread, apple cider. Zweiback, applesauce, and ice cream for Vedran Smailovich Cooper. Molly sat in the glory seat between Veronica and Jessie, poking them and saying, "Youwannaknowwhat, youwannaknowwhat?"

After dinner, Jessie pulled all the packages out of the trunk and they opened presents. There were new clothes for everyone, toys for Molly, a Jolly Jumper for Vedran, and a new laptop for Charlie.

"And here's the big news," Veronica said. "Tomorrow, Jessie and I are taking you shopping for a new car." Catherine hugged her mother and whooped; Charlie looked overwhelmed; Molly stomped around the kitchen in her new winter boots shouting, "New blue car, new blue car." Vedran dozed on Jessie's chest.

After the celebration, Charlie and Jessie washed dishes while Veronica helped Catherine put the babies to bed.

"This is the nicest thing anyone has ever done for us," Catherine said. "Charlie's so shy, and everybody always takes him for granted. That's why it's so cool you're treating him like family. Thanks, Mom."

Later, while Catherine and Jessie whispered on the sofa and Charlie fiddled with his new computer on the kitchen table, Veronica excused herself.

"I'm going out for a while," she said, trying to sound as casual as possible.

"And where do you think you're going?" Catherine asked, squinting like a momma skeptic.

"Just out," said Veronica.

"Do we know the people you'll be with? Did you leave a number where we can reach you?"

Jessie was enjoying this. "Yeah, just remember," she said, wagging her finger. "Your actions have consequences."

"I hope so," Veronica laughed, heading out the door and giving Charlie a pat on the shoulder as she slipped past him.

Veronica drove around the empty farmhouse and dark barn, across the field behind the empty Barringer estate. Above her, the night sky shone—more stars than space. She bounced the Camry down the narrow path through the woods.

It was eleven o'clock. Hope it's not too late, she whispered to the windshield.

She saw the Christmas lights and heard the mariachi music before she made the last two turns in the path. She parked her car in the wide space before the clearing and walked through the trees toward the commotion.

The clearing looked like a Tijuana truck stop. The old RV was outlined with strings of bright Christmas lights, and there was a set of speakers on the roof, playing Spanish guitar and fiddle music, complete with chirping vocals. In front of the camper, Doc stood behind a half dozen pots and kettles that were simmering on a long rack over the campfire. A wooden table across the front of the RV was heaped high with piles of tomatoes, peppers, and greens.

He hadn't heard her come through the woods, so he was still singing and dancing to himself when Veronica sneaked up beside him. She hugged him from behind.

"Hi, Jimmy," she said, close to his ear.

"You're here!" Doc said. "I knew you'd make it." He poked around in a cooler under the table and fished out a bottle. "Here," he said. "Try this. Chihuahua beer."

"Is this a theme party?" Veronica asked.

"We're making salsa," Doc said. "I've wanted to do this for years, but I never had all the right spices. I grew everything except the lemon."

"Where did you get the recipe?"

Doc pointed to the pots. "I'm improvising," he said. "Whichever batch we don't like, we can use for fuel in the truck."

"What can I do?"

"Whatever you want," Doc said. "Chop some tomatoes, roll some tortillas, or just sit and talk."

Veronica took her beer to the table and started dicing greens. "How much salsa are we making?"

"Gallons," he said. "I got seven cases of Mason jars as trade for a broken ankle. I'm going to prescribe it at the clinic. Doc Barringer's Chunky Fire Cure. Actually, salsa is good medicine. It's a great cleanser."

Veronica put a pan of tortillas on a stone to warm; Doc stirred the salsa. They sipped Chihuahua beer from the same bottle.

"What's this?" Veronica asked, holding up a shock of greens with purple fringe.

"I don't know. I found it growing near the llamas. I like the way it smells."

"Should I put some in?"

"Sure. Toss a pinch into the sixth pot. It could use something."

They fussed over the bubbling brew like two kids making mud pies. They danced in the firelight to "Mexicali Rose" and chased each other around the camper, throwing tomatoes.

Sometime between midnight and the last Chihuahua, they stopped mixing the pots. Doc put a blanket on the ground, and they lay side by side, holding hands and watching the moon float by.

"It's the strangest thing," Veronica said. "It's like there are two worlds. There's the world I live in, where people scheme and do anything they want—and even kill themselves in hospitals—and then there's the world of Catherine, Jessie, and Dr. Jimmy, where people are happy with life and follow the rules. They help each other and they respect themselves. I don't like my world anymore. It's too vicious. It's eating me alive."

"Sounds like you need a world transplant. Move to Crawfordsville. Take a leave of absence and get a short-term rental. I know some nice places in town. Work a couple days a week at the clinic, spend the rest of the time reading, hiking around, and playing with the kids. Try it for a few months."

"Yeah," she said, smiling at the bright night sky. "Maybe I will."

"When can you do it?"

"I don't know. It all depends on Wes and his problems with the town. Soon, I hope. Let me think about it."

They lay on their backs, watching sparks sail upward, into the stars—and shards of Heaven flashing downward in the darkness, streaking to earth.

"I'm so tired," Veronica said. "Bone tired. Are we going to try the salsa?"

"Before bed?"

"Why not?"

Doc peeled a tortilla out of the pan and spooned a bowl of salsa from the last pot. They sat cross-legged on the blanket and dipped salsa with pieces of tortilla.

"Interesting," said Doc. "How many peppers did you put in this?"

"A handful of the red ones."

"Yikes." He looked a little dizzy. "What's that flavor?"

"That green and purple stuff from the llama pen."

Doc looked at the tortilla, then dropped it on the blanket.

"What's wrong?"

"I don't know," he said. "I feel funny. My fingers felt weird touching it."

Veronica laughed. "Too many Chihuahuas," she said, but when she took another bite of salsa herself, she felt a rush of touch on the rim of her lips as the tortilla slid into her mouth. Her skin felt electric. She could feel the folds of the dough inside her mouth, and with her tongue she could feel the pulpy flesh of each piece of pepper, the ragged tips of the cilantro stems, and the smooth rounded crown on each kernel of corn. As she chewed, bursts of each spice exploded in her mouth.

Her skin felt raw, too sensitive. She could feel everything—the night air brushing the hairs on her arm, the threads of her clothing shifting and sliding over the hyper-tactile nerve endings in her skin.

"What's happening?" she asked.

"I think my synapses are wired open," Doc said. "I can actually feel the underside of my watchband." He held out his hand, and when their fingertips touched, an electric jolt passed between them. Their eyes locked as Veronica brushed the balls of her fingertips over the palms of Doc's hands.

"I can feel the ridges of your fingerprints," he said.

Veronica leaned into him, sucked his bottom lip into her mouth, and unbuttoned the front of his shirt. She slid her fingertips across his chest, then lightly pinched his nipples with her fingernails. He shivered and caught his breath.

They fell sideways onto the blanket, pulling off their clothes, tasting, touching, and sliding into each other.

It was electric—everywhere they touched—at the edge of pain.

When he brushed the tips of her labia, she exploded in a spine-twister of an orgasm, clutching at him, pulling him inside. He couldn't hold himself. Before he had entered her halfway, he burst in a dozen savage spasms, each one locking him rigid, out of control.

There was no finishing. After an hour of of strainings and release, they were still aroused. When they exhausted one cycle of coaxing each other to serial orgasms, they began again. Lying on the blanket, naked under the harvest night, they gasped and shuddered as they writhed around each other, rolling under and over, tangling themselves in impossible knots like teenage wrestlers. They nibbled and teased, kissed and squeezed, talking, giggling, and moaning in waves of heat for three hours straight.

By daybreak, the effects of the aphrodisiac salsa were starting to wear off. They still couldn't stop touching each other, but the pace of their lovemaking had settled into a lazy and easy, middle-aged groove.

As the gray-blue dawn washed over the clearing, Veronica and Doc sat shoulder to shoulder, still naked, watching the colors come up in the garden.

"So beautiful," said Veronica. "How can everything be so beautiful?"

They dressed and fed the animals together. They collected eggs, and Doc showed Veronica how to milk one of the nannies.

She made breakfast while he watered the fire and dismantled the sound system on the roof.

He came into the camper, carrying an armful of ladles and dirty pots.

"Breakfast time," said Veronica, setting the plates on the table. "We're having omelets. Western style." Dribbled across the top of the eggs was a spoonful of salsa.

"For the love of God, no," Doc said, clutching the doorway in mock terror.

At two thirty in the afternoon, Veronica meandered through the door of Catherine's kitchen. Her hair was wild, her eyes were glazed, her shoes were untied, and her T-shirt was on backward. She was wearing a pair of Doc's jeans.

"Who dressed you?" Catherine asked.

"We made salsa," Veronica said vacantly, heading for the shower.

"Cool," said Jessie. "Can I have some?"

"I don't think so," said Veronica, shutting the bathroom door behind her.

Charlie was giddy over the new wagon. It was large enough to carry Catherine, the babies, his practice cello, his performance cello, and his viola da gamba. It had a killer sound system, and—wonder of wonders—it actually started every time he turned the key.

When they returned home from the auto spree, he gave Jessie a ride into town to meet her new friends; then he sat in the driveway listening to Brahms and reading the owner's manual cover to cover.

"He's never had anything nice," Catherine said, standing inside the cabin window with Veronica, watching him test the car. "He's a true artist. He cares more about beautiful things than he does about money. That's why I married him, you know. Anybody can buy flowers, remember birthdays, and order the right wine. Only Charlie stays up all night and writes me sonatas."

Veronica felt like crying. "I'm sorry I was so evil before," she said. She hugged Catherine. "I didn't understand."

"No problem," Catherine said. "I was a little scared of the whole thing myself."

"You did the right thing. You've got a beautiful family. How would you feel about Jessie and me moving up here?"

Catherine yelped. "You're kidding! When?"

"I don't know. I guess if we do, it will be after all the trouble with Wes gets settled. Maybe in the spring."

"That will be so much fun," Catherine said. "You can watch the babies grow up. I need a good friend for a mother."

Doc met them at the concert. Molly wanted to sit on his lap, and when she got sleepy she stretched herself across Doc's and Veronica's legs.

It was a perfect concert. The ensemble was tight and polished. There was a family vibe in the audience of musicians, students, and friends. Charlie's pieces were the most vibrant, decorating the spare soul of Renaissance music with his sweet lyrical inventions. The encore was titled "A Nocturne for Catherine."

Doc carried Molly around the reception while Catherine held Vedran. Charlie stood with his group, awkwardly accepting compliments.

"Do you see those three people over there?" Catherine asked Veronica. "They're the committee from Boston who want Charlie to write a concerto for their museum. And they're going to pay him," Catherine said, bugging her eyes.

When the reception was over, Jessie and Doc loaded equipment while Veronica and Catherine held the babies. After Charlie locked the auditorium and Jessie left to spend the night with friends, Catherine and Charlie drove off in the new wagon, and Veronica went back to the clearing in the pickup with Doc.

26

It was a shock, seeing Earl's old car at Wes and Sister's house; then I remembered that Reggie was driving it while he stayed at Veronica's. Good, I thought, the more people we have going through the boxes, the more credible my fake discovery of the map will seem. My little scheme could actually work.

Sister was making cookies in the house, so I waited in the kitchen for a fresh batch to take to the barn.

"They've been out there since this morning," she said. "Your father has been looking forward to this for days. Have you got a little time? I still need to talk to you."

"Sure. How about after we finish?"

Perfect, I thought. Wes finds the map and I never have to admit I lied to Sister. I still don't trust Beth not to tell her about it.

I took the cookies out back. The barn looked like Frankenstein's lab. Wes had cranked up his old root beer machine—a five-foot steel pressure cooker sitting on a barbecue rack over a propane flame. There were pipes, valves, gauges, and faucets sticking out of the body of the still, and they dripped and sputtered with bursts of steam. It looked like a giant carburetor. The air was rich with a sassafras smell.

"Hey, buddy," Wes yelled. He was wearing his overalls, a raccoon coat, and a fire chief's hat. He was tapping a tire iron on a gauge that looked like an alarm clock. Reggie was chopping sassafras roots on the workbench with a machete. He was wearing tails, a fez, and a pair of aviator's goggles. They were standing in a puddle of dark brown root water.

"Oh boy, cookies," beamed Wes. The top of the tank rumbled and belched. "We're making the mash," he yelled above the hiss of the contraption. "It's almost thick enough. When it gets like mud, we'll drain off the syrup, add water, carbonate it, and put it in bottles."

"How do you know when it's done?"

He shrugged. "I lost the directions," he yelled.

"Mash, mashie, mash," Reggie shouted, grinning and whacking roots.

"I thought we were going to sort through your evidence boxes," I said.

Scattered around the barn were remnants of Wes's various collections and projects: parts for his ancient maroon Chevy, the Chevy itself, his log-cabin houseboat prototype, an abandoned earthworm farm, a huge papier-mâché bust of JFK that looked exactly like Bette Midler, his phone-booth sauna, his recording studio, trays of arrowheads, and his fourteen badly carved twenty-foot totem poles. It was obvious that his costume collection had caught his fancy today. There were open boxes of Elizabethan clothes, cowboy gear, and World War II junk everywhere.

"It can wait," he said.

"It's kind of important, don't you think?"

"I don't go to court for a while."

"It's next Monday," I said. "Where's the stuff they subpoenaed?"

"Over there," he said, waving the tire iron toward a stack of cartons. "But I want to make root beer now. Get suited up and punch in. We're at a very critical juncture in the project," he yelled, saluting me, then Reggie.

"National Security," Reggie shouted, waving the machete. "Viva le car-bonacion."

"Do you mind if I go through the boxes?"

"Knock yourself out," Wes yelled.

I went back to the boxes, pulled up a wobbly chair, and opened the first one. It was full of Veronica's childhood knickknacks: diaries, homework, cards, and pictures of forlorn-looking animals. I opened a diary to a page titled "Why I Hate My Family."

My mother always walks around talking in Latin or something and my younger brother teases me. I wish he was dead somehow very painfull. My father is never home and when he is, he tells jokes that are so stupid I want to puke seriously. The only one I like in my family (besides Quincy Rabbit) is my big brother who always pays attention and agrees with me about everything.

There was a box full of Reggie's sports awards and another with pictures of me and Wes dressed for our colonial show. There were letters from Rotary clubs thanking us for our inspiring presentation of heritage and history. There was a reel of tape—"Boone, 12, practicing The Show." It probably had vastly incriminating consequences for Wes—and me, as the town's future chief of police, testifying to a colonial holocaust.

There was a box of love letters from Wes to Sister, and notebooks in her handwriting that described her visions over the past fifty years.

What was I thinking? This was personal, family history. How could I violate these memories with something so profane as a map from the Devil? And besides, if we turned over these boxes, we would never see them again—after some snotty lawyer smeared them across the front of a jury box. After the trial, they would stay locked in an evidence room for thirty years. Our family history would be wiped out, gone forever.

I left the map in my pocket. This was a stupid idea; there had to be a better way to beat the Devil.

I was restacking the boxes when a blast shook the barn. It was so powerful, it pushed me over the pile, onto the floor. The barn filled with smoke, dust, and a choking smell of root beer. I pulled myself up and looked through the haze to the other side of the barn, where Reggie and Wes had been standing.

It was a mess.

The top of the pressure cooker had blown off, straight through the roof, over the backyard, and fifty feet into the woods.

The two wizards were standing on either side of the ruptured tank, bug-eyed and completely covered with sassafras mud.

There was sludge everywhere—stuck on the ceiling, blasted across the barn, and over all the windows.

"Are you guys okay?" I yelled.

They were already laughing—shrieking like lunatics, pointing at each other, at the hole in the roof and the three inches of root beer paste that covered everything within forty feet of where they stood.

I made it to their side of the barn, slipping twice in root goop. They were completely out of control, falling all over each other in roaring hysterics. After ten minutes of Moffatt delirium, they tried to clean themselves. They rubbed at the reddish-brown gunk that covered their faces and hands. The blast had power-dyed every inch of their skin—except for four-inch circles around Reggie's eyes where the goggles had been. My father and brother were exactly the color that two white guys would paint themselves if they wanted to really piss off a bunch of Indians.

I helped them put a tarp over the hole in the roof, then tried to slip out the door. Reggie followed me to the car. He wanted to talk.

"What a scream, huh?" He was still trying to wipe the stain off his face and hands. Sister was inside the house, and I knew she wanted to see me. Since I had scrapped my plan for discovering the map, I wanted to leave— go somewhere and reconsider my options.

"Boone, there's some things I've got to say." With his new Root Boy look, it was hard to take Reggie seriously. "I'm sorry I was such a burden all these years. I know it was hard, cleaning up after me, and I want you to know how much I appreciate it. I was selfish, and I want to make it up to you."

"That's okay. We're just glad you're back."

"I want to help," he said. "Whatever needs to be done. I want to help with family stuff."

"Everything's under control at the moment," I said. "But if anything comes up—"

"I'm serious," he said. "Anything."

"Alright. I'll let you know."

He hugged me. I was afraid he would feel the heat from the map in my pocket. I tried to angle away, toward the car.

"There's more," he said. "I want to apologize for all the bad things I did."

"Don't worry about it."

"No, it's important to me. There's a lot you don't know about. Remember the time all your tapes went missing from your car?"

"You did that? You stole my tapes?"

He shrugged. "I sold them. I needed the money."

"You told me Jerry Schmidt did it. You let me beat him up. Dammit, Reggie, now I've got to go apologize to him. He's been avoiding me for forty years."

"I know, I know. That's what I mean. I'm sorry. There's more."

I saw Sister standing in the window, waving me inside.

"Maybe we can do this later?" I said. "I've got some things I need to take care of right now."

"Need help?"

"No. Police stuff."

"Well, I'm going to stay here for a while," he said. "Help clean up, have some dinner. Call me later, okay?"

I walked to my car with my head down. I couldn't face my mother.

I spent the night at the station. I told Beth I needed to stay close to the action. Before my trip to Disney World, Beth and I had never spent a night apart. Tonight, here I was, sleeping at the jail in my own hometown, a mountain away from my guardian angel. I tried to sleep on the cot in the break room, but I couldn't stop scheming, crafting new plans to save my life. Nothing came to mind. I had to wait for the Devil's next move.

27

After he led the closing prayer for the Friday night Bible study, Ronnie Dolan approached the assistant pastor.

"I can't talk to anyone about some of the things I'm going through," he said softly. "Instead of giving me advice, they just write everything down. I can't be honest about my feelings, and it's a hindrance to my progress."

"What kinds of feelings?"

"I feel like God wants to lead me in certain directions, but I can't connect with Him at that deeper level. Do you know what I mean?"

"I do," said the pastor. "And you've tried prayer."

"I pray all the time," said Dolan. "I think it's a question of discernment."

"I'd be happy to pray with you," the young man said.

"Would you? I know a place where it's quiet," said Holy Hell.

Before they found the assistant pastor's naked body on the supply room floor with his head nearly sliced off, Ronnie Dolan had escaped. He had unscrewed the window frame two floors above his flowerbed, sprinted the length of the narrow, long room, and dived out the tiny window. He sailed into the night, thirty feet or more—over the space between the building and the sidewalk, over the sidewalk, and onto a cushion of loosely packed earth six feet deep and very soft. He jumped up, brushed himself off, and, wearing the assistant pastor's clothes, picked the lock on the Grounds shed door, pulled out a ladder, dragged it to the wall, and scrambled over.

Saturday morning at the station, I got the call.

"Moffatt, we've got trouble." It was the guy from the attorney general's office. "Real trouble. That guy Dolan got loose from Concord. He killed a man, and now he's out. Do you have any idea where he might be?"

I hope in your basement, I wanted to say.

"How did he do it?" I asked.

"He killed some preacher and took his clothes. He must have had a key to the toolshed. He stole a ladder and threw it against the wall."

I felt dizzy. I could actually sense Ronnie Dolan's darkness rolling toward me through the woods, across the hills, over the creeks and valleys.

"Do you think he's coming my way?" I asked.

"I hope not. Especially with that town full of tourists you've got now."

My chest hurt.

"Get me something on the wire," I said. "Description, anything. I'm going to hit the road and look for him."

"We're getting a statement and a picture ready now. I'll fax it."

I called Beth.

"Oh, no," she said. "Benny's driving down from Henniker this afternoon. He's in the middle—between here and Concord."

"I'll go up and get him. I'm leaving now."

"Do you think that man is coming this way?"

"I wish you knew how to use a gun," I said. "Go to Wes and Sister's. Stay there until I get back."

"Did you get rid of that map?"

"First thing this morning," I lied.

"Thank you," she said.

I called all units back to the station, Xeroxed the flyer, and distributed it. Prison had been good to Ronnie Dolan. He didn't look much older in his picture. If anything, he looked tougher, more vicious.

My backup is my old Colt Python. When I need it, I keep it in a black doctor's bag on the seat beside me. I grabbed the bag and a 12-gauge off the rack and took off in the cruiser, lights on riot burst.

Sixty-five on Route 6. Crazy. It's one of the oldest roads in the state, and it banks and bends like a snake on a rockpile. I gunned it on the straights, then let the weight of the big car and the rise of the road slide me through the turns.

This was bad. Ronnie Dolan on the loose was poison in the ground—death to everything around him. This was the Devil's final move, turning Holy Hell loose to stalk my family. This game had turned against me, and I could lose everything now—my family, my life, two generations of righteous hard work—torn away in a day by this beast on the road. We could all be gone by nightfall.

This isn't about faith anymore. It's survival. I'm circling the wagons now, protecting the women and children.

How can I even think about faith while evil roams freely, stalking innocents on Route 6? The third time I saw the Devil, he *was* Ronnie Dolan.

Today is the rematch and I know I'm going to lose. I'm speeding to my death, driving right into his trap—delivering my soul in a Crown Victoria. It's over. He can get me when he wants; I just want to find Benny before Ronnie finds him.

As I drove, I scoped the front and back of every shack I passed. I watched for two things: my son, and the Devil himself. Benny was at school in Henniker, exactly halfway between me and Concord, and Holy Hell was on the run, probably heading south. I imagined him above me, coming downhill on this same road, in a stolen car and already armed, stopping in the college town for a bite to eat. He would submerge for a few hours and trim off a couple of college kids; and before anyone noticed they were missing, Ronnie would have money, a new car, and clothes that fit.

The Devil was calling the shots now. I knew if he wanted to kill Benny, he could put Ronnie next to him. I remembered what he said on the plane.

Just like you've got family—he's my boy.

I drove faster. I made it to Henniker in under an hour.

I went to Benny's place. One of his roommates told me where he was.

He was sitting in a coffee shop with some of his friends, looking at a laptop. A small girl with long dark hair was nestled into him, one of her legs draped over his, her hand under his jacket. When I walked to their table, they all looked up.

"Benny, you need to come with me."

"Benny?" said one of his friends.

"I'm kind of busy here," he said, his face going tight.

"What's this about?" asked his girlfriend, talking to me, looking at him.

"We've got an emergency, and I came to pick you up. Give you a ride home."

"Is my mother okay?"

"She's fine, it's something else. There's a prisoner, and he's escaped from Concord."

"Well, shouldn't you be picking *him* up?" Benny said.

"It's not that simple. He's very dangerous, a killer, and I think he's on the road."

"Is his brain squirming like a toad?" Benny asked.

His girlfriend laughed.

"This is serious," I said. "He has a grudge with me, and I'm making sure everyone is safe. Your mother knows about this."

"I'm not coming," he said. "I'll be there later."

"Benny—"

"He doesn't want to go with you," said his girlfriend. "Do you have a warrant or something?"

"Yeah, let's see the warrant," said a boy in a Tool sweatshirt.

"I'm not arresting anybody," I said. "I'm asking. As a father."

"Stepfather," said Benny.

"You're not even Henniker police," said Benny's girlfriend. "You can't just go to another town and pick somebody up."

"I'm not a cop here," I said. "This is family business."

"If you're not on cop business, you shouldn't be wearing a uniform," said a girl with dreads. "Or a gun."

"Benny," I said, reaching around his girlfriend and touching him on the shoulder.

The girl took my picture with her cell phone.

I took my hand off my son's shoulder. "This is for your mother and me," I said. "Please."

"Call your mother," said the girl with the phone. "Get the real story."

"Okay, okay," Benny said. "I'll go. This is already too weird." He closed his laptop and put it in his backpack. He hugged his girlfriend, who gave me the stink-eye over his shoulder. I followed him out the door. He got in the front seat of the cruiser and slammed the door.

"Could you at least turn off those lights?" he said.

We were halfway home before I spoke.

Thanks for coming," I said.

"Thanks for coming? You fucking *arrested* me. In front of my friends, in front of my girlfriend. Unbelievable." He whacked the dashboard with his hand.

"If you'll give me a minute to explain."

"Explain what?" He turned to face me. "About how the Devil is chasing you from Franklin Freaking Notch and you need me to hold the wheel while we go on a high-speed chase with you shooting garlic bullets out the window? How about we drink holy water and turn invisible, then sneak up behind the bad guy and knock him out with that big pole the Pope carries around?"

"Benny—"

"Don't call me Benny. My name isn't Benny. And it's not Moffatt, either.

We have nothing in common. Don't get me wrong, I love Sister and I think Wes is a trip, but you're all crazy. I'm not like the rest of you. I wasn't born into this freak show."

"Listen," I said, "I'm just trying to protect my family. You don't understand what's going on here. You're still just a kid."

"No, *you* don't understand, because you're a dick. Do us all a favor. Stop trying to run everybody's life. You act like you're always helping everybody, but it's so obvious—you're a control freak. After you do something, you get this look like 'Hey, everybody, look at me. I just saved the world.' "

We were three miles from Franklin Notch. In front of us was a flatbed loaded with hay. When I slowed down, Benny jumped out. I pulled over, lights flashing, and chased him into the woods. For a skinny kid with a backpack, he was fast. I lost him running down the backside of a gully. I slipped on a patch of gravel, and when I got up he was over the top and gone.

"You let him out of the car?" Beth was angry—hands-on-hips angry.

"He jumped out. We were arguing. I chased him for a mile. I couldn't leave the cruiser in the middle of the road. I had a shotgun on the front seat."

"Oh, that's good. At least you didn't chase your son down Route 6 with a shotgun. What would people think?"

"Beth—"

The phone rang. She waved me off and picked up the call.

"No, honey," she said. "You have to come here. I know, but you were coming down anyway. We'll go out tomorrow and buy some clothes. Just come here and we'll work everything out. Don't worry, I'll drive you back after the party."

She hung up and faced me.

"Did you really get rid of that map?" she asked. "Did you burn that map?"

I couldn't answer.

"I can't believe this," she said. "What's happening to you? You need to think about what you're doing, Boone. I'm going to pick up Benny now, and I don't want any fighting when I bring him back."

I got my guns out of the cruiser and called the station. No news on Dolan. I was off-shift anyway, so I went upstairs and changed into my jeans. I looked in the mirror. The whole left side of my upper body was inflamed.

Bright red streaks snaked from the burnt skin over my heart, across my chest, and under my arm. It looked like blood poisoning.

I put on a workshirt and slipped the map into the pocket. Even with the burning pain, I felt safer keeping it with me—like having fake credentials behind enemy lines.

I heard Beth's car returning, so I grabbed my guns, went downstairs to the den, and shut the door behind me. From the den, I could only see the backyard and a slice of the woods behind the house. To get a fix on the whole perimeter, I needed to have access to every downstairs window. I sat on the sofa, shotgun across my legs, Ruger on my belt, Colt in the black bag beside me.

Beth knocked on the door, came into the room, and sat in a chair facing me.

"Do you want to be left alone?" she asked.

I nodded.

"Should I worry about you? All these guns?"

"I just need some space," I said. "Until I know what Dolan is doing."

She nodded. "I talked to Benny, and I don't think you did anything wrong, picking him up. He shouldn't have made fun of you. I'm sorry."

"Thanks."

"Can I get you anything?"

"No. Did you make your appointment?"

"I go in Monday," she said. "Thanks for asking."

I tried to smile. "Sorry," I said. "I don't know what to say."

"It's okay. We'll stay upstairs for a while."

"Okay. That's good. I need to get around down here, anyway. You know this is real, don't you?"

She nodded and smiled. "Most of it," she said. "Unless you're going to shoot something for dinner, I'm making spaghetti."

I heard them settling upstairs, watching the news on Benny's TV. I went from room to room downstairs, checking sightlines. I went outside and moved Beth's car into the garage. I turned the cruiser around so it was facing the street. I called Wes and Sister's house, and Reggie answered the phone.

"Custer household."

"That's not funny."

"Yes, it is. What's up?"

"Is everybody inside?"

"Well, we're sunbathing on the roof. Does that count?"

"Can you be serious for just a minute?"

"It hurts my head," he said.

"Reggie, just listen to me. Don't let anybody leave the house until we catch this guy. He won't go near Sister, so stay together."

"Okay, boss. We'll get back under her apron, me and Wes."

I tried to take a nap. I couldn't relax, so I smoked cigarettes instead. Standing in the hall between the kitchen and the porch, I blew smoke into the backyard through a slit in the doorway.

Beth made dinner and brought me a plate.

"Honey, don't you think you're overreacting a little?"

"Until they catch him, we're in danger. All of us."

"Do you really think he'll come here? This is where he got caught last time. Between all the police in town and the TV crews, everybody knows him. It doesn't make any sense."

"I know it looks like that, but he's nearby. I can feel it."

I could tell she wanted to talk about the map, so I looked down at the floor.

"Okay," she said. "Alright."

She kissed me and went back upstairs. Every forty minutes, I made my rounds with all my guns. With the lights off, I started in the den—staying low, looking out the windows—then I crouched through the kitchen to the garage, where I could see around the back of the house and the side of the neighbor's yard. I worked my way through the downstairs—living room, dining room, bathroom, and den. Upstairs in Benny's room, I could hear Chico Marx clowning around.

At eleven o'clock, Beth came to the top of the stairs.

"Are you coming up?" she asked.

I guess I looked dangerous. She ducked behind the banister.

"Boone," she said, "you're really scaring me."

"I know. I'm sorry, but I can't take any chances."

For six hours, I slinked around my house. I really believed Ronnie Dolan was coming for us. Every half hour I called Reggie.

"Are you still awake?"

"No. I'm splitting shifts with Wes. It's his turn."

"Wes? He can't handle this. He's probably asleep."

"Yeah, he probably is. Everybody is. You should be, too."

"How can you say that? You people don't understand."

"You *people*? Boone, I'm worried about you. I'm coming over."

"No. Don't leave. I don't want anybody outside. You don't understand how this fits together."

"What fits together?"

"Everything. Ronnie Dolan, my seventh visit, the treaty, Wes and the Indians. Even the anniversary party and you coming back have something to do with it. And there's other things you don't know about. It's all the same thing."

"No, it's not. This is just some bad guy who escaped from jail. If he was coming here, he'd be here."

"He *is* here. I can feel it."

"Do you have any weed?"

"What?"

"You need to calm down, man."

A few hours before sunrise, I started to fade. I pushed the living room sofa against the front door, put the kitchen table against the door to the garage, and piled cushions at the back door, where I lay down with my guns and my map.

I awoke to the sounds of Beth leaving for church. She and Benny were in the kitchen, moving the table away from the door.

She came into the living room and saw me sleeping on the floor with three guns. "I guess you're not coming to church," she said.

"I don't want you going out."

"I know, honey. Why don't you take a shower, change your clothes, and come with me?"

"I think I'll stay."

"I think you need to go to church."

"I'll stay here."

"Okay," she said, giving me a lame little fingertip wave. "Bye."

Benny slipped past her, back upstairs.

I've reached the point where I need to do something, anything—even if it's wrong. Like the way they deal with avalanches in ski country—somebody goes to the place where all the snow is jammed up and lays in a couple sticks of dynamite. Blow it up, let it settle.

My mind is made up. I'm going for the treaty today. I'm taking this little map and I'm going to use it. It's all I've got now. I traded it for my mother's wisdom and my wife's common sense. If I get into a scrap with the Devil and lose my life, and lose my soul—at least I tried. Maybe I'm making a mistake, rearranging the landscape, and I'll get buried under the whole mess. I don't care anymore. I can't go on like this.

I'm not running away from this fight. Like a good cop, I'm going in the front door—taking it to the bad guy. I'm tired of worrying about his next visit and how many times I have left. I'm down to my last chance, and I'm not going to cower in a corner with a loaded shotgun, fretting about Mr. Sticks and his legion of bullshit characters. I'm going to take my chance on my terms. This is my life and I'm in control.

I called the station. No word on Dolan. It figures. They're looking for him where they want to find him. I took a shower, put on a clean shirt and my uniform. I put the map in the bag with my old gun. I sat in the kitchen, finishing Beth's cup of coffee, waiting for her to come home from church, waiting to say good-bye.

She came home around noon, carrying a crumb cake and the *Sunday Times*. When she saw me sitting in my uniform, her face went cold.

"Boone, no," she said.

"Can we just talk for a minute?"

She sat at the other end of the table.

"How was church?"

"Alright," she said. "I sat with Reggie."

"Reggie was in church?"

"Sure. Why not?"

"No reason. Did they get that junk off their faces?"

"No. They're calling themselves the Fizz Kids."

We shared the smile.

"Well," I said. "All I wanted to say is that I'm sorry I've been so paranoid. And I'm sorry I lied about burning the map."

"Thank you. Apology accepted."

"And I don't want to be remembered for trying to control things. I never wanted to run anybody's life. I just wanted to make sure everybody had what they needed."

"Okay. Now can I say something?"

"Please."

"What you're doing is really stupid."

"That's it?"

"That's it."

"Well, I have faith that this will turn out okay. I'm determined to make it work."

"Those are opposite things."

"From where I sit, it fits together."

"From where I sit, you're screwed. We're screwed. You think you can beat the Devil, and you can't see he's the one who put that idea in your head. What does that tell you?"

"That I can't win."

"So why are you doing it?"

"Because if he thinks I think I can't win, then I've got a chance—as long as I really think I can."

"Boone, you're not making any sense at all. You can't play his game and win. He's got that evil logic that looks like it makes sense because it pretends to never completely cancel itself, but the solution is real simple: The only way to beat him is not to play his game."

As she spoke, I could feel myself slowing down and letting all the confusion in my head roll on without me. My father's problems, Beth's test on Monday, Ronnie Dolan, my seventh visit—but as I took inventory of the chaos, before I knew what was happening, I was back in the muddle, pulling away from the last thing she said.

"But these problems won't fix themselves."

"Oh, Boone," she said. "When we got married you asked me if I really wanted to. You said it gets crazy around here. Remember what I said?"

"Forever and ever. On earth and whatever comes next."

"And I meant it, Boone. I'm on your side. I've kept your secret because you asked me to. But now, I think it was the wrong thing to do because I helped the Devil confuse you. Have you talked to Sister?"

"No."

"You need to. Don't be embarrassed. Call her."

"I'll stop by."

"And do what?"

"Tell her everything."

I knew she didn't believe me.

"Boone, this is my last shot: If you don't tell her what you're doing, I will."

"You're going to tell on me to my mother?"

"Yes, I am."

I needed to leave, to get this over with.

"I'll drive over now," I said.

We hugged at the door. She was already crying.

"I'll see you later," I said, but it was just something to say.

I drove to the top of West Mountain and worked my way down, block by block.

I remember when this mountain was all forest and there were only three streets crisscrossing the bottom of the hill. I hiked this ridge with my dad. Over the years, the town has crept up the mountain, and now there are fine new homes on the crest with paved driveways that wind through the pines, and gates with cameras and speakerphones. Now I couldn't walk through here without a warrant.

At the bottom of the mountain was an alley that ran behind the stores on Main Street. Behind the sub shop, the bank, and the hardware store were the places where kids always gathered. Today, the alley was empty; everyone was up East Mountain at the ball field, watching the imaginary Indians. I remember the night Reggie and his buddies tipped all the dumpsters in the alley and when Ronnie Dolan spray-painted the Rolling Stones lapping tongue on the back of Town Hall. I remember getting drunk in the alley behind the drugstore and Sister walking me home, pulling me up the mountain by my belt.

I cruised north on Main Street, then south. The curbs were solid with cars; people were sitting on the benches and waiting in line for Sunday supper outside the Bob-O-Link. As I drove past, everyone paused to watch me.

I went up to Talbert's Ridge and worked the streets down East Mountain. I drove around the ball field fast enough to avoid the news crews. The Indians with walkie-talkies scowled at me as I drove past. They were eating pizza.

I drove to Wes and Sister's house.

"She's inside, praying," Wes said. He was lying on his back in the driveway, wedged under his truck, tying the tailpipe to the muffler with a collection of coat hangers.

"When are you going to get a new truck?" I asked him.

"When I run out of coat hangers. What are you doing in uniform? Today's still Sunday, isn't it?"

"I'm feeling restless about tomorrow—your court date, remember? Aren't you worried?"

"Sure," he said. "That's why I'm working on my getaway vehicle."

I was quiet for a moment. For the first time, his good nature was pissing me off.

"Did you call an attorney yet?"

"They're all home, drinking blood," he said.

"What if you're indicted? What if this goes to trial?"

He wriggled his belly out from under the truck and looked at me from the ground. His forehead was smudged with rusty grime. "Well, then, I guess I've got trouble," he said, wiping his hands on his shirt. "Until that happens, I'm sticking with the advice of my current counsel."

"Sister?"

"Yep," he said. "Fifty years on the job and she hasn't steered me wrong yet." He stuck his finger in the air and tried to quote her. "Since His love is all we find, we feel so comfortable in our minds."

"Do you mean:

In His Love He has divined
The Healing Comfort of Our Kind?"

"Oh, yeah. I guess that makes more sense." He grinned, then humped himself back under the truck. There was a wrenching sound and a loud clunk somewhere near the engine. "Dammit," he said. "There goes the front end."

"Have you seen Reggie?" I asked.

"He's splitting wood over at Veronica's. He said he was coming over this afternoon with a load for us. Hey, let's do something later—the three of us. Maybe we could go through those boxes. I bet there's some good stuff in there."

"Maybe I'll stop by."

I saw Sister standing in the window. She waved, and I went inside. We sat at the kitchen table.

"I'm glad you came over," she said. "We haven't talked in a while."

"I came to apologize. I didn't tell you the truth before—when you asked if the Devil gave me something to hold. He did."

"I know. Thanks for 'fessing up."

"Did Beth tell you?"

"No. I saw some things the other night. I haven't figured them all out, but that part was pretty clear. I'm glad you told Beth. What did he give you?"

"A map."

"A map? To where?"

"To find Talbert's Treaty."

"And that's where you're going now?"

"Yes. It's not the real treaty."

"Of course not. Your father made that up."

"You know that?"

"Doesn't everybody?"

"He doesn't."

She laughed. "Oh, Daniel," she said. "I never imagined it would turn out like this—so complicated, with you in the middle. I was just a girl when this started, and things seemed so simple then."

"It's never been simple," I said. "At least not for me."

"And I'm sorry, honey. I know it hasn't been easy."

"Am I going to die? I don't want to die. I'm only forty-nine."

"I don't know, Daniel. All I can tell you is what I've seen."

"Is this your vision?"

"Yes. It came to me during Scrabble. There is going to be a terrible battle of iron and spirit colliding—with smoke and the roaring of fire on stone. There will be death and blood all over the mountain, a great battle between the legions of evil and the Army of Saints."

"It sounds like the end of the world."

"No. Afterward there is a smell of strawberries."

"I've got to go. I'm more confused than before."

"Let's pray your Axis Mundi."

She reached across the table and laid her hands over mine.

> *"Heaven and Hell, forever apart,*
> *Met for battle in my wavering heart.*
> *While Goodness and Evil struggled within,*
> *Faith was the sword that brought death to sin."*

"You were my first baby," she said. "I was so happy. You were the answer to all my prayers, but I'm afraid I gave you too much to carry."

"It's a little late for that."

I could see the sorrow rising.

"I should be going," I said. "I need to get up there before it gets dark."

"And I should be praying."

As I was walking away from the house, I heard the phone ring. I knew it was Beth calling.

The picnic at Doc's had just entered the watermelon phase. Jessie was teaching Molly how to spit seeds. Charlie and Doc were playing duets—Doc on his homemade bazooka-flute, Charlie on mandolin.

Veronica and Catherine were sitting in lawn chairs, talking, watching the sun and moon share the midday sky. Vedran was asleep on Veronica's lap, and she was brushing her fingertips lightly through his fine brown hair. He was smiling in his sleep.

"Are you guys ready for the anniversary party?" Catherine asked.

"Everything's up in the air," Veronica said. "Wes goes to court tomorrow, and all the guests are canceling. At least Uncle Reggie is back."

"Do you need help?"

"Probably. I'm sure something didn't get done."

"Charlie's off tomorrow and Tuesday. We'll drive over in the morning."

"Thanks, sweetie. No matter what—we'll have a good time. At least the whole family will be there."

Molly ran to Catherine.

"My spitter hurts," she said, touching her tongue with her fingertip.

"I was watching you," Veronica said. "You spit far."

"I hit the moon," said the little girl.

"Oh, boy," said Catherine. "Next year we can have moon-melons."

The girl pouted.

"Molly Coddle," Catherine said, snuggling her. "You're so tired. We need to go home for a nap."

"So do we," said Veronica. "We've got two hours ahead of us."

"When can I see you again?" Doc asked Veronica. They were leaning against the Camry, his hands on her hips, her hands on his shoulders.

"Next weekend," she said. "I'll bring the chips."

They kissed.

"What's this?" Doc asked, looking over her shoulder, through the back window of the car. He reached in and picked up the newspaper from the backseat.

"That's Wes," Veronica said. "Not a real good picture. He doesn't usually look terrified."

"No. Who's this?" Doc asked, poking the picture of Sarah Running Doe.

"She's the Indian woman who's causing all the trouble."

"Indian, my ass. That's Lucy Wrinkles. She was my office manager in Syracuse. We caught her stealing meds and had her arrested. She has warrants out all over New York state."

"Lucy Wrinkles?"

"Wrinklachofski. Lucinda Wrinklachofski. She's bad news."

"Warrants?"

"Yeah. She skipped town."

"Come on," said Veronica. "We've got to call Boone."

They jumped in the Camry and high-tailed it over the mountain to Catherine's place.

Veronica called Beth. Beth was crying. "He went looking for the Devil," she said. "I know I'm not supposed to stop him, but I don't know what's going to happen now."

"We're coming home," Veronica said. "We've got to find him." She grabbed her purse and tossed Jessie her backpack.

"Can you ride with us?" Molly asked Jessie.

Doc and Veronica rode in the Camry; Jessie rode in the backseat of Charlie and Catherine's new wagon, sitting between the two car seats. She sang old hippie songs to the babies until they fell asleep.

28

I drove to the north edge of town where the road narrowed and turned to the backside of East Mountain. Ahead of me were thirty-seven miles of lightly traveled two-lane blacktop that connected a few smaller towns to the north before wandering through the center of Henniker, then eventually to nowhere.

The road had been cut through a skull of a hill, and the gray slab cliffs rose from the rubbled berm to the blank crown of the ridge. Scrawny shrubs clung to the side of the pass, their roots exposed, their branches bending away from the stone face of the stark walls.

Past the cut was a stretch of lowland forest. A mile up the road, I saw my marker: a pointed black stone, a natural obelisk with a white quartz edge. Beside the stone was a beckoning of a road, overgrown and unremarkable— barely a road, more of a path through the trees. I edged the cruiser past the stone, into the dark woods. I turned on the headlights and looked at my map.

The vegetation closed around the sides of the car—too close to open the door if I needed to bail in a hurry, so I backed up the cruiser a few feet, then shut off the engine.

According to the map, I had to circle back through the woods, skirting a bog to the right, then climb a hill—back to the butt of Talbert's Ridge, where I would find my path leading to the Devil's Tree.

It was hard hiking in my cop shoes, and the ground felt spongy beneath my feet. I had to keep moving to avoid sinking.

I thought I knew my way, but as I circled the swamp, I found my path bending farther to the left, then back upon itself. I struggled over a stand of fallen trees and through eye-high brambles an acre deep, then found myself looking at the wrong side of my car.

I struck out again, keeping closer to the brim of the bog, going into mud over my ankles. I watched the woods around me for any movement, any shadow of motion. An hour later, soaked and scratched, I was at the back-side of East Mountain, looking up at a trail I had never seen before.

It was late afternoon, and I was on the dusky side of the ridge. I started climbing over the rocks at the base of the hill, pulling myself forward by the skeleton brush. After another hour, I was standing at the beginning of a deeply worn footpath scraped into the stone by generations of shuffling pilgrims. I checked my map again.

For a distance of several hundred yards, procede with prudence midway acrost the highest pointe of Talberte's Ridge to a place marked by a great stone hewn in halves.

This territory should have been familiar, but it wasn't. I recognized all the landmarks, but they had been rearranged. The *"great stone hewn in halves"* was the split rock where I had met the Devil when I was eighteen years old. Today, the crevice was facing the wrong way—instead of short-cutting to my parents' house, the narrow path ran through it, toward a domelike copse of tangled lifeless trees that had no natural place on Talbert's Ridge, or on this earth.

I followed the path through the crevice, looking above me for the Devil's ambush. I was being watched, I could feel it. I sat on a rock and tried to clear my thoughts. I was muddy up to my knees and worn down to my bones. A bad smell came from the dark dome of trees, like the funk of Gehenna on a wrong-way breeze. I sat on a rock and smoked.

"Reggie, this is Doc," said Veronica. "What happened to you? You look like a raccoon."

"Exploding root beer incident. You oughta see Wes. Glad to meet you," he said to Doc, shaking hands.

"I've heard a lot about you," said Doc.

"I'll bet. Thanks for coming to help."

"Where do you think he is?" Veronica asked Beth.

"He said he had to 'get up' somewhere before it got dark," said Sister.

"There's only one way up," said Wes. "The ridge."

"Then what?" said Veronica.

"Then I bring him back," said Reggie, heading for the collection of cars in the driveway.

"I'm coming," said Veronica.

"Mom, take my lucky jacket," said Jessie.

Catherine came out of the house as they pulled out of the driveway. "Where are they going?" she asked.

"To fight the Devil," Wes said.

"Isn't that dangerous?"

"Yes," said Sister. "For him."

I walked across the stony field to the clutch of trees. They had grown together thick as a barricade, their twisted trunks barely a foot apart and their thorny branches snarled tight as wire.

I pulled myself into the thicket, twenty feet on my hands and knees, squeezing through the narrow spaces between the trunks, jabbing myself with thorns, ripping my uniform, and cutting my hands. I swept the den of thorns with the beam of my flashlight. It was closed all around me, and the ground was hard like stone, pounded down by a thousand dancing demons.

The Devil's stomping ground. The spidery branches were a tangle, woven above me into a latticed web, thick enough to stop the daylight.

There was an empty space like a mausoleum in the center of the chamber, with a dirt floor worn into the clawlike roots of the twisted little trees. Set like an altar in the middle of the chamber was a bone white deadwood stump, chest high and six feet across.

"The so-called Tree of Life."

I crawled to the empty space and tried to stand. The thorny branches formed a low ceiling above me, forcing me to stoop, keeping my head bowed.

I played my flashlight across the floor. The dirt had been scratched out between the knuckles of the roots, making hundreds of depressions like tiny graves. In each hole was an object. There were pieces of jewelry, a moldy withered finger, photographs and hand-drawn caricatures, a miniature hangman's noose, and needles crusted with rust and blood. There was money everywhere, crumpled, folded, and stuffed into the little graves. There were snatches of hair and dried ribbons of skin flayed like jerky. I could see folded documents like birth certificates and deeds, IOUs and hand-drawn pictures of copulating figures. There were weapons half-buried between the roots—knives, bullets, little amber bottles with drawings of skulls. There were painted carvings and clay figures snapped in half and small bowls with crusty residues and pieces of bloodstained cloth.

I bent over the stump.

The surface was flat and smooth as gravestone marble, and it was covered with delicate etchings of several thousand names.

Tabor Quincy, consecration by self-drowning. Eleanor Tibbetts, admission by murder of daughter. Leo Szizjiak, by commission of blasphemy. Rita Pole, hypocrite.

The list was endless, and it seemed to grow as I watched. As I read the roll call of the sinned and soulless, I felt a breath of cold wind sweep across my legs. I turned my light on the thorny walls of the chamber. I saw nothing, but felt the draw of evil at my feet.

At the base of the trunk was a hole the size of my fist. The lip of the hole was worn shiny, and when I bent down and touched it with my finger, my hand eased in, up to my elbow. I tried to pull my arm out of the stump, but it had become wedged inside, deep into an open space that was wet with cold rot between the roots. I felt something like a thick rope lock around my wrist. It jerked me like a leash, pulling my arm into the hole, up to my shoulder, knocking my head on the stump.

I fell to my knees and braced myself against the tree, pushing back with my free hand against the grip of the hole. My arm was pulled deeper into the belly of the earth and I was stuck, kneeling on the ground with the side of my face jammed against the bark. I panicked and jerked backward in great grunting heaves like an animal caught in a steel trap.

The harder I pulled, the tighter the slipknot pinched my wrist. Then, deep in the hole, something began twisting my arm. It twisted one way, then the other. It twisted my arm like a turkey bone, to the point of breaking, then gave it another half-turn. Something snapped in my shoulder, and I could feel the gristle separating from my bone. Pain shot across my chest, up my neck, and behind my eyes. Under the tree, my arm was being twisted off my body, and there was nothing I could do. It felt like the whole weight of the earth itself was hung on the hinge of my shoulder.

I felt the point of a large nail pressing against the palm of my hand. I held my breath as the Devil teased me, tracing my lifeline with the tip. He backed off, then drove the spike straight thought the center of my hand. I howled and cried like a man cut in half.

The serpent released my wrist, and I pulled my arm out of the hole. A thick rusty spike seven inches long had been driven clean through me, nailing a sheet of brown parchment to my palm.

Dizzy with pain, I sat on demon ground with my back to the stump. My shoulder was twisted out of its socket, and I couldn't bend my elbow or move my fingers. I turned my dead hand over with my good one, and, using my knee as a brace on my wrist, I pulled on the head of the nail until it slid out of the hole in my hand. I closed my eyes and gasped in tight vicious breaths.

My arm smelled like rotted meat.

The piece of parchment was several pages thick. I opened it on my lap.

A Declaration of Good Faith Composed for the Mutual Benefit of Sagaweh and Free Men Alike.

This was it—the real fake—an authentic document verifying a fictional event. This parchment would vindicate my father, redeem my family, and save our town. It would preserve the peace. It was also the receipt for my soul.

I hunched myself upright. Like a battered supplicant, I laid my head on the cold slab of petrified wood and closed my eyes, reaching for strength. My body was shaking; my legs were too weak to hold me. An acid lightness was slipping through my head, and I knew I was dying; the sounds of my own beat and breath were sinking beneath the hold of my senses. Behind my eyes, the darkness was coming.

I could feel the heat from my chest being drawn out of my body, into the cold dead stone beneath me, and I heard my own name coming up at the bottom of the growing list.

"Now comes Daniel Moffatt, by pitiful lack of faith."

The sound that spoke my name was like a mother's voice, soft and sweet, singsong and gentle; a bedside whisper—someone who had known me for my whole life.

"Welcome home, Daniel, my son. You have done well. You have fought the good fight, and now your deliverance is at hand. Rest yourself on my tree; I will come for you and bring you home."

Comfort me, I thought it said.

"That, too," it said, in a voice no different from any god.

There were stirrings, vibrations coming from chambers beneath the stump. So this is how it ends—my name on the slab of the Devil's Tree, cold as stone on the roster of Hell. This the price of my soul, the final cost of faithlessness—of honoring duty while worshipping nothing. I was born to carry the load, then die under its weight.

Universal mule, Reggie used to call me, and tonight my family would find my body, dead on the ridge with proof of my father's claims folded in my pocket.

"You think too much," sighed the Devil. "It doesn't matter how it ends. It simply ends."

"And after I die?"

"You're already dead. You just don't know it yet."

Maybe he was right. I was exhausted beyond the reach of reason, broken in body and spirit; and I just wanted to slide away, to fade beneath my pain and defeat, into the nameless haven of a timeless dusk. In the pain of life, what is the point of Heaven or Hell? Living like this is too hard, anyway.

"Now you're talking," said the Devil. "It is too hard, trapped between Heaven and Hell—forever a part of the fight."

"What did you say?"

"Nothing," said the Devil. "Forget it."

I tried to let it go, but some faithful notion wouldn't pass away. Something the Devil said sounded like a verse. *Heaven and Hell, forever apart.* I opened my eyes, and the warmth of a life-long memory crossed my heart as I hoped to die. I remembered sitting at the kitchen table, my mother's hands over mine, reciting some sing-song Sunday School rhyme. My Axis Mundi.

> *"Heaven and Hell, forever apart,*
> *Met for battle in my wavering heart.*
> *While Goodness and Evil struggled within,*
> *Faith was the sword that brought death to sin."*

Then something happened. Call it faith, spirit, or a simple longing for the comfort of my kind; but after I said my prayer, a surge of strength rose up like a flash of redemption, shining like steel—a sharp edge of light, pushing back against the darkness.

In an instant, I was washed with a bright new power that swept me above my pain. I felt focused and desperate to finish the fight. The Devil could take my arm; he could have my whole body, curled like a worm in the dust, but I still owned my soul. And it was mine to keep.

I raised myself, dropped the treaty, and kicked it back into the stump. Then, with my good hand, I unzipped my pants and pissed in the hole.

A burst of yellow steam, hot as acid, exploded out of the hole and scalded the side of my left leg. It would have done more damage, but I was already moving. Holding my bad arm with my left hand, I jumped away from the stump and barreled into the barricade of trees with my good shoulder, fighting my way out.

I heard dry sliding sounds beneath me. He was coming through the hole. I pounded myself through the unholy grove to the twilight outside and charged across the field of stones, stumbling, falling twice, holding my right arm tight against my chest. With every step, waves of dark pain clouded my sight.

My clothes were shredded. The skin was torn across my head, dripping blood into my eyes. I had lost my belt, my gun, both shoes.

Something was running behind me, howling with the voices of a thousand men thundering to battle, its claws scraping the stony ground. I looked over my shoulder and saw a beast with the face of a scarlet dog and seven legs, six of them clawed, and the seventh like the arm of a man growing from its breast. With its six legs the beast ran, its claws digging into the ground, and with the seventh leg, it grabbed stones as it ran and hurled them at my back. As the stones flew around me, they became melted iron. Three of the stones hit my back and knocked me sideways. A fourth stone hit the back of my head, and I heard the skin sizzle behind my ear.

Bending forward and clutching my ruined arm to my stomach, I ran across the top of the ridge to a line of trees.

As I ran, the noise of iron-on-stone stopped, and in its place was the sound of one person running and roaring like a furnace. I turned and saw the beast had become a small man with long, dark, thinning hair and a gray beard. He was wearing a dirty denim jacket, black jeans, and scuffed workboots with pointed toes. He was snarling as he ran, the spit dripping into his beard. His eyes were hard black points in his sallow face, and his hands were stretched toward me, his dirty fingernails only several inches from my neck.

I tried to run faster, but my legs were weak, and my bloody feet slipped on the stone and gravel. I turned and looked over my shoulder again. The Devil had divided and become two people. Running beside the old man was Ronnie Dolan, strong and healthy, coming up fast on my back. He was waving a nine-inch gut knife. "Hiff, hiff." He pounded toward me, closing in. "Hiff, hiff."

Around us was a terrible clatter of iron and steel, like a thousand swords clashing, and when I turned to see Wes's pickup careening around the backside of my vision, I stumbled and fell forward, out of its way. As the two Devils slowed down, looking to their left, Reggie nailed them both, flat-on with the front of the truck. Dolan went down with a curse and a grunt, folded like trash beneath the Ford. Reggie dragged him a hundred feet before bothering to slow down, and when he backed up to run over him again, Veronica jumped out of the passenger side and sprinted across the field to help me.

Pinned beneath the truck, Ronnie Dolan thrashed and shrieked. In his struggle to get loose, he pulled off the muffler, and clouds of dark smoke rose around the old roaring Ford.

The truck went straight through the old man, and now he ran across the open space to where his boy lay, jerking and bleeding on the ground.

Veronica half-carried me to the pickup and pushed me in. I saw she was wearing Jessie's jacket. I slumped against Reggie, holding my arm in my lap.

"Let's go, let's go," she yelled. Reggie gassed the truck, and we cut across the field in a wide loop. As we passed the place where Ronnie Dolan lay, I raised myself and looked over the dashboard. He was sprawled steaming on the rocks, torn nearly in half, one arm bent beneath him, the other arm over his face.

The Devil stood over his son, bent at the knees, his head pulled back, arms out straight and his hands jerking like snakes snapped in half. He started wailing at the sky and dancing as if he were standing on hot coals. He hopped from one foot to the other as fast as he could; then, still dancing, he started spinning—slowly at first, then faster and faster, until he turned to dust. Still roaring like a dog on a hook, he disappeared.

"Boone, you okay?" Veronica asked. "Here, lean up," and she took off Jessie's jacket, draped it across my chest, and tucked it under my chin. I smelled the scent of patchouli, weed, and strawberry shampoo.

The collision with the Devil had jarred everything loose in the cab of Wes's truck, and Reggie groped around the floor, clearing the rubble from around his feet.

"Hey, look," he said, holding up a month-old Entemann's box. "Anybody want a donut?"

I passed out.

29

I woke up on Sister's sofa in a shock of pain. A thin man with glasses was standing over me, holding my elbow and pushing on my collarbone. Behind him stood Veronica and her family. Wes and Sister were standing at my side. Sister was crying; Wes looked scared. Reggie was at the foot of the sofa.

"Thanks, man," I said.

"No prob, bro."

The thin man laid my arm gently across my chest. "I'm a doctor," he said. "We just popped your shoulder back in. How does it feel?"

"Okay," I said. It hurt like hell. I tried to lift my hand, but it slid over my chest toward my face instead.

"Limited oblique movement," the thin man said. "That's hopeful."

Veronica's hand was on his shoulder.

"How did this happen?" he asked.

"Wrestling match," I said. "I actually won."

"What happened to your clothes?" Wes asked.

I raised my head to see myself. My uniform was shredded, and my body was raked with deep scratches.

"I'm sorry," I said.

"Sorry for what, sweetie?" Sister asked. She was holding my left hand, stroking it gently.

"I let everyone down. I couldn't go through with it."

"Let who down?" Veronica asked. "Us?"

"Everybody," I said.

Tell him, I heard Jessie whisper. Tell him.

"Tell me what?"

"Doc has news about Sarah Running Doe. He knows her."

"She's got warrants," Wes said. "That's why she's running."

"Warrants? Where?"

They told me the whole story—about Doc seeing her picture in the *Union Leader* and recognizing her as the office manager at his clinic in Syracuse who stole meds for nine months before he caught her in the act.

"Tape me up."

"You're not going anywhere," Veronica said.

"Yes, I am, and you're driving me. I'm going to the station. I'll be alright."

"Not if you don't go to the hospital," Doc said.

"Help me up."

Beth rode with me in the backseat of Veronica's car, and Doc rode shotgun. Wearing a pair of Wes's sweatpants and one of his Red Sox jackets, I slipped in the back door of the station. With Doc's memory of dates and events, we downloaded the book on Lucinda Wrinklachofski. Grand larceny, theft of a controlled substance, intent to distribute, failure to appear, and interstate flight—as well as additional warrants from shoplifting to solicitation trailing down the East Coast to Miami. It would be a while before Sarah Running Doe saw the inside of a ski lodge.

I e-mailed and copied every jurisdiction.

My shoulder was killing me. I was having spasms the length of my spine.

"Now you're going to the hospital," Veronica said.

Beth and I sat side by side in our bed, leaning against the headboard. My right arm was taped across my chest, and I had fifty-nine stiches in my scalp. I couldn't shift my weight or even breathe without bolts of pain ripping across my back and shoulders. My arm was ruined; I would never have full use of it. Lying with Beth, I had never been more happy, just to be alive.

The AG's office called to congratulate me for finding Holy Hell for the second time. There was a reward for his capture, and although Reggie wasn't the first person in New Hampshire history to break up a fight with a pickup truck, we all agreed that the reward was his—for assisting an officer in the apprehension of a felon. Indeed.

I'm going on medical leave, and after Wes's hearing tomorrow morning, I'm retiring from law enforcement. I'll take the citation, the farewell banquet, and the pension. I'll never wear another uniform; I'll never sit in another cruiser. And just for good measure, I've taken a vow against donuts.

Beth and I shared a cup of lemon tea. She held the cup and fed me crackers and cheese. We talked about what comes next.

"I don't know how to be retired," I said.

"It's easy. You wake up in the morning, make a pot of coffee, and hang out with me. And then later in the day you go hang out with somebody else—Reggie or Wes. Wes will keep you busy with his projects, and when you come home, we'll have dinner and hang out again. We'll lie in bed, drink wine, and eat crackers."

We tried it some more.

"Does this mean I don't have a brain tumor?" she asked.

"I think we can still get sick. You should go to your appointment tomorrow."

"Don't you want me to go to court with you?"

"There's nothing more to do."

She felt the bandage on my chest. "Does this hurt?" she asked.

"Just inside. I can't believe I treated you so badly. I'm sorry, Beth."

"It's alright, honey. Looking back, I can't believe it wasn't worse—all the pressure you were under."

"That's no excuse. I really lost my way. Thanks for sticking with me."

"Everybody gets confused," she said. "That's how we know when we're not."

In the morning I collected my paperwork; then I called Sister.

"We'll meet you at the courthouse," she said.

I thought she meant just Wes and herself, but when I walked into the lobby, I saw the whole crew: Sister and Wes, Reggie, Veronica, Doc, Jessie, Catherine and Charlie and their kids.

I took Eddie along for backup in case Sarah Running Doe tried to bolt. I couldn't catch and cuff her alone with my arm in a sling.

We waited outside the door of Courtroom C. The lobby was full of news sharks chumming on scraps of speculation. Wes stood beside me. He looked like a buckeye. For once, he kept his mouth shut.

At nine o'clock the front door opened and a wave of phony Indians charged into the lobby with Sarah Running Doe and her two attorneys at the head of the pack. She was wearing a fringed buckskin jacket and had feathers in her hair. Cameras hummed and flashed.

One of her attorneys bullied his way into my face.

"Why isn't this man in handcuffs?" he yelled, pointing at Wes.

"Because this is a small town and we only have one pair," I said, stuffing a copy of the warrant inside his suit coat.

"Lucinda Wrinklachofski," I said, turning to her. "I'm placing you under arrest for grand larceny, theft of a Class D substance with intent to distribute, failure to appear, interstate flight to avoid prosecution, shoplifting, and prostitution. I'm placing you in custody until you can be remanded to the proper jurisdictions."

She wanted to hit me.

Eddie read her her rights, cuffed her, and marched her back through the crowd. The rest of the Sagawehs stood around looking confused.

Tomorrow, the headline of the *Union Leader* would read NEW WRINKLES IN FAKE SQUAW AMBUSH.

Case dismissed. No plaintiff, no case. Three minutes before the judge, and Wes was off the hook.

We stood outside the courthouse, gathered around Wes, who grinned and gaped over his good luck. Sister wanted to have the anniversary party that night, so we agreed to gather at the house around six o'clock. In the meantime, I had paperwork waiting at the station, and Veronica needed to stop by the hospital for a few hours.

"Hey, Danny, can I do my show tonight?" Wes asked.

"Sure. Do you want some company?"

Wes turned to his youngest son. "How about it, Reggie? Do you want to help me with my show? We'll have some fun."

"You bet," said Reggie.

Jessie, Catherine, Charlie, and the babies went to Veronica's house. Sister went home to set up for the party. Wes and Reggie stayed at the courthouse to goof on the camera crews.

Doc offered to cook.

. . .

It was over. The news wagons and imaginary Indians packed up and mo-
seyed down the valley. The Channel 6 helicopter rose like a dark angel,
banked over West Mountain, and sputtered away. Sitting at my desk on the
second floor of the station, I watched the caravan head out, looking for The
Next Big Thing. I could feel the calm settling again on Franklin Notch, and
now all that remained was the true nature of our town—and whether the
people could forgive Wes.

At five thirty, Reggie walked into the makeup room at the tiny cable station. Wes was sitting on a folding chair, looking at himself in the mirror.

"Hey, pal," he said, giving Reggie a hug. "Have a seat. Are you settled
in?"

"It's been hectic. I think there's three people in New Hampshire I
haven't apologized to. I went to see Carolyn."

"How did it go?"

"Not so good. I tried to apologize, but she didn't believe me. She had
some papers for me to sign, so I guess I'm divorced now. She gets everything we owned before she threw me out. God knows, she deserves it."

"The house?"

"Just a box of bad memories, Dad."

"I suppose so. Still, it's a shame you couldn't work things out. Is she doing anything with her life yet?"

"No. She hired a good lawyer instead."

They were sitting next to each other, both facing the makeup mirror and
talking to each other's reflections. They looked like one man speaking to
both sides of his own life.

"I'm so glad you're back," said Wes. "I was worried about you. I knew
you were going through a bad time before you left, but I didn't know how
to help."

"Nobody could help me. I was a mess. I was so proud of the wrong
things—what I owned and who I knew. Keeping score was killing me, and
after forty years I still turned out like everybody else. I just owned more
stuff and knew more people."

"I know what you mean," Wes said. "I thought I was king of the mountain, and all I did was dig a big hole and push myself in. It's always a shock to find out what an asshole you really are."

"I just want to make it better," Reggie said. "Apologize to everyone and make up for lost time."

"Not to me, I hope."

"To everybody—you, Sister, Boone, Veronica—but especially to you. I'm sorry I called you an idiot. That was really cruel."

"You don't owe me an apology, Reg. It's my fault. I was too busy with Danny and I didn't spend enough time with you. I was wrong, and I'm sorry you had to struggle so hard for attention."

Reggie put his arm across his father's shoulders and gave him a squeeze.

"I'll trade apologies," he said, smiling. "Now let's make up for lost time."

30

At Sister's house, everyone was settling around the television to watch *This Is My Town.*

Sister, Beth, and Catherine were sitting on the sofa. Catherine was holding Vedran, who was asleep with a wooden spoon in his hand.

Jessie was on the floor with Molly, who was swabbing cookie dough out of a big bowl with both fists.

Veronica and Doc were wedged into an easy chair like teenagers. Charlie was sitting cross-legged on the floor, tuning a ukulele.

Aero Kierkegaard was sitting in the kitchen with an open laptop, scowling at the screen.

The air was rich with the scents of fresh-baked bread, peppered gravies, cinnamon, turkey, stuffing, sweet potatoes, cookies, and pies—mixed with hints of mint and curry, garlic and sage.

"Here we go," Veronica said, as the show started.

As the intro fades, Wes and Reggie are sitting together at the table, smiling at the camera. Reggie whispers something to Wes. It looks like "good luck."

"Good evening. I'm Wes Moffatt, and I used to think this was my town.

The truth is, I acted like I really owned the place, and now I'm embarrassed about my behavior. Because of that, tonight's show is going to be a little different.

"First, I want to apologize to everybody. This whole episode was all my fault. I made up a bunch of stories to make myself look important, and then I was too proud to admit it. I didn't mean to cause any trouble; I thought they were just good stories. I wish I could go house-to-house and apologize in person—maybe rake leaves for everybody, or something.

"I can't say 'I'm sorry' enough, but since I've got this show, I'm going to open the phones in a minute and let everybody vote if I should keep doing it. If everyone thinks I should leave the air, I will.

"Before I go to the phones, I want to welcome a special guest tonight. This is my son Reggie. A lot of you may remember him from when he was older and was a sportscaster on WNAU-TV. He's been living in Disney World for the past eight months."

Reggie smiles and nods at the camera.

"Alright," says Wes. "We'll go to the phones now and see what the weather's like."

He pushes a button and picks up. "Hello, caller."

"Wes. Consider this a vote for you to get off the air—and out of town, if possible. I'm embarrassed to tell anybody where I'm from. You made us all look like idiots. And what's wrong with your face?"

"Well, I'm sorry you feel that way," Wes says. "I wasn't trying to, but if that's the way you feel—"

Click. Dial tone.

Town, one. Wes, zero.

He hangs up, pushes another button. "You're on the air."

"I'm with that guy," the caller says. "Things are tough enough without lies from you guys in the media. People don't know what to believe anymore. If there are any lawyers listening, isn't there some way for a city to sue for defamation of character or something?"

Reggie leans forward.

"Hold it," he says. "Let's slow down for a second. You can't have it both ways. We can't believe the stories, then shoot the storyteller if we don't like the ending. We can't eat all the cookies, then blame the cook when we run out.

"We're all in this together, folks. We all bought the book. We can't all move out and start a new town somewhere else, so let's cut the big guy some slack. Nobody said this was science. Look at it this way: This is just another good story about our town."

For a full two minutes, no one calls. The phone finally rings.

"Hey, Wes. What if somebody actually found that treaty? How much would it be worth?"

"Well, I don't know. Since it doesn't exist, you couldn't really put a price on it."

"So what you're saying is, it's priceless?"

"I guess you could see it that way."

"And you don't have it?"

"No. I never had it."

"So it could be anywhere else?"

"What do you mean?" Wes asks.

"Well, if you don't have it, then you can't really be sure it's not somewhere else."

Wes rolls his eyes. "Let me know if you find it," he says, punching another button. "You're on the air."

"Hi, Wes," says a woman. "No hard feelings, by the way, but you're welcome to come over and help rake leaves any time you want."

"Thanks, Dottie. What's your question?"

"Is it true when those Indians were camped up at the ball fields they put some kind of curse on the ground? I mean, if the ground is actually cursed, could this be why the high school has never had a winning season—and does that mean they could never win a home game again? Maybe Reggie can answer this: Is this like that Babe Ruth curse on the Red Sox, and if so, do you think we should move the ball fields to some other flat place that doesn't have a curse on it? I'm curious to hear if any other listeners agree with me."

Reggie considers the question. "Well," he says, "The Red Sox didn't move out of Fenway."

"Good answer, Reg," Wes says, patting him on the back and hitting another button. "You're on the air, caller."

"What's up, Wes?"

"Doing fine. What's your question?"

"Do you think it's possible that the Indians never left East Mountain?"

"What?"

"Well, I saw a show on TV about some Pilgrims that lived in Virginia and the whole colony disappeared. And then they did some DNA tests on the Indians who live there now, and they discovered that they were related to the Pilgrims."

"What are you saying? Do you think we should DNA-test everyone who lives on East Mountain and see if they're related to some Indians I made up?"

"I don't know. It's just a thought," says the caller. "Thanks, and keep up the good work."

"I love this job," Wes says, grinning at the camera.

Aero Kierkegaard walked into the living room for snacks. When he saw Buckeye and Raccoon Boy on TV he stopped cold. His eyes bugged out, his mouth flopped wide, and he bent over, wheezing and clutching his stomach with one arm, pointing at the screen with his other hand. He made little squeaking sounds as droplets of spit sprayed around his head.

Molly ran to Catherine and grabbed her leg. "Mommy, what's he doing?"

"I think he's laughing, honey."

On TV, Wes and Reggie yukked it up, clowns on the loose.

And so it went—caller after caller contributing to the legends of happenstance. As usual, the show was fun to watch, and tonight was a triumph with the rare parade of quirks and crackpots. Nobody cared about history; everybody just liked the stories. Wes had been forgiven.

I went to the kitchen to sample the food. Doc joined me.

"This is a remarkable family you've got."

"Believe me, I know. Thanks for the ID on Wrinklachofski."

"What are the chances?" he said.

"In this town? Inevitable. This is the coincidence capital of the world. Did you cook all this food?"

"I did. Veronica said you liked peanut butter cookies." He handed me a plateful.

I already liked this guy.

Beth found me.

"Good news," she said. "Veronica's friend runs the CAT-scan machine, and she saw my test. She's not supposed to say anything, but she knows what a good brain looks like. Mine was clear. She said I had a happy brain."

With my bad arm, we held a half-hug twice as long.

When the show was over, Sister went into her bedroom to change clothes for dinner. She looked inside her chapel and noticed the Scrabble tiles still arranged in promise on her altar. When she picked them up, she only meant to say a prayer, but as she closed her eyes she felt herself being drawn away again into the sweetly scented mist, pulled out of the moment and into the sky.

"I really need to get back," she said, as she sailed dreamlike toward warm and wide familiar plains, with lazy rivers below and a cloudless sky that arched above a towering range of grand and gentle mountains.

She returned to the mountaintop where she had planted her promise tree more than fifty years ago. Ten days ago, the tree was a gnarled caricature of neglect. Today her tree was the largest one in a lush green forest that grew for miles across the top of the mountain, down its sides and into the valleys.

There was a ground covering of thick green grass and patches of sweet-smelling brush with delicate purple flowers and bright red berries. There were singing birds of amazing shapes and colors. Beyond the mountains were peaceful cities, shimmering silver in the sunset.

Even though she had a house full of family waiting for a dinner party, Sister sat beneath her glorious tree of life, breathing the clear air, leaning against the smooth trunk, and basking in the glory of a covenant well kept. Above her, the branches were strong and healthy, loaded with rich, perfect, ripe fruit—bananas, mangoes, figs, and oranges—all growing together on the same tree.

All was well. Her family was safe and complete, her promise fulfilled. God was pleased.

Wes and Reggie returned from the station in high humor, making plans for a father-son call-in show named *Granite State Storybook*. It will be a show for people who have good stories to tell about their families or towns. Guest artists will sketch the scenes as callers read their tales on the air.

We collected at the dining room table—thirteen of us, including the babies. Wes and Sister sat together at the place of honor.

Sister said prayers.

"Father, we're gathered tonight to thank You for Your promise of this family made over fifty years ago. We hope we have served You well, and we pledge ourselves to the continued increase of goodness on Earth for as long as you see fit. Please bless this food, protect us in the moment, and watch over us all forever. Amen."

It was a wonderful dinner. Turkey and stuffing, glazed ham, vegetarian lasagna, green salad, pasta salad, sweet potatoes, garlic mashed potatoes, curried rice, persimmon-corn chutney, dill sauce, coconut-mushroom soup, sage bread, corn muffins, and ginger marmalade. For drinks, we had herbal teas, milk, buttermilk, coffee, and a case of Moffatt's Famous Sassafras Fizz.

As we ate, Reggie told us the story of his exile, Charlie explained the concerto he was writing for the art museum, and Molly assaulted Aero Kierkegaard with endless variations of the same chicken-crossing-the-road joke.

Wes recapped the Ball Field Indian Wars.

"She never laid a glove on me," he said.

"That's bold," I said. "Humility in the face of disaster."

"What disaster? It turned out fine," he said. "It gave people something to talk about, and we learned who our real friends are."

"Yeah. All thirteen of us," said Veronica.

"I'm glad it's over," Beth said. "I thought that woman was scary."

"I wasn't worried," Wes said. "She couldn't get me."

"I guess not," I said. "Since I had you locked up in the back of the cruiser."

"I thought that was our little secret," he said, laughing along with every-one else.

I watched my mother. A few times during the meal I saw her close her eyes and rock slowly from side to side on her chair, a childlike smile cross-ing her face. I knew she was enjoying some secret communion, floating in her mystic bliss between the present and forever.

"I want some root beer, too," she said, pulling out of her reverie.

"Root beer for my bride," Wes said, popping the bottle-top with the clasp on his suspenders. "It's time for toasts."

He stood and raised his bottle of Sassafras Fizz.

"Root beers up," he said. "Speaking of friends: Here's to the man who saved the day—"

"And saved your ass," said Reggie.

"And that's no small job," said Wes, laughing. "Thank you, Doc. And welcome to the family."

Doc beamed and bowed; Veronica looked shy.

"Bottoms up," said Wes.

Molly laughed.

And we all chanted:

"Through the lips and past the gums,
Look out, belly, here it comes."

"Another toast, folks," Wes said. "Another toast before we take the picture."

Everyone was quiet.

"Here's to my bride," he said. "As beautiful as the day we married, and the only reason we're a family today. I've said it a million times, and I'll say it again: She saves my life every day. Thank you, sweetie, for having faith in me."

He put his arm around Sister, bent down, and kissed her gently.

The moment hovered like a returning dove.

"I love you all so much," she said. "This is even better than I dreamed."

We toasted the stories of the past fifty years, then arranged ourselves for the picture.

Wes and Sister sat in front. Veronica, Reggie, and I stood behind them.

The light flashed, an image of revelation—proof of eternal favors like Faith, Hope, and Grace, living like dreams in our fragile souls, protected and nourished by the comfort of our kind.

As Sister says, it's a pretty puzzle.